THE KEYS OF HELL AND DEATH

Charles Cordell has been a career soldier and diplomat on the ground in the Middle East, South Asia and North Africa. He has seen humanity at its best, its worst and its most desperate. His novels draw both on time spent on the fraying margins of civilisation and studies of the great political and religious crises of 17th century Europe.

The Keys of Hell and Death is the second novel in the *Divided Kingdom* series, which chronicles Britain's Civil Wars between 1642 and 1653.

Also by Charles Cordell:

GOD'S VINDICTIVE WRATH

THE KEYS
OF HELL
AND DEATH

CHARLES CORDELL

MYRMIDON

Myrmidon
Rotterdam House
116 Quayside
Newcastle upon Tyne
NE1 3DY

www.myrmidonbooks.com

First published in the United Kingdom by Myrmidon 2024

A catalogue record for this book is available from the British Library.

ISBN 978-1-910183-33-5

Set in Minion Pro by
Falcon Oast Graphic Art Limited,
www.falcon.uk.com

Printed in the UK by CPI Group (UK) Ltd, Croydon, CR0 4YY

1 3 5 7 9 10 8 6 4 2

For Muzvuru and Malone

You are the dawn piper, the swirl of dust,
    the shining gift of water;
The jewelled light of an eastern dusk, the
    fast-falling night;
The infinite scent of a desert wind.
Yours are the Gates of Basra.

Contents

PART THREE: REDEMPTION

MAPS

Character Notes

THE KING'S ARMY

Prince Maurice's Regiment of Dragoons

Colonel Henry Washington*	commanded after Colonel James Usher was killed at Lichfield
Captain Henry Norwood*	commissioned to raise a troop of dragoons in December 1642
Sergeant O'Brien	fought in Flanders, France and Germany, from Limerick
Ralph Reeve	stepson of Mr Reeve*, gentleman of Westleton, Suffolk
Luke Sherington	son of Thomas Sherington* yeoman of Westleton
Clement Tooley	son of Katherine Tooley* of Westleton

Colonel Henry Lunsford's Regiment of Foot

Lt-Colonel Nathaniel Moyle*	younger son of John Moyle* MP, of St Germans, Cornwall
Corporal William Stokes*	of Shepton Mallett, served with Lunsford's from September 1642
Moussa 'Moses' Dansocko	enslaved son of a Bambara numuw of Gao in Songhai

Sir Bevil Grenville's Regiment of Foot

Ensign Anthony Payne*	the 'Cornish Giant', of Stratton, Cornwall
Morgan Pascoe	husbandman of Morwenstow, Cornwall

Sir Nicholas Slanning's Regiment of Foot 'The Tinners'

Ensign Teage Mohun* gentleman of Boconnoc, Cornwall

Kendall Tremain St Ives fisherman and Tamar tinner of Metherill, Cornwall

The King's Train of Artillery

Mr George Merrett* younger brother of the scientist Christopher Merrett*

Mr Nicholas Busy* professional gun captain at Edgehill and Bristol

Mr Berkeley* professional gunner at the Siege of Gloucester

THE PARLIAMENT'S WESTERN ASSOCIATION ARMY

Colonel Nathaniel Fiennes' Regiment of Horse

Major Hercules Langrish* served with Huguenots in France, saviour of the 'five members'

Francis Reeve son of Mr Reeve*, gentleman of Westleton, Suffolk

Lord St John's Regiment of Foot

Theodore II Paleologus* descended from Constantine XI, the last Byzantine emperor

Nathaniel Dunkley apprentice shoemaker, from Northampton

Colonel Nathaniel Fiennes' Regiment of Foot

Major Edward Wood* on the line and in the sally at Bristol, 1643

Lieutenant Thomas Taylor*	Lieutenant of Major Wood's* company at Bristol, 1643
Jeremy Holway*	Bristol Mercer and city trained bands musketeer
John Friend*	stonemason from Westerleigh, Gloucestershire, at Bristol, 1643

City of Bristol Citizen Volunteers

Dorothy Hazzard*	founder of Broadmead Baptist Church, Rector of St Ewen's wife
Enid Powell	maid to the family of Mr George Boucher*, from Monmouthshire
Abel Cowans	disabled sailor, Bristol docker and gun matross, from Newcastle

City of Gloucester Citizen Volunteers

| John Barnwood* | pewterer, bell founder and bullet maker, freeman of Gloucester |

* denotes a character known to history.

The Western Campaign, 1643: The Battle of Lansdown Hill to the Storming of Bristol

The Keys of Hell and Death is a work of historical fiction. However, the story is as accurate and authentic as reasonably possible. It does not play loose with history. There is no need. The events of the British Civil Wars and the personal stories within them are extraordinary enough as they are. These stories just need to be told.

Their voices are those of ordinary men and women facing each other in the chaos of Britain in civil war. They are both relatable and sharply relevant today in reflecting the very many parallels between the current global situation and the crises of the 17th century. Ultimately, the British Civil Wars were the bloodiest conflict in British history; a war fought in our fields, villages and towns; a war that forged the United Kingdom and its political divide today.

The Keys of Hell and Death is the second novel in the Divided Kingdom series. It is now the second summer of civil war, July 1643. Some of its characters have survived the first campaign – from the shockingly brutal Battle of Edgehill to the barricades at Brentford in autumn 1642 – the scenes of *God's Vindictive Wrath*. The Reeve brothers clashed again at Winchester in 1642 (the setting for the short story,

Desecration, in which Francis Reeve managed to take his bother Ralph's horse). Others are about to be dragged into the war for the first time.

The Parliamentary cause is in peril. The Earl of Essex is in retreat, his army ravaged by disease. The King's Army is dominant in the North. His Catholic Queen, Henrietta Maria, marches south with her own army and fresh munitions to reinforce him at Oxford. Another Royalist force has fought its way from Cornwall to Bath. If it can reach Oxford, the King will have the forces he needs to turn again on London – or to seize Bristol, England's second city and port, stoking Parliamentarian fears of an Irish Papist Army to invade and ravage Protestant England.

Part One

Lansdown

Then Granvile stood,
And with himself oppos'd and check'd the flood.
Conquest or death was all his thought; so fire
Either o'ercomes, or does itself expire.
His courage work'd like flames, cast heat about;
Here, there, on this, on that side, none gave out.
Not any pike in that renowned stand,
But took new force from his inspiring hand.
Soldier encouraged soldier; man urged man;
And he urged all; so far example can;
Hurt upon hurt, wound upon wound, did call;
He was the butt, the mark, the aim of all.
His soul, this while retired from cell to cell,
At last flew up from all, and then he fell;
But the devoted stand, encouraged the more
From that, his fate ply'd hotter than before;
And proud to fall with him, sworn not to yield,
Each sought an honour'd grave, and gained the field.
Thus, he being fallen, his actions fought anew,
And the dead conquer'd whilst the living flew.

WILLIAM CARTWRIGHT, 1643

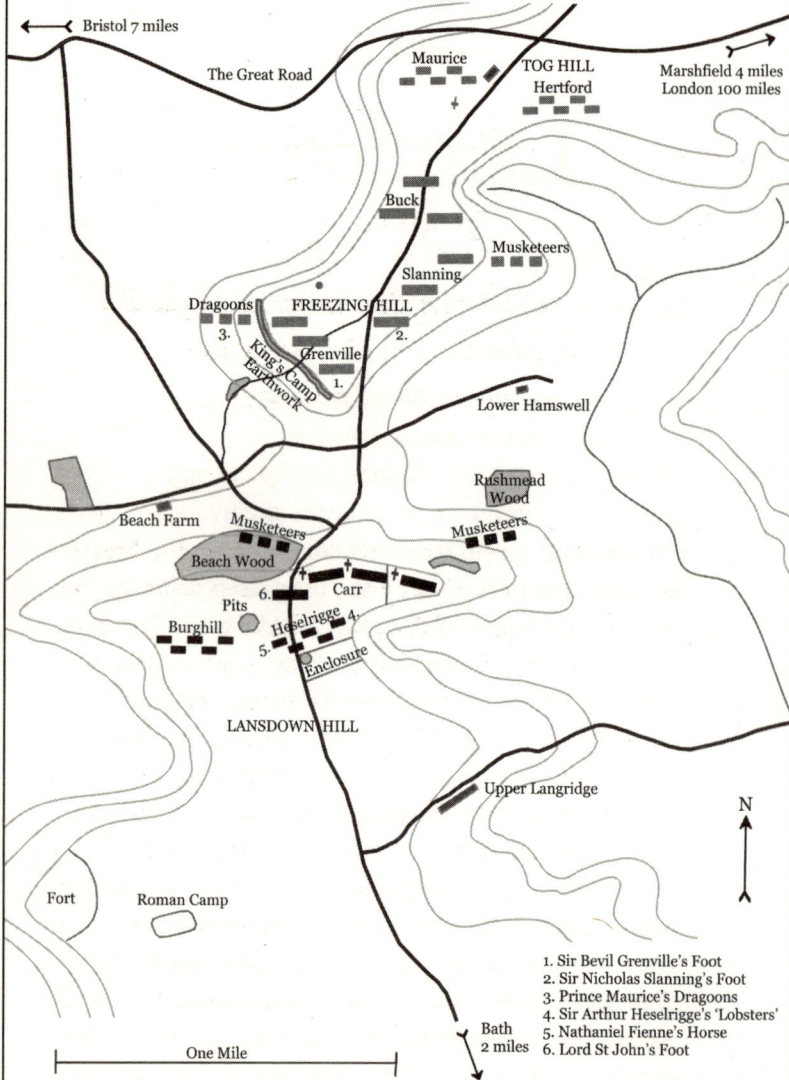

The Battle of Lansdown Hill: 5th of July 1643, 5 o'clock in the afternoon

Bristol 7 miles

The Great Road

Maurice

TOG HILL

Hertford

Marshfield 4 miles
London 100 miles

Buck

Musketeers

Slanning

Dragoons

FREEZING HILL

3.

King's Camp
Earthwork

Grenville

2.

1.

Lower Hamswell

Rushmead
Wood

Beach Farm

Musketeers

Musketeers

Beach Wood

Carr

Pits

6.

Burghill

Heselrigge

4.

5.

Enclosure

LANSDOWN HILL

Upper Langridge

N

Fort

Roman Camp

1. Sir Bevil Grenville's Foot
2. Sir Nicholas Slanning's Foot
3. Prince Maurice's Dragoons
4. Sir Arthur Heselrigge's 'Lobsters'
5. Nathaniel Fienne's Horse
6. Lord St John's Foot

Bath
2 miles

One Mile

Copyright (c) 2023 CHARLES CORDELL

I

Mount Zion

Francis Reeve

Lansdown Hill, Langridge, Somerset, England
Wednesday the 5th of July 1643, five
o'clock in the afternoon

The gun stood on its platform, staring out over the breast-work of earth and timber, out across the steep valley to the hill beyond; a flat-topped hill, a great field of wheat laid over it, ripening and shimmering in the late afternoon sun; a cornfield filled with an army, a Cornish army, a superstitious, idolatrous army; an army of half-wild, barbarous heathens; a cornfield and an army to be cut down; a sacrifice to be reaped. *For they have sown the wind, and they shall reap the whirlwind.*

Francis Reeve gathered the reins of his horse as the gun captain stepped forward, smoking linstock in hand. The burning match came down on the gun's breach. Priming powder flared in a burst of sparks and smoke, the great saker leaping backwards in a ball of yellow smoke and thunderous roar to send its five-pound iron ball shrieking across the valley towards the cornfield and the Cornish, the ground shaking as the gun crashed back down, iron ring-bolts, locks and rivets clashing.

Francis held his horse in check, twisting the iron bit in its mouth, hauling its head down, spurs pressed against its quivering flanks. It had been his father's horse, Breda. He had recognised it instantly, taken it from his bastard half-brother, from the unworthy sinner, Ralph. Somehow, the bastard had escaped him at Winchester, a common prisoner let loose, ejected from that cleansed city like the worthless shit that he was. God alone, in his infinite wisdom, knew why the reprobate had been spared, where he was or in which whore's bed, ditch or shallow grave he now lay. Francis did not care. It meant nothing to him. He turned the spurs slowly against the horse's ribs, felt the beast shake, snorting, the sharp rowels piercing its skin. The horse was his now. It would obey him and it would serve God.

All along the line, horses tossed, whinnied and stamped, the gun smoke rolling back to rankle in dust-filled nostrils and dry throats. All day they had stood on the edge of Lansdown Hill, fixed, static, unmoving while others, horse and foot, skirmished back and forth between the two hills. A forlorn hope of Godly horsemen and covenantor dragoons had reached that cornfield, throwing back the apostate cavaliers in chaos, only to be forced back again. Now the whole heathen army stood amongst the wheat, within range of the great guns, a crop to be reaped, as the forlorn hope returned, cresting the escarpment, and the gunners threw themselves into their devilish craft to reload the gun.

God had ordained that the battle should be fought upon this hill. This was as Mount Tabor. He had made it so, given them this hill, guided Sir William Waller to ring it with fortifications, to make it as much a fortress as Mount Zion. Now was the time of slaughter, now was the time to turn back the tide of evil that washed against them.

For this was surely the place of reckoning. The Earl of Essex was in retreat, his army sick, defeated, his resignation offered to Parliament while cavaliers from Oxford raided as far as Wycombe, terrified London. John Hampden, the better man, was dead, a volunteer martyred fighting to throw back the apostates. The North was lost. Only Hull stood between the King's northern army of Popish brigands and the eastern counties.

Even now, the papist Queen, the *Deviless*, marched south with her own Roman army, an army of recusants, French mercenaries and Jesuit priests. It was said she carried with her enough guns, powder and match to equip the King's army in Oxford twice over; arms she had procured in Flanders by whoring herself, by hawking the crown jewels like a common jade, a procuress. The spice merchants of Amsterdam had them now – England's regalia had been sold, for just £200,000 pounds.

And here in the west, the heathen Cornish horde was loose, free to rape and pillage, to infest the land like a plague of pestilential caterpillars. For they were an alien race. Not truly English but a wild and Godless tribe, a nation of lawless, faithless, drunken seamen and miners, damned creatures that moved between hellish cavern and tempestuous sea, slippery and amphibian; neither men nor fish, but devils.

Savage rovers and wreckers, they drowned ships' crews, carried away the cargoes of Godfearing English merchants, the hard-won toil of the Godly planters of New England. They plied an illicit trade with Catholic France, Portugal and Spain, running their forbidden cargoes and Jesuit priests ashore at night. And they consorted with the Moor and the barbarous Turk across the sea, harbouring renegades and secret Mohammedans, those with the barber's mark of the Beast upon them.

If they were not stopped here, they too would join forces with the King in Oxford and swell the ranks of Satan's horde. Together, combined, the armies of Ahab, his Jezebel queen, Popish north and barbarous Cornwall would overwhelm what was left of Essex's blighted, plague-ridden army to march on London once more.

Worse, they could take Bristol, England's second city and port, a Babylon of whoring merchants that held the key to the West Country. Its great harbour lay open to any ship, any crew or cargo, an inlet for all the delicacies, temptations and plagues of the world. Nathaniel Fiennes held it now for Parliament, a bulwark against Welsh malignancy and the threat of Irish Papist invasion. But it was a nest of vipers, a city that fornicated with Satan. Half the merchant venturers of Bristol plotted with the cavaliers. Any of them would sell their city for earthly profit. Even now, the King's Lord Lieutenant in Ireland, in league with Rome and the Antichrist, sought to unleash upon England the forces of darkness that ran amok in that savage isle.

Surely here, now, upon this hill, the true and righteous must make a stand, hold back this heathen Cornish horde. *For thus hath the Lord spoken unto me. Like as the lion and the young lion roaring on his prey, when a multitude of shepherds is called forth against him, he will not be afraid of their voice, nor abase himself for the noise of them. So shall the Lord of Hosts come down to fight for Mount Zion, and for the hill thereof.*

And he was chosen to stand with them. *Oh Lord, Thou preserved me from the carnage of Edgehill, saved me from the terrible tide at Brentford, plucked me from Winchester's gutter. Thou sent the righteous Mistress Bennett to take me in when I had nothing.* He could not return home. He had renounced his drunken father and his family, his college at Cambridge

8

and their ways of sin. The Godly Widow Bennett had taken him in, tended him, clothed him, armed him with a fresh pair of pistols and her husband's Bible. She had brought him anew unto the Lord, raised him up as a two-edged sword to lay waste to His enemies that they may be cast aside as dung to fat the land.

The gun reloaded, its crew set about laying it, levering it into line with a hand spike under the trail and shoulders against the wheel spokes, the wedged quoin tapped under the breech for elevation. With a nod and touch of his hat, the gun captain stepped back, pulled the smoking linstock from the ground and blew upon its lighted match.

Francis pulled back on the reins of his horse, touched his spurs to its bloody flanks. He was chosen, dedicated to the King of Heaven in body, soul and spirit; chosen of Him from the beginning; justified, sanctified and received into a communion with Christ that could never be broken. For was not the End of Times at hand? Was this hill not a fitting place to be gathered in? *Up! For this is the day in which the Lord hath delivered Sisera into thine hand. Is not the Lord gone out before thee? So, Barak went down from Mount Tabor, and 10,000 men after him.*

II

Keskerr!

Morgan Pascoe

*Freezing Hill, Cold Ashton, Gloucestershire,
a quarter past five o'clock*

Morgan Pascoe was a Cornishman. And he was damned if he was going to stand about all day while bloody rebels blasted them with great shot. It didn't matter that they sat on top of their hill, all fortified behind breastworks. He and the rest of Grenville's pikemen had fought their way up Stamford Hill, beaten the rebels from the rings on its top. That was at Stratton, in Cornwall. *Home.* Well, they'd do it again here – Lansdown Hill they called it.

They'd had bugger all to eat since daybreak. Roused out of quarters in an alarum, they'd marched backways and forth all day long; while bloody cannon racked them from that hill. Now it was near supper time and they'd had neither breakfast nor *croust*. And all along of their own bloody prinked up cavaliers not doing their pissing job. First, they let their horse guards get all scat in. Then they fell foul upon their own foot, riding amok through the ranks, all in retreat from a few damned pioneers in the hedges. Now they came streaming back from the rebel hill with their tails between their legs. Runaway horse they were. And they called themselves gentlemen? They were worse than a pack of dogs. All they'd done was trample the corn.

It'd been a wonderous great field of wheat, still a mite green, but coming on for a handsome harvest. Lord, what would he give to have a field like that? Not like their scrubby little Cornish fields all huddled up against the sea and wind between hedge, rock and furze. And those wheat ears were heavy and soft as a maiden's purse – no barley spikes, barbs or prickling dust to rub a man's arms and neck raw. But now the field was ruined, half flattened, trampled underfoot. A crying shame it was. A crying, bloody shame.

For years, he'd worked as man and boy beside his father to clear, hedge, break, burn, drain and manure the piddling little enclosures they leased in Morwenstow, every bit of it by hand. He'd dragged sea-wrack and sand up cliff and down lane to feed the soil. Day in, day out, he'd tilled the land; broken his back dragging stones, clods and weeds from the ground; driven oxen and plough, gulls wheeling and diving to rise shrieking from the fresh furrow; harrowed, sown and harrowed again; chased off craw, pigeon and starling with stick and stone, hands and feet raw in the Atlantic wind and rain; he'd fed and tended store-cattle through each winter to calve, suckle, wean, milk and herd them in the spring; and he'd hoed, row upon row, back and forth, willing the seedlings to grow through drought and flood; and then reaping, raking, binding, carting, stacking hay and barley in the summer heat to cry the neck, glean, thresh, winnow, pick and mill the grain; only to start over again each Michaelmas.

But then came the bad years. It started in summer of 1630. Hot and dry, there was not a drop of rain from March through

August, the corn all shrivelled, dead before it was formed. They lost half the crop that year, the rest was nothing but dust and broken straw. There was a terrible dearth in all Cornwall, across all the West Country. It killed his father. It was as if he just wasted away, worn down to nothing after a lifetime of hard lowster on the land. They buried him that winter, in the wind and rain, a withered husk wrapped in an old shroud.

Thanks be to God, Sir Bevil had let him and his mam stay on, though he was not much more than a boy – just seventeen years old. Sir Bevil had given them seed-corn, had seen them right to start again. He understood them, shared their troubles. He might have been born in a fine house, but he was one of them, as much a Cornishman as any other. Besides, Sir Bevil was grandson to old Sir Richard Grenville, captain of the *Revenge*, the ship and crew – a West Country crew – that alone defied a Spanish fleet in battle. Morgan would follow Sir Bevil anywhere.

But God knew how he'd missed his father. They were hard years, with only one good harvest in ten and that no bumper. It was as if the Lord was punishing them. The worst was '37, the summer hot and airless after a winter and spring as cold as ice. It left them with near enough nothing, reduced to scavenging hedgerow and cliff to stay alive. And then came the ague. He'd held Betty in his arms as the burning fever racked her, her breath quick and rasping, her body tortured, burning, the sour bile spewing from her until there was nothing left. They'd been married no more than a year, the babe dead in her arms, its little body blotched and scabby with pustules. She'd given the poor mite all she could until she milked herself dry, empty, exhausted, lost. He'd touched the Nine Stones, fetched holy water from Saint Morwenna's, Saint John's and Saint Anne's wells – even carried Betty and the babe to Saint

Juliot's Cross. But it was no good. Mother and child were buried together in the churchyard above the cliff, next to his father and so many more who died that year.

And it was all his fault – he'd not paid his tithe. What with the wedding and the babe, there'd been nothing spare. God had punished them for it. It should have been him, not Betty and the babe, but God had chosen them and left him alone, in earthly purgatory. He'd never not pay the tithe again. Even his last bean, he'd pay God and the church first.

Mind, there were others who'd answer come the Day of Judgement. First would be the corn merchants, mongers and engrossers who forced farmers to sell their hard-won grain for next to nothing, held onto it in time of want, then sold it back to poor folk all musty and rotten at twice the price. Then there were the unchristian brokers, up-country townsmen, city folk – gamesters who played cards with the poor – for profit. It was July now, the worst of the hunger months before harvest, when nothing was left and purses were empty. There were plenty who would feel the pinch of want before the corn was ripe and they could enjoy their first bellyful of Lammas bread.

Worse even than them were the bloody preachers who smashed statues, carvings and stained glass, who white-washed the churches and buried the old granite crosses. They said such thing were idols, weren't Christian! They filled in the holy wells and broke down the ancient chapels. They banned the miracle plays, their Beltane bonfires, their Mazey Days and Obby Oss. They even tried to ban their saints. What did they know of saints? They knew nothing of Saint Meriasek, Saint Petroc, Saint Piran or any of the other twenty-score Cornish saints, saints who lived and preached in Cornwall long before Saint Augustin set foot in bloody Canterbury, when the Saxon English were still heathen savages.

Besides, Cornwall was sacred. Jesus Christ had blessed the land with his own feet, trod Cornish soil as a boy beside his uncle trading tin – back amongst his grandmother's people. It was written over a church door, inscribed in stone. In ancient letters. In runes. Christ's uncle, Saint Joseph of Arimathea, carried the crown of thorns to Cornwall, after Christ was crucified upon the cross. He'd carried it on to Glastonbury where it took root, rose up, grew anew. If it wasn't true, how come that thorn bush flowered every Christmas? There was none other like it. It was sacred.

What did these so-called 'ministers' from London know of Christ and Cornish saints? They were foreigners, from town and city. They might be educated in a fine university, but they were ignorant of Cornish ways, of the land and its past. Country folk kept the knowledge alive, passed it from memory to memory – piously taught, from father to son and grandson. These *ministers* were nothing but a gaggle of sour, Bible clutching preachers in their stiff hats and black coats set upon running and reforming everything. They knew nothing of beauty, of God in all His infinite glory. If they'd only stop and listen – sit a while and feel His presence about them, in the wind and rocks, in the trees, the running water and crashing waves.

By rights, they'd no business poking their long noses into Cornish affairs. Cornwall was a duchy – independent, not some sodding English shire nor county neither. It had its own parliament, the convocation of the Stannaries, granted by King John, that made their own laws and taxes. No statute, nor ordinance nor proclamation made by King or Queen of England had writ in Cornwall, unless by assent of the Stannary. Good Queen Bess had affirmed it by Letters Patent, as had old King Harry – though it took a Cornish army to march on London, to fight and die for what was their right and due.

They'd risen up and marched again, in the time of young King Edward, taken Exeter twice over, fought the English in pitched battle. But then came the hangings. The bloody English hanged the mayors of Bodmin and St Ives, six men of God, including the vicar of Poundstock, and four thousand poor souls in cold blood. And all because they kept to the old words, to *Kernuak* and Latin, in church. They weren't Catholics; they just didn't speak English! It wasn't the King's fault; young Edward was just a boy. But English ministers and their Parliament had whispered in his ear, usurped his power, made proclamations in his name, forgot the word of old King Harry and those that went before him.

It wasn't as if Cornwall was rebellious. Cornishmen had always fought for their king – when asked. They were loyal subjects of the crown, a royal duchy. But they knew what was their right. And no Cornishman was going to listen to a ruddy Saxon parliament telling them what to do. An English king was one thing, but an English parliament was another. Cornwall had its own kings in ancient times, from Corin of Troy, to King Mark and King Arthur. King Charles might be an Englishman, but he was their king. And they'd fight any bugger that said different.

Now Cornwall marched again. They marched for their king against a rebellion that wasn't lawful. Twelve good men and true had said as much – judged the case in a court of law in Truro and found for King Charles. Well, that was good enough for every true Cornishman, one and all. It was time again to show what Cornishmen could do. Damn standing about in the corn while bloody rebels blasted them from yon hill. It was time to fetch off those cannon. They'd done it before. They'd do it again.

The air about them shook with the rumbling blur of

another screaming cannon ball as it ploughed through the corn and a file of musketeers, flinging both aside to leave a blood strewn, steaming swathe across the field. A ball of yellow smoke and thumping explosion crashed out from a rebel breastwork in defiance.

Grenville's line of Cornishmen swayed and lurched, a low growl running through the ranks like a storm far out at sea, the boulders grinding as the waves built. And then it burst, men yelling, shaking their weapons in the air, the pikes clashing, thumping the ground, shouting, demanding, exclaiming. *'Kernow vedn keskerras!'* Cornwall will march!

And then came the shout no Cornishman could resist, an ancient cry, a battle call, that rich or poor, nobleman or labourer, one and all were bound to follow. *'Kernow kensa!'* Cornwall first! Together, as one, they yelled their answer. *'Kernow kensa!'* Again, they shouted it out. *'Kernow kensa!'* Again, together. *'Kernow kensa!'*

All across the cornfield, every Cornish regiment took up the cry: Godolphin's, Trevanion's, Slanning's and Lord Mohun's, the ranks heaving, shaking, on the point of bursting. It was now or lose all discipline. Cornwall would march. It would storm that hill, it would fetch those guns, with or without its officers.

Sir Bevil Grenville stood before them. He held up his hand, turned to face Lansdown Hill and stepped forward, waving them on. With one final great yell the Cornish army surged over the edge of the cornfield and down into the valley.

III

Indenture

Nathaniel Dunkley
Beach Wood, Lansdown Hill, half past five o'clock

Nathaniel Dunkley heard the savage yell. He stared out from between the trees.

'Nat, they're comin.' It was Billy, his friend. Billy would be afeared. He was only young.

'I know, Billy. I seed them.' He needed to be strong, for Billy. They were both young. They said he was seven years old when the parish put him as an apprentice shoemaker to the master in Northampton. He'd served ten years. Billy must have started a year after.

'What'er we goin to do?' Billy looked up at him.

'Ah reckon we do like corporal said. Keep our heads down, keep out of way of sergeant and give fire when he tells we.'

'Thuz thousands on 'em.'

'I know, Billy boy. Thou and me'll be alright. Keep thy match lit.' He checked his own match and gave it a gentle blow. The coal glowed bright in the shade beneath the great beech trees.

He and Billy had mustered a year back, when Lord St John's Regiment beat the drum in Northampton Market Square. In

17

truth, they'd run away to sign up, broken their bond. There'd been no point asking the master. The old bastard wouldn't have let them go. He'd have kept them apprentice till they served their term. Well, they couldn't go back now. The bloody town guild wouldn't let them back, wouldn't let them earn their own crust – not in Northampton. Besides, they'd each taken a pair of shoes and a snap of bread. They'd hang for it if they were caught.

But they'd find a place to set up. When they'd made a bit as soldiers. He'd learnt about all there was to know about making shoes. There was nothing more the old git could teach him. He just needed a place to set up shop, and the tools, and a lapstone, and wooden lasts, and a bit of good shoe leather – a bit of soft cordovan for best. Maybe they'd set up in Bristol, or London even. They could make shoes for the army! Half the soldiers he saw needed new shoes. They wore them something terrible with all the clomping about. Then, when they'd made enough, they'd take ship to the colonies. He'd heard tell how a man could set up for next to nought – do well out there. And there were plenty of ships leaving Bristol for Virginia. They'd make their fortune yet, he and Billy. They just needed to make a bit as soldiers first.

The master wasn't a bad man. He taught them their prayers, let them take their stools to church to hear the minister. There were plenty worse. He was old, used, worn through, squinting in the gloom. He'd belt them when they made a mistake, or spoke out of turn. But he was alright if you knew how to keep on the right side of him. You just had to watch and copy – in silence. It took years before he let you hammer a tack or stitch a piece of leather, years of sweeping, scrubbing and fetching, years of chores before he let you work on a bit of leather.

But the mistress was different. She was a mean, nasty

woman. She beat the little ones, treated them like slaves, never a kind word from her. She kept them all at their work from five o'clock in the morning till gone seven at night. She fed them on nothing but slops and let them go hungry when she wasn't pleased. They slept where they could in the shop, cold, hungry, fit to drop. Even then, she wouldn't let them rest. She had her favourites – taught them to snitch and bully at night.

It'd killed poor Walter. He was kind, quiet, shown him what to do when he was little. But then he'd got sick, coughing till the blood came. She wouldn't fetch the apothecary or light the fire. Then she wouldn't feed him – said he needed to work to earn his crust. He died one night shivering and coughing on a pile of dirty old castoff shoe leather, among the rat piss and spiders. They buried him in the rain, wrapped in his shift, like a sack of bones; not even a nail spared to make a cross of sticks to mark his grave.

The parish had never come back, never looked in to check on Nat. The mistress said his mother died a whore, that she'd died a sinner, that she deserved to die. There was nobody else that he knew of. Nobody had come for him. She'd told him he was alone, that nobody loved him, told him nobody wanted a parish bastard. She said he was born of sin, that he was sinful. He didn't care. She couldn't hurt him. But then she turned on his butty. He'd been afraid she'd kill Billy next. He couldn't let her. He had to get him away before she killed him. So, they'd run away to muster. There'd been nowhere else to go.

Billy and he'd been alright. They'd gotten by. They'd learned to soldier, to keep out of the way of sergeant. Billy still struggled a bit on the march, what with carrying his musket, powder and shot and all, and on guard at night. But they'd done alright, looked out for each other – a pair of butties.

They'd barnished on good food, feasting like lords on beef, pork or chicken near every day. And they'd swilled ale like real men – till Billy puked his guts out. They'd been given a coat each and they'd had a bed to share in garrison, at Worcester and at Bristol – a real bed with a blanket and all.

They'd missed the battles at Kineton and London. But they'd taken Malmesbury, by cunning more than storm. And they'd beaten the Welsh at Highnam – dumb, mullocking malignants, they were a 'mushroom army' that rose up and then laid down its weapons. They couldn't even speak proper. Most of them didn't have shoes either – they went barefoot! That'd been with Sir William Waller. William the Conqueror they called him.

They'd rooted out Papists, whores and 'reprobates' and those who hid them, made them all pay. They'd purified the country churches, tearing down altar rails, smashing stained glass, lewd pictures, statues and benches; danced in the road with organ pipes for trumpets and priests' vestments for drapes; slept in the aisles, butchered their meat on the altar, pissed in the pulpit, crapped in the chancel and tore up the prayerbooks to wipe their arses and wad their muskets. It was all good sport. And it was in the name of Christ and Parliament.

Now, Sir William had called for them again out of Bristol, gathered his army at Bath to face the Cornish invaders. The sergeant said they were worse than the Welsh – half-wild heathens in league with Spain and the Devil. He said their womenfolk were worse, murderous sea witches that would lure a boy into water, then slit his gizzard. Now they were coming, pouring down the road that led across the valley to climb Lansdown Hill. More streamed down through the fields and lanes, cavalier horse among them, their path towards the wood where Billy and he squatted. He'd not thought it'd come to this.

'The're gerin closer, Nat.' Billy was afeared.

'I know, Billy.' He needed to be strong. For Billy. 'Check thy match is lit.'

IV

Dragoon

Ralph Reeve
Freezing Hill, a quarter to six o'clock

They were moving over the ancient earthwork at the end of the cornfield and down the steep field beyond, descending the hill into the valley below. Ralph gripped his musket and blew on its smouldering match as he stepped out. God, what would he give to have Ned's old carbine now, but he had lost everything at Winchester: carbine, pistols, sword, money and horse. His weapons surrendered, a rebel trooper stole his hat and what was left of his purse. But it had been his brother, Francis, who had taken Breda and the broken rapier from him – precious gifts from their father given to him when he joined the King's army. Francis had left him with nothing save the clothes on his back.

Now he was a lowly dragoon with a matchlock musket, a tuck sword and a pony. It was not the first time he had lost everything and had to start again. He'd failed at school – at most things. He'd left London with nothing but disgrace, failure and shame: his indenture, future and four long years of sweat and grovelling thrown away – for a woman. But this time there was no going home for help from his father; the rebels held Suffolk and all of the eastern counties. He'd be hunted down and thrown into gaol before he got there. He had to fight on and hope that the King beat the rebels soon. Only then could he go home to his father and to Susanna. But until then he had to serve as a soldier, as a lowly dragoon.

But he was not alone. Most of his old division were still together. They marched beside him now: Jack, scarred and grim; Sam, scanning the hedge and lane ahead; Luke, his earnest friend – God only knew how he depended on Luke – and Clem, dear Clem, still smiling. Hodge and the boy were back beyond the cornfield, holding the ponies. They'd only lost Brown, poor bloody Brown, his thigh smashed, twisted and bleeding amongst the rubble in the breach at Lichfield, beside Colonel Usher and so many more.

Somehow, they'd made their way from Winchester to Marlborough, on foot across the windswept plain in winter, without horses, money, weapons or cloaks. It had almost killed the boy. They'd begged and stolen like vagabonds, avoiding the rebel patrols and village watchmen. On the road outside Marlborough, they'd taken a stable of nags and ponies and ridden to Oxford. Lord Grandison had found them a place amongst his brother's troop of dragoons, in Colonel Usher's Regiment. It was a step down, but it was still better than trudging with the soldiery of a foot regiment.

Others had joined them, marched with them. He looked across the slope at them now. They were a mixed bunch, each a volunteer for their own distinct reason. Tandy was an ostler at a Burford inn, a gambler, always ready with his cards. Perhaps he'd only joined them to escape the constable, but he was generous as well as lucky, and a good soldier. Then there was Jewkes, dirty, drunken and easily riled. He'd been a porter at Worcester Docks. Dangerous in a brawl but fearless in a real fight, Jewkes scowled at the world as he marched, matchlock musket gripped in his fists. Last was Kibler, a Warwickshire trained bands soldier. Always smart, he knew his drill and his military articles. He was Sergeant O'Brien's pet and knew it – quick to challenge when the sergeant's back was turned. He puffed, panted and grumbled at the back now as they descended the hill in the sun.

Lord Grandison's brother had been taken prisoner at Cirencester. Captain Henry Norwood commanded them now. He'd made Ralph a corporal and put him at the head of his division. He was not sure that Sergeant O'Brien approved. The big Irishman was a Grandison favourite, an experienced soldier from their Limerick estates. He never seemed to have much of a good word to say. Perhaps he'd prefer Kibler as corporal.

Ralph gripped his musket, his back wet with sweat. This was his first real test, the first time he had led them into battle. There had been marches, billets and skirmishes, but this was different. They'd been commanded to the West Country, detached to join Prince Maurice while the rest of the regiment waited with Prince Rupert for the Queen's march south.

Now they were advancing to storm a hill, a table-topped escarpment defended by rebel foot and horse behind gun platforms and breastworks, the way up its slope flanked by woods filled with rebel musketeers. Ralph led them downhill, quickly, steeply, their strides descending the slope in great steps towards the valley floor and the slope of Lansdown Hill beyond. There'd been almost no warning. After a day of skirmishing backwards and forwards the Cornish foot suddenly started yelling wildly in their strange tongue then plunged forward, their officers unable to hold them back, to drag the rest of the King's Western Army with them.

Grenville's Regiment of Foot led, their pike block striding down the road that crossed the valley to climb Lansdown Hill and pierce the centre of the rebel defence and on to Bath. Their musketeers moved as a single wing out to their left. Beyond them, more musketeers advanced towards the wooded eastern slope. Behind, the rest of the Cornish foot swarmed out over the edge of the cornfield and down the slope, drums thrashing, colours streaming and ranks cheering in the late afternoon sun. To Grenville's right, two squadrons of horse descended the open field. Beyond them, on the far-right flank, Ralph moved with the dragoons in open order.

There was no time for orders. But it was clear that they must protect the horse and foot from any rebel charge or fire from the flank. They moved quickly, trying to keep pace with the horsemen to their left; bandolier and powder bottles swinging, rattling as they stepped downhill. The sun burned, the grass shimmering with heat in the still, clammy air of the valley. High above, larks still sang; larks, drums, cheering and cannon thundering between the hills.

At the foot of the slope, they crossed a road and dropped into a lane, forcing their way through blackthorn and bramble. On the far side, the ground sloped upwards as they started to climb Lansdown Hill. Above them a great wood loomed. It covered half the slope on this side of the escarpment, dark and still under its canopy. It would be filled with rebel musketeers who would rake their horse and foot as they climbed. The wood had to be cleared. But first they had to get to it.

'A'right, now. . . we need to get up this hill and into that wood.' Sergeant O'Brien was beside him. 'Reeve. . . take Sam, Tandy and Clem, and lead the way up.' Was the sergeant testing him? 'I want yiz t' find a way up through these here enclosures that keeps us out of sight and out of the fire from

25

that wood or the top of the hill. I'll foller with Luke and the rest of them. We move in file, hidden behind the hedges.'

Thank God. At least it was clear what he was to do.

'Well now. . .' O'Brien waved them on. 'Let's be gettin' on with it.'

V

Lansdown Hill

Morgan Pascoe
The bottom of Lansdown Hill, six o'clock in the evening

Morgan strode out on the road, pike butt clasped in his right hand, the steel tip rising to the sky sixteen feet above on its blue and white painted shaft – Grenville colours. The drums beat out the time as they marched, half-boots crunching in the dry gravel and dust. He marched in the second rank, six feet behind old Jago and only a few paces behind Sir Bevil himself.

He was glad to follow Jago. He was a fine file leader, a husbandman, a farmer like himself, of the next tithing, the next parish. He was church warden and he was Betty's uncle. He'd been like a father in difficult times. Beside Morgan stepped Anthony Payne, Sir Bevil's ensign, towering over them all, the standard clutched in his fist. The Cornish Giant they called him. Seven feet four inches tall he was and built like an ox. He'd never been beaten at wrestling, nor in any other fight. And yet a kinder, better yeoman you could not find.

The road ran flat and broad across the valley floor, wide enough for eight pikemen abreast as they marched in a great column. Out to their left, their musketeers kept pace whilst their bloody cavaliers moved across the open fields on their right. Overhead, another cannon ball thundered, only to bury itself in the hillside behind them with a great cheer from those that followed. The rebels could shoot all they liked; they weren't going to stop Cornwall.

Slowly, steadily, the road began to climb, turning across the hill as the slope steepened. It ran deeper now, a great bank cut into the hillside to their left, the cannon fire shrieking harmless overhead. They leant into the hill as the drums changed, thrashing out the Preparative, the call to close ranks, to make ready, to prepare to close with the enemy. Sir Bevil's orders followed, ringing out in time with the march. 'Ranks! Close to... the front! To your... order!' Now they marched just a yard, a single pace, between rank and file.

'You with me Morgan?' It was Jago, his file leader.

'I'm with ee, Jago. I'm right behind ee.'

'Come on, then. Let's be fetching them there bloody cannon.'

'Hold your horses, Jago.' It was Anthony, beside him. 'Wait up for the rear ranks. Now, together boys, one and all... march on!'

A great iron ball burst through the top of the bank above them, crashing through the pikes in a shower of splinters, shattered wood, dust, grit and flying stones. And then the bank was gone, a lane crossing their path, the brow of the hill above them, open, in plain view, smoke wreathing from the breastworks, a rebel foot battalion between every gun platform.

The ridge above exploded in flame and smoke, the first musket volley tearing the air apart in a wave of lead that smashed into the front ranks. They staggered at the blow, men cursing and swearing as they stepped over those that fell writhing on the ground in pain, but they kept going. They did not stop. They put their heads down and stepped into the hill.

Sir Bevil's orders came thick and fast now. 'Pikes! Pikes will double their front. . . by divisions!' This was the order to change formation, from a marching column to a broad pike block for combat. 'Pike divisions! Double your front. . . to the left entire. . . by divisions!'

'The Colonel's Pike Division, step short!' Anthony was calling them back, ordering his division to slow their advance on the road. 'Step short! Hold your ground!' They marched on the spot as the divisions behind moved up the hill into line beside them. 'Forward. . . march!'

Again, a volley crashed out from the ridge above. Again, men fell screaming in agony, ounce lead balls smashing flesh and bones, showering splinters that sliced cheeks and eyes as they rattled through the pike shafts. Again, they hunched their shoulders, kept going as Grenville's musketeers answered with a volley of their own.

The drums thrashed out the Battaile, the call for the ranks to close up, to form a solid block of steel, wood and bunched flesh for the final charge. Over the drums came Sir Bevil's orders to close in, to draw together. 'Pikes! Files, close to your. . . centre. To your close. . . order!' Morgan stepped inwards as he marched, his shoulders brushing the next man.

The hillside erupted in flame, thunder and shrieking cannister shot as a cannon fired down from the breastwork above. Its hail of tight-packed musket balls scythed a bloody, mangled path through the pike block. 'Close in! Close in! To your centre!' Again, they stepped inwards to close the gap, the ground blood strewn, churned, steaming.

'Pikes! Port your. . . pikes!' Morgan let his pike swing forward, up over the front rank, its weight in his left hand, right arm forcing the base down behind as he marched. The slope was steeper now, men cursing, stumbling as they stepped off the lane in their tightly packed ranks.

More volleys crashed out, the sky darkening, storm clouds blotting out the sun. The flash of musket and cannon was brighter now under thick wreaths of sulphurous gunsmoke, the thunder almost constant, deafening. Men groaned, cursed and spat as they pressed on.

'Pikes! Charge your... pikes!' Morgan levelled his pike, still stepping forward, staring down its length, past Jago, the breastwork and great gun only forty feet above them. The pikes of those behind ran past his cheek or over his head.

Again, the ridge exploded in a blaze of musket fire. Jago staggered, stepped forward once more, his pike dipping, unsure, slowing. Morgan's shoulder was forced up against him, pressed on by the ranks behind. 'Go on, Jago! I'm right with ee!'

'Get on, Jago!' Anthony reached out to clasp him.

'I... I can't see.' Jago turned, his face ripped open, a single eye bulging, staring wildly, his nose and other eye gone, blood running down his front, still trying to march.

'God damn! I'm sorry, Jago.' Anthony kept a hand on Jago's shoulder. 'Leave that pike go now.' He turned Jago around. 'Get back down the hill. Try to stay on the lane. God bless ee. Let old Jago through now boys!'

Morgan pressed back to let Jago past as best he could, the other man's blood thick and warm on his coat sleeve, down his arm, across his hand. Poor Jago was knocked and buffeted as the ranks behind moved past. Morgan turned away, faced the front, stared at the gap before him, the front rank empty where Jago had marched.

'Get on, Morgan!' It was Anthony. 'You've got to fill that there gap now. I'm with ee. Come on now boys! One and all!'

Morgan stepped forward, his shoulders were level with the front rank, his pike tip with theirs, the rest of his file pushing forward behind him. 'Come on then!' Together they pressed on, stepping steadily towards the breastwork.

Above them, the bloody rebel gunners worked feverishly about their charge. One fell, slumped over the breastwork, only to be replaced by another ramming home their cannister.

All along the line men yelled, urged, pushed each other on. Above all, Sir Bevil besought them to follow him, keep with him, stay with their cause. 'Come on, keep together my brave boys! One and all! For the King! For God! For Cornwall!'

'Let's be having that bloody cannon!' Anthony drove them forward, the standard in his fist. 'For Jago! For one and all! For Cornwall!'

The rebel gun ran forward, its muzzle thrusting out over the breastwork. The gunners were levering the breech up, forcing the muzzle down, its dark mouth gaping.

And then the shout that none could resist, their ancient cry, their battle call. Loud and clear, it rang out across the hillside, over the rattle and crash of muskets, piercing the dark clouds of smoke. *'Kernow kensa!'* Cornwall first! Together, as one, they charged. *'Kernow kensa!'*

A rebel gunner leaped forward, smoking linstock arcing down. The gun muzzle exploded in a sheet of flame, white light and searing heat.

VI

Beach Wood

Nathaniel Dunkley
Beach Wood, Lansdown Hill, half
past six o'clock in the evening

'The're right close, Nat.' Billy was afeared, whispering.

'I know, Billy.' The cavalier horse were close now, climbing the hill towards the wood. Sweat ran down Nat's back, cold and damp under the trees. Hunger and worry gripped his innards. But he needed to be strong. For Billy.

Billy looked up at him. 'What'er we goin to do?'

'We've got'er wait for sergeant, give fire when he tells we.' He'd not thought it would come to this. 'Check thy match is lit, Billy.' Nat checked his own match, flicked the ash off and blew gently on it for the umpteenth time that day.

They'd watched the Cornish foot pour down from their hill across the valley and march up the road through a hail of cannon fire and shot. It was as if nothing could stop them. A battle raged along the ridge to their right in flame and thunder under dark clouds of gunsmoke. Now the cavalier horse came on up the hill to join them.

They were supposed to be on the edge of the battlefield, out of the way – *safe*, the corporal had said. It was dark and still here under the trees. Maybe the cavaliers wouldn't see them. Maybe they would just let them go on by.

'Stand up!' It was the sergeant, striding along the line with his damned halberd. 'Make ready to give fire by salvee!' All along the edge of the wood, officers were stirring their plotoons of musketeers into action.

'Blow on thy coal, Billy.' He whispered so sergeant wouldn't hear. *Oh Lord, don't let Billy misfire. Let them hit their mark true, like real soldiers.* 'And try thy match.' He looked to see that Billy's match was firm in its cock and trimmed to come down onto the priming pan.

'Present!' The sergeant raised his halberd. 'Aim low boys! Aim for their bloody horses!'

'Guard thy pan and blow, Billy.' One last blow and the match spluttered bright and hot in the gloom. 'Open pans!' He flicked open the pan cover to lay bare priming powder and touch hole bare beneath the match.

The first troop of cavaliers were only yards from the edge of the wood, their horses straining at the hill. An officer in plumed hat and lace led them on. His horse waivered in front of Nat's aim, the barrel heavy, shaking. He leant against a tree, braced his left arm against its trunk, steadied his breathing.

'Give fire!'

Nat shut his eyes and squeezed the trigger arm. The great musket exploded, thumping into his shoulder with a vicious kick, ball of smoke and terrifying roar. He knew he should keep his eyes open, but he couldn't help it. The musket's kick always hurt, left him bruised and sore. All about him, the trees were filled with stinking, choking sulphurous smoke. Nat's eyes burned as twigs and leaves fell from above.

'Make Ready!' The sergeant's voice echoed in the gloom. 'Give fire at will!'

Billy looked up, grinning. Together they reloaded their muskets, holding them across their chests, the match pulled free, its smouldering ends between the fingers of the left hand. Together, they whispered the command for each posture, checking for any mistake, one eye out for their sergeant, a pair of butties watching out for each other.

'Clear pans!' Together they stuck a thumb into warm priming pans, wiping gritty burnt powder away from touch holes. 'Prime pans!' They poured in fresh powder. 'Shut yorn pan!' They shut their covers firmly. 'Cast off your loose corns. Blow off your loose corns.' They shook and blew loose powder grains from the pan and breech.

'Cast about your musket. Open your charge.' Musket butt on the ground, right foot forward, Nat gripped the first powder bottle on the bandolier, wiggling its cover up and off with thumb and forefinger. Billy pulled his off with his teeth. He still struggled to get the caps off with just finger and thumb.

'Charge with powder.' Upending the bottle, each tipped a charge into the muzzle of their musket. 'Charge with bullet.' They took an ounce lead ball from their bullet bags and dropped it down the barrel. 'Charge with wad.' They each pulled out a scrap of torn prayerbook. Nat unfolded his, stood straight, pretended to read it, solemnly, like a real minister. *And He shall deliver their kings into thine hand. And thou shalt destroy their name from under heaven.* With a shared grin, they stuffed the scraps down into the muzzle of their musket.

'Draw forth your scouring stick.' They pulled the stick out from under their musket barrels. 'Shorten your stick.' Each turned their sticks, put the rammer head against their chest and slid their hand down to grasp it near the end. 'Ram home your charge.' They pushed the stick into the muzzle and thrust it down, ramming it home three times to be sure there was no gap between charge and shot that could burst the breech.

Already, others were giving fire, firing at will as soon as they were loaded. But Billy needed more time than others. He was only young. The sergeant was looking at them, striding through the trees, his great halberd in his fist.

'Withdraw your scouring stick. Shorten your stick. Return your stick.' They whipped the stick out, turned it and slid it back into its groove beneath the barrel. 'Draw forth your match. Blow your coal. Cock your match. Try yorn match.' They took the end of the match in the right hand, blew the ash from it, pressed it into the jaws of the cock and checked it would come down over the priming pan. Finally, they were ready.

'Yo' two! Stop lorpin' about an' gerron wirrit!' The sergeant was behind them. 'Nat, Billy, present an' give fire! Bloody cavaliers aren't waitin all day for yo' pair of daft 'apeths!'

Another quick blow, the match crackling bright, pan cover flicked open and up to the present, arm braced against the tree. Nat peered through the smoke. The cavalier officer and his horse were still there, closer now, almost passing the edge of the wood. Nat pulled the butt into his bruised shoulder, aimed for the horse's breast, low against the musket's kick. Eyes wide open, he steadied his breathing, squeezed the trigger.

Again, the musket crashed out, smashing into his bruised shoulder with its terrible thunder, flame and blinding smoke.

'Cock-bod!' Billy was jumping, pointing. 'Nat, thou'st killed that bloody 'oss! Thou hast!'

Nat stepped forward, peered through the smoke. The horse was on the ground, kicking, whinnying, the cavalier dragging himself to his feet. He'd done it! He'd hit his mark, struck home, knocked down a bloody cavalier horse.

Beside him, Billy's musket exploded in a deafening roar and ball of choking gunsmoke. Billy staggered, almost knocked from his feet by the blast, his muzzle waving in the air.

They shared a grin as they set about reloading: clearing the pan, priming, shutting the cover; casting and blowing off the loose corns; charging with powder, bullet and wad; ramming home; drawing forth the match, blowing the coal to finally cock the match again. All about them, the wood rang with crashing muskets, thick with smoke under the trees and lowering sun. Together, they gave fire again. As the smoke rolled back, the wood filled with cheering, shouting, men pointing.

'Look!' Billy was jumping. 'Thee's runnin, Nat! T' bloody cavaliers is runnin!'

'Alright!' The sergeant paced along the line. 'Make ready! There'll be more on 'em yet!'

A shot rang out amongst the trees.

'Who were it?' The sergeant glared at them, shaking his halberd. 'Speak up! I'll bat the next lairy bugger that doesna guard theirn match! Have a care, or you'll ger a bastin'!'

Again, a shot crashed out. Then another, the ball clattering through the low branches, smacking into a tree above; a shower of twigs, leaves and splinters softly falling. The shot had come from behind them, from inside the wood.

'Shit! About face!' The sergeant was pointing, yelling. 'About face! Cavaliers in the wood!'

VII

'Kernow Bys Vycken!'

Morgan Pascoe
The top of Lansdown Hill, seven o'clock in the evening

The blinding light cleared, the noise of battle returning, Morgan Pascoe was alive, still standing. The file beside him was gone, swept away, churned to bloody pulp as the cannister shot tore through them at point-blank range.

A deep growl swept up from the ranks behind, a wave of anger swelling up from the ocean floor to burst upon the dark cliffs above, cascading over the breastwork in a foaming torrent of yelling, stabbing, hacking Cornishmen.

Morgan thrust his pike into the body on the breastwork, deep into the wood behind, pulled it free to charge on, clawing his way up the bank. At the top, rebel gunners and musketeers ran from the gun platform – chaos, burning powder, flame and smoke. A rebel officer tried to rally them, a fat city merchant in silver lace and plumed helmet, a rich monger, an engrosser, a bastard broker that preyed upon the poor for profit.

The tosser twisted and parried, pushing the pike away with his spear-headed partizan. But he was fat and slow. Morgan drew his pike back, balanced its sixteen feet of ash and steel in his hands and lunged. The pike sank deep into bastard's belly. He drove it deeper still, the monger doubling over, sinking to his knees, the pike head thrusting from his back. Morgan drew his knife and slit the pig's throat, spilling his blood on the trampled ground.

He dragged his pike back, soaked with gore. He looked up; the lowering sun lanced through black clouds of sulphur. Beyond the merchant's body stood a squadron of horse, rebel horse, Saxon English horse; armoured horsemen clad in iron; helmets, breast and backplates, buff coats, gauntlets and long boots; on great chargers that pawed the ground, wreathed in smoke; a shaft of sunlight glinting on armour, harness, carbines and pistols. There was nothing between him and them but flat open grass down. He stepped back. He'd come too far.

'Form Battaile!' Sir Bevil was yelling, pushing men into line. 'Prepare to receive horse! Pikes, on me!' The drums beat the call to the colours, to reform the ranks. 'Form Battaile!'

Anthony Payne stood like a rock beside his colonel, Sir Bevil's standard held high against the dark storm. 'The Colonel's Pike Division, to me! Morgan, stand with me. Front rank now.'

Morgan took his place in the front rank again as the files filled behind him, the drums still beating. Their musketeers were locked in fire with rebel foot battalions left and right, flaming volleys behind banks of gunsmoke, sergeants pushing them into line with their halberds.

'Battaile, advance your arms!' Sir Bevil stood with them. 'Port your arms! Pikes, charge your pikes!' Morgan hefted his pike up to grasp it in the right hand, swung its head forward and then down again. Beside him, from behind, the pikes came down in a thick fence of ash and steel. If they stood their ground, together, as one, no horse would charge them, no matter how hard a rider spurred it. It wasn't in their nature. He stared out along the length of his pike.

A blare of trumpets, the rebel squadron coming on through the smoke; a hundred or more men and animals tight packed in ranks; beasts snorting, tossing heads; hooves drumming the dry ground in a steady trot, harness clashing, louder as they came on, drowning out the crash of muskets. Flame ripped along their line, carbines crashing out. Beasts and riders burst from the cloud of their own swirling gun-smoke to reign in hard only a pike's length away; teeth bared, eyes wild, spume flying from champing bits; a dark wall of iron, leather and stamping horseflesh.

Each horseman drew a pistol, levelled it. Again, flame tore along their line as the pistols exploded, this time closer, louder, more vicious. A pike dropped beside him, the man clutching at his arm. But Grenville's pikemen stood firm; only the curses of those struck and a low growl of anger. Beside them, their musketeers answered with a volley of their own. It was ragged, half rushed, but a rider and three horses fell writhing and kicking on the ground, the rest of the squadron turning to ride away, back into the smoke that surrounded them. Almost before they'd gone, musketeers dashed out, leaped upon the fallen horsemen, musket butts and knives rising and falling, before rifling pouches, pockets and purses.

'Stand straight!' Sir Bevil held the pikes in check. 'There'll be more of them!'

Where were their own bloody cavaliers? Why were they not with them now, on top of the hill, driving back the rebel horse? Was this fight too hot for them? The rest of the Cornish foot still struggled to get up onto the top of the hill, the battle raging along the ridgeline to their left. Grenville's alone stood on the summit, wreathed in stinking sulphurous smoke, clinging to their edge of the down.

'Here they come again!' Sir Bevil stood beside them, his partizan raised.

Another squadron of rebel horse advanced out of the smoke, firing their carbines as they came. This time, they swung against the musketeers with drumming hooves, crashing pistols, great mortuary swords and poleaxes. There were curses, yells and shouting, the musketeers unable to protect themselves from the beasts that charged them with volleys of shot, steel and flailing iron hooves. There was nothing more they could do. Their ranks broke to clamber under the pikes, into gaps in the ranks or back behind the breastwork.

Morgan looked down at the musketeers sheltering under his pike, tending bullet wounds, binding scalps sliced open, bleeding arms and severed fingers. He looked along the line of pikemen. Bloodshot eyes stared out, red, tired, slumped over their pikes, bodies torn, battered and bloody. '*Sows* bastards!'

'Stand firm with me now, boys.' Sir Bevil moved amongst them. 'Stand firm.' He reached out to a wounded man, touching another's shoulder. 'We stand together now. One and all.' He was limping, hobbling, leaning on his partizan.

Already, again, another dark rank of shadows loomed out of the smoke, took shape. Another squadron of damned rebel horse tossing and snorting, pawing the ground.

Sir Bevil took a place in the front rank, amongst them, beside his standard. 'Stand firm now, boys. Stand firm for your King. For God. For each other.'

The rebel horse came on: lobsters, armoured from head to knee, closed helmets, shot-proof cuirass, arms vambraced, thighs covered by steel tassets; mounted on great warhorses.

'Stand firm!' Sir Bevil coughed, recovered, raised his

partizan high, tears and hurt in his eyes, blood dripping from his sleeve. 'Stand firm!' He coughed again and spat. 'For Cornwall!'

The ground shook under the drumming iron hooves, the armoured ranks packed knee to knee, rank upon rank of them, pistols in hand, the air about them thick with smoke.

A murmur swept across the mass of pikemen and musketeers, forty-score voices whispering a prayer, a *hireth* longing, an ancient pride that swirled, twisting in men's souls to burst forth in one determination, one yell. *'Kernow bys vycken!'* Cornwall for ever!

VIII

'Upon the Hill'

Ralph Reeve
Beach Wood, Lansdown Hill, half past
seven o'clock in the evening

The rebel musketeers were up ahead on the far edge of the wood. Ralph Reeve stepped between the trees as quickly and as quietly as he could. Another stick cracked beneath a boot, brambles catching in his spurs. Already there were shots down to their left, another division engaged. They would be too late, too few, the King's horse galled, thrown back by the rebels that raked them from this wood. Beyond the wood the battle raged, the ridge still in rebel hands as they poured shot and cannon fire down upon the Cornish foot from their breastworks.

Ralph gripped his musket, his back cold with sweat beneath the trees, the late sun struggling to pierce between its shadows. He blew on the match till it crackled bright in its cock as he led his little division of dragoons forward between the trees in open order. Beside him, the hunter in his element, Sam stepped lightly. Tandy moved beside him, alert, ready. There was Jack, scarred and grim, and Jewkes glowering, uneasy, dangerous, his matchlock gripped in gnarled fists.

Dear Clem still smiled, and there was Luke, blessed Luke, his lansprizado.

Sergeant O'Brien followed. He still did not know what the big Irishman thought of him. He never had a good word to say, always keeping himself apart, even in quarters. They said he'd fought in Flanders. Some said he'd been with Buckingham at La Rochelle, others that he'd served with O'Neill's Irish *Tercio*, for Spain, that he'd fought at Breda, Arras and Gennep. At least he knew what he was doing in a fight like this. Somewhere behind him was Kibler, lagging again, his bandolier caught in a bramble bush at the edge of the wood.

Ahead, dark figures moved amongst the trees and smoke. He needed to tell his division what they were to do, give them his orders. 'We get as close as we can. Then fire at will. But we skirmish in pairs. In files. One man giving fire while the other loads. We stay high, up the slope. I want to get above them. If we can, we cut them off.'

'I'm with ee, Master Ralph.' Clem watched his back as ever.

They moved closer, stepping from tree to tree, the firing down to their left more intense now. They pushed on, across the slope. Ahead, figures moved, shouting, a sergeant with halberd pointing up at them, turning musketeers to face them. They had been seen.

A flash of fire, ball of smoke, shot clattering through the trees and the thump of a musket firing at them. Then another. And another, the ball smacking into a tree next to Clem. They had to move carefully now. 'Keep to the cover and keep your heads down!'

The rebel sergeant was directing their fire, pointing them out as targets. Ralph tucked behind the next tree, blew his match to a crackle and flicked open the priming pan, edging around the trunk to raise his musket. The fool stood in the open below him. Ralph steadied his breathing, aimed low to compensate for the slope, exhaled and steadily squeezed the trigger.

The cock snapped down, the match stabbing into the pan in a jet of sparks. The musket crashed out in a ball of smoke, flame and thumping recoil. No time to wait for the smoke to clear to see if he'd hit his mark.

He turned, his back against the tree as he reloaded, Clem stepping past with a nod. Luke and Sam fired then Jack, followed by Tandy, Clem and Jewkes as they moved slowly forward, giving a steady fire, skirmishing from tree to tree.

Ralph thrust the scouring stick back into its groove, pressed the match back into its cock and was up, moving past Clem as he poured powder down his barrel, his back to a tree. There was no sign of the rebel sergeant below. Perhaps he'd thought better of standing in the open, or he lay under a tree with a bullet in him.

Ralph searched for another target, a musketeer beside a tree, ramming home his charge. Again, he took aim, fired and loaded as Clem stepped beyond him, aimed and fired. Again, Ralph moved across the slope as Clem loaded his musket.

Ahead, along the slope, figures were moving, climbing the hill, the rebel musketeers retreating up the edge of the wood to the ridge above. Down the slope to their left, the other dragoon divisions were pressing forward, squeezing the rebels into the corner of the wood. Together, they were forcing them out.

The rebels were running, scrabbling up the hill to get away, not even returning fire now, intent only on escape. 'Come on!' Ralph stepped out, moving quickly. 'They're getting away!' Together, they pressed forward, no longer moving from tree to tree. No longer halting to cover each other. They would be the ones to cut off the rebel retreat and win the wood.

'Look out!' Sam threw himself against a tree, musket raised. 'Behind that tump!'

Something moved, a rebel coat, half hidden, a musket levelled. At Clem! 'No!' Ralph's musket exploded in his grasp. 'Bastard!' Leaping forward through the smoke, he swung the butt high, the barrel hot and smoking.

The body lay on its front behind the upturned roots of a tree, blood seeping amongst the dead leaves, torn roots and broken soil. Ralph turned it over with his boot, ready to smash the skull if it moved. It rolled on its back, arms open, cap thrown back, face staring up from a collar that was too wide, a coat made for a bigger man, cuffs that swallowed tiny hands, skinny legs and shoes that did not fit.

It was a boy. A kid barely bigger than his musket. Ralph stared, the musket falling to his side. He'd killed a child.

'He were all cooched down.' Sam stepped forward. 'As if he were hiding. Poor little nisgal.'

'I thought. . .' Ralph stepped back. He wanted to wretch. 'I thought he was going to shoot. . . to shoot Clem.'

'Perhaps he were.' Sam closed the child's eyes and gaping mouth. 'His match were out, mind. No use moithering on it now.'

'You weren't to know, Master Ralph.' Clem stood beside him. 'Tint right he bein' here.'

'A'right now, Reeve.' It was Sergeant O'Brien. 'Stop your dawdlin' and let's be g'ttin' on with it! We need to be clearing this bloody wood of rebels, so we do. Not standin' about weepin' over them now!'

IX

'A Heavy Stone on the Very Brow of the Hill'

Francis Reeve

Lansdown Hill, eight o'clock in the evening

Praise God! Finally, they were moving. They were to take up the fight.

Francis pressed spurs against the trembling flanks of his horse. Now, the beast would serve the Lord, it would carry him into battle against the unrighteous. All day they had stood on Lansdown Hill, unmoving in the heat, dust and gunsmoke while others threw themselves at the Cornish host. Even now, these devils stood on the very edge of Lansdown. For now was the moment, before God and the setting sun, here on this mount, to turn back the tide of evil that threatened to engulf them.

He was chosen. He and the Godly troopers of Colonel Nathaniel Fiennes' Regiment of Horse were chosen to reap the harvest, to offer up the sacrifice. They had charged the guns at Edgehill, taken Aylesbury and stormed Winchester as a troop with Sir William Balfour. Now their Puritan captain was a colonel and Governor of Bristol, and they were his regiment. Now, after others had been cast back, they were chosen to destroy this evil that clung to the walls of Zion. For he was chosen of God, an Israelite dedicated to the King of Heaven – justified, sanctified and received in communion with Christ. And they would glory in His name.

Francis pulled down the barred faceguard of his helmet, steel bars meeting iron breastplate. Spurs turned against the beast's bloodied belly, he lurched forward. All along the line, horses tossed their heads, stepped high, champing at their bits. Tight-packed, they surged forward, three ranks of horsemen, booted legs pressed between heaving horse flanks left and right, a mighty squadron of iron zeal, steel and stamping horseflesh.

———

Sir Bevil lay a-dying, his soul departed, skull split open by a bloody lobster with a poleaxe. He'd fought beside them in the front rank, with them, one of them; until he fell, along with so many more. The Saxon bastard died under a barrage of musket butts, his horse stuck through with a pike. The animal lay before them now, blood bubbling from its nose, muzzle and ripped belly, shattered ash sticking from its chest. Other horses still writhed on the ground kicking feebly, whinnying in their pain, eyes wide and tongues bare. All about them lay dead and dying men, damned Saxon English lobsters and brave Cornishmen, the ground strewn with the truck of war: bits of armour all stove in, equipage, helmets, swords, muskets and a broken drum.

Here and there, a man picked through the chaos in search of powder, shot or a weapon. But most, those of Grenville's men that still stood, leaned on their pikes and muskets staring blankly out through eyes shot with blood. Those that could no longer stand sat or lay slumped on the ground trying to staunch their wounds, trying to hold together their lacerated bodies, trying to hold on as they coughed, moaned and spat out their lifeblood.

Morgan Pascoe touched the arm tucked into his coat and winced at the pain. It was broken, shattered by a pistol ball, wet and sticky, the blood thick on his ripped sleeve. It would have to be severed, sawn through, amputated. God knew how he would drive a plough, reap, stack or thresh corn with one arm. He was a cripple, maimed and useless. But he wasn't going. *He weren't turning. Not now, not never.* None of them was going. They'd sworn to stand with Sir Bevil. He'd stood with them, shown them the way, held them together. He'd taken wound upon wound, been the butt, the mark, the aim of all that came at them. They weren't yielding now, not to no bloody Saxon English bastard, not to no bugger. The dead didn't desert him. Neither would the living. They'd stand or fall beside him, Cornishmen one and all.

Anthony Payne stood towering over them like a rock upon Bedruthen Sands, the standard ripped and holed in his grip while the tide swirled all about. He pulled off his morion helmet and filled his great chest. With eyes closed, his voice rang out in song, a deep slow chant that rose and fell, the words lifted to the setting sun that burned fierce and red through the black sulphurous clouds about them.

'Ellas, kyny a rama ha cana coll,
Marow a Arleth, a'gun pernaz pub ol.'

Together, as one, they sang, following his lead. They filled the air with the ancient hymn, a chant in the old tongue, a lament for their lord. As one, they sang the *Kan Marya*, the song of Mary Salome, she who saw her Lord crucified, who found his tomb empty, mourner of Jesus Christ, sister to the Blessed Virgin, daughter of Saint Anne, daughter of a Breton queen.

'Ellas, kyny a rama ha cana coll,
Marow a Arleth, a'gun pernaz pub ol.'

Morgan let the tears fall down his face. They ran in streaks through the dust and powder soot, staining his ragged collar as the old words seeped into his being, wrapped themselves about his soul, dragging at his *hireth*, his longing for home and what might have been. For their lord was dead.

Alas, morning I sing, morning I call;
Dead is my Lord, that bought us all.
"Ellas, kyny a rama ha cana coll,
Marow a Arleth, a'gun pernaz pub ol.'

They were singing! The bloody Cornish were singing, chanting their defiance in a strange, heathen tongue. Nat gripped his musket tight.

'Give. . . fire!' The rank ahead gave the barbarians another volley of lead. 'To the rear!' They turned and filed past. Now it was his turn, the sergeant staring, halberd held high. 'Second rank!'

Nat stepped forward.

'Present!'

He blew his match coal bright and hot, flicked open the priming pan, levelled the musket at the swirling smoke.

'Give. . . fire!'

With one deafening roar, the line of muskets exploded in a sheet of flame and yet more choking, sulphurous smoke; Nat's shoulder bruised and burning with pain again.

'To the rear!'

He turned to the right and marched back through the ranks, a grin from Billy as he passed, to take his place at the rear. He and Billy had got out of that wood. They'd run, dodging between the trees. Others weren't so lucky, killed or trapped by the damned cavaliers. Now they were back with the rest of Lord St John's Regiment, back safe in the ranks, in battalia, back where Billy wouldn't be so afeared, giving fire to the heathen Cornish.

———

The rebel battalion lay ahead. It straddled the road to Bath, one wing of musketeers bent back, firing on Grenville's Cornish foot where they clung to the edge of the down.

'We need to get closer.' Ralph turned to look at his division. They'd cleared the wood of rebels, cutting off their retreat, forcing the last of them to surrender. Now they huddled around the edge of a hollow, a shallow pit or old scraping out beyond the wood on the down. 'There are more pits like this further on. The sun will be behind us. It should blind them. But keep low and move quickly.'

He led the way, bent double, musket in one hand, his boots flapping as he ran sliding down the bank of the next pit. They worked their way closer, to within range, until there were no more pits to occupy, just open down. 'This is as close as we can get.' Other groups of dragoons followed, fanning out to fill the pits left and right. 'Fire at will, but work in pairs, in files. One man giving fire while the other loads. If you can hit them, aim for their officers.'

———

They were singing! The accursed Cornish were singing, chanting a satanic hymn in their devil's tongue; a witch's incantation, beckoning the night, hidden in fiery dark smoke, summoning Satan himself and his forces of darkness.

The trumpets blared over the din of musket and cannon.

Francis ran spur rowels down his horse's flanks, lurching into a trot. Yanking back on the reins, he twisted the iron bit in its mouth, holding the beast in check. He drew a pistol from its saddle holster, pulled back the cock, releasing the doglock. Another touch to Breda's bloodied belly and they sprang into a canter.

Billy marched past him, back through the ranks, with a grin and smoking musket almost taller than he. He was alright; he wasn't afeared. He'd fired in his rank and now he'd be safe at the rear while he made his musket ready again. Nat stepped forward another rank closer to the front. If only he could be next to his butty, to whisper each posture, to watch out for the sergeant. The boy's shoulder had to be bruised something terrible, worse than his own.

A scream, shouting, men affrighted, pushing from behind. Another cry, the rear rank under fire, cavaliers behind them. 'Nat!' Billy's voice – Billy was calling for him. 'Nat?' He was afeared.

'Billy!' Nat turned. His butty needed him. 'Billy!'

Francis stood high in his stirrups, levelled his pistol, took aim at a pikeman, a heathen Cornishman to be cut down, a harvest to be reaped and offered up to the Lord.

Pistols crashed and flared along the line in a ripple of fire. His gauntleted finger closed around the trigger, the pistol whipping back and up as the charge exploded in his grip.

His horse shook, tossed, stamped, ears flat. Francis slid the smoking pistol into its holster, grabbed at both reins, hauled the beast's head back and down.

51

The pikeman sank to his knees, clawing at his chest, gasping, choking, spitting blood, his lungs flooding – drowning in his own sin.

Francis drew his sword, the heavy mortuary blade rasping from the scabbard, his gauntleted fist tight around the hilt. It was time to reap God's harvest, to scythe the last stand, to cut it down with steel before the sun finally set. Already, it was dipping, a great fiery disc burning over Bristol.

———

Morgan pulled the blade from the ground and lifted the sword, the last of the sun running red down its length. It was an English horseman's sword, a beautiful piece of steel. Now the bastard and his horse lay dead on the ground in front of them and the sword was his. He couldn't weald a pike with a shattered arm, nor fire a musket, nor load a pistol – so, a sword it was.

A pair of wounded musketeers sat propped against the animal's carcass, bound in bloody bandages, their muskets ready across their laps. All about Morgan, men braced themselves against the next Saxon onslaught. They weren't yielding. Sir Bevil hadn't yielded and the dead didn't yield now. They'd stand their ground with their lord and brothers, alive or dead, day or night, forever true Cornishmen, one and all! *'Kernow bys vycken!'*

———

Ralph raised his head again, up over the lip of the pit. He took aim at an officer, sunset bright on his partizan, gorget and lace, and fired. They were turning. The rebel battalion was turning away from Grenville's Cornishmen, turning and retiring! It was beating a retreat back down the lane across the down, back towards Bath. 'Don't stop now. Keep firing. Keep them moving. Break them if we can!'

———

Francis dug spurs into Breda's bloodied flanks, forced the beast at the heathen horde. They huddled, clinging to the very edge of the down, surrounded by their dead and dying; a heap of sullen devils, reeking of death, saltpetre and sin. In their midst was a giant that held aloft Satan's banner. All had to be cut down. Sacrificed. Flung from Mount Zion, thrown back into Gehenna and the bottomless pit from which they came.

He turned aside a pike, leaped a dead horse, his own terrified beast flinching, rearing from the flesh and anarchy that carpeted the ground. A one-armed creature hacked at him with raised sword. He parried and slashed back. Again and again, he brought his blade smashing down upon the faithless sea-devil until he sank to his knees. With one final blow, he smashed the fiend's sword away. And drove his own blade deep into its chest.

———

Morgan breathed in the sweet smell of warm grass, the tang of dry soil, the summer evening hum of bees, the metal taste of his own blood, the stench of sulphur, saltpetre, the noise of battle all drifting away with the last light of the setting sun. He'd gathered in his last harvest. He'd cried the neck. No more would he plough, drag sea-wrack, stones nor clods against a winter gale. He was going home to his Lord.

Betty was calling, waiving him to follow, laughing as she ran ahead while his father held the babe. She'd take him by the hand, run him to the clifftop, lay him down among the bracken, yarrow, betony and furze. She'd kiss him, love him, hold him tight. Until the sun finally sank below the ocean.

X

The Dead Conquered whilst the Living Flew

Ralph Reeve
The Pits, Lansdown Hill, eleven o'clock at night

Ralph lay against the side of the pit, stars filling the sky above. It was dark, silent, clear. Both armies drew breath in the cool night air. The heat still rose from the earth beneath Ralph's back while the stench of gunsmoke lingered in the grass and seeped into the pit. There was no moon – and no firing, just the moan of the wounded, of men broken, dying where they lay.

The two armies had fought themselves to a standstill. Grenville's stand had clung on long enough for the rest of the King's foot to claw their way onto the edge of Lansdown, followed by their guns. The rebels had fallen back from their breastworks to a wall that crossed the down. And there the two armies had stood pouring great shot at each until the last light had finally gone and darkness stopped them. Thank God there was no moon to let them continue. For an hour or more each army had waited, exhausted, in silence.

There were whispers that the rebels were just waiting to charge, to push the battered Cornish foot back down the hill.

They'd knocked gaps in the wall for their horse to charge out. There was nothing to stop them. The cavalier horse had refused to stand on the down. They were hiding now, somewhere back down the hill, beyond the reach of the rebel cannon, ready to run. Ralph and his dragoons lay in the pit from where they'd galled the end of the rebel line, half way between the wood and their wall.

The glow of match coals faintly lit the others in the pit – his division, his band of dragoons, his duty and charge. They were all shattered... beat... drained... their powder, shot and match almost spent. Weeks in the field, weeks of constant marches, guard duty, scouting and skirmishing had taken their toll. They slept where they lay, slumped against the side of the pit, twitching in their sleep. Luke had organised the watch. He stared out over the lip now, keeping watch while the others slept. They would need to conserve their match if it was to last the night. He stubbed his out, closed his eyes and tried to shut out the image of a face staring up from amongst the dead leaves and torn roots of the wood – a child's face, tiny hands and skinny legs poking from the collar and cuffs of a coat made for a man.

———

The night exploded in flame, lead shot crackling through the cool air, tearing the grass and turf about the pit in a crashing volley. Then another. And another. The down alight with flashes of fire and thunder.

Luke! Oh God, he was watching out, over the lip. 'Luke?'

'I'm alright.' Luke slid back down the bank. 'But the whole rebel line is giving fire.'

'Thank God. The rest of you, keep your heads down.' Ralph lit his match from Luke's. He blew on it till it spluttered bright and hot. 'If you are not already, make ready. Get your match lit.' The thunder of the last volley rolled away, dark and quiet returning Each man held his breath, straining to hear. Silence. No trumpets, no drums, no yelled orders. The rebels weren't charging.

'That's strange. No cannon.' Luke was right. 'Just muskets.'

'Well.' Jack shifted. 'If they ain't charging, what are they about then?'

'I reckon I hears hosses a-moving.' Clem whispered. 'But they ain't a-gettin closer.'

'Tha' as maybe.' Sam was at the pit edge, looking out. 'But their matches is still a-lit all along that there wall. And there're stands of pikes. None on them is movin' mind. Tis like they're just standing there, stock still.'

'Ralph. . .' Luke sounded earnest. 'Maybe it's some sort o' ruse, a subterfuge.'

Each one offered up their thoughts, the noise rising. 'Alright.' Ralph sat forward. 'Maybe they are up to something. Either way, we keep down and we keep quiet. We watch and we listen.'

There was a noise from behind, someone moving, a figure at the edge of the pit, sliding down the bank. 'A'right now, Reeve.' It was Sergeant O'Brien. 'We need to find out what the bloody rebels are up to. The captain wants yiz to send out a scout.'

'I'll go, Sergeant O'Brien.' Ralph laid his musket down. He could not ask any of the others to do it. He had to do it. Alone. 'I will go myself.'

'I'm a-goin along o' you, Master Ralph.' It was Clem, dear Clem.

'No, Clem. It will be quieter with just one.'

'And what do I say to your father? I promised he I'd stick by you.'

'You tell him I gave you an order.'

'Well bugger it. I dunno. . .'

'Please, Clem, guard my musket. I will leave it behind. The bloody match will give me away.' Ralph unbuckled his spurs and sword belt, pulled off his hat and bandolier. 'And my spurs and scabbard.' He drew the short tuck sword. 'It will be easier moving with sword only.'

'A'right, lad. Very well. But take this here pistol with ye.' Sergeant O'Brien pushed a wheellock horse pistol into his hand. 'It's spanned and ready. I'll be wantin' it back, mind. It was. . . *given* to me by a French officer at Leuven, so it was.'

Ralph weighed the pistol in his hand. It was a beautiful weapon. 'Thank you.'

'A'right now. On yer way.'

With a nod from those around him, Ralph pushed the pistol inside his coat and crawled up over the edge of the pit, out across the down. The grass was cool and fresh beneath the stars. He crawled, crept, stole across the open ground, as low as possible, parallel with the road. Finally, he was level with the end of the wall. Slowly, carefully, he crept towards it, pausing every few feet to listen. The great Plough and pole-star hung silently above the wood, the pits and his friends, watching, waiting. A fox barked in the distance.

He slipped into the ditch beside the lane and peered across it. Lit match coals stretched away along the wall's length, the smell of saltpetre hanging in the air. Pike shafts stood dark against the bright eastern stars. But something was not right. They all stood in one rank along the wall. It was as if the rear ranks had lain down, grounded their weapons, as if they were lying asleep. Or was this some sort of trap? Were there rebels hiding, waiting, ready to spring up?

Ralph gripped the pistol and sword. Slowly, cautiously he

stood, sweat prickling the base of his spine, running down his back, lifting his hair in the cool night air. Carefully he stepped out across the lane, feeling with his boots for loose stones. He slipped back down into the ditch and hollow on the far side, exhaling gently. Nothing moved. Silence. No sleeping rebels and no ambuscade.

Lit matches hung, draped, dangling over the wall top in a line. It was not a rank of musketeers that they had seen from the pit, but a ruse, a clever trick to make it seem so. He stuffed the pistol in his coat and pulled the sections of match from the wall, tossed them into the grass behind. He worked quickly. But there were scores of them. He couldn't pull them all down, there was not time.

The pikes stood propped against the wall, as if they were the front rank of a pike block. He pushed them to the ground, let the ash poles clatter and crash against each other. Let others hear him, let them know it was all a ruse, that the rebels had run, that there was no enemy waiting to charge.

Finally, he stubbed out and picked up more of the match, filling his fist. The pieces were short, only long enough to burn for a few hours. But his dragoons had so little left of their own and these pieces would replenish what they had. He tucked the sword under his arm and plucked up more of the matches in his right hand, left them alight to let those watching see him return to the pits, see he was a friend, that he'd taken the match from the wall.

With his fists full and the sword under his arm, he set off to walk back the way he'd come. He walked upright, strolling in the night air, the stars above and glowing match in his hand dimly lighting the way home.

XI

Prisoners, Powder and Pipes

Ralph Reeve
Tog Hill, Thursday the 6ᵗʰ of July 1643,
ten o'clock in the morning.

Ralph leaned back against his horse, the reins in his hands. It was good to be back with her, even if she was only a pony and not Breda. They stood in the warm sun, larks singing in a clear sky above, as the army assembled on Tog Hill. It was good to be alive. His tongue was dry, his body ached and his stomach groaned for want of food, drink and bed. Dust and grime chafed at his collar and his grazed hands stung with saltpetre. But they had won the day and he and his dragoons were unhurt.

They stood in almost the same positions they had started the battle the day before. They'd stayed in the field all night, masters of Lansdown Hill, the foot plundering what they wanted in the morning light. He'd hoped to find a carbine on the field, but the Cornish were in savage mood, threatening any that came close to their spoil. Now the army rendez-voused back on Tog Hill. The rebels were nowhere to be seen, retreated into Bath.

But victory had come at a terrible cost. Sir Bevil Grenville lay mortally wounded, his major, captain-lieutenant and two hundred of his brave Cornishmen already dead. Three hundred more were grievously wounded. Almost every foot regiment had lost men dead or wounded. Sir Ralph Hopton, the Field-Marshal-General, had been shot through the arm. Lord Mohun had lost a foot smashed by a cannon ball. Lord Carnarvon, Colonel Bennett and Colonel Vaughan were all hurt. Others among the horse were missing, some no doubt fled back to Oxford.

They waited for an ammunition cart, the prisoners and the last of the rear-guard to follow up the lane from the cornfield below. The cart was loaded with wounded prisoners and barrels of powder left behind by the rebels when they abandoned the hill. The powder was badly needed. Ralph touched the bandolier over his shoulder; only six charges remained and precious little match. Thank God he'd carried back what he could from the rebel wall. No doubt, the Field-Marshal would see the new powder distributed when they got back into their billets in Marshfield.

Sir Ralph Hopton sat astride his horse, surrounded by officers, smiling, joking, beside the lane, waiting for his rearguard, despite his wound. The Cornish foot loved him. Next to Sir Bevil Grenville, he was their hero. He'd led them to victory at Braddock Down, Sourton and Stratton. With him, they'd subdued Devon and secured Somerset. Now they'd beaten Sir William 'the Conqueror' Waller, fought their way up Lansdown Hill, thrown his Western Association army from its breastworks and sent them packing into Bath. They would attempt anything for him.

But before that, Sir Ralph Hopton and Sir William Waller had both been served together in Frederick of Bohemia's bodyguard, escorted the King and Queen in their escape from the Battle of White Mountain. It was Sir Ralph Hopton who carried the Winter Queen pillion on his horse, through the snow when she was heavy with Prince Maurice and Prince Rupert still just a babe in arms, as they fled the rape of Prague. He might have known Ralph's mother, perhaps something of his father. She'd served the queen in Prague, been part of that terrible flight. He had to find an opportunity to ask. She'd died so young, without telling him of it. And his stepfather would not speak of it, although he knew the Hoptons when they lived in Suffolk, in Yoxford, the next parish to Westleton.

Ralph fidgeted with the reins. Could he, should he, approach the Field-Marshall? He wanted – needed – to know. His discovery of the rebel retreat at night had to be worth something. The cart was closer now, almost past the Field-Marshall and his party, the wounded prisoners smoking a pipe in the sun. The opportunity to ask would soon be gone. The Field-Marshall would be busy again, the credit of his night scouting forgotten, lost in another day's march and duty. Fuck it! Ralph stepped forward, pulling the reins, the mare twitching awake.

The cart disappeared in a burst of searing white heat, burning light, shrieking wind. Again and again, shattered barrel staves, iron hoops, boards, limbs and torsos were hurled outwards by jets of blazing gas as barrel after barrel of gunpowder detonated. Burning wind scorched, charred and blistered, leaving skin, throats, lungs stripped raw, thrown bodily by its force to roll in the dirt and soot. As the last barrel was flung into the air to burst like a second sun, a deafening cloud of smoke, ash and dust blackened the sky, hiding all within it.

Ralph clung to the mare's reins. All about him horses reared and tossed, whinnying and shrieking in their terror. In front of them, a horse rose from the dirt, its face bald, neck, flanks and hair smouldering, breath rasping, only to fall to the ground again a steaming, blistering heap of meat. Another horse bolted past, its body singed of hair, like parched leather. Men staggered from the smoke, their hair, beards and clothes scorched, smoking. Others: officers, prisoners, rear-guard crawled screaming amongst the scorched grass and blackened dust of the lane.

Sir Ralph Hopton was dragged, burnt, blind, hairless from the smoke to be carried away towards Marshfield. In shock and horror, his Cornish foot watched yet another of their beloved heroes pass, before dragging themselves after him.

Part Two

Devizes &
Roundway Down

That great God who is the searcher of my heart knows with what reluctance I go upon this service and with what a perfect hatred I detest a war without an enemy...

We are both on the stage, and we must act the parts that are assigned us in this tragedy.

Let us do it in a way of honour and without personal animosities; but whatever be the issue I shall not willingly relinquish the dear title of Your affectionate friend and faithful servant.

SIR WILLIAM WALLER, To my noble friend,
SIR RALPH HOPTON, 16 JUNE 1643

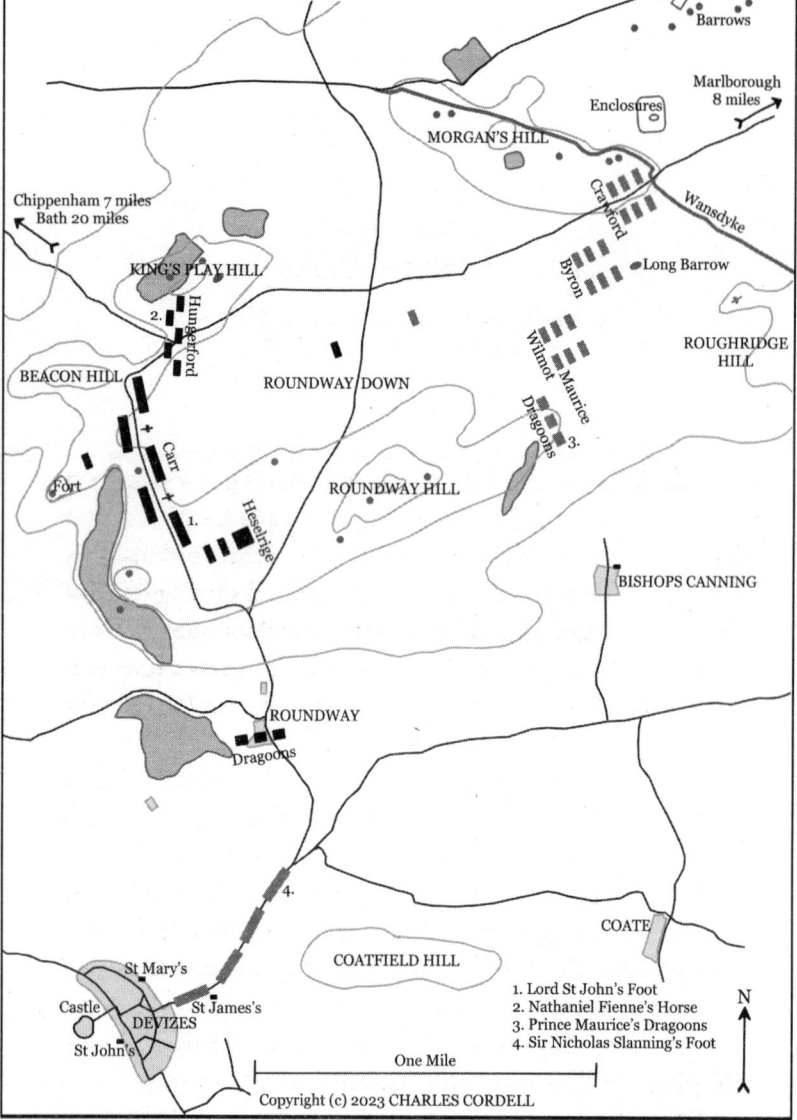

The Battle of Roundway Down: 13th of July 1643, 4 o'clock in the afternoon

Barrows

Marlborough 8 miles

Enclosures

MORGAN'S HILL

Crawford

Wansdyke

Chippenham 7 miles
Bath 20 miles

KING'S PLAY HILL

Byron

Long Barrow

ROUGHRIDGE HILL

Hungerford

2.

Wilmot

Maurice

BEACON HILL

Dragoons

ROUNDWAY DOWN

3.

Carr

Fort

1.

ROUNDWAY HILL

Heselrige

BISHOPS CANNING

ROUNDWAY

Dragoons

4.

COATE

St Mary's

COATFIELD HILL

Castle

St James's

DEVIZES

St John's

1. Lord St John's Foot
2. Nathaniel Fienne's Horse
3. Prince Maurice's Dragoons
4. Sir Nicholas Slanning's Foot

N

One Mile

Copyright (c) 2023 CHARLES CORDELL

I

Chippenham

Kendall Tremain
Chippenham, Wiltshire, Saturday the 8th of
July 1643, four o'clock in the afternoon

Kendall Tremain pulled the wool cap from his head and wiped his brow with his sleeve. It was hot, terrible hot, with hardly a breeze to ruffle the corn or grass. His feet ached and his bandolier hung heavy, pressing his sweat-soaked shirt against his chest. They'd stood in battalia facing the bloody rebels since morning, with no dinner or rest. It was near supper time and now they said they were staying put, standing in the field for the night in case the *Sows* bastards attacked.

They were supposed to be marching to Oxford to meet their king. They'd got as far as Chippenham on the King's Great Road from Bristol to London. But then Sir William bloody Waller and his rebel horse caught up with them. They'd had one night of rest before turning back over Chippenham Bridge to face the rebels. And still they stood there staring at each other: rebel horse and Cornish foot. Their own horse were no use – half of them still scattered after the fight for Lansdown Hill. Tossing 'run away horse' they were.

They'd beaten the bloody rebels, taken Lansdown Hill,

stormed its slope against great shot, grape shot and small shot. But what good had it done them? What was it all for? Sir Bevil Grenville was dead, Sir Ralph Hopton half burnt to death. Others dragged themselves on the march with bloody, bound wounds festering in the heat – yet more dead and missing. They'd seen bugger all powder, shot or match since they marched from Marshfield. The quartermaster's boy said there was none. And there was no welcome from the towns-folk in Chippenham, nor the villages along the way. What sort of victory was that?

Kendall looked along the ranks of Sir Nicholas Slanning's Regiment of Foot, 'The Tinners'. Musketeers and pikemen stood leaning on their weapons, heads bowed. They were all dirty, caked in dust and sweat, coats tattered, many of them lousy, others wrapped in bloody rags. They'd not stopped marching and fighting since they'd beaten the rebels from Stamford Hill, outside Stratton. That was back in Cornwall, before Pentecost, in the middle of May; near two months without a rest. When was it going to end? When were they going to get back home? Back to Cornwall?

God, what would he give to be there now? To be back at sea again? The smell of salt on a cool breeze, calm lap of water, tug of canvas, the shimmer of fish coming in over the gunwale. There'd be shoals of mackerel in St Ives Bay now, gleaming darts of silver and green. And then, in a month, the lookout crying *hevva* from the cliffs. . . the sea alive with pil-chards, liquid silver under the harvest moon. . . Morwenna shining, singing, chanting with the *mozzi* as they helped haul the catch ashore.

He'd always loved going to sea with his father, uncle, brother and cousins, as man and boy. It was true enough that he'd not always seen eye to eye with his elder brother. Jack knew how he loved Morwenna. But she was promised to Jack. Jack had just laughed in his face and downed another ale. They'd come to blows, onboard and on land. In the end, he'd left, took himself off. He couldn't bear to see them wed.

He'd sailed with the Newfoundland fleet, aboard a barque out of Fowey, spent near a year away, from March to November. From May to September they'd fished, gutted, drained of oil, salted, dried and packed cod, ton upon ton of dried white fish; fishing in open boats amid icebergs, whales and the *Lethowsow* swell, sheltering ashore in makeshift shacks, the howl of wolves and Beothuk in the hills about. They landed the cod in Spain, at Bilboa, then shipped home with a cargo of wool, wine, iron and timber, and a pocket full of Spanish *El Dorado* gold. That was the Year of Our Lord 1635.

But when he got home it was to find that his father, uncle, brother Jack and his cousins had all been taken by Salé rovers, Barbary corsairs, to be sold into Turkish bondage – enslaved, cut, circumcised. Their beloved *Borlewen* was found drifting, deserted, her sails flogging on the swell off Pendeen, half the catch still over the side. He'd found his mother, aunt and sisters packing fish and living off scraps, the boat sold to pay off debts they said.

He'd found Morwenna on Carn Naun, silent, wild, half starved, staring out to sea. They said she was *mescack*, crazed, daft with grief. But he wed her still; fed, clothed, cared for her. They'd been alright while his Newfoundland money lasted. But it barely kept them for the first winter. He couldn't afford a boat of his own and nobody wanted another fisherman. Nobody wanted to put out to sea – not with the corsairs off the coast. Eighty-seven Cornish crews were lost to pirates that year alone. More than a thousand men, women and children taken, the corsairs running ashore at their will.

He'd tried his luck again in Fowey, hauling seine nets filled with pilchards. But then came news of Jack. An English fleet sailed into Rabat, bombarded the Salé rovers' fortress and freed three hundred poor wretches. They told of men herded like beasts in the marketplace, chained, branded, beaten, violated, only to be marched away, sold into slavery. Women, girls... boys stripped naked, offered to satisfy every vice, their purgatory only relieved by death.

But they said Jack was different. He wasn't chained to a galley oar, nor whipped to build great palaces for the Moorish Sultan. He wasn't sold a slave. Jack had turned Turk! He was a renegade! He'd joined the bloody rovers – was one of them, a pirate. Worse, he'd taken the turban and turned Mahometan, his soul blackened and damned for eternity. They said he dressed in flowing robes, silks and calicos, and went by a new name. They called him Tariq al-Aselti or Salatik, said he sailed with the great pirate captain, John Janszoon – Murat Reis.

They said that Jack would come back for Morwenna. That he'd return to claim her for his own. That he'd come in the night to lead his heathen Moorish crew ashore. They said Jack would kill him, enslave all with him, take them from their beds. They said that Morwenna and he were Jonahs, a curse on them all. *And nobody wanted 'a Jonah aboard along of 'em'.*

They'd had to leave Fowey, fishing and the sea for good. He'd had to get her away – find a place inland, as a tinner. It was hard labour. And he did miss the sea something terrible. It wouldn't leave him: the smell washing up the great Tamar River to Danescombe on the top of the tide. It hadn't been easy. He'd had to teach Morwenna to speak *Sowsnack*. She'd only ever known *Kernuak*, their own tongue. But it was only a few old folk that still spoke it up East. They'd made do alright in the end.

They'd built a cottage. Built it themselves in a single night on a patch of waste at Metherell – got the cob walls up, roof on and fire lit before dawn to claim the lease for their life-times. It was only one room, a pig's *crow*, a furze rick and a scrap of garden, but it was theirs. He could see Morwenna now, tending the garden, she'd be weeding between the beans and onions, barefoot in the sun, pushing her hair back like she did, Hedrek playing with his little sister, Merryn.

But God knew how he missed the sea. He missed it in the sun, in the wind and the dark. He even missed the hiss of rain sweeping across it. He missed the dancing sunlight, its ever-shifting tint and hue, scudding cloud and shadow – dap-pled, ruffled, heaving, waves ridden by white horses, spume streaked, fierce and shrieking. He missed its limitless, open call, its ungoverned, unchecked freedom, the pull of the hori-zon, an unknown shore, clarity and unfathomable deep. Most of all he missed the *mordroz*: the sound of the sea, its sooth-ing whisper, its pounding drum, its howling fury. For the sea called to him still; it was in his blood, wanted him back, sucked at his soul, clawing, smothering, dragging him down, a restless lover, a shining temptress that could never be sated.

But he couldn't go back, not without Morwenna, and no one would have her back. Not until the threat of the Turks was gone, not until the King's navy had driven them off. And that wasn't going to happen without Ship Money. It wasn't right that just Cornwall and the coastal counties paid it. They were the ones that suffered, manned the navy's ships, lost loved ones. Every county and shire needed to pay their share. And that wasn't going to happen until they'd beaten the *Sows* rebel bastards in Parliament that refused to pay.

II

Rowde: Redemption and Revenge

Francis Reeve
Derry Hill, Studley, Wiltshire, Sunday the 9th
of July 1643, three o'clock in the afternoon

They were turning south, leaving the Great Road to London, turning away from Calne. Thank the Lord! The heathen Cornish horde was turning away. They were deflected, dragging themselves away, retreating.

Francis pulled the helmet from his head and mopped the sweat from his hair. It was hot, the sun beating down on iron breast, back and helmet; sweat soaking his shirt, breeches and hose beneath heavy buff coat, boots and gauntlets. Steam rose from Breda's flanks.

But the accursed were retreating, recoiling, running like the wounded beast that they were. Half their horse was scattered or taken and their foot was no longer filled with stubborn, superstitious pride. It was a mighty deliverance. For the Lord's own hand had saved His army. Surely, this was providence, God's trial of their faith. He had brought them out of the fire, anew, golden, the dross cleansed from them in its heat. *His mercy endureth for ever! We called upon him in the day of our Trouble. He delivered us. And we will glorify him.*

The heathens may have taken Lansdown Hill, defied the Lord upon its summit, but He had punished them for it. He had sent a spark to destroy the powder they had taken, to burn the apostate Hopton, to leave them with scarce any ammunition after the battle. *A fire goeth before Him and burneth up His enemies round about. His lightnings enlightened the world; the earth saw and trembled.* For the Lord would root out and destroy all who move hand or tongue against the children of the promise. *And in thy great glory, thou hast overthrown them that rose up against thee. Thou sentest forth thy wrath which consumed them as stubble.*

Sir William Waller had shielded his forces, slipped them away from Lansdown, cloaked in the dark of night, drawn them back into Bath to rest, repent and pray anew. Refreshed, they had marched out again to reoccupy and reclaim Lansdown Hill, the apostates leaving it, abandoning their gain to fall back on Marshfield and lick their wounds.

They had followed the Cornish horde as it marched to Chippenham, scattering their rear-guard of horse outside the town. Sir William had forced the apostates to stand in battalia before Chippenham all the next day and night, denying them any rest or comfort in that town.

Now they marched again, not stopping to refresh themselves, but marching on towards Calne and London until they turned aside from the Great Road, dragging themselves south between the woods and hedges towards Devizes. They were wounded, hurt – a desperate, hunted beast. Soon, the beast would tire. Then, would be the time to finish it.

Francis pulled on his helmet – bucking it tight under his chin. They were moving forward again. Troop by troop they descended the hill to follow the heathen horde south, shadowing their march. For two miles they wound their way between woods and hills, parallel with the road, gaining slowly but surely on the heathen column that followed it.

And then the country opened to heath and field; the Cornish army was exposed along the road, ragged and staggering in the listless heat of the day. A body of cavaliers led them: six strung out battalions of foot, artillery, baggage train and camp followers dragging behind, a rear-guard of three more battalions, their ranks thinned, another squadron of cavaliers and a troop of dragoons covering the rear. And behind them all limped a long, trailing column of stragglers; a procession of wounded, exhausted and lame; struggling foot soldiers, horseless cavaliers, serving boys, sutlers, camp followers, wives, whores and brats.

Francis pulled down his barred visor as his troop moved forward; Breda snorting, jolted by his spurs, the line of horses stirring into a trot. He reached forward to draw a pistol from its holster, cocking it, the dog lock released, long barrel held high. They surged forward, gathering pace.

The damned dragoons were dismounting, taking up positions in the ditches that lined the road. Let them waste their time. They were not the target. The line of godly horsemen was turning, arcing across the open heath to fall on the road behind the dragoons.

They leaped the ditch, Breda lurching forward, landing on the wide, open way. The line swung around to face north, back up the road, the dragoons behind, the stragglers before them, horses steaming, snorting in the heat and dust.

Slowly at first, they began to walk forward, the first stragglers parting, dragging themselves into the ditches. A pistol crashed out, then another. A woman screamed, men yelled and children cried. A trooper broke away to pursue a hobbling man across the heath.

Ahead, a knot of men stood firm, pressed together in a rough block across the road. They were dirty, shabby, foul, bestial – half without a pike or musket; heads, arms, torsos bound and stained with blood. They dared to stand. '*Molla Duw warnaz!*' They spat and cursed God in their heathen tongue. '*Ha whei a toaz nebbaz nes – me venga pilya gus pedn!*' They cast their witchery – conjuring their devils. '*Cawgh an Jowl y'th vin!*'

A ripple of fire burst along the line of horsemen. Francis reigned back, holding Breda in check, holstering the smoking pistol. He drew his sword, the long mortuary blade grating from the scabbard, and dug spurs into the horse's flanks to send them crashing forward. A foul, cursing beast fell yelling and snarling under the horse's hooves, another cast aside by the heavy blade.

Scattered now, they rode on, sweeping the road of more of its vermin. He and there, a pistol crashed out. But mostly, the Lord's work was done with the sword; troopers cutting down and flinging aside the sinners that were before them.

A defiant devil stood before him, hunched over a rough-hewn crutch, one leg bound in a bloody cloth, a rusty tuck sword raised. '*Ke the veaz! Horsen!*' Behind him stood a she-fiend, a foul, dirty, uncombed creature – long hair and long knife bared in the sun. A nasty little vixen stood beside her while another familiar clung to her back.

Francis smashed the tuck aside. He turned his blade in the air to bring it down upon the devil – the crutch jarring, splintering. Again and again, he hacked down until the stick and devil gave way under the horse's hooves.

'*Bylen!*' The witch sprang at him, wild hair and knife

flailing. The horse reared, backing and stamping as he slashed back, the long blade slicing across the bitch's chest and face to send her and her screaming familiar sprawling in the ditch where they belonged. Wife or whore, it mattered not. She was a heathen sinner, beyond redemption.

Only the little vixen remained, alone on the road, barefoot, spattered with her mother's blood, shaking – glaring at him. To leave her would be to let the pestilence of sin grow, spread, infect yet more souls. Sin begat sin. She would only grow to be another sinner. Too soon, she would be a breeder of sin, a whore, a whelping bitch to yet more heathen sinner curs; swelling the ranks of Satan's hordes before the final battle.

He urged Breda forward. But the horse backed, stamping. He raked spurs back across bloodied ribs. The animal bucked, reared, shaking, tossing, turning on the road. *Damn the beast for its defiance!* Again, he dug sharp spur rowels deep into bloody flesh. The horse leaped forward, dragging the reins through his gauntlets, twisting and turning, thrashing its head. He could not control it. The beast was bewitched. The child still stared, mumbling, chanting its curse, controlling the horse, making it dance. Satan was close at hand, here on the road.

He let the horse have its head to turn and canter away from the little witch, away from her curse, leaping the ditch back onto the heath. The trumpet was calling retire, calling them back to their colours. Up ahead on the road, the rear-guard battalion were making a stand where the road crossed a ford, a red-coated battalion with yellow colours: Lord Mohun's Cornish foot. They stood while the rest of their accursed army carried on up the hill to stand before the town of Devizes.

III

The Vies

Kendall Tremain
Town Ditch, St Mary's Church, Devizes, Wiltshire
Monday the 10th July 1643, two o'clock in the afternoon

Kendall Tremain stood up, stretched his back and slapped a horsefly from the sweat that ran down his neck. His back was stiff and aching. And he needed sleep. He and others from Sir Nicholas Slanning's Regiment of Foot had been digging out the town ditch since morning. 'The Tinners' they called them. Well now they were digging a stinking ditch to keep out rebel horse instead of mining for Saint Piran's *stean du*. God give him a proper Cornish shovel, not the poxy little *Sows* spade he'd got out of a garden.

They'd barricaded the ways in and now they dug the old town ditch deeper. Only God knew why the folk of Devizes couldn't dig their own bloody ditch. They only seemed interested in hiding their bales of precious pissing woolcloth, scurrying about like rats in a barn, in and out of alleys and doors. Well, there'd be a few hungry, sore and tired tinners filling up their billets soon enough. It was well past dinner now and they'd had nothing, no *tabm* nor drink nor rest since breakfast.

It was hot and close. No breeze to cool the air. Just hot, clammy air, dust and flies that prickled the skin with sweat. Like others, he'd stripped to the waist. But there wasn't even enough match-cord to put about his breeches. He'd had to tie them up with his shirt. God knew what they were supposed to do if the bloody rebels attacked now. They'd bugger all powder nor match between them.

They were supposed to be marching to Oxford to meet the King. But it was all open downland, a sea of grass for near twenty leagues – horse country. They'd be taken abroad by the bloody rebel horse, without hedge nor ditch to protect them. Their own damned cavalier horse were only good for taking what they wanted, spoiling what they didn't and turning when they shouldn't. Bloody 'run away horse' they were. How was it that the bloody horse troopers always got to stay in the best inns, while the foot that did the real work were billeted on the likes of poor weavers who'd hardly got bed or board between them.

Now they were stuck fast, grounded, stranded in a bloody town, building barricades and digging ditches to keep out rebel horse. Sir Bevil Grenville was dead, laid out in his coffin. Sir Ralph Hopton was blinded, burnt, confined to a chair. Others lay half dead on the floor of the Correction House, their wounds black and stinking. Too many more were missing or dead. They had near enough no powder and bugger all match, with the rebels ranged all about them. Up on the hill above the town, the Puritan *Sows* bastards were preparing a battery of guns. No doubt they'd soon be starting their bloody bombardment.

God, what would he give to be back home, back in Cornwall, back holding Morwenna, stroking her hair, Hedrek and little Merryn on his knee. And what would he give to go to sea again, hauling the catch in over the gunwale, bright silver in the sun, the cool breeze on his face as the boat lifted on the swell. God, but he missed it, its smell, taste and sound, its infinite variety and endless, heaving pull. It was in his blood.

But there was no going back to sea without Morwenna. And no seafaring folk would have her back until Jack and the corsairs were a threat no more. The King needed Ship Money to build a navy strong enough to beat the Turks once and for all, a navy that could protect Britain's waters and shores from attack or invasion, that would protect its fishermen and merchantmen, wherever they sailed and traded.

The weavers of Devizes needed Spanish wool to make their precious bloody broadcloth. How did they think it got here? Everyone knew there wasn't enough wool in all England to keep the weavers in employ. And how did they think they sold their drapery to Flanders, Spain, Italy or Virginia if it did not go by ship over the sea? Didn't they drink wine from France, Spain and Canary? Eat fish from the sea, near and wide? Eat oranges, lemons, Barbary fruits and spices from the Orient? Didn't they smoke Virginia tobacco in their pipes? They depended upon trade across the sea as much as any man, only they didn't risk their lives by it.

Cornish folk had lived and died at the mercy of the sea. They risked their lives upon it day in, day out. They'd stood against Spanish galleys that plundered Mousehole, burned Paul Church, Lulyn and Penzance, defended Marazion and the Mount against invasion. And now they couldn't sleep for fear of the Salé rovers that occupied Lundy Island, took their menfolk, burned their boats, raiding ashore from Mousehole to St Keverne, Penryn, Looe and Padstow, seizing their women and children. From out of the chapel at *Marhasyow*, they'd dragged away three-score folk at prayer. They left behind only the old, the infirm, corpses, burnt cottages and ruined churches.

Cornwall needed a navy to protect them. A navy with proper ships, not just the little whelps they had. But that needed Ship Money. It was a Member of Parliament, William Noy of St Ives, a Cornishman, who proposed all counties pay their fair share. But others, tossers like John Hampden, made an argument of it, stirred up opposition to it, voted against it. They knew it was only right and fair, but they refused to pay their share. It wasn't the King's fault. He'd tried to get what was right and proper to protect his people. They used it against him, said he'd used *arbitrary powers*, that he was a tyrant. Instead of fitting out a navy to fight the heathen Turks, Parliament had raised an army against their own king and the true people of his kingdom.

Now they were digging out a stinking town ditch in the heat of the day to keep out Parliament's iron-clad horsemen while rebel gunners built a battery for their cannon on the hill above. There was bugger all powder and sod all match left. Kendall's back ached, he was hungry and he needed sleep. And he was parched, *mar zeh vel conz lenez!* It was well past time for dinner.

The air crackled above them, thunder crashing out from the hill above as the first of the rebel cannon belched dark sulphurous smoke, its iron ball passing overhead to smash against the old castle mound.

'*Abarh Deew!*' They'd started. Already.

IV

Ambuscade

Francis Reeve
Silbury Hill, Avebury, eleven o'clock at night

Silbury Hill towered above them, the halfmoon casting its black shadow across the highway, the Great Road from London to Bristol, from Marlborough to Calne, the way to Devizes. They sat silent, waiting for the convoy to reach the base of the hill, waiting to spring their ambush upon a convoy of powder, match and shot sent from Oxford for the heathen Cornish trapped in Devizes.

Francis unbuckled and re-buckled the chinstrap of his helmet, shifted in his saddle. This place was unnatural, impure, ungodly, the wind about it warm and fetid. Evil lurked in its dark shadow, a malevolent eye watching, waiting. Ancient spirits lurked deep within the giant mound. It was said that a golden king sat on a golden horse was buried within, that the mound was raised by the Devil. The hill was alive, its sides rippling in the moonlight, the grass sighing, whispering, muttering curses under its breath. And then darkness swept over the ground. Black night, a cloud passing across the moon. This was a place of trickery, of witchery.

All about were the marks of sin, of heathen practice.

The hills and downs were scarred with depraved workings: mounds, barrows, dykes, ancient ways and standing stones. Not a mile from this place the villagers of Avebury lived amidst a ring of ancient, twisted stones within a heathen temple, a place of diabolical practice, of evil summoning, of human sacrifice. Across the downs ran roads as straight as pike shafts, mile after mile of open, windswept way; the works of ancient artifice, the Devil's highways. These were not the Lord's creations. They were the marks of man and Satan.

Francis reached within his breastplate, touched the bible that lay within. He needed to feel its strength, to fortify himself with God's word, to armour his soul against the evil that abounded this night. Already, it had touched them, cast a curse upon their endeavour, wreaked chaos and havoc amongst them. They had met with another troop on the march, a troop of Sir William Waller's own regiment of horse transported, disguised, their true colours veiled in darkness. They had been confounded, bewitched, fired on each other, scattered in the confusion.

He shall cover thee with his feathers, and under his wings shalt thou trust;

His truth shall be thy shield and buckler.

Thou shalt not be afraid for the terror by night; nor for the arrow that flieth by day;

Nor for the pestilence that walketh in darkness; nor for the destruction that wasteth at noonday.

Something moved on top of the giant mound. A man, a trooper, a scout sliding, tumbling down its side. The convoy was coming. There would be cavalier horse on the road before and behind it, the ammunition carts between them.

He pulled down the faceguard of his helmet, the steel bars bright in the moonlight. They were to wait for the signal, wait until the lead cavalier horse were trapped on the road as it climbed between Silbury Hill and the high down beyond. Then they were to sweep out, fall upon the carts, seize the road as it crossed the River Kennet and block any retreat or reinforcement. He gathered up his reins, drew a pistol and waited.

His horse twitched. Silence. The night air ruffled its mane. The animal's ears pricked – and then he heard it, carried on the wind: a horse snorting, an iron shoe striking a flint, the jangle of harness, the clop of hooves on the road. They were almost at the crest, almost upon them, behind them. They would be seen.

Shots crashed out on the road, horses whinnying, yelling, crying out – the ambush was sprung. Francis clapped spurs into the horse's flanks as they surged forward, sweeping around the base of Silbury Hill. They thundered across the flat meadow, hooves pounding the sod; willows swaying in the moonlight, the river to their left. The convoy was on the road ahead. Drivers yelled. Horses reared, shrieking. Cavaliers scattered. *And the light shineth in darkness; and the darkness comprehended it not!*

They leaped the ditch and bank, horses scrambling up onto the road. Five ammunition carts and a coach were trapped on the road between Silbury Hill and the River Kennet, unable to turn, unable to go forward or back. More shots rang out as the cavalier rear-guard were forced back from the river.

Francis yanked open the coach door. A woman screamed – a maidservant sat within. A cavalier shrunk back into the dark beside her. Francis reached in, grabbed at the apostate. Booted legs kicked and squirmed, the woman's arms wrapped around the reprobate. He thrust deeper, gauntleted hand closing upon breeches and pointed doublet. By God, he would drag this coward out by his balls, hang the immoral sinner!

'Unhand me, sir!' A woman's voice.

'Lay your hands off of her, sir!' The maid's arm was raised, a pistol in her hand. 'Or by God I'll shoot!'

'I say unhand me!' A lady's voice – the booted legs subsiding, submitting. 'Unhand me and I give my word we will step down.'

Francis let go, stepped back. How could this be? Was this yet more trickery; some hidden spectre; a shapeshifting witch within? He grabbed up his pistol and held it before him.

The maid stepped out of the coach, her own pistol still in hand. Behind her the cavalier emerged, long boots stepping down into the moonlight, fine hands smoothing silk, slashed sleeves, lace and ribbons, one arm crooked akimbo upon the hip. The plumed hat was swept off – long hair tumbling down about shoulders, slender neck, throat, heaving chest, scented breath, flushed cheeks, lips and glistening eyes.

A woman dressed in cavalier's apparel! Some lewd strumpet out of Oxford's academy of bedlam, a courtesan to their courtiers and commanders, a harlot come to lie with Prince Maurice, the Marquis of Hertford or Sir Ralph Hopton.

Francis stepped back. God protect him. This night stank of sin, of debauchery and moral turpitude!

'Please present me to Sir William Waller. I am Mistress. . . Parsons.'

V

Escape

Ralph Reeve
Market Place, Devizes, a quarter to midnight

Ralph mounted his horse. The little mare sagged under him. She was tired, thin and out of condition, her coat showing dull and dusty in the torchlight. She needed feeding up and rest. They all did. They'd not stopped since they'd joined Prince Maurice and the Western Army. Every day had seen them on the march as outguards, scouting or skirmishing.

Clem stood beside him, his hand on the bridle still. 'I'm sorry, Master Ralph, her ain't lookin' her best. She'd be glad o' some oats. And a bit o' rest. She needs a-puttin' out to grass for a bit. Them all do. That's as no good a-working they every day and just feedin' them of hay.'

Ralph gathered his reins and leaned down. 'I know, Clem. We all need rest. Thank you for looking after her. How is the boy?'

'Oh, he's alright. Tired mind. He do need his sleep. And that Kibler do needle he something terrible.'

'I know. Keep an eye on him. This march will not be easy. They say we must make Marlborough by morning and maybe Oxford after that. And the rebel horse may yet be about this night. They will not want to let us get away without a fight.'

'Well, leastways we ain't a-walking to Marlborough this time, or stormin' it.'

'No, thank God, Clem. I don't know which was worse. I wouldn't want to make that walk again. And it was no easy fight to take the town.'

The market place was filled with horses and men, every horseman and dragoon of the Western Army, all preparing to march. They were leaving Devizes, breaking out of the town, escaping Waller's encirclement before it was too late. They were going before they ran out of powder and match, before they ran out of fodder. They were escaping while they still could, before they were trapped for good.

There was not enough powder and match for the foot, let alone every horseman and dragoon as well. Thank God, they still had some of the rebel match he'd taken from the wall at Lansdown. There was not much left, but his division had more than most. Even now, they dared not light it. They could not afford to burn it. Besides, it might be seen in the dark and give away their stratagem. Sergeant O'Brien alone carried a lighted match concealed in a tin case.

Ralph clasped the tuck sword at his side, drawing it out an inch, easing it back down, checking it would run smoothly from its scabbard. It was all that he would have in an alarum until he could get his match lit. God, what would he give to have back his old wheellock pistols and Ned's snaphaunce carbine – to be a proper horseman again, not a lowly dragoon with a tuck sword and matchlock musket.

But Christ, how he missed Breda! He would give anything to have his horse under him again, to feel his strength and power. God only knew what Francis would have done to that horse, goading him with spur and bit. The last Ralph had seen of them was Francis forcing Breda in through the doors of Winchester Cathedral.

Ralph leaned forward and patted the mare on the neck, ruffled her mane. She'd done well enough, carried him far. But could she carry him through this night march? They'd struggle to keep up with the bigger horses. If there was an alarum or charge, they'd not be able to stay with the horse regiments, they'd be left behind. He could not bear the thought of being taken prisoner again – not that.

Clem was right. The horses needed oats, grass and rest. Thank God the hay at the Talbot was fresh cut, not some musty scrag-end from last year's crop. They all needed rest, not a long night march through rebel lines. He looked across at the other file leaders, exchanged a nod with each: Jack, Sam and dear Luke. He turned and smiled at those behind: Hodge and Kibler, Sam's lad and Tandy, Jewkes – then a gap where Brown had once rode – the boy and Clem. Gaunt shadows and red eyes stared back. Only Clem managed to crack a smile.

And then they were moving, the great mass lurching forward to form a single column. They rode out of the market place, down Long Street and out towards the old South Gate, regiment after regiment of horsemen. The little troop of dragoons followed Prince Maurice's own regiment of horse. Behind them trooped the rest of Prince Maurice's brigade of horse: the Earl of Carnarvon's, Howard's, Hamilton's, Bennet's. Then came the Marquis of Hertford's Regiment, Vaughan's, Basset's Cornish Horse, Hopton's Horse, and finally Hopton's troop of dragoons followed on.

They rode in silence, at a steady walk, out beyond the edge of town, out into the darkness, the last of the moon disappearing behind the rooftops and castle. They were heading

South East, not North, away from the highway that led to Marlborough, away from Waller's strength about Roundway. A mile from town, they turned east off the Salisbury road. The lane climbed between fields and downland to skirt the village of Etchilhampton – a dog barking, candle wavering at a cottage window.

There was no halt to tighten girths or check hooves. Any horse or rider that could not keep up had to fall out of the column, stand by the wayside and join the stragglers behind. Musket, carbine and pistol shots crackled back down in the valley – the rear-guard fighting to keep the rebels off their backs. There would be no stopping until they were free from Waller's encirclement, beyond his horse patrols.

They rode on turning northeast, the Plough above pointing the way across level open country as they slipped past the church and houses at All Cannings. Beyond the village, they climbed slowly, breaking out onto open grass downland, on and up, the track winding amongst steep sided hills.

A warm breeze hissed amongst the grass, chattering in the lonely clumps of buckthorn, dogwood and whitebeam, gnarled, twisted trunks and clawing branches reaching out to snare the unwary. The horses twitched and tossed, treading stiffly as they climbed the hard dry chalk slope. From the hilltops above them, ancient earthworks, barrows and burial mounds stared down, the slopes and hollows dark and impenetrable below the skyline of black clouds sweeping across the stars.

Finally, they crested the ridge, the track rising and falling as it crossed a great earth bank and a ditch deep enough to swallow a horse, a bank and ditch that ran as far as the eye could see along the ridge, disappearing into the darkness left and right. An earthwork of colossal scale, the Wansdyke could only have been built by giants, or by an ancient people more organised than any that had ruled this land since.

The track led on across open down, slowly descending, the wind warm and close, the tang of dust and iron sharp in throats and noses. The horizon flashed and crackled with lightning; a thunderstorm growling far to the north. The horses stiffened, tossing heads and whickering.

The first tinges of grey half-light turned almost impercep-tibly to shards of orange, the wind fanning night embers to glow bright and warm, until the sun burst above the eastern horizon, coal black clouds flaring into a blazing dawn. They'd been in the saddle for four hours without a halt and covered near ten miles in the dark, half of it across open downland. Ralph shifted in the saddle. He was tired, stiff and sore. God alone knew how the horses were feeling.

He turned to look back at his division. The boy was sway-ing, half asleep, rolling in his saddle, Clem holding him to keep him from falling. Jewkes muttering under his breath, uncomfortable, exposed under the open sky, away from his familiar rat runs of town and dockside. Kibler was falling behind, his pony stepping stiffly, one leg lame, the clink of iron telling of a loose shoe. They needed to halt, rest and tend their horses.

They descended the long gentle slope to the valley and River Kennet below. At the base of the slope, they clattered past a church and cob cottages in the morning sun to join the King's highway, the Great Road that ran from Bristol to Marlborough and on to London. The horses pricked up their ears, stepping out bravely in the sun.

They were almost at the edge of Marlborough, the Great Mound and Lord Seymour's House in view. They'd stormed the town, fought their way between the earthworks, fired a barn and broken through an inn onto the High Street. But the townsfolk had kept firing from windows, barricades and St Mary's Church. And then some fool set fire to the market stalls; tons of precious broadcloth, lace, rope, Marlborough cheeses and half the town were lost to the flames.

That had been before Winchester, before he lost everything, before his brother took Breda and they had to walk back across the plain in winter. Now Marlborough was held for the King, an outpost astride the Great Road, protecting Oxford and controlling the flow of traffic between Bristol and London. Surely, they would halt and rest here.

A volley of shots crashed on the road ahead. Horses whinnied, men cursed and officers yelled. The column staggering to a halt. *Oh God, no!* The rebels couldn't be here, not in Marlborough! Not again!

'Dismount!' Sergeant O'Brien leaped from the saddle. 'File leaders to me for match! Horse holders and horses to the rear! The rest of yiz, make ready!'

Ralph slipped from the saddle, thrust the reins into the boy's startled hands and ran stiff and stumbling to O'Brien, musket in hand. Each file leader lit their match from the sergeant's and passed it on to the others. But before they could move forward, past the horse troops of Prince Maurice's own regiment at the head of the column, there were more yelled orders. 'Hold your fire! Hold your fire! As you were!'

This was not a rebel ambush. It was a jittery outpost of Lord Crawford's Regiment of Horse. They'd been ambushed the evening before, bringing a convoy of ammunition to relieve them in Devizes. They'd thought Prince Maurice was Waller pursuing them, come to seize Marlborough for Parliament.

Ralph hauled himself stiffly back into the saddle as the column moved forward again, finally turning into the High

Street. They passed the White Hart Inn and Blind Lane, the sweat suddenly prickling down his back at the memories of breaking into the town, bursting out through the inn to yells of *A town! A town for King Charles!*

At last, they dismounted at the far end of the High Street. Prince Maurice was served a glass of sherry before he and an escort of officers mounted fresh horses. With a final wave of hats, they clattered out of the High Street to gallop the forty miles across the downs to Aldbourne, Lambourne, Wantage and on to Oxford.

Thank God, the rest of them were to remain in Marlborough.

VI

Beleaguers and Bed Cords

Kendall Tremain
St John's Alley, Devizes, Tuesday the 11th
of July 1643, half past five o'clock

It was hot, humid and stinking in the alleyway, despite the shade under its overhanging storeys. Kendall Tremain pushed open the door and stepped under the low wooden lintel. The rhythmic clatter, clack, thump of the weaver's loom fell silent, as treadle, shuttle and lathe stopped their motion. His eyes struggled to adjust in the gloom; the air hung with dust, wool and carding fibre, all floating and twisting in the dim light.

A hunched old man peered over his loom coughing nervously. A boy stood gaping, his arms full of yarn. A woman sat at a spinning wheel surrounded by ragged children combing wool at her feet, alarm and fear in every eye. '*Dohajeth da.* Sorry, Goodee. But I needs thy beds.'

The woman dropped her distaff. 'But we've already got two soldiers billeted on us.' Red eyes held back tears. 'I can't hardly feed them and us as it is.'

'*Re Ia.* Goodee, I in't here t' sleep. Though I do dearly wan'it. I needs thy bed cords.'

'Our bed cords!'

'Thy bed cords.'

'But what do ee want with poor folks' bed cords? We've only got the one bed and the soldiers have taken that. Are they going to sleep on the floor along of us?'

'Us is here to fetch every bed cord in town. They're to be boiled to make match cord. Tis ordered by Sir Ralph Hopton himself, God bless him.'

'Good Jesus, preserve us.' The poor woman stood slowly, brushing the dust and loose wool from her apron, and led the way to the one chamber above.

The room was strewn with soldiers' clutter; two muddy snapsacks lay open on the floorboards, soiled shirts and holed hose, a horn mug, wooden spoons, a comb, a broken powder bottle and a pair of dice scattered across the floorboards around a simple oak bed. Kendall laid his musket on the floor and pulled back the blanket and straw mattress, pushing them against the wall. He drew his knife. It was his old fishing knife, long and curved. The one he'd used to gut and fillet so many mackerel, pilchards, herring and cod in happier times. The bed cord parted with a single cut of the blade.

He pulled the cord through the wooden side rails, head and foot boards, dust scattering on the floor, coiling it in his hand as he went. The bed frame stood empty, useless. He swept up his musket and stepped quickly from the room. 'I'm sorry, Goodee.'

It was one thing cutting the bed cords of rich merchants and clothiers, or fine inn chambers. But he didn't like to take from these poor weavers. They had so little as it was. Most of them were in debt to the richer clothiers and market-spinners who engrossed wool and yarn, selling it at an unfair price and buying back the cloth for next to nothing. These weavers and their families were not much better than slaves, working themselves to death over their looms late into the night, half-blind, their lungs filled to coughing with dust. They dare not stop, even when a battle raged all about them. Thank God he was a Cornishman, born to breathe freely in the sea air.

But they had to have more match cord. The quartermaster's boy said there were no more than seven-score and ten pounds weight of it left for the whole army. And just two barrels of powder. While they were beleaguered about on all sides, the rebels had been trying to storm the barricades and ditches with horse and foot since daybreak, cannon playing upon them night and day. There was not enough powder for their own cannon to reply. They sat useless, pulled inside the castle in case the town was taken.

There wasn't much hope of relief either. A rebel trumpeter had come that afternoon – from Sir William Waller himself. He told how their horsemen had captured a convoy from Oxford bound for Devizes with powder, match and shot then offered a treaty for terms of surrender. And it was no good waiting for their own bloody cavaliers. They'd run away to Oxford in the night.

Well, Sir Ralph Hopton had accepted a ceasefire. But they weren't going to surrender. Not while they still held the out-works, town ditches and barricades. Not while there was even a yard of bed cord in Devizes that could be boiled up to make match for their muskets. Sir Ralph was playing for time, he was. Leastways, it'd spared their powder and shot and given them a couple of hours rest to gather more of the precious bloody bed cords!

Outside, others emerged from doors carrying lengths of cord cut from every bed in the alley. Together, they picked up what they'd already collected and stepped out onto St John's Street. They marched back towards the market place to turn into Castle

Road. Yet more joined them as they marched carrying sheets of lead torn from the roof of St John's Church for shot.

This was Saint John the Baptist's Church. It was barely more than a fortnight since Saint John's Tide – since *Golowan* – when every hilltop in Cornwall, from Land's End to the Tamar, would be ablaze with midsummer bonfires – cattle driven round them, children swung over them. There'd be swinging torches, young men and women leaping through the flames, the sharing of sweet bread, cheese and ale, singing, chanting and dancing into the night. Then it'd be down to the sea and church for blessings and baptisms, processions and holy well dressing; every door hung with yarrow, fennel, rosemary, rue, birch, bracken and Saint John's wort.

They'd need to pray they hadn't angered Saint John by tearing up the roof of his fine church. There'd be plenty more needing the Baptist's protection and healing before they escaped this siege. The castle, Yarn Hall and the Correction House were packed tight with bleeding and broken men already.

The smell of seething tar filled the castle walls as the bed cords were beaten flat and boiled in resin. It smelled of pitch pine, boatbuilding, oakum and bright sunlight on warm wooden decks. But there was no fresh sea breeze, no sail casting shade, no calm lap of water, no *mordroz*. The air in the castle yard was stifling, hot and clammy, thick with black smoke, steam and the noise of men feverishly hammering out, seething, stirring and hanging out match cord to dry. Overhead, dark rain clouds hid the sun, threatening storm and thunder.

The air above split with a clap, crash and roar, the ground shaking. The rebel battery on Coatefield Hill had started up its bombardment again. The ceasefire had ended.

VII

Storm

Nathaniel Dunkley
Spitalcroft, Devizes, Wednesday the 12ᵗʰ of
July 1643, ten o'clock in the morning

Nat blew on his match. It spluttered, smoking, steaming, the match wet with rain. 'Blow on thy coal, Billy.' He whispered so the sergeant wouldn't hear. *Oh Lord, don't let Billy's match fail him.* Billy was cold, shivering, sniffing. They'd got soaked through in the thunderstorm, sentinels on guard that night, with nothing but a windy barn to sleep in after. If only he could be next to his butty, to help him with each command, to watch out for the sergeant.

They stood in file with the musketeers of Lord St John's Regiment of Foot, ready to storm the church. The cavaliers had fortified it, made it an outwork of their defences, an outguard that raked any who tried to storm the town ditch. Sir William Waller wanted it seized, cleared out, destroyed. But first, they had to wait for the great guns on Coathefield Hill to do their work, to prepare the way by to bringing down the church tower.

———

Kendall Tremain stood on the roof of St James' Chapel. He didn't like to smash a hole in the fine glass windows for a place to give fire. Besides, he'd got more space on the roof, the better to see and fire down from. It was almost like the battlements of a castle or a ship's fighting top. Except when it rained, then he had to retreat back into the tower.

They'd defended the church for two days now, an outwork beyond the town ditch, raking the rebels who tried to get by to attack the town. But they needed more powder. They'd got enough shot and match now, what with stripping the church roofs and boiling up bed cords. But they badly needed more powder. He only had three charges left.

St James' was a grand, great chapel, as big as half the churches in Cornwall. They'd be celebrating the feast of Saint James inside a fortnight. But half the roof had gone, the lead stripped off of it for shot. It was a crying shame to see the rain and wet running down the inside walls to flood the nave floor. Mind, it was washing away the Puritan whitewash to let the old colours come through again, bright and shining. And there were scallop shells, waves and a fisherman's net in hues of red, blue and green.

The air about him shuddered as another cannon ball shrieked across the roof in a rumbling blur. Yellow smoke and thumping explosion crashed out from the rebel battery on Coatefield Hill as the iron ball ploughed into the town ditch behind. They were trying to hit the chapel tower. To left and right, rebel foot and horse waited in the sodden fields.

———

Francis shifted in his saddle. The leather was wet, clinging to his damp breeches, water dribbling in at the tops of his long boots. It dripped from his nose, seeped down his neck, soaking his tight collar, his back damp and sticky under buff coat and armour.

They stood waiting in the rain, waiting on the hillside for the cannon to bring down the church tower and the foot to clear it of heathen Cornish. Then would these horsemen of God be unleashed upon this nest of miscreants. They would be free to cross the green and fall upon the barricades and their Godless defenders. *And their carcases shall be meat for the fowls of heaven, and the beasts of the earth.*

But God sent thunder and rain. He hindered their efforts. He punished them. The Lord punished them because they were unworthy. They had sinned in His eyes. They had not kept His commandments. And their iniquities were deliverance in the hands of their enemies. Each one must search himself for his sinning. They must justify themselves anew in their faith, search their souls, bodies and spirit for His truth. *And they shall answer, because they have forsaken the Covenant of the Lord God of their fathers.*

———

The church shook, the tower swaying, stone, mortar and iron crashing down into the nave below. Kendall clung to the stone parapet. A dark hole pierced the tower's traceried stonework, a dark hole where the cannonball had struck, the chapel bells clanging in discordant alarm.

The rebel battery on Coatefield Hill had hit its mark, its dirty yellow smoke billowing in the wind and rain. It was the second direct hit on the tower. How many more could it take before collapsing upon those of them who still defended the church?

———

'Cock-bod!' Nat cheered with the rest of St John's Regiment of Foot as the great guns struck the church tower again. Soon it would fall and then they would storm what was left of the church. Already, the drums thrashed out the troop, beating away before they marched. 'Billy, did you see it? Did you see the tower shake?'

———

They should trust in the Lord. Francis gathered up the reins of his horse. They wasted time waiting for the cannon, waiting for the foot to take the heathens' outworks. God had punished them for their sin, for their self-righteousness, for their confidence in their own supposed strength of arms, for not trusting in His perfect obedience. *Thus saith the Lord, cursed be the man that trusteth in man and maketh flesh his arm, and withdraweth his heart from the Lord.* They should charge now, trust in God's promise to Abraham, trust in Christ's salvation of the righteous. It was time to storm the barricades, to scatter and destroy the enemies of the Lord.

———

Kendall ran, his half-boots splashing in the sodden grass. They all ran, all that could get away from the outwork. They ran as fast as they could, across the open green. Better to run than let the church be destroyed about them. God, let them make the town ditch before the bloody rebel horse were amongst them.

———

The drums beat the march as rank after rank strode forward. Nat shouldered his musket and stepped off six feet behind his file leader. He kept pace with the drum and the man to his right. Billy would follow in his rank, three ranks behind, one rank before the rear.

They were marching past the church. It was empty, abandoned. The damned Cornish were running, like the irreligious cowards they were. Lord St John's Regiment was marching on towards the town, towards the ditch and barricades.

Oh Lord, don't let Billy drop his match in the wet.

———

Francis pulled down his barred visor and clapped spurs into his horse as the line lurched forward. They swept across the Green at an awkward trot, water and mud splashing up to coat Breda's belly.

They ignored the heathens running from their fallen outpost, aiming instead for the far end of the Green, the southern end, where a row of houses spilled out from the edge of the town, poor cottages encroaching onto the common. Here there was no town ditch, just a barricade across the end of the street.

Musket smoke thumped out from the barricade. A horse and trooper fell, sliding, kicking, crying out in the wet grass. But it was not a well-ordered volley – a few ragged shots alongside misfires and wet match in the rain. More reprobate musketeers tumbled from an alehouse, running down the street to man the defences.

The Godly horsemen halted in front of a jumble of an upturned cart, timber and broken furniture and levelled their pistols. Flame and smoke banged out, the flint snapping forward in the lock, pistol barrel whipping back and up in Francis's gauntleted hand. Lead and thunder crashed in the street, reverberating between tight-packed buildings and wet cobbles.

His horse stamped, shook, backed. Francis drew another pistol as Waller's foot ran past, tearing at the barricade, pulling it down, dragging it aside. And then they were pushing forward again, horses and men crushed one against the other as they forced their way past the barricade and into the street. They were through! The dam burst. They careered forward, iron shoes smashing down on wet stone as they poured into the town.

At the end of the street was an inn and crossroads. Cornish pikemen and musketeers ran from houses to block the way left and right. Ahead, a lane lay unguarded, a cut-through to the next street, to the centre of the town.

Francis dug brutal spurs into Breda's bloody flanks, the horse leaping forward, plunging into the narrow lane. They charged between tight packed weavers' hovels, turned a corner and burst out onto the broad street, hooves skittering, sliding, pounding on cobbles slick with rain.

Across the street stood a great church, set back. To the right, fine houses stretched out to the edge of the market place, to the centre of the rats' nest. Already, heathen Cornish pikemen blocked the street, advancing slowly, their pike shafts levelled. More pikemen and musketeers filled the way behind.

Slowly at first, one by one, the other troopers turned and disappeared back up the lane. And then the few became a rush until Francis stood alone on the street, his horse shaking, twisting, turning, desperate to follow the herd. He yanked at the reins, twisting the iron bit in the horse's mouth, hauling its head back and down. Eyes wide, ears flat in fear and pain, it backed down the street, iron shoes rasping on the cobles. Francis turned spurs into its bloody, twitching flanks, dug the roules deeper – raking the beast's ribs. The horse bunched, lurching between spur and bit, instinct, pain and terror. He held it there, neck arched, pulsing, sweating, steaming in the rain, its head held down to its chest, haunches quaking.

———

Kendall Tremain stepped forward down Long Street beside the pike block. A single ironclad rebel horseman stood defying them, pistol raised, his horse pawing the cobbles under him, glaring at them through the rain.

'Accursed sinners!' the horseman snarled. 'Burn in Hell!' And then he was gone, back down Morris Lane towards the edge of town and the Green.

VIII

The Strife is O'er, the Battle Done

Kendall Tremain
Market Place, Devizes, two o'clock

Kendall Tremain stood at the edge of the Market Place, his musket under his left arm, clubbed, reversed, muzzle pointing back and down in mournful tribute. They were bidding farewell to Sir Bevil Grenville, the whole army lining the route for him and the procession that would carry his corpse back to Kilkhampton, back to Cornwall, that would carry him home. They lined the route from the castle, through the Market Place, down Northgate Street and out beyond the town ditch, their heads bowed, silent. Wet cobbles steaming in the sun.

Even the rebel cannon dared not disturb the peace. Sir Ralph Hopton had procured a ceasefire, for his friend's safe passage out of Devizes, away from the close siege, away while he could, before it was too late. Over all the town and rebel lines beyond, the church bells tolled, slowly, steadily, rhythmically, marking the pace of the cortege. Not a bird, not an animal nor human spoke, just the steady tolling of bells, the slow tramp of feat, the beat of muffled drum and the solemn chant of a hymn.

First came a sergeant, halberd reversed, axe head pointing to the ground. Then came two divisions of musketeers, rests painted in Grenville colours of blue and white, muskets turned back and down, followed by two divisions of pikes, shafts of blue and white, pike heads reversed, all of Sir Bevil's own company, a black ribbon in every hat.

A drummer followed, his drum covered in black cloth, its dull beat in time with the bells. Behind him walked Sir Bevil's chaplin, a bible before him, chanting the funeral hymn.

'Finita iam sunt prœlia,
Est parta iam victoria:'
Two lines between each toll of the bell.
'Gaudeamus et canamus,
Alleluia.'
Two lines of Latin to mark each pace.
'Post fata mortis Barbara
Devicit Iesus tartara:'
Two lines in the old language of their church.
'Applaudamus et psallamus,
Alleluia.'
Lines of an ancient, solemn funeral hymn.
The strife is o'er, the battle done;
The victory of life is won;
Lines of Latin to mark a Grenville's passing.
The song of triumph has begun.
Alleluia.

The hearse creaked, drawn by four horses, all draped in black – Sir Bevil's own colour, his partizan and helmet laid upon the coffin. His horse followed, stepping slowly, saddle empty. Behind it walked Sir Bevil's ensign, Anthony Payne, the Cornish Giant, stepping slowly, trailing his staff draped in black ribbon. Behind him stepped Sir Bevil's groom, clerk and page and then a rear guard of the last two musketeer divisions of Sir Bevil's own company.

All that was left that could march went with him. So many carried wounds, torn and bloody, limping, dark eyed and thin, the ranks gapped and missing. But they marched with their heads and arms held high, those that had stood with him on Lansdown Hill, proud Cornishmen, one and all, men of Stratton, Kilkhampton, Morwenstow and Launcells, his men, his retinue and household, taking him back, taking him to Cornwall, taking him home.

The rest of the foot stood in silence, lining the route, arms clubbed, reversed as they passed. Colonel Bamfield's little regiment stood at the castle gate. Colonel Buck's Hampshires, Sir Ralph Hopton's regiment, the Marquis of Hertford's Somersets and Prince Maurice's Devons lined Castle Street and into the Market Place. Then stood Trevanion's, Slanning's, Lord Mohun's and Godolphin's, Cornishmen all, out of the Market Place and along Northgate Street.

Out beyond gate and town, Grenville's own regiment had the final honour, the last guard, the final salute and farewell to their colonel and his company. They stood watching them go, until they were out of sight, a single company, alone on their march through the rebel lines, alone on their march across Wiltshire, Somerset and Devon, alone on their march to the River Tamar and Cornwall.

There was nothing more they could do. All would've dearly loved to go with them, to accompany Sir Bevil on his final journey, to attend his funeral, to go home. But it was no use. They were stuck in Devizes. All they could do was drink his health, to wake him. It was only right and proper to do so.

Kendall walked into the taproom of the Lamb Inn. It was already filled with Slanning's men, *onen hag oll*. He was *dogluthez* – worn out. He should sleep. But he wasn't missing this. Sleep would come later, when he'd drunk his fill. At a proper funeral they'd have warm sweet poker ale, *shenagrum* or sugared *shrub*. But the bitter taste of Wiltshire beer would do to break his thirst.

'Kendall! *Yow!*' His corporal beckoned. '*Kemerew, evew an cor!*' A pitcher of beer was thrust into his hand. 'Sir Bevil!' Together, as one, they drank his toast. '*Re bowasso en crees!*'

IX

Repentance

Francis Reeve
Potterne, Wiltshire, outside Devizes,
six o'clock in the evening

It was raining. Again. The sky was black, angry. A summer deluge that flattened the wheat poured from rooves, running in channels down the lane. Francis pushed back the visor of his helmet and slipped from the saddle, his boots sinking in the mire, to wait in file outside the graveyard, the rain dripping from a great yew tree above.

Why did the Lord send His flood to hinder them in His work? The ways of Heaven were beyond the comprehension of man. But this was a sure sign of divine displeasure, the controller of nature's ire, the Lord's anger. *O Lord have mercy on us. We have waited for thee. Be thou their arm in the morning, our salvation also in the time of trouble.*

He must fast and pray. There were still too many amongst them who lacked true faith, who doubted Christ's promise of redemption. Too few were justified in and through Christ, lacking absolute trust in him, his life and resurrection. Only Christ's absolute freedom from sin and his sacrifice for man's salvation would bring the gift of grace.

Even Sir William Waller had shown weakness. He had demeaned himself in front of the Lord; wasting time in treating with Hopton, consenting to allow the Grenville's cadaver to be paraded in a Popish ceremony, when it should have been cast aside with all the other malignant sinners and heathen Cornish as meat for the crows.

Everyone knew that Hopton had fought beside Sir William in Bohemia, that together they had helped rescue Elizabeth of Bohemia, the Winter Queen, snatching her away from the grasp of the imperial *tercios* and the Catholic League. Francis's own mother had served the queen in Prague. Perhaps they knew something of her.

Now, Sir William was resolved on a general assault on Devizes in the morning, promising Parliament that he would make Hopton his prisoner. But, thus far, Sir William had been too friendly, too gentlemanly, too free to exchange letters and courtesies with Hopton, the apostate. It was as if he colluded with his enemy.

They had to redeem themselves in the eyes of the Lord, turn to Him in perfect trust and obedience. Only true and utter faith would bring the gift of grace. Man's so-called good works were as filthy rags to the righteous. Only Christ's grace could erase the dark stain of original sin, eradicate man's natural sinfulness, earn acceptance into the Kingdom of Heaven. *Remember not against us former iniquities, but let thy tender mercies speedily prevent us. For we are brought very low.*

Francis led Breda forward through the lychgate and down the stone path between the tombs and gravestones, the rain sliding from the horse's face and sides. Past the south transept, they turned to step through the little porch and over the threshold into the church.

The horse's hooves crashed out on the stone floor, echoing

in the high arched nave as the rain hammered on the roof and lancet windows. The church was filled with horses, in the nave, chancel and north and south transept. It was nothing but a stable filled with beasts of burden, their hay, steaming horseshit and piss strewn across its flagstones and tombs.

He dragged the saddle from Breda's steaming back, hung the bridle to drip from a memorial and let the horse feed. The animal showed its pleasure with tossing wet mane, dusty snort and pawing iron hoof. Let the beast enjoy its stable out of the rain. There was nothing holy or sacred about this building. No more than any other.

Thus saith the Lord, Heaven is my throne and the earth is my footstool: where is the house that ye built unto me and where is the place of my rest? The idea of a temple to God was profanity. Paraphernalia, ceremony and singing were the work of the Antichrist – Popish magic, learned by rote to lure sinners. Faith alone could save the righteous. This was no place for prayer. It was a stable.

With one last glance towards the chancel, Francis strode out of the church, his boots and spurs ringing on the stone floor. They must trust in the God's promise of succour in their hour of need. They must trust in Him only, in Him wholly and to Him forever, dedicate themselves to Him in soul, body and spirit. Not as the wicked of the world, or the hirelings of a Church profanely called by His name. But as a sword in the hand of a vengeful Lord wherewith to lay waste His enemies. For now was the time to follow Him. *Lay hand upon the sword and buckler, and stand up for mine help!*

X

Relief

They were moving again, leaving Marlborough. Prince Maurice had returned, brought with him Lord Wilmot, Sir John Byron and two fresh brigades of Oxford horse. They were going back to Devizes, to break Waller's siege, to free the Cornish foot trapped within the town.

Prince Maurice had galloped the forty miles and more across the downs to Oxford to raise the alarm. The King, Prince Rupert and almost all the Oxford Army were gone – gone north to meet the Queen and her convoy of arms. But Lord Wilmot had gathered twelve hundred cavaliers and two guns from what was left of Oxford's garrison to ride back with Prince Maurice.

They joined those who had escaped Devizes with Prince Maurice and those of the Earl of Crawford's force that had survived the night ambush. Together, they'd rendezvoused at Marlborough, many riding through the night to get there.

Now they were moving, together, two thousand horsemen pouring out of the High Street and onto the King's highway, the Great Road from London to Bristol, the way to Bath and Devizes. Horses snorted, tossed, jostled, crapped and farted as they left, troop after troop, Ralph's little mare stepping out brightly in the clear sun. Two day's rest had done her more good than a bag of oats.

Ralph turned in the saddle to share a nod and a grin with his division, his little band of dragoons. Dark shadows still ringed eyes that had seen and done too much, but sleep, good food and heady ale had eased their strain.

The road ran west, following the river, out past the Great Mound and Lord Seymour's House, through Fyfield and Little Kennet, past standing stones and ancient burial mounds, fields of wheat and acre after acre of downland grass, green and rustling in the brilliant, fresh light, washed clean after summer rain. The hedges and roadside gleamed with flowers, fairy flax, boomrape, dropwort and hawkbit – tiny turquoise butterflies rising and falling as they passed.

They climbed the slope past great Silbury Hill and on through Beckhampton. Leaving the village behind, they turned off the Great Road onto the road to Bath, the broad way climbing slowly up to Roundway Down, the road empty and desolate, just wind and grass, sky and lark song. The way ran across the down, a great sweeping bowl between hills. At its centre, a byway led South, down through Roundway village to Devizes.

They crossed the great ditch and bank of the Wansdyke, halting to fire their two small cannon from a hilltop, a signal to those in Devizes that they were coming. A signal to Sir Ralph Hopton and his western foot to be ready to march out, to trap the rebels between their two forces, to catch William the Conqueror Waller.

They stood listening, waiting, hoping. There was nothing

but the sound of larks singing and the wind in the grass. Were they too late? Had Devizes fallen already? Had they left their foot without powder and match to be overrun by the rebels? Were they now prisoners, the brave Cornish foot and Western Army lost? Was all hope of joining with the King's, Queen's and Northern armies gone, all hope of a combined march on London thrown away?

And then they heard it. Two cannon shots, faint, flung on the wind. But the town had answered with its precious powder, returned the signal from four miles below. The Western Army still stood. The Cornish still held Devizes.

XI

Roundway Down

Nathaniel Dunkley
Roundway Hill, two o'clock

The sergeant urged them to march faster with his halberd. The hill was steep. It would be terrible hard on Billy. Nat ran to catch up with his file leader again. The musket was heavy, digging hard into his shoulder – his shins, calves and thighs burning with the pace of the march.

They'd all heard the cannon. The damned Cornish were signalling to their bloody cavaliers on the hill. Two thousand of the King's cursed horsemen were on the road from Oxford. They thought they were going to trap Sir William Waller and his army between them. Well, Sir William had a trick of his own to play them.

They'd heard tell of the cavaliers just as they'd been getting their dinner. They had to pack their snapsacks and fall in on the road outside with just a mouthful of bread to eat. Now they were marching up Roundway Hill – the whole army – as quickly as they could. They marched without drum or trumpet, just the sergeant calling out the pace, forcing them on.

They'd marched through Roundway village behind Sir William and half the horse regiments, their shit all over the lane. The rest of the foot marched behind, with Sir Arthur Hesilrigge and his iron lobsters at the rear. All that remained about Devizes were a few dragoons to keep the bloody Cornish cooped up behind their barricades.

Now they climbed Roundway Hill, the lane steep and narrow. Sweat soaked Nat's shirt, despite the cool breeze. If only he could slip back in the ranks to help his butty. *Oh Lord, don't let Billy fall behind.*

'Come on lads, keep up now!' It was the bloody sergeant. He was next to them. 'Bloody cavaliers aren't waitin all day for us.' He was looking back. He'd see Billy struggling. 'Billy, lad! Billy!'

No! Not his butty. He'd slit the bastard's gizzard if he hurt Billy.

'Billy, lad. . .' The sergeant spoke softly. 'Give us thee musket an' gerron up the front for a bit.'

———

Francis Reeve crested the hill. Roundway Down stretched before them and out to the right, a great empty, shallow bowl of grass downland sat between four hills, God's light and a clear sky. They followed Sir William Waller and his regiment of horse out onto the down. Behind them followed Burghill's and Popham's Somerset Horse, the foot in five battalions, Sir Arthur Hesilrigge's armoured cuirassiers and Gould's Devon Horse.

Across the down on its northern rim ran the road from Bath to Silbury Hill and Marlborough. To the right, spilling out from that road, were the accursed cavaliers. They spread like locusts across the down, crawling out between Morgan's Hill and Roughridge Hill to infest the plain; three brigades of cavalier horse – no foot with them, just two small guns.

Sir William did not turn to face them, to charge them immediately; he rode straight on, heading north, holding the high ground. They had reached the down in time to stop the enemy in their tracks, to marshal the whole army of the Western Association against them, horse, foot and cannon on Roundway Down.

They would forestall the cavaliers' artifice, overturn their devilish intent to trap them between their horse brigades and the heathen Cornish in Devizes. Instead, this Godly army would block both the road to Bath and the way down to Devizes, crush this infestation upon the down.

And then they would finally be free to destroy the heathen horde that hid behind its barricades. Put an end to this Cornish incursion, avert their swelling of Satan's ranks, save London, hold Bristol fast against demonic Irish invasion, hold back the forces of darkness that threatened England – keep locked the gate to Hell.

———

Ralph Reeve urged his little mare on. The bloody rebels were up on the down already. Somehow, Waller must have known of Prince Maurice's return, abandoned his siege of Devizes, marched up Roundway Hill and onto the down. The whole damned rebel army was there, foot and cannon between two wings of horse.

Prince Maurice's Regiment of Horse moved forward at a full trot, already formed for battle, in line, three deep. They led Lord Wilmot's brigade, out across the down. Sir John Byron's brigade came on in the centre, with the Earl of Crawford's force following rear right, a reserve on the Bath road. Ahead, a forlorn hope of commanded troopers cleared the way – a lone squadron of horsemen in a sea of grass under blue sky and hovering larks.

Ralph urged the mare on into a canter. He and his dragoons rode on the far left of Prince Maurice's Horse – on the far left of all the King's horse. Now, they were moved forward ahead of Wilmot's brigade – ahead to seize Roundway Hill before the rebels occupied it. They were to seize it, hold it, protect the left flank of the prince's charge and watch for Hopton's foot coming up from Devizes.

They cantered up the slope of the hill, the ponies labouring, wheezing, lathered in sweat. God, what would he give to ride Breda again? They halted just below the crest.

'Dismount!' Sergeant O'Brien was already jumping from his saddle. 'Horse holders and horses to the rear!'

Ralph threw his reins to the boy and unslung his musket. Hodge would take care of him and the other horse holders, leading the ponies back down the slope into the shelter of a gully.

'The rest of yiz, make ready!' Sergeant O'Brien strode ahead, sword and pistol in hand. 'Let's be movin' now. . . skirmish order!'

Ralph blew on the match between his fingers and pressed it into the musket cock as he stepped forward. Beside him, Jack strode out, scarred, grim, musket at the ready. Jewkes glowered at the hill, ready to strike. Sam moved like a wolfhound, low and fast, scenting the air ahead. Tandy was with him, alert, sharp. A nod from Luke, a smile from Clem. Kibler fiddled with his bandolier at the back. Together, they moved forward towards the summit.

———

'Lord St John's Regiment will wheel to the right. . . by divisions!' It was their Lieutenant-Colonel, Colonel Theodore Paleologus the Second. They said by rights he'd be the

Emperor of Constantinople, if it weren't for the Turks. Well, he was commanding a regiment of Christian English men and boys now. 'Wheel your battle. . . to the right!'

Orders rang out from captains, ensigns and sergeants as each division wheeled to the right, turning them to face the bloody cavaliers, no longer marching across the battlefield in column they turned to form a battalion in line. 'Billy lad. . . take thy musket now.' The sergeant handed the musket back to Nat's butty and raised his halberd. 'Division will wheel to the right! About!'

Nat followed his file leader in a tight arc, stepping up off the lane, across the long down grass, turning about the sergeant and his halberd, Billy following.

'March on!'

They stepped forward again, letting the files behind straighten after their turn.

'Stand!'

Lord St John's Regiment of Foot stood in battalia, pike block and musket wings, six ranks deep, division after division in line. They looked out across Roundway Down, down the slope to the advancing cavaliers. To their right, four more battalions turned off the lane and into line; Popham's Somersets, Sir Robert Cooke's poor Welshmen, Colonel Nathaniel Fiennes's Bristol city militia and Sir John Merrick's London greycoats – a chequerboard of battalions. Between the front battalions, the great guns were wheeled into line, pair after pair. Beyond them, on the far right, Sir Arthur Heselrigge's iron lobsters were turning off the lane from Roundway. To the left, Sir William Waller already waited with his horse regiments.

The whole Western Association army of Parliament stood ready for battle. They'd beaten the damned cavaliers at their own game, seized the high ground on Roundway Down before they could spring their trap. To the rear stood the prisoners taken at Lansdown Hill, on the march and at Silbury Hill – more than a hundred of them. And up the lane trooped crowds of country folk, gentlemen and their ladies, masters and mistresses come to see the great victory, to see Parliament's soldiers vanquish the King's accursed cavaliers, come to see the spectacle.

'Make Ready!'

Nat took the end of the match in his right hand, blew the ash from it jammed it down into the jaws of his musket cock. He pulled the cock back to check it would bring the match down on the priming pan. He was ready. *Oh Lord, don't let Billy misfire. Don't let his butty be afeared. And, Lord, thank thee for making sergeant carry Billy's musket up the hill.*

———

Francis pulled down his faceguard and gathered his reins. Already, an advance guard of Godly troopers was moving forward, descending the slope towards the apostates. Soon they would follow. Soon they would crush these accursed cavaliers, wipe them from the down, end this heathen Cornish invasion, shut fast the gate to Hell.

He touched spurs to Breda's flanks, the beast flinching under him, iron bit holding it back, twisting its head down. His brother's horse would carry him to victory. It must be ready, it must feel God's spirit, know the sweet irony as the cavaliers were crushed under its hooves.

He sat in the front rank of Colonel Nathaniel Fiennes' Regiment of Horse, on the slopes of Bagdon Hill beside the road to Bath. The whole army of the Western Association stretched out across the high ground to his right. At the far end of the line, Sir Arthur Heselrigge's cuirassiers were swinging into line, moving forward, six ranks deep, a great armoured block of horseflesh and steel, advancing across Roundway Hill.

How could just three brigades of dissolute and sinful cavaliers stand against this army of the Lord? They had thought to surprise them, catch them from behind between Roundway and Devizes. Now the tables were turned. Now was the time to crush them. *Now will I arise saith the Lord. Now will I be exalted. Now will I lift myself!*

———

The summit was clear, the top of Roundway Hill theirs. Ralph pulled off his hat and sucked in cool air. They had beaten the rebels to it: an empty, unoccupied hilltop, just the sound of larks hanging in the air.

Below them, Roundway Down stretched out on three sides. But to the south, the ground dropped away steeply. Ralph traced the course of the lane that crawled up that slope, following it down through Roundway village and on to Devizes. It was empty. Nothing moved on it save what looked like a country gentleman and his family out for a visit.

Where were the foot? Where were the Cornish, Grenville's and Slanning's tertias? Where were Colonel Buck's tertia of Somersets and Devons? Why weren't they marching? Why were they not coming to join with Prince Maurice on Roundway Down? They'd answered the signal guns. Why were they still sat behind their barricades in bloody Devizes? Did some other force hold them there or had the unruly Cornish finally mutinied? Surely, they hadn't surrendered?

He looked back across the down. Their cavaliers were moving forward at a full and steady trot, Prince Maurice and

117

Lord Wilmot's brigade almost level with the hill, three small brigades of horse – no more than two-thousand troopers riding uphill against an army of armoured horsemen, foot and cannon, an army more than twice their strength.

Fuck! Prince Maurice must be told. He must be warned, advised that the foot were not yet marching to his aid, that he and the Oxford horse were alone; alone and unaided against Waller's army of the Western Association. Already Wilmot's forlorn hope was engaged, locked in combat with the rebel advance guard. Prince Maurice was almost past Roundway Hill. Ralph would never make it on foot. And his little mare was back down the slope, tired and blown from the march and canter to seize the hill.

The near wing of rebel horse stood ready to meet Prince Maurice and Lord Wilmot, a deep block of horsemen, troop after troop. Each troop was five – no, six ranks of armoured horsemen, lobsters in shot-proof armour from closed helmet to tasseted thigh, mounted on heavy warhorses, their ranks packed knee to booted and steel plated knee. Against them, Prince Maurice came on, his cavaliers just three ranks deep.

The forlorn hope was pushing back the rebel advance guard, forcing them to turn about, driving them to retire into their own lines. Carbines and pistols flashed amongst the front rank of lobsters, their gunsmoke whipped away on the cool breeze. And then Prince Maurice crashed against the tightly packed horsemen, his regiment and Wilmot's brigade wrapping themselves around Heselrigge's flanks, their own pistols hammering against steel at point blank range.

Like waves washing around a headland, the cavaliers chipped away at the armoured block. Here and there a lobster fell or turned and ran, gradually the grains of sand brought down boulders as larger knots and a troop turned to follow, disappearing behind the shelter of the rebel foot. But the cliff of tempered steel and horseflesh still stood on the shore, battered and knocked back, but solid still as the wave of cavaliers washed back down the hill.

Beyond them on the far flank, Byron's brigade of Oxford horse came on. They moved forward, up the slope, at a full and firm trot beside the Bath road.

———

Sir Arthur Heselrigge's lobsters had held the cavaliers on the right. Now the King's horse came forward on the left. The damned cavaliers were coming on to charge Sir William Waller and his horsemen. Nat gripped his musket tight. Already the great guns beside them were crashing out.

'Give. . . fire!' The front rank gave the cavalier horsemen a volley of lead. 'To the rear!' They turned and filed past. Now it was his turn. The sergeant held his halberd high. 'Second rank!'

Nat stepped forward.

'Present!'

He blew on his match coal till it flared hot and smoking, flicked open the priming pan and levelled the musket at the ranks of trotting horses.

'Give. . . fire!'

Two hundred muskets crashed out with a deafening roar of flame and smoke, the heavy musket butt thumping back into Nat's already bruised shoulder.

'To the rear!'

A turn to the right and he marched back through the ranks, Billy grinning back at him as he passed. Another turn and he was in his place at the rear, making ready, stepping forward with each motion done. Billy wasn't so afeared this time.

Three more volleys crashed out and then Billy was marching past him again, back through the ranks, with a great wide grin and smoking musket. He was alright. He wasn't afeared. He'd given fire with the rest of his rank and now his butty was safe again at the rear. He wasn't just a boy any more. They were near men – like true soldiers, he and his butty.

———

Praise God, they were advancing, moving forward! Francis raked spurs across Breda's bloodied flanks, lurching into a trot. Hauling back on the reins and iron bit to hold the beast in check, he reached forward, drew a pistol and pulled back the cock.

They surged forward, boot against boot, held between heaving horseflesh left and right, tossing heads, high stepping, stamping hooves, champing at the bit. Three ranks of Godly horsemen, an invincible iron squadron of faith and fervour.

For they were chosen; chosen to break the accursed cavaliers. They followed the Bath road towards Marlborough, outflanking the apostate horde that dared to advance against Sir William Waller and his horsemen. An Angel of the Lord, he would swing down upon the foe, drive in their flank and execute His wrath.

And they shall know that I am the Lord, when I shall lay my vengeance upon them.

———

Ralph blew heat into his match coal, held his breath, aimed low, aimed at the horse and squeezed the trigger. The cock snapped down, stabbing the match into the priming pan. A jet of sparks burst upward, the musket thumping into his shoulder, smoke whisked away on the wind.

There was no point in aiming at the man. The lobster was encased in shot-proof armour, closed helmet, cuirass, vambraces and tassets to the knee. But the horse was vulnerable, unprotected. It crashed to the ground, writhing, kicking, shrieking, the lobster crushed beneath its bulk. It was a handsome animal. But there'd been no alternative.

Ralph stepped forward, reloading as he went. They'd moved down the slope of Roundway Hill, running down the ridge to fire into the flank of Hesselrigge's lobsters as they came forward to charge Prince Maurice and Lord Wilmot's brigade a second time.

Now they were turning, running, leaving the battlefield. The great façade of tempered steel and solid warhorse was crumbling, melting away, running behind their foot and riding for the road to Bath in a wild, headlong dash.

On the far flank, Byron's brigade was locked in a melee with Waller's horsemen. Beyond them, the Earl of Crawford had thrown his cavaliers into the battle, breathing new spirit into them, leading them in a charge along the Bath road, a charge to avenge their night of humiliation at Silbury Hill, crashing into a rebel regiment that threatened Byron's flank.

———

'Nat?' Billy was calling out to him from behind. 'Nat!' He was afeared. Horses and horsemen streamed past them, charging towards the rear. His butty needed him.

'I'm 'ere Billy!'

'What's happenin, Nat?'

Sir Arthur Heselrigge's lobsters had disappeared behind them. The country folk were running in all directions. A woman screamed. Now Sir William's horsemen were turning, crashing back against their own reserve, their second line, all running in chaos, riding for the rear, leaving the foot alone on Roundway Down.

'Nat! What's happenin?'

'It's alright, Billy. Thou and me'll be alright. Keep thy match lit and do as sergeant says.'

———

Francis pulled at the reins, hauling back on them, twisting the iron bit, feet braced in the stirrups, but the reins slipped through his gauntleted hands. He was not strong enough. He could not slow Breda's charge. The beast was uncontrollable, wild eyed, ears flat, neck outstretched as it tore headlong. All about him, riders clung to their mounts in a terrifying, thunderous gallop.

Tears whipped back from his face, eyes swimming as he held on to mane and saddle. They were not charging to victory; they were running from God's enemies, fleeing in defeat and disgrace, born along upon a wave of base fear, animal panic, herd instinct. God had forsaken them, abandoned them to this bestial stampede.

They careered across the down in a cloud of dust and flying grass, the ground gently rising, hooves tearing at the sod, the pace unslacking, furlong after furlong. And then the ground was gone, a precipice dropping sharply away. Breda plunged, whinnying, flailing, kicking legs, belly and saddle over twisted neck, rolling under flying hooves, dust and stones.

XII

The Conqueror

Kendall Tremain
Roundway Hill, four o'clock

They were marching up through Roundway village, up onto Roundway Down to join their cavaliers returned from Oxford, sallying out from Devizes to beat the bloody rebels once and for all. Kendall Tremain shifted the musket on his shoulder. The hill was steep, the pace fast, the sun hot on his sweat-soaked back.

There were plenty who'd thought it was one of Sir William the bloody Conqueror Waller's tricks, a ruse to lure them out from behind their barricades. They said that he'd fired the signal guns from up on the down. But it wasn't so. It was Prince Maurice, come back from Oxford with fresh cavaliers.

Prince Maurice was up on Roundway Down now, charging the bloody rebels. The battle was half won. Now they were late for it. It'd be over before they got up there. There'd be nought left to pillage or plunder, the prizes all taken. They should have listened to old Sir Ralph Hopton when he told them to march after the signal. He might be blinded and hurt, but he was still a soldier who knew what was what.

They crested the ridge, Slanning's Foot leading the way, with Mohun's, Trevanion's, Godolphin's, what was left of

123

Grenville's and Hopton's Somersets following, and Colonel Buck's tertia bringing up the rear. Ahead, the down stretched out before them: a sea of grass, waves rippling across it under wind and sun.

The grass swayed about dead horses, like boulders half submerged. Beyond them, the rebel foot still stood, a great square of pike and musket washed up on the shore, clinging to the high ground and the lane that ran across the battlefield. All about them were cavaliers.

———

'Nat!' Billy was afeared. 'What's happenin, Nat?'

They'd stood against the bloody cavaliers' charge, thrown them back. They'd done alright, just the foot alone on Roundway Down, their own horse and gunners gone. But now the Cornish foot were on the down, marching up the lane from Devizes. Men whispered all about, fear and worry in their voices, faces black and creased like worn out leather.

But Sir William still stood with them. And Colonel Popham. And Colonel Paleologus. Sir William would get them out of it. The Conqueror knew what to do. He always knew what to do. They just needed to hang on for their horse to come back. It was all part of his plan. It was one of his tricks, a subterfuge to lure the cavaliers away.

'Nat! What's happenin?'

'It's alright, Billy. It's alright. Just do like sergeant says.'

A drum rattled out a call then stopped.

'Have a care!' The sergeant raised his halberd. 'Listen in now. Shoulder your muskets!'

'Lord St John's Regiment will move. . . to the left!' It was Colonel Paleologus. He knew what to do. 'Battaile, face to the. . . left!'

Every man turned to the left, turning on the ball of his left foot, the battalion facing what was the flank.

'Prepare to march! By your right. . . march on!'

The drum beat out the call to march, the drums of every company taking it up, beating out the steady pace as they stepped off. Nat marched three feet behind his number in the next file. Billy was no longer behind him, but beside him.

They were marching across the down, away from Devizes and the Cornish foot, the sun on their backs. They were marching towards Bagdon Hill and the road to Bath, a great square of foot: Lord St John's, Popham's, Cooke's, Colonel Nathaniel Fiennes' and Sir John Merrick's; the Western Association foot as one. They'd march all the way to Bath like this if they had to.

More damned cavaliers stood ahead of them, they swarmed about them, ahead and on the flank, the Cornish foot closing behind. They marched on, in silence, just the beat of the drum and the noise of larks singing on the wind, the pace quickening, stepping out over the long down grass. Billy stumbled, almost dropping his musket.

The air about them shrieked as a cannon ball hurtled overhead, yellow smoke and thumping explosion ahead. And then another. This time, there were screams, cursing and yelling as the iron ball ploughed through a battalion to the left. The cavaliers had taken two of Sir William's own cannon and turned them against him and his foot. The pace quickened yet more, men stumbling and cursing, the ranks ragged, Billy running to keep up.

Again, the cannon crashed out, smashing a path through the ranks. Nat stepped over a body – twisted, mangled limbs, guts steaming in the grass. The wounded man looked up at him, old enough to be his master, bloody stumps and torn cloth where legs should have been. Clawing at his shoes. Billy retched, pale and shaking.

Sir William was on his horse with a pistol in his hand. Beside him, Colonel Popham and the other field officers were mounting. Colonel Paleologus hopped beside his horse, pulling himself up into the saddle. Sir William was going to charge the cannon, kill the cavalier gunners.

Together, the officers galloped forward. They charged towards the cannon, riding low, bent over their horses' necks, turning, racing – past the cannon, past the cavaliers and on towards the Bath road, disappearing past Bagdon Hill.

Sir William was gone. He'd left them. Perhaps he'd gone to fetch his horsemen, to bring them back. It was all part of his plan. He'd come back.

The pace slowed. One by one, the drums fell silent, the ranks breaking apart as grown men dropped their pike or musket and turned back. They tried to push themselves to the centre of the block, a mass of lairy, leaderless wretches. A fountain of blazing smoke shot into the air; a quartermaster burning his budge barrel of gunpowder. All about them was chaos.

'With me, lads!' The sergeant held his halberd high.

'Nat! What's happenin?'

'I'm with thee, Billy!' His butty needed him. 'Stay with sergeant!'

'With me, lads!' The sergeant forced his way through the mass. 'Stay close with me and we'll be alright!'

Men were moving towards the edge of the down, moving in knots about an officer's partizan or colour – others running in ones and twos. Already, the cavalier horsemen were charging past, dashing in amongst them, pistols barking, swords flashing in the sun, blood streaked, cutting, hacking, screaming, yelling, iron hooves thundering, chasing down leather shoes, bodies crawling in the grass.

Cavaliers swirled around them – smoke, steel and sweating horseflesh. Standing back to back, the sergeant swung his halberd. Beside him, Billy swayed, his musket upturned, the heavy butt above his head. Others thrust with smoking barrels or tuck sword.

A pistol crashed out; thunder, flame and tossing horse. The sergeant fell to his knees clutching at his chest, gasping, spitting blood, his back ripped open, bone and gore, lungs filling with blood. Nat grabbed his halberd, lunged at the horseman. Billy swinging his musket, falling beneath flailing hooves, scrabbling for his weapon.

'Billy!' Nat leapt forward. 'Leave it!' He pulled Billy back – held him close. The others were running, running for the edge of the down. It was just him and his butty.

Billy slipped from his grasp, dropped beside the sergeant on all fours, put his arm around him, trying to pull him up, to drag him to his feet again.

The older man shook his head and spat. 'No, Billy lad.' His voice a whisper. 'Run. Run now.'

Billy looked up, cheeks thick with dust and gunsmoke streaked in tears.

'Do like sergeant says.' Nat stepped forward, halberd thrust out. 'Run, Billy lad. I'll be right behind thee. Run as fast as you can. Now, Billy! Run!'

Billy ran, tears whipping back in the wind, skinny legs and outsized shoes flying over the grass. A boy running from a battle, running from things he should never have known.

Nat watched him go, then threw down the halberd and ran after his butty. He could see Billy no more through the smoke and cavalier horsemen. He ran as fast as he could, lungs bursting, leaping and stumbling in the long grass, blinded by tears.

Iron hooves drummed out a canter behind him. He twisted and turned, leather shoes loose in worn through hose, the sword slicing the air beside him.

The cavalier slowed, turning his horse back across his path. Nat pulled the bandolier from his shoulder and flung it at the beast as he ran. His shoe slipped – twisting over. He rolled on the ground, ankle burning with pain, the sword flashing over his head. He dragged himself up, gasping down air. He stepped forward, pain shooting up his leg, eyes flooding, ears pulsing. He could run no further. The cavalier stood before him, beast snorting, steaming, lathered in sweat, blood dripping from his sword.

The blade pierced coat, shirt, skin and flesh, driving between ribs. It ripped open a path of torn lung and severed blood vessels, dragging with it dirty cloth, deep within a boyish chest, a chest that had known no woman's love. Blood, pain, tears, life spilt out upon the down. He would never make another shoe.

XIII

Bloody Ditch

Ralph Reeve
Rear of the Parliamentary Foot,
Roundway Down, five o'clock

They were following the lane towards Bagdon Hill and the Bath road, behind what was left of the rebel foot. Ralph picked his way through the jumble of discarded equipage, dead and dying, fleeing rebel foot cut down by cavalier horsemen. They'd worked their way north, keeping ahead of the Cornish foot who eyed them with suspicion. More than once, he'd had to yell, show the colour ribbon in his hat, make cavaliers and Cornishmen see that they were Prince Maurice's dragoons, not more rebel foot.

To their left, the down ended sharply, falling away suddenly, steeply, a precipice three hundred feet deep, Rowde village and its ford below. They slipped around the end of a great gully filled with wounded and wary rebels, some still running past, others crawling in the grass and calling out. Terrified eyes amid tear-streaked cheeks peered out from behind a furze bush – a boy looking back across the down as if waiting for a friend that did not follow, too frightened to go on alone, too afraid to go back amongst the chaos of the battlefield.

And then they were past, the down opening out again. A great promontory hung above the plain below, its far end enclosed within an ancient earthwork. A company of rebel foot still stood within the earthwork, a company of foot and a coach. Waller's reserve, still guarding his carriage? Was he, or some other rebel officer with them, lying wounded in the coach? There would be papers, letters of import, prizes, perhaps even coin.

Ralph led the way towards the coach. It was madness to advance on a company of foot with just his little division of dragoons. He should go back, find Sergeant O'Brien and the rest of the troop, re-join Prince Maurice's Regiment. And yet, these rebels were not formed as a company. They did not stand in ranks and files, ready to defend themselves or their charge. They stood about in groups, in shifting clumps, as if they were unsure of friend as well as foe.

These were not rebels. They were prisoners, cavaliers captured by Waller and held here at the rear of the rebel army during the battle. Some were foot soldiers taken on the march from Landsdown Hill to Devizes, at Chippenham and Rowde. But more were cavaliers, Oxford horse, gentlemen of the Earl Crawford's force that was ambushed and captured at Silbury Hill. All were held here waiting to be joined by yet more from Devizes and Roundway Down, waiting to be marched to Bristol or London in shame.

A cavalier stood before him, between him and the coach: plumed hat, silk jacket, sleeves slashed open to show fine linen – no sword or pistol. 'Thank you, my man, but you should come no closer.'

Ralph halted, his dragoons behind him. What lay within this coach? Did it carry disease, some sort of pestilence or plague, the sweating fever? 'Why so?'

'I cannot allow you to see within this coach. I would be grateful if you and your men will escort the coach and myself at a distance, as I direct you.'

Ralph flicked the ash from his match, the heat rising within him. This damned coxcomb stood before him, a prisoner, disarmed, dishonoured, clean and fresh, without a scratch, powder burn or dust from the battlefield and addressed him as a servant. 'I assume you are a prisoner, sir. Upon your parole?'

'That is not of your concern.'

'I rather think it is, sir. You appear to have neither warrant nor weapon upon this battlefield. I will take charge of this coach and its contents.'

'Have a care, my man. Do you know who I am?'

'Do you know who I am, sir?'

'I do not.'

'Good. Now, stand aside!' Ralph pushed past the fop. 'Good day, sir.' Gunpowder, grit and grime chafed at his collar, dust showering from his tattered soldier's coat and scuffed boots.

'I must protest!' The fool shook, almost stamping his foot as the rest of Ralph's dragoons followed, stepping past with a grin.

'Clem. . . Tandy. . . take hold of the lead horses.' He was almost at the coach. 'Sam. . . watch the driver and footman. Luke. . . Jack. . . round the other side, please. Don't let anybody out of the coach and don't let anybody near.' Musket at the ready, he flung open the coach door.

A woman sat within, pistol at the ready. Beside her cowered a cavalier – unarmed. Slowly, eyes adjusting to the gloom, Ralph surveyed them, his match hissing, smoking in the doorway and wind, mingling with the smell of scent within. The woman was dressed as a maidservant. The cavalier was another dandy, a fop in ostrich plumed hat, slashed sleeves, lace and ribbons, fine boned hands and long calfskin boots. The hat was lifted slowly as soft long hair tumbled down around fine shoulders, slender throat, swelling chest, high cheekbones, full lips and flashing eyes – a lady cavalier in silk and leather, strange and sensual. Ralph stirred, an eyebrow raised.

The maid raised her pistol. 'Touch her, sir, and by God, I'll shoot ye dead!'

Ralph stepped back, sweeping off his hat. 'My lady, I am at your service.'

'Thank you, bold sir.' The lady cavalier looked him in the eye. 'Bridget, dear, there is no need to shoot him. He is one of Prince Maurice's brave boys – one of our own. Besides, he is rather handsome, do you not think? And much more gallant than those fools who let us be captured. He has come fresh from the battle.'

'Aye, my lady.' The maid lowered her pistol. 'It'd be a pity for tae shoot him. But he's no so fresh. He's needing of a bath.'

'Thank you, madame.' Ralph smiled. 'I am one of Prince Maurice's dragoons.'

'Well, I would be grateful if you would take me to my Prince. We are. . . acquainted.'

'And may I know who we have the honour of escorting?'

'I am. . . Mistress Parsons.'

'Very well, my lady. Please keep within the coach. The battlefield is not yet secure.' He shut the door and climbed up beside the worried-looking coachman. 'Clem. . .Tandy. . . climb up on the rear with the footman.'

'We're with ee, Master Ralph.'

Ralph turned back to the prisoners. 'Luke, I am sorry. . .

you had better stay here with the others and make sure no harm comes to these prisoners. We will be back as quickly as we can.' He turned to the driver. 'Drive on!'

The coach lurched forward, swaying as it passed through the entrance to the earthwork. They worked their way back across the down towards the lane, wary of wounded rebels lying in the grass. The last remnants of Waller's foot battalions were laying down their weapons and surrendering their colours. As they went, they gathered about them a mounted escort of cavaliers, all interested in the coach, wanting to know what lay within, wanting to be part of its prize. Ahead stood a knot of horsemen about Prince Maurice's standard, his regiment reforming behind.

Ralph stopped the coach short on the lane and waited for an officer to approach. It was Major Atkyns of Prince Maurice's Regiment, his horse's muzzle, cheek and bridle cut and bleeding. Ralph leaned forward from the driver's seat. 'Sir, I have a Mistress Parsons in the coach. She asks to be taken to His Highness – to the Prince. I believe she was taken prisoner by the rebels at Silbury Hill.'

'Well done! Well done, my boy! Wait here.' The major turned to go. 'And do not let anyone approach this coach, unless it is His Highness.' He cantered back to Prince Maurice.

Ralph jumped down from the coach, stepping quickly to stand in front of the door. 'Clem, guard the other door. Let no one near the coach.'

'Right you are, Master Ralph.'

'Tandy, hold the lead horses steady.'

The knot of horsemen cantered forward, Prince Maurice jumping from his saddle. Ralph held the coach door open as the lady's maid stepped down and the Prince leapt into her place. The door shut firmly behind him, the coach swaying.

133

There was a moment of silence before Major Atkyns coughed and drew the other horsemen back. Ralph stood awkwardly in front of the door.

'Thank you for yer. . . discretion.' The waiting-maid looked at him, young and sure in her tight bodice and open lace collar. 'My lady asked to know yer name.'

'Ralph Reeve, corporal of dragoons.'

'My lady also asked me to give you this.' She pressed a coin into his hand, a golden crown – near two day's pay. 'A wee token of her gratitude, for you and yer lads' service. She is grateful for what you did.' She looked him in the eye. 'And this is from me.' Leaning forward, she kissed him. 'Now, away with yersels. And find a bath.'

———

Ralph led them back across the down to the earthwork, Luke and the prisoners. They'd found the rest of their troop, received pats on the back and a hundred questions as to who she was that lay within the coach. Even Sergeant O'Brien had a smile and a nod for him, telling him to gather up his division and catch up with the troop before nightfall. Already, regiments were reformed, marching back down the lane to Devizes.

With Hodge, the boy, Sam's lad and the spare ponies, they rode in silence, the sun low in the sky ahead of them. They were tired, dirty, hungry and thirsty but happy to be alive, unhurt, and the darlings of Prince Maurice's Regiment of Horse. There were others with the freed prisoners now, cavalier officers and sergeants forming them into bodies and marching them off to re-join their regiments. Thank God, he would not need to face the coxcomb fop again.

Luke stood apart with Sam, Jack, Kibler and Jewkes at

the edge of the earthwork. He looked tired, earnest – grim. 'Ralph, I'm sorry, but you'd better see this.'

They stood on the earthwork bank staring down the slope that fell away from the edge of Roundway Down: a steep, sudden drop; a precipice three hundred feet deep. The grass scarp was scattered with dark shapes, twisted and unnatural shapes; the bodies of horses and men – scores of them, and more hidden in the deep folds, gullies and shadows that ran down to the plain below. Here and there a body moved, horses still kicking, trying to rise, men crawling, rolling, a scavenger picking over the dead, crows rising and falling. This was where Waller's horse regiments had left the battlefield, riding over the edge of the precipice in blind panic, aiming for the Bath road only to fall to their deaths in a charnel house of broken necks and mangled limbs, a terrifying ride in dust and chaos over the edge into this now bloody ditch.

They left their ponies with Hodge and the boys, descending the hill in silence, each picking their way across the slope, from body to body. They all knew what they were looking for, what they hoped to find: a firelock carbine to replace their matchlock muskets, a good pistol or mortuary sword instead of the short tucks they were issued with. But they also knew what they feared to find: a wounded man or, worse, an injured horse. Ralph shivered as a single shot crashed out in the evening sun as another broken animal was dispatched.

A body lay in the gulley below, an ironclad trooper, facedown, helmet torn back. Ralph slid down the grass and chalk bank. A flintstone rattled on iron backplate, bouncing on down the slope. The rebel trooper's body was unmoving, dead. He turned the body over, the head rolling, neck twisted, bruised, awkward, broken – thrown from his horse. Beside the body lay a carbine on a crossbelt.

He unclipped the carbine, turning it over in the glowing sunlight, brushing away the grass and chalk that stuck to it. It was not a firelock, but a snaphaunce – almost as good. He drew back the lock, pulled the frizzen down, flipped open the priming pan cover, squeezed the trigger. It had lost its flint and needed cleaning and the stock was scratched and dented from the fall, but the action worked. He brought it up to his shoulder and sighted along the barrel. It fitted him well, came naturally into the aim. Thank God! He had a carbine again.

He pulled a powder flask on its cord out from under the body, searched under the breastplate and buff coat for spare flints, shot and purse, pocketing each in turn. The sword was missing, the scabbard empty, lost in the flight or fall, and there was no pistol. But he had what he needed. He had a carbine again. His matchlock musket could go back to the quartermaster. He no longer needed to carry and keep alight the stinking match. He had a weapon that would fire in rain or snow, a weapon that would not give him away in darkness. It was a pity it was not Ned's old carbine. Some underserving bastard rebel had taken that at Winchester. But now he had another like it. He climbed up out of the gulley, carbine and musket over his shoulder, to stand in the sun.

'Oh Jesus!' The shout echoed across the slope. 'No!' It was Clem's voice, ahead and across the slope. 'It can't be. Oh, my poor beauty! What has he done to ee?'

Ralph ran, sliding and scrabbling, down and up the next ridge. 'Clem!' His hands were raw and bleeding, holding both carbine and musket, dragging at grass tufts, chalk and flint. 'Clem!' Again, he charged down into a gully, clawing his way up the other side.

'No, Master Ralph!' Clem blocked his way at the top, held

him back. 'You can't! You mustn't! I tell ee, you don't want to see it!'

'Clem, what is it? What have you found?'

'I didn't doubt no good'd come on it. He never could manage he proper. I reckoned he'd do him no good, spoil him if he didn't mind his ways. But I didn't think he'd kill him!'

'Who Clem? Who is down there?'

''Tis Breda!'

'Breda? My father's horse?'

'The hoss your father gave to ee.'

'Are you sure?'

'I'd know that hoss anywhere.'

'Is he dead?'

'No. 'Tis worse. You don't want to know it, Master Ralph. I beg ee. Go back. Let him be.'

Ralph dropped the musket and carbine, pushed Clem aside, tore himself away to slide down the next slope. Breda lay at the bottom, head raised, ears pricked, a whickering snort to greet him. The great charger rolled, trying to raise himself, only to fall back, his foreleg broken, twisted and bloody, shattered bone jutting through severed skin and blood matted hair, fetlock and hoof hanging, dragging, useless.

'Alright boy.' Ralph slid down beside his horse. 'Lay still now.' He cradled the big head in his arms, let its weight fall on his chest, felt its warmth, his fingers stroking behind ears, under his mane, brushing the hair away. Hot, moist, rasping breath blew dew across his coat, whiskers twitching, eyelashes fluttering, calming, soothing. 'There now, boy. Lay still.'

Tears slid down Ralph's cheeks as he held tightly to the horse, the horse he had grown up with, the horse his stepfather had given to him, a precious gift from the only father he'd ever known, the horse that had carried him safe across the battlefield of Edgehill, outrun their pursuers, got him safe through the gates of Winchester, the horse that had been taken from him, taken by his own brother, Francis.

Where was Francis now? Had he been riding Breda when he fell? Was he lying dead or hurt down the slope? 'Clem, is there any sign of my brother?'

'No. He ain't down that there slope, if that's what you mean. He *were* here, mind. That's his snapsack on your old saddle. There's one pistol in the holster there too. Other one's gone. Taken it with him. In a hurry I reckon. Didn't stay with Breda here, did he?'

Breda coughed, a great rasping, wheezing cough, rocking on the hard ground. His own weight was slowly crushing him, pressing down on him, drowning him in a slow painful death. He needed to stand. But he couldn't stand, he couldn't get up with a broken foreleg. He would never stand again, never walk, trot, canter, never gallop again, never feel the ground rushing beneath him, never again run like the wind.

'Master Ralph, please. You've got let me do the right thing by Breda now. God knows I don't want to. But it's got to be done. You leave Breda with me now. Go back to the others.'

'No Clem. I must do it. Breda is my horse. I owe him that.'

'Are you sure, now? Nobody will think the worst of ee. Everyone knows what you thought of this horse. You don't need to put yourself through it.'

'Thank you, Clem. But I must do it. Bring me that pistol now. Is it loaded?'

''Tis loaded.'

'Cock it for me. Please, Clem.'

Ralph slid back a little, took the pistol in his hand, placed it against the horse's head. Breda whickered softly, ears twitching, great dark eyes looking up, eyes he knew better than any

others, eyes that had shared so much, deep wells of under-
standing, knowing pools, trusting, trusted, loving. He could
look into them no more, tears flooding his face, his own eyes
screwed shut. 'Goodbye old friend.'

The pistol exploded, whipping back in a shower of blood.
The horse twitched, convulsed, kicking, then lay still, a bubble
of blood rising from its muzzle. Ralph lay back, the great head
heavy on him, his face spattered in blood, hot, salty and sticky,
mingling with his tears, running down his neck and soaking
his collar and chest.

Clem took the pistol from him and wiped it clean. He shut
Breda's eyes and held the horse's head while Ralph slid out
from underneath, laying it gently on the ground. Together,
they removed the bridle and bit, undid the girth, pulled the
saddle away and brushed Breda clean. Ralph shook the horse
blanket out and laid it carefully over Breda's head. He was
damned if he would leave his old friend's eyes to be pecked
out by the crows.

When there was nothing more they could do, he gave his
horse one last stroke before climbing back up onto the ridge
above the gully. The sun was low, setting towards the West.
Somewhere out there was his brother Francis, making his way
to Bath or Bristol. What was he even doing here? He'd been
with Balfour's Horse at Winchester. They weren't with Waller's
army of the Western Association. But there were reports that
some of Balfour's had gone with Nathaniel Fiennes to form a
new regiment of horse at Bristol. Well, the shit would have
a fucking long walk home.

He'd promised his mother on her deathbed that he would
look after Francis. His brother was somewhere out there, on
foot, perhaps hurt. He filled his chest and yelled, long and
hard. 'Francis!'

But, damn him, he had taken Breda from him, taken his beautiful horse and ridden him to his death. He'd done it knowing he was not a strong rider. 'Francis Reeve!'

Worse, he'd left Breda for dead. He didn't stop to do the right thing. He didn't shoot him, put him out of his misery. He ran away – left Breda to die alone, a slow and painful death. Left him as crowbait. 'You bastard!'

Part Three

Redemption

This glorious day, for it was a day of triumph, redeemed the king's whole affairs, so that all clouds that shadowed them seemed to be dispelled, and a bright light of success to shine over the whole kingdom.

EDWARD HYDE, *The History of the Great Rebellion*, 1667

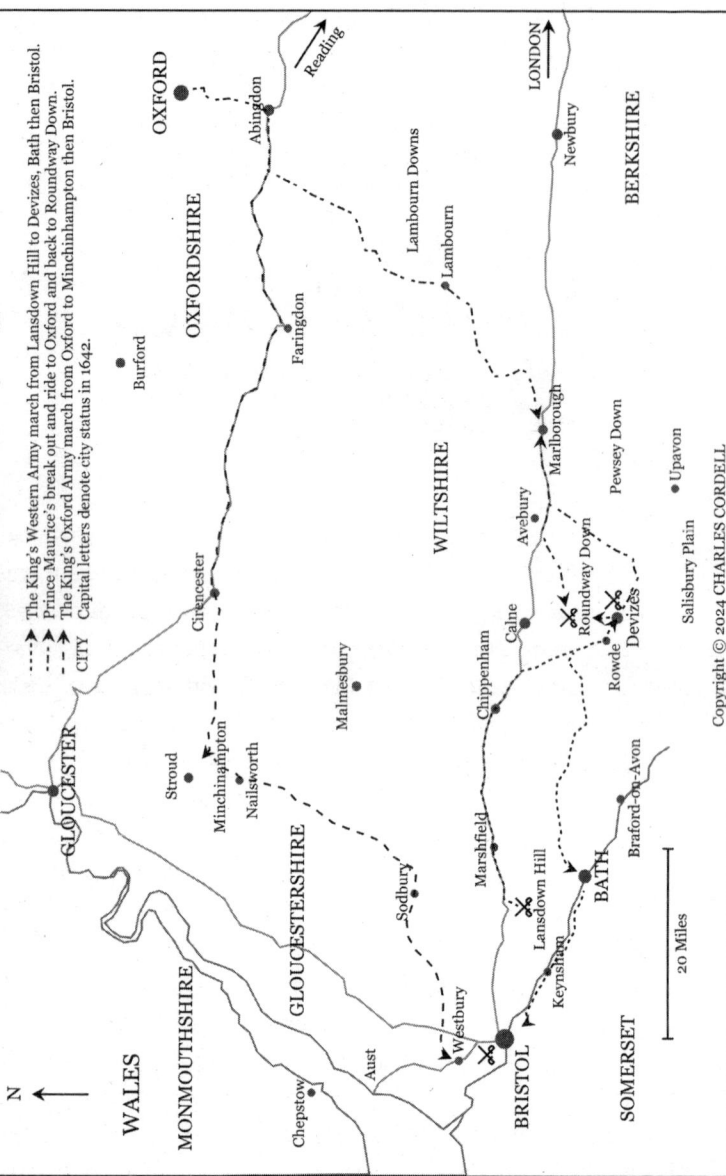

Western Campaign: 5th to 26th of July 1643

- - - - - → The King's Western Army march from Lansdown Hill to Devizes, Bath then Bristol.
- · - · → Prince Maurice's break out and ride to Oxford and back to Roundway Down.
········→ The King's Oxford Army march from Oxford to Minchinhampton then Bristol.
CITY   Capital letters denote city status in 1642.

N

WALES

MONMOUTHSHIRE

Chepstow

Aust

GLOUCESTERSHIRE

GLOUCESTER

Stroud

Minchinhampton

Nailsworth

Cirencester

Burford

OXFORDSHIRE

OXFORD

Abingdon

Reading

Malmesbury

Faringdon

Sodbury

Westbury

BRISTOL

Marshfield

Lansdown Hill

Keynsham

BATH

Braford-on-Avon

SOMERSET

Chippenham

Calne

Avebury

Rowde

Devizes

Roundway Down

Pewsey Down

Marlborough

WILTSHIRE

Upavon

Salisbury Plain

Lambourn

Lambourn Downs

BERKSHIRE

Newbury

LONDON

20 Miles

Copyright © 2024 CHARLES CORDELL

I

St Swithin's Day

George Merrett
New College, Oxford, Saturday the 15th
of July 1643, a quarter to midnight

George Merrett felt for the watch in his pocket, pulling it free. He flipped open the silver lid and held it to the candle. It was almost midnight. He had not rested since the King and Queen entered Oxford, his table still strewn with papers, lists, calculations. They had arrived in triumph, to the ringing of bells, singing of *Te Deums*, the blaring of town bands and cheers of rejoicing crowds. The candles still burned bright with carousing in the hall across the Great Quad of New College and in every college, inn and tavern in the city. Christ, how he longed to be free to drink, discuss, dispute, to sing drunkenly, to be a student in Oxford again. But there was still so much to be done.

Prince Rupert had returned with the Oxford Army, filling their quarters once again. They had successfully thrown off the Earl of Essex and joined with the Queen. He had met her Majesty at Stratford-upon-Avon, in the house of the great bard himself, after her brave march from York. The *She Generalissima* herself had shared the march with her troops, eating in the field with them. And she had taken Burton upon Trent in bloody battle. Together, they had marched to Kineton to be received by the King on the field of Edgehill. She brought to Oxford her own army, three thousand foot and fifteen hundred horse, all needing yet more billets, fare and fodder to be found. And every musketeer now in Oxford needing fresh match.

Of more import, the Queen brought with her a second train of artillery and one hundred and fifty wagons filled with munitions purchased at The Hague and landed at Bridlington on the Yorkshire coast. She had endured the bombardment of the Parliamentary fleet, sheltering in a ditch as bar-shot and twelve-pound cannon balls tore through the house in which she was staying, showering her in dust and killing a sergeant nearby. Every new artillery piece and wagonload had to be housed, unloaded, inspected, itemised, accounted, allocated, issued, crewed and supplied with powder and shot.

And the same day, Lord Wilmot had returned from Devizes with Sir John Byron and Prince Maurice. They brought news of victory, joyous news of victory over Sir William 'the Conqueror' Waller – a *complete* victory. Parliament's Western Association was no more. Sir Ralph Hopton and the King's Western Army were finally free to march and join with the King about Oxford. But they needed yet more powder and match, and shot of every size, calibre and weight for their pistols, carbines, muskets and old fowling pieces; for their robinets, falconets, falcons, minions, sakers and seven brass pieces captured at Roundway Down.

They had already consumed so much precious powder and match on their march. What they had taken had been lost, burnt by Waller's quartermasters or blown up by some fool smoking a pipe of tobacco. George had prepared powder bags, on the King's order, to be sent to Devizes on the backs of dragoons. The order was countermanded. In their place, barrels of powder were dispatched by cart with the Earl of Crawford, only for them to be lost in an ambush. Thirty-seven more cartloads of munitions had been sent after Lord Wilmot.

God alone knew what was left or how he was to find, manufacture or create yet more gunpowder. Every possible mill about Oxford had been pressed into service, grinding the volatile mix. But it was dangerous work that needed supervision, care and time – *precious* time, let alone the sulphur, charcoal and saltpetre needed to make it. All had to be roasted, burnt, dug, procured, transported, mixed and ground to precise instruction. A single spark could destroy a month's labour – worse, an entire mill.

Sir John Heydon, the Lieutenant-General of the Ordnance, required a report before morning. A report for the Council of War with the King. The council was to decide whether to march immediately on London, or to take Bristol first. For the first time, the King had men and guns enough to win the war outright. Thirty-thousand men now lay under his command, ready to march upon the capital, to envelope it. Hopton's Western Army was finally free to march through the Southern counties whilst the King's Oxford and the Queen's armies advanced down the Thames Valley. And in the North, the Earl of Newcastle had defeated the Fairfaxes, besieged Hull, was poised ready to invade East Anglia. Surely, now was the time to strike, while the Earl of Essex's army lay weakened by fever, while Parliament was split.

But there were those who argued that the West must be secured first, that Bristol should be taken before London, that England's second city and port was ripe to fall. It was true that some in Bristol were ready to support the King. But their plot to deliver the city to Rupert had ended in failure. The Parliamentary governor, Nathaniel Fiennes, had hanged the leaders and built new defences. And now he would be reinforced by those who had escaped from Roundway Down. The King still hoped for peace in Ireland, to bring his army there back to England. Bristol was the principal port for Ireland. But Parliamentary dogs would use it against them, say that the King treated with Catholic rebels instead of crushing them.

Surely, London was the mark, the prize, the centre of the Parliamentary party's strength? Without London, the rebellion would be nothing. The King should fall on London now, with all that he could muster – whilst he held all the cards. Now was not the time to divert attention, to allow the Parliamentary dogs respite, to dissipate the King's hard-won concentration of forces in a costly siege or storm. Already, there were those who contrived, manipulated and plotted within the court for personal gain. The arrival of the Queen with her own factious party only added discontent and jealousy, perhaps even division within the council. It was said that she had denied the King a private interview until her own favourites were granted rank and advancement.

Prince Rupert had ordered the army be ready to march again within two days. He was right, of course. It was St Swithin's Day and the weather would be fine for the next forty days. And it was a new moon, the Hay Moon, the first since the solstice. Now was the time to start out on a new enterprise, the time to strike. The stars were aligned. But there was still so much to do.

He would speak with Nick Busy in the morning, ensure that the two culverins were ready. The old gunner would know what to do, but they would need greasing and reaming out again. And the powder checking. And the King wanted every soldier in the Oxford Army to be issued with their new coat, breeches and montero cap before they marched!

He should go to his wife, comfort her, spend time with her before he marched away again. He had put her through so much already, the failure of his iron smelting enterprise, creditors, lawsuits, smallpox and the loss of their child, not to mention the cramped conditions, squabbling and petty tyrannies as the wife of a lowly officer of the ordnance. She lay in the bed across their borrowed chamber, waiting for him, heavy with child again.

But he dared not upset his master. He could not afford to. He longed to purse his own designs once more. But there were so many ready to prostitute themselves for favour, to backstab and climb over him. And ruin was but one step away.

The table was piled with inventories, legers, orderbooks, requests, demands and receipts. Once it had been a place of study, the repository of ideas, of invention, of *philisophia naturalis*, the pursuit of wisdom, reason and virtue. It had been filled with Plato, with Servetus, Galileo and Helmont, with hope and belief in a better world. Christ, how he had loved Oxford then. He had loved its soaring spires, colleges, libraries, halls and taverns, the discourse, debate and joy of life unbounded.

He gently pressed the watch closed, an instrument of wonderous precision, a perfection encased in silver, held in the palm of his hand. If only the natural world could be so regulated, ordered to conform. If only time itself could be held. He rubbed his eyes and picked up his quill again. It was almost midnight. And there was still so much to do.

II

Bath

Ralph Reeve
The King's Bath, Bath, Somerset, Sunday the
16th of July 1643, two o'clock in the afternoon

Ralph stepped carefully into the water. It swirled, warm and green about his legs. He took another step, the water and its vapours rising around him. Slowly, gently he stepped deeper, descending, lowering himself into the great King's Bath. His toes found the gravel floor, the spring bubbling up hot and strong under the soles of his feet, the water about his chest. He walked on, his arms paddling the water aside as he waded through the crowd. A brass ring hung set in the sidewall, he grabbed it, pulling himself onto a stone seat jutting out from below the water. He lay back against the warm, smooth stone and let the water lift his legs. The weight, cares, aches and bruises ebbed from him, his body floating.

The great bath was thronged with men and women. They sat around the sides, stood uncertainly, the water up to their necks, their shifts and smocks billowing about them. A few braver soles paddled out to the domed temple that stood over the bubbling, seething spring in the centre. The 'Kitchen' they called it. Others had buckets of the hot water poured over their heads or afflicted bodies. But most simply stood and let the waters cleanse their skin, sooth aching limbs, bathe away sickness and worry, the vapours steeping heads and sinews, soaking away rheums, palsies and cramps.

He recognised many as soldiers – officers mostly. More than should be were wounded, lowered into the waters by their friends and the guides that waited about the baths for a gratuity, hoping that its curative powers would bring relief to their pain and hurt. The King's Western Army had occupied the town as soon as Waller abandoned it after Roundway Down. Now they rested for the first time in weeks. He and his division of dragoons had not stopped marching and fighting since the beginning of June, six weeks in the saddle.

He'd found nits, lice eggs, in the seam of his coat, felt the first itchy prickling, the rash of their bite in the pit of his arm. He'd washed and combed his matted hair, pealed the sweat-sodden shirt from his back and taken his coat, breeches, hose and foul linen to the washhouse to have the lice soaked and seethed away. Thank God it had not been worse, that there were not more. He let his legs float out from under him, his head sinking beneath the steaming water, felt it strip him clean. He came up spluttering. It tasted of sulphur and iron.

There were others in the water, those who weren't soldiers. A few old men – wrinkled lechers and rakes mostly – their bodies pickled for too long in the stew. There was a cripple and an old woman with her maid and hook-nosed hag of a guide. But there were others: ladies, women and pretty maids, half shy, flushed with excitement and the heat. They feigned shock and nervous glances. Wanton girls and whores flaunted their looks with unchaperoned freedom and flashing eyes. Over them all watched the statue of King Bladud, descendent of Brutus and the spring's ancient discoverer.

Onlookers looked down through the steam, watching from balustraded balconies and inn windows on every side. They gossiped, gasped and pointed, torn between admiration, jealousy, temptation and horror. Common soldiers gaped and prodded each other. The Cornish seemed to show no deference; not giving a damn for rank or station, they were familiar with their officers, thought themselves the equal of any gentleman and laughed out loud at the spectacle before them. In a quieter corner, an old sodomite threw ha'penny bits into the water, drooling as a line of naked boys, smooth skinned and shining wet, dived from the rail to retrieve them, surfacing again with the silver coins between their teeth.

He'd come hoping to see, to meet Mistress Parsons and her waiting-maid, Bridget. He'd seen them in the street, Mistress Parsons promenading on the arm of Prince Maurice in her ostrich plumed hat, slashed sleeves, men's breeches and long calfskin boots, all silk and leather, one gloved hand on her hip and arm akimbo as if she was the perfect bold cavalier. And he'd seen them here about the King's Bath and in the Queen's Bath beyond the rail. He'd stood watching them and caught the maid's eye with a sweep of his hat. But they were not here now.

He'd been foolish. He should not have come. How did he think he was going to approach, let alone talk to her. He could not afford to tip the keeper of the baths to introduce him. Even if he could, he would not be allowed near. Prince Maurice was away, in Oxford. A lady like Mistress Parsons would be surrounded by others, chaperoned and escorted by officers. Not even the waiting-maid would consider him seriously. He was simply an amusement, a trinket that was once toyed with, no longer needed and now discarded. He was a lowly corporal of dragoons with a tattered and lousy coat that needed boiling clean after weeks in the saddle.

Dragoon corporals were supposed to receive two shillings a day pay. He'd been worth more as a trooper of horse, two shillings and sixpence, half-a-crown per day. Still, at least the dragoons got paid on occasion. As a trooper of horse, he'd seen nothing after Shrewsbury and then had his purse taken at Winchester. All that was left of it was a lead token from a London inn, discarded in the dirt. His pay was at least a month in arears. And he'd rarely received more than half-pay. After deductions for board, lodging and hay, he was lucky if he saw four shillings a week, just seven pence per day for beer and extras. At this rate he could hardly afford a fresh shirt, let alone a new coat and breeches or a carbine at thirty shillings. Perhaps he should be diving for the sodomite's pennies with the little boys.

Was it really worth it? He was risking life and limb, exhausting himself as a common soldier with nothing to show but lice and a few pennies. It was not as if he felt deeply for the cause. He believed in the natural order of things, a hierarchy of dependency, the shared fellowship of the village, law and order. But, in truth, he'd joined the King's army to appease his stepfather, because he'd failed at everything else. He'd hoped, dreamed of becoming an officer, a cornet of horse. Instead, he was a lowly corporal of dragoons.

He was not even sure that he was worthy of that. He was still not sure what his division thought of him: Sam hardly spoke, was impenetrable; Jack just grim; Tandy more interested in gambling and what he could pick up; Jewkes glowering and angry with the world; Kibler only ready to show off in front of Sergeant O'Brien. Thank God for Luke and Clem – dear Clem.

They'd all be laughing at him now if they knew where he was, who he had come hoping to see. He should be with them, talking, sharing his time with them. Instead, he'd slunk away to hide in the King's Bath, chasing a foolish dream. He was no better than when he'd been a child, never sure, never settling, ever since his mother died. He lay back and closed his eyes, letting his body float gently in the warm water, the vapours enclosing him. Perhaps one day he would know who he was, what he was, where he was going.

A movement, a scene on the steps, brought him up out of the water, rubbing the steam from his eyes. Guides clearing a path, officers fussed – someone of importance. Carefully, slowly, guides and officers helped a man descend the steps into the water, a man with livid pink skin, a man feeling his way, a hunched old man burnt and blind. Sir Ralph Hopton!

The guides were clearing a path through the bath, leading Sir Ralph across it towards him. They were bringing him to sit against the wall. Ralph slid along the seat to make room. Perhaps he should leave, swim away, make room for the retinue. An officer was glaring at him. Fuck it! It was a public bath. He was here first. He'd made room for the Field-Marshal.

Sir Ralph Hopton groped for the brass ring in the wall, eased himself onto the seat. 'Ah, that's better.' He settled back against the wall. 'Thank you for making way, young man. Forgive me, I cannot yet see well, or move far. The doctors tell me the bath will aid a recovery.'

'I know, sir.' Ralph ignored the officer staring at him. 'I was close by when it happened. We all wish you a speedy recovery.'

'Ah, one of ours are you. Well, thank you. Who are you with?'

'I am with Prince Maurice's Dragoons, sir.'

'Ah, an officer of dragoons. You did well at Lansdown Hill clearing that wood. It was you dragoons that occupied those pits on the flank. And I hear one of your fellows discovered the rebels had quit the field. That was good work. I am grateful. Might I presume you were with the prince at Roundway Down also?'

'Yes, sir.' Ralph saw the officers looking at him, searching, questioning. Should he admit now that he was just a lowly corporal. Fuck it! Let them challenge him in front of their field-marshal. Let them hear that he was the one who crawled forward to that damn rebel wall on Lansdown. He settled back against the warm stone wall. 'We were on the flank.'

'I am sorry that the foot were a little late in joining you on the down. I am afraid that some of these officers here thought that it was another of Sir William Waller's stratagems. It would not have been unlike him. We were friends once you know. I knew him well.'

Ralph sat up. Was this the opportunity he'd hoped for? Could he, should he ask? Sir Ralph had been with the Winter Queen and the Bohemian court when they fled Prague. He might remember Ralph's mother, perhaps know something of his true father. Fuck it – he needed to know. There would be no better time, perhaps no other opportunity to ask the Field-Marshal. 'I believe, sir, that you carried Her Majesty, Queen Elizabeth of Bohemia on your horse during the retreat from Prague.'

'Ah, yes, that I did. That was after Nymburk. We thought we were safe beyond the River Elbe. But the damned imperial Cossacks caught up with us. And some of our own allied troops took to pillaging the baggage. We were forced to abandon the carriages in the snow. Her Majesty rode pillion on my horse. It was bitterly cold and she was heavy with child, you know, carrying the unborn Prince Maurice. An incomparable lady, she bore it all with an unchangeable temper and queenly dignity.'

'May I ask, sir, where did you carry her?'

'We rode on East to Glatz. Then to Breslau, where King Frederick remained to organise the resistance of his Silesian provinces. From there, some of us escorted Her Majesty north to Berlin. It was thought the Margrave of Brandenburg would accommodate his sister-in-law during her confinement to child-bed. But he sent us on to Kustrin, on the river Oder. I believe he feared Emperor Ferdinand and his Imperial ban too much. The castle at Kustrin was half a ruin, crawling with rats. And in that place, the Queen was delivered of his Highness Prince Maurice, on Twelfth Day, the sixth of January 1621.'

'Thank you, sir. My mother served the Queen in Prague. I believe she too accompanied her on that journey. Before coming to England.'

Sir Ralph Hopton stiffened. 'There were a number of ladies, Bohemian and Palatine, who fled with the royal household and court.' He continued to stare ahead of him. 'You will forgive me if I do not remember. I am afraid I feel rather fatigued. The doctors tell me I should rest.'

'Of course, sir.' Ralph slipped from his seat. He was being dismissed. He wanted more, but the Field-Marshal was ending the audience. 'Forgive me, sir.' He stepped back. 'I should not have presumed to take so much of your time.' The officers were staring at him.

'What did you say your name was?'

'Reeve, sir.' He stepped back further. 'Ralph Reeve.' He slid below the surface, swimming under its warm green hue, away from the wall, out into the bath, out to the centre and its steaming *kitchen*.

III

Westward

George Merrett
Boxwell, Gloucestershire, Saturday
the 22nd of July 1643, midday

It was Bristol. They were marching on Bristol. The King's Council of War had declared that the army was to prosecute the reduction of the West, bring it to the obedience of His Majesty, before they turned on London, before they struck at the real prize.

George pulled the watch from his pocket, held it carefully in the palm of his hand and flipped open its oval silver case. It was midday. They still had another ten miles to march before they would reach Sodbury and quarters for the night. There had been hardly an inn, let alone a village on the road since they had left Minchinhampton early that morning – and nothing since Nailsworth. They had stopped to let the draught horses drink their fill of water after negotiating the twisting road down into the town and to slake their own thirsts. But now there was little chance of finding dinner, let alone feeding an army on the march. The road ran straight, open, deserted under the endless blue sky and blazing sun, for mile after mile across the Cotswolds, southwest towards Bath and Bristol. It was an ancient road, a Roman road, recorded in antiquity by Antoninus. It was the Fosse Way.

They had left Oxford on the Tuesday, with Prince Rupert at their head. He carried with him an army of fourteen regiments of foot, divided between three tertias under Lord Grandison, Colonel Wentworth and Colonel Belasyse respectively. Each regiment marched in their new coats, breeches and matching montero caps, either all in red or all blue. No longer were they a ragtag and bobtail posse comitatus, but an army that even King Gustavus Adolphus would have been proud to have on parade. Even the Welsh foot regiments looked smart, though half of them still carried their shoes wrapped in their home-spun blankets rather than wear them on the march.

The horse regiments were placed in two wings, one at the head of the army and one as a rear-guard, whilst the Prince's own troop formed his Life Guard. Ever active, ahead, on the flanks and guarding the rear were the dragoons, Colonel Washington's whole regiment and another two other troops of Sir Robert Howard's. They were maids of all work, the unsung heroes of the army. Too many looked down upon them as their inferiors. But the army needed them. And, in so many ways, they showed more discipline than most horsemen.

But more importantly, the army carried with it a train of artillery that consisted of both a siege train and a battery of field guns. In pride of place were the two huge demi-cannons, each weighing near three tons apiece, with their twelve-foot-long barrels that fired a twenty-seven-pound ball six inches across. Then came a pair of two-ton, fifteen pounder culverins, the two nine pounder demi-culverins, a pair of six pounder sakers and a mortar that fired a thirty-pound bomb. With them, they dragged a full ammunition train, the makings of a petard, cartloads of equipage, shovels, pickaxes, wooden planks, nails, engineers, fire-workers, artificers, smiths, carpenters, wheelwrights, coopers, clerks, a ladle maker and a company of pioneers. For the first time since the rebellion had started, they had enough artillery, shot, powder, equipment and expertise to besiege a city.

It had taken months to assemble this army and its munitions, endless days and nights of work to fund, purchase, manufacture, assemble, store, account, allocate, issue, equip and man. Finally, they were marching. Not to take London, but Bristol. They needed to take it for the King, secure the West Country and the port for his army in Ireland. And then they could focus on the real prize. Then they would strike at London.

They needed to seize Bristol quickly and efficiently. They could not afford to lose time, troops or equipment in a costly, long-drawn-out siege. Look at what siege work had done to Essex's army. The King might have lost Reading, but Essex's siege of the town had almost lost Parliament its last effective field army. What was left of it lay sapped of strength and racked with sickness from weeks of digging, living and fighting in the mud and filth of its own siege trenches. And now the Parliamentary armies in the North and West had been scattered.

They had to take Bristol quickly. They had to take it and turn on London – strike at the capital while the rebel armies lay scattered or sick with fever, while Parliament was riven with faction and doubt. They had to seize London before the summer was out, before Essex and Parliament had time to recover, to build up their strength again over winter. There would not be another such opportunity as now. The Hay Moon was full. Now was the time to gather in the hay. In four weeks, it would be time to reap the wheat, the real harvest.

But they needed to break the defences of Bristol and seize the city without undue loss. They had to safeguard the King's precious foot and keep their regiments intact for the assault on London. For the capital would be a harder nut to crack. They could not afford to weaken the King's foot regiments in a siege. But neither could they afford to risk them in a rushed and costly storm against a city prepared with defensive works.

The artillery would be the key. They must use it efficiently, effectively. The foot must wait while the great guns, mortar, petards and fireworks did their work, while they broke down the defences; whilst they wore down the defenders. Only then, when the defences were broken and the defenders on their knees, should they send in the foot to secure the victory. Even better, let the bombardment work to force a surrender. This was how a modern, efficient army should take a city. This was the lesson of Prince Maurice of Nassau and his well-planned victories over the Spanish in Flanders. Now Prince Rupert had to apply that lesson to seize Bristol.

The whole Oxford Army was strung out on the road, a wing of horse and dragoons up ahead to clear the way, the vanguard tertia of foot, general officers and centre tertia before the artillery and baggage train, rear-guard tertia of foot and wing of horse bringing up the rear. They had lost precious days in a feint towards Gloucester, driving in its horse troops and forcing the Parliamentary garrison to flee Malmesbury. They had left Oxford on Tuesday the eighteenth of July. It was now midday on Saturday – midday, the twenty-second of July.

George turned in the saddle to look at the nearest gun crew following on the road: two gunners and four matrosses behind their great culverin and its nine draught horses. Mister Busy strode out at their head, watching over his precious gun. Christ knew what George would do without Old

Nick, without his knowledge and experience. The gun captain had been with him at Edgehill, at Brentford and in the mine tunnel under Lichfield Close. Behind him shambled Flash, the boy they had saved together from under the gun at Edgehill. God damn, they had all come so close to death that day when the King's battery was overrun by vengeful horsemen – young Squit cut down trying to hold them back.

George snapped the watch shut and pushed it back inside his pocket. 'Mister Busy, we must make gabions, prepare them for the siege work ahead. We will need them to protect the guns.'

Old Nick looked up, gave a curt nod of the head. 'Flash, lad. . . run to the conductor now. Ask him if we can have a bundle of withies when we get to quarters, for the hurdling of gabions.'

IV

Slavery

Moussa Dansocko
The Marsh, Bristol, Saturday the
22nd of July 1643, two o'clock

Moussa Dansocko stood in line with the others, waiting to be marched away. They waited on The Marsh, below the town, the smell of the sea on the wind, ships surrounding them, along Bristol's quays, backs and grove and riding at anchor down the River Avon to the ocean. Sweat soaked his shirt, despite the cool wind ruffling the water. He was near to retching, the stench of the ocean rankling in his nose. It reeked of dank foul air, sickness, shit and salt. It stank of slavery.

They were looking at him, hundreds of them, serving men, apprentices, labourers, journeymen and poor shopkeepers, watching him, whispering about him. But they did not see him. They saw only his *foro*, his skin. They saw only a black-amoor. A blackamoor in fine clothes, a page to a merchant venturer. They looked at him as if he was an animal, something they wanted, but feared, that attracted and appalled. He was ugly, ignorant, dark, a dangerous inhuman savage thing. But they knew nothing of him, of his *hakili*, of his *ni*, his *dya*, his inner self, his mind, soul or spirit. They called him

Moses, said that he was a black Ethiopian belonging to Mister Boucher. But he was Moussa Dansocko, son of a Bambara *numuw*, a blacksmith, of Gao in Songhai. What did they know of the world, its many lands and peoples, or of God?

He was not there of his own free will. He did not come to dig the city defences because he wanted to. He was there because he had to, because he'd been sent, because he had no choice. It was no better than standing in the slave market at Timbuktu. At least there he was not alone. One day he would be free again, free to go home, to walk in the clear sun, to sit in the still shade, to read the Holy Quran, to heed the muezzin's call in the dawn and dusk light and to pray out loud to God.

He would give anything for the smell of home, the infinite, dry scent of a desert wind, the perfect, pure, clean light of the new day, the chatter of paradise-birds rising from acacia bushes, bread and watermelons sold in the street, old men beneath ancient baobab trees, the swirl of dust, the shining gift of water, the jewelled light of dusk, the moonlit Sahel night. To look again across the rooftops of Gao, to see its grand mosque, minarets and markets, to gaze upon the great River Niger, to walk into the family *du*, wrapped once more within its warm adobe walls.

Moussa's hair prickled, sweat running down his temple at the memory of being taken. They came with the evening shadows: Tuareg raiders, 'blue men' wrapped in flowing scarfs and boubous, with swords and lances. He was supposed to guard the *siri* charcoal, watch out for his mother and sister as they gathered *dogora* firewood, waiting for his father to return. But he strayed, looking for shea nuts in the shade. And then they were there, emerging from a cloud of dust, dark shadows in the evening sun, great blue *jinn* on fearsome mounts. He tried to run but he was too small, too slow. They took him with his mother and sister, tears streaking his dusty face, the horses snorting and camels grunting as they carried them away. That was in the dry season, in the month of *Sha'ban*, in the year 1042, ten years before. He was just a boy, no more than ten years old, waiting for his father.

He'd always dreamed of going to Timbuktu. To pray in the Djinguereber Mosque, to read, to learn from its endless libraries, to study astrology at Mansa Musa's great Sankore Masjid – not to stand in its slave market like an animal. He'd watched helpless, weeping, whipped as his mother and sister were dragged away, sold to a Marrakechi camel caravan for a block of salt. Ahmad Baba al-Massufi, Timbuktu's greatest scholar, had taught that Muslim should not enslave Muslim. And yet they were sold openly in the market place. He was not some ignorant, savage *mushrik*. He was schooled in a madrassa, read and wrote in Arabic, could recite almost all of the Quran, knew his *hadiths*, used al-Khwarizmi's calculations, spoke four languages and understood more. *In the name of Allah, the Most Beneficent, the Most Merciful; be you not exalted against me, but come to me as Muslims.*

And yet he too was sold as a slave in Timbuktu's market, sold to a Wangara merchant for a handful of gold dust worth just six ducats. He and others were marched to Djenne, following the waters of the great Niger, sold to fearsome tall Fula warriors for a calf and sixty cowry shells to be herded with their precious *nagge* horned cattle, tattooed women and their *jihad*, west, always west, to the Senegal River. He was sold for a dusty piece of English woollen saye cloth, bound in the bottom of a Wolof canoe and paddled downstream to be paraded in front of the great *Waalo Lingeer* queen, then on downriver to Guet N'Dar and the dreaded ocean. He was traded for a jar of brandy by a pale elegant *mullata senhora*, part Tukulor, part Portuguese. She ruffled his hair, patted his head, listened to him sing, then left him to rot in a stinking French factory on Bocos Island, in the wet and fly-ridden filth of the rainy season. She exchanged him for just two yards of pretty cotton cloth.

But then the shimmering heat and the ship came, towering over them all. For one brass manilla, he was sold to a Dutch slave ship, made to climb its side, forced into the hot wooden hell of its hold; row upon row, rack upon rack of manacled men, women and children. The whispering prayers and chants turned to screams as the ship lurched, the deck tilting to the wind; the hull creaking, water surging past, masts straining, shadows swirling as the whole ship pitched and rolled; manacles clanking, an endless wailing moan lost on the sea.

But it was the smell that stayed with him, that clung to him, that he could never wash away. Sweat ran from him at the arresting shock of smelling it again, here in Bristol. A simple errand that took him down to the quays for his master, just another French ship unloading wine. He stood staring at it, transfixed by the smell, transported back to its horror, the reek that came from deep within its timbers: the stench of shit, piss, sweat, vomit and fear; the ghostly scent of a slave ship, a smell that could never be washed clean, that bore witness to the hell that had been held within its wooden walls. The sailors watched him, their look knowing: incarceration, torture, rape and death on their hands and in their eyes.

He was sold to an English planter in Virginia for eighty pounds of tobacco, the icy wind whipping down the James River, taken to a lonely homelot cut from the forest. The planters called themselves Godly. But all they cared about was their precious tobacco leaves. They drove their servants to work on the land, day after day of backbreaking labour, with just boiled pounded maize hominy to eat. They exhausted the land and those who worked it just to grow and sell tobacco, to make their precious profit. They cut, burned and killed as they pleased. And they ruled their homelot as a *shaitan*.

They said there was no slavery in English law, that they were only indentured servants, bound to their master for just seven years. But the master used them like slaves, *Bidan*, *Sudan* and native, white, black and red man, indentured bondsman or maidservant. Young Englishmen and boys arrived with every ship. Poor illiterate skinny white boys, they were worked to their deaths in the freezing winter and summer heat, dying of disease, exhaustion and hardship. And pale, flat-chested young girls sold to planters as wives for one hundred and twenty pounds of best leaf tobacco, with no older women or *harem* to protect them from the eyes, desires and lust of the men about them.

Within the Songhai Empire, all peoples had their place under the great *Askia* king. There was equal justice for *Sudan* as well as *Bidan*. But not in Virginia. The white boys had Saturday afternoon and Sunday to rest. Blacks and red men were given no rest on a Saturday; they worked in the field or in the barn. It was the Oquiock boy who had the worst of it. From the Kickotank tribe, they took him as a child, killed his elders with muskets and disease. They said he was a savage. But he was just lost, confused, everything alien to his way of life and belief, his world cut down, burnt, dug up, nature forced into straight lines. It was they who were beastly to him.

They said that all blacks were descended from Ham, son of Noah; that they were cursed. They said John Punch tried to escape and sentenced him to be bound by indentured servitude for life, that all blacks were damned, that it was God's will that they should be consigned to perpetual bondage. There was no slavery in English law. But what was the difference? It was just a pretence, a legal nuance, a twisting of the law. To be consigned by law to work for a master as his bondsman, day in, day out, for life, was nothing other than slavery.

He'd worked on that homelot for five long years when his master gave him to a ship captain, his indenture lost in a play of cards, his life gambled then discarded in a game of chance. He'd learnt to serve the captain, wait on him at table, to read his books, study the charts in his cabin. He made sense of the coast of Africa, the Atlantic Ocean, America, Europe, the Mediterranean Sea – memorised the way home. He learned the Barbary ports of Morocco, the camel routes from Marakech to Mandinca – had laughed at the map of the River Niger, Timbuktu and the image of the great Mansa Musa sat on his gold.

But when they reached Bristol, he was given to a rich merchant venturer, to Mister Boucher, as payment for a debt. He'd been Mister Boucher's footman, his bondsman for two and a half years. By law, his seven-year indenture had ended in December, at Christmas. It was now the sixteenth of July. He should be free. But he was still a house-slave, forced to dig Bristol's defences. And Mister Boucher was dead – executed, hanged by the neck as a criminal.

They were finally moving, marching off to dig the defences, one man from every household in Bristol. They passed the ships along the Backs to turn up the High Street. At the High Cross and Tolsey, they crossed Wine Street. He shivered at the memory of the crowds, men and women jostling, pushing, shouting at Mister Boucher and Mister Yeamans; the families paraded, forced to watch; the master tortured, starved, pale and cowed on the scaffold; the ministers preaching their *jihad*, refusing to listen to his prayers; the soldiers drumming; the bodies swinging, legs kicking, thrashing, choking; faces, eyes, tongues bulging, red, dark with blood; the mistress heavy with child, fainting; Mistress Hazzard yelling, shrieking, calling on the crowd to kill the children, to smash their heads, to scatter their brains on the street.

They marched on down Broad Street, between Christ Church and the church of St Ewen, the Governor's House and on under St John's. They crossed Jewrie Lane, marching past the Boucher House on Christmas Street. He looked up at the chamber, hoping, wanting, praying for Mistress Elizabeth to be there, to catch a glimpse of her. There was a figure in the window – she had come to see him! She had been waiting, watching for him to march past! But it was not her, but the maid, Enid Powell, smiling – gloating at his humiliation. She would delight, revel in the fact that he was forced to dig the defences for her parliament, for her rebellion, for her Jesus, for the horse soldiers that were now billeted in the house, who watched their every move, ready to arrest him at the first provocation.

It was Enid who brought the soldiers, told them of the master's plotting against them. She'd loved Moussa before that, come to him in the night, as the seductress Zulaikha beguiled Yusuf. She slid naked into his bed, wrapping herself silently about him, laid her hot slick lust upon him. Night after night, she fucked him. He did not resist her. He let her take his frustration, his longing; let her teach him to satisfy the need in them both, turn him from boy into man, leaving them both sated and sleepy. She knew that he did not love her, that he longed for Mistress Elizabeth. But still she came to him, needing, wanting his body, an insatiable *qarinah*, a succubus, goading him, draining him. And then the soldiers came. Her love for him turned to jealousy and hatred. She turned to another to spite him, brought evil upon the house, betrayed their master.

Sweat ran down his back, his *dya* stirring at the memory of the soldiers smashing down the door on the night of the plot, of the chaos within. Mister Boucher had argued with them, refusing them entry. The soldiers charging in as forty of his plotters tried to hide or escape across the roofs, garden and river, the mistress screaming, children crying. Instead of opening the city gates and ringing St John's church bells to welcome in the King's men, the night ended in misery and horror as the master was dragged away to the Castle dungeon amid smashed furniture and torn curtains.

Praise be to God that Mistress Elizabeth had stayed strong. Together, they'd shut up the door, kept her mother and the little ones safe inside the house. So many of the other servants had left the house, abandoned the family. He worked beside her every day. She'd listened to his stories, asked questions of him, pored over maps of Africa and America, and shown an interest in the peoples and ways of those lands. She marvelled at his descriptions of Gao, Timbuktu and Djenne, was amazed at the blue Tuareg raiders, the long-limbed Fulani women with their ink-black lips, the great *Lingeer* queen of Waalo, graceful *mullata senhoras* of Guet N'Dar, Kickotank hunters and Nanticoke warriors, Virginia and the wide ocean. And he'd done everything he could to help and protect her and her family, day and night. He could not bring himself to leave her.

They marched on across Frome Bridge, between the tall houses that lined its sides, out through Frome Gate at its far end. The death of his master had not brought him freedom. He was mentioned in Mister Boucher's will, but not as a recipient or beneficiary, not even as a valued servant to be thanked, but as an item, an article, a property among many to be inherited. There was no mention of an indenture or its ending. He was just another chattel, an object to be passed on, to be exchanged or sold. He was a slave once more.

They crossed Horse Street and climbed Christmas Steps. Already, there were other merchant venturers, lawyers and creditors that circled, called with their condolences, presented their petitions, claimed their due, whilst eyeing the fine furnishings, drooling over Mistress Elizabeth, watching him – weighing him as a payment. They would take him if they could, seize him if they couldn't, hold him as their page boy, show him off as an exotic trophy. There were others who would send him back to work in the Virginia tobacco fields. Or worse, ship him to Barbados, force him to work on one of the new sugarcane plantations, to work him to death as a slave.

At the top of the steps, they crossed Steep Street to march on up Stony Hill, while others turned up St Michael's Hill and Maudlin Lane. They passed the Essex Work, the new fort built out from the side of the hill overlooking the Red Lodge, the city and its approaches. Now the Parliament had granted their governor of the city, Colonel Nathaniel Fiennes, authority to seize the estates of the plotters, those belonging to Mister Yeamans and Mister Boucher. He was a chattel belonging to Mister Boucher's estate, an asset to be seized by the governor and sold, sold into slavery, *permanent* slavery, to be worked as a slave until dead. They marched on beyond the suburbs, beyond the last of the houses that lined Stony Hill towards Clifton and the line of defences that stretched from Brandon Hill to St Michael's Hill.

He had to escape, to leave Bristol before he was seized,

before he was enslaved forever. He would find a way back to
Africa, a way back to Gao, his father and family *du,* find a
way to rescue his mother and sister. He would join Fa Sine
Kulubali, fight for the Bambara people, fight for Songhai. The
jali said he had the *ni* of his grandfather, his spirit; that he had
received his grandfather's *zahan*; his grandfather who had
fashioned armour for the noble *horo* Songhai horsemen, *jelew*
axes and the chief's *dugutigitama* iron spear; his grandfather
who fell with the last of the Songhai rear-guard at Tondibi,
fighting against the guns and cannon of the Moroccan Sultan
and his Spanish mercenaries. One day he would return. He
would return like Sundjata, the Lion King, first *mansa* of
Mali, great uncle of Mansa Musa. He would return and make
Songhai great again.

It would mean leaving Mistress Elizabeth, leaving her
to care for her mother and the little ones alone, leaving her to
face the creditors and soldiers without him. But first he must
learn from the English soldiers, master their *daliluw*, the
secret of gun making, complete his apprenticeship, become a
numuw, carry the knowledge back to Gao and the Bambara.
Then, he would be Moussa Dansocko once more, not Moses
the slave. He would be free again, free to walk in the clear sun,
to sit in the warm shade, to inhale the infinite, dry scent of the
desert, to revel in the shining gift of water, to drown in the
dusk call of the muezzin.

V

The Mark of The Beast

Enid Powell
St Ewen's Rectory, Broad Street, Bristol,
Sunday the 23rd of July 1643, eleven o'clock

Enid Powell sat in the rector's parlour, silent. They all sat there – in silence, bibles clutched in their laps, sat round in a circle. It wasn't like any church service she'd ever seen, not in her whole life. She wanted to speak, to hear the Lord's word within her. But the words never came. He didn't speak to her, didn't speak to the others through her. She wasn't worthy. She wasn't holy, wasn't Godly, wasn't pure.

It'd always been the same. She wasn't a great speaker, wasn't clever like Mistress Hazard or the others. She knew her letters. But she could never make sense of them on a page, not like educated people. Truth be told, she wasn't much of one for the Bible. She knew her prayers and a few psalms, but she couldn't read it. She'd followed him into the rectory because she couldn't leave him. Because she wanted to be near him. Because she loved him. Because she wanted him to see her, to love her, to tell her she was worthy. She'd taken the bible they'd given her, held it on her lap. But she dared not open it. She'd held it and kept her eyes tight shut.

He sat across the room from her now, in his soldier's buff coat and leather boots; young, pure and handsome. Not much more than a boy, he was shy, hurt and vulnerable, despite the battles he'd fought and his faith in the Lord. She'd seen his confusion, his discomfort, his inner struggle and self-loathing. She saw it in him, recognised it, knew it like her own. She'd caught him looking at her, met his eye, saw him turn away, his cheeks reddening. He'd looked at her the way all men looked at her, with lust in his eyes, like a dog that smells a bitch on heat.

She didn't hate him for it. Not like other women. It wasn't his fault. It was her. Ever since she'd been a girl, ever since her mother died, men looked at her that way. They saw it in her, smelled it on her, sensed, felt, knew the lust that lurked deep inside her. Her stomach knotted, tightening, aching. The dirt lay thick within her. She could feel it, hear it, taste it. No matter how much she washed herself clean, it was still there, gnawing at her insides, seeping from her. She couldn't remember when it started. As far as she knew, it'd always been there, dark and hot, writhing in her belly. It'd been a secret back then, something special, not for others. She'd known no better. She knew it was wrong, now – bad, sinful. But she couldn't stop it, even if she wanted to. She craved it, needed it, had to have it. Even when it hurt.

Men knew it. They all did. They all wanted her. It was not their fault. It was her. It was the lust she carried within her, that oozed from her. It touched them, infected them, twisted itself around them, left them lustful, stiff and aching, needing her, wanting it. She'd left home when she saw it in her own father's eyes after her mother died, ran away bare-footed in the dawn, away from the farm, the hills and cattle, away from Llanvaches, away from Monmouthshire, from Wales and the

Welsh Marches. She'd followed the drovers, begged a place on a ferry across the River Severn, walked to Bristol, found a place as a maidservant in the city, in the house of Mister Boucher.

The mistress had been kind to her back then, taking her in, giving her an old shift and a pair of cast-off shoes. Even Mistress Elizabeth had smiled, spoken kindly to her. She'd been happy for a while. And she'd had Moses. He was no older than her, a boy far from home, hurt, angry and alone. She knew that the night was a torture to him too; he was restless and crying out, haunted in turn by sleeplessness and night-mares. She'd gone to him, soothed him, stroking, holding him tight. Night after night, he'd taken her in his arms, his smooth, dark skin shining in the moonlight, his body firm, strong and muscular, driving their demons away to lie together in perfect sleep.

But then the mistress was with child again and the master began to look at her that way. He watched her, sent for her, asked, begged, demanded, threatened to throw her out on the street, forcing himself upon her, sweating, drooling, grunt-ing as the candle guttered in his chamber. She dared not tell the mistress, dared not even tell Moses. She'd kept it hidden, secret and dark like before; the dirt filling her, turning her insides black again.

She'd watched the old bastard choke and gasp, swinging from the scaffold. She'd made sure he saw her in the crowd before he dropped, watched him stumble over his prayers, pale and shaking. It was she who had told the soldiers about his plot to open the city gates. He couldn't keep from brag-ging about it. Never suspected she'd guide the soldiers to his door. Served the bastard right it did. But Moses never forgave her. He'd still believed the master would free him from his indenture, did not care what the bastard had done to her. But she'd show Moses. He'd see what he was missing.

Some of the soldiers had stayed in the house, four Godly troopers billeted on them to keep watch on Mistress Boucher and her family. They'd frightened her at first with their iron helmets, boots and bibles. But this one was different. She saw the loss within him, knew his pain, felt it touch her own. And then they were gone, called away to Bath to fight the wild Cornish horde.

He'd come back to Bristol from the battle, shattered, hurt and limping, without a horse, his armour scratched and dented, coat tattered, his faith torn – tormented. She'd tended him, minded over him, served him. She washed and mended his clothes, fetched food for him, showed him where the master's pistols were hidden, showed him the best horse in the stable. And she'd followed him to Mistress Hazzard's door, to her congregation, to see his faith mended. Now she couldn't leave him. She'd do anything for him. She loved him, wanted him.

But he didn't see her like that. She'd seen the way he looked at her. And she'd seen the way he looked at Mistress Elizabeth. It was the same with all of them. They all loved Mistress Elizabeth. She was beautiful, tall and lithe, pale, pure, shining – perfect in every way, not a blemish or speck of dirt upon her, her very scent fresh and clear. What would she give to be in her skin for just one day, to be clean and pure, to be loved, not lusted over?

But Mistress Elizabeth was cold and untouchable, like a statue made of smooth stone. She'd never lain with a man, felt the heat within him, let it fill her till she was afire with him. What would it be like to lie with her. . . to touch her. . . to run hands over her smooth white skin. . . to rub against her cool, hard hips, breasts, lips. . . to slide over her belly. . . down deeper, legs and arms entwined. . . to warm her, to feel her blood rising, the fire lit within her, swelling dark and red. . . to be the first. . . to take the virgin. . . to sully that perfect body. . . to leave it hot, wet and dirty.

Was that what he wanted? She dared to open an eye to peep across the room at him, handsome, young and devout in his buff coat and prayer. She closed her eyes tightly shut again and whispered his name to herself, rolling it in her mind and heart, the ache tightening and twisting within her belly. . . *Master Francis Reeve*. The heat rose in her, her breasts swelling, paps pressing against her bodice, inflamed, sore, hard and hot. She squeezed her thighs together, the wetness coming.

A chair scraped. The worthy Reverend Walter Cradock stood up. He knew! He knew her from Llanvaches, knew her sin. He'd seen the heat within her, smelled the dirt dripping from her. She'd be cast out, whipped for the sinner she was – humiliated. Master Francis would see, know her for what she was. She must go, now, leave, run away!

'*Then Judah looked!*' The pastor was staring. '*And behold the battle was before and behind them. And they cried unto the Lord!*'

He was staring at her, looking at her.

'Are not the Books of Chronicles come to pass? For the hour has come. Are we not now surrounded by the Lord's enemies? Are we not besieged by an army of apostates, by the forces of darkness, by the host of Satan himself? For the day of battle is upon us – the great battle for the souls of the world. And all must cry unto the Lord from their hearts, in the very instant of this battle before us!'

Enid sat stock still, sweat running cold down her back. She dared not move.

'*And it came to pass, when the captains of the chariots saw Jehoshaphat, they said, it is the King of Israel and they compassed about him to fight. But Jehoshaphat cried out. And the Lord helped him. And God moved them to depart from him.*

'For we must consider that sometimes God's people are worsted in battle. That sometimes they have the worst of it, worse even than the enemies of the Lord about them. All of us must consider that, though God's people have the worst, yet it cometh of the Lord Himself! *Who gave Jacob to the spoil and Israel to the robbers? Did not the Lord? He against whom we have sinned.* For their iniquity, God's people are delivered into the hands of their enemies!

'*Even nations shall ask, wherefore hath the Lord done this unto this land? What meaneth the heat of his great wrath? Then men shall answer. Because they have forsaken the Covenant of the Lord God of their fathers!*

'For is it not plainly writ in scripture? All God's people must seek out their sins. We must all search within ourselves. Let us ask whether we are truly convinced of our sin; convinced of our lost state without Christ the Redeemer. Let us ask ourselves if we are truly brought to the Lord Jesus Christ. Let us search for that which defiles us, that which angers the Lord. Let us root out the sin that infects us. Let us cast out the evil that hides amongst us.

'*Up therefore, sanctify yourselves against tomorrow. For thus saith the Lord God of Israel, there is an accursed thing in the midst of thee, oh Israel. Thou canst not stand against thine enemies until ye put out the accursed thing from among you!* Amen.'

'Amen!'

'Amen.' Enid gasped out her response after the others. She blushed and sat rigid. They were looking at her, ready to accuse her, ready to cast her out. For was she not filled with sin? Was her life not accursed from childhood?

The pastor sat, smiled at her.

She dared not breathe, her eyes clamped tight shut. *Please God, not here, not now, not in front of him, not in front of Master Francis.* She'd never sin again. She'd be good and pure and clean. Anything but to be found out in front of him for the sinner she was.

Another chair scraped; the sound of petticoats stirring. Mistress Hazzard stood, her bible open in her hands. *'If any man worship the beast and his image, and receive his mark on his forehead, or in his hand. The same shall drink of the wine of the wrath of God!* Are there not some living amongst us that hide their sins – because they are too heinous to show?

'Within this city, this Babylon, abide heathens – nay, infidels! Secret worshipers of Mahomet! Surely, the Lord punishes us for not rooting out this sin. Not two streets from this house lie blackamoors, in every direction. One, a Barabbas, was with them that plotted to open the gates to the same accursed cavaliers that now surround us!

'I say, is this not the *accursed thing* of sin, the evil that must be put out?'

'Amen!' The congregation stirred, alive, roused in their agreement.

Mistress Hazzard was talking about Moses! Surely not. He was a blackamoor. But a Mahometan? He was just a boy far from his home.

Reverend Cradock was on his feet again. 'The merchant venturers of this city do trade with Spain, the Levant, with Barbary – lands thick mingled with Mahometans. The heat and unrest of such lands doth render a man vulnerable, doth change his humours, opening his soul to possession. The fruits, fripperies and spices they carry back tempt the weak to sin, to burn with lust!

'There are, amongst those that return, renegades and blackamoors. They may profess their repentance. But the heart of a heretic is hardened. The soul within stained black with sin, shrivelled dry by the humours of those dark, melancholic lands.

'For theirs is a monstrous, devilish religion. A patchwork cloak, a cento, a chimera of discredited doctrines, of Nestorian fopperies created by Sergius the lapsed monk and Abdalla the Jew. It only serves to lure the cruel, base and covetous to serve the mock-god Mahomet!

'They may hide their sin in seemly clothes. But they are ready to put on the turban again. To rise up in league with the malignant hordes that even now sit outside our walls, that will open the gates to the heathen Irish, the Spaniard, the Pope and the forces of the Antichrist!

'Like the chameleon of Africanus, they would eftsoons change their element, their shape, their being. They sit ready to spread like a plague of caterpillars that would infest the land, poison the nation of the Godly. They will crawl out to pollute us with their sin, with their sodomy!

'They will take possession of our very souls, their corruption a contagion. They wait amongst us to welcome in their Turkish Doom. To bring about an End of Times!

'They may hide amongst us. But they will be known for what they are to the Righteous Judge, from whose eyes nothing is hid, nothing is secret. For they have the Mark of the Beast upon them! As it is writ. *If ye be circumcised, Christ shall profit you nothing!'*

'Amen!' The congregation were on their feet, waving their bibles, shaking the pastor's hand, applauding Mistress Hazzard.

Enid stood slowly, quietly, shakily. She placed the bible on the chair. Mistress Hazzard smiled and nodded towards her. Master Francis was looking at her. He saw her across the room. She would not sin again. She would be good, clean and pure. For him.

She felt God's light upon her, the sun streaming through the rectory window. She was saved. Saved from heinous sin, saved from immortal damnation. She was saved from the clutches of Barabbas, from certain sodomy. She knew Moses for what he was now. He was accursed, a Mahometan!

He'd hidden it from her, called himself Moses, let her think he was one of them, like her. But beneath his fine clothes his skin was shaven, his manhood cut, cut with the Mark of the Beast. His heart was stained black, shrivelled, hardened with sin.

VI

Reconnaissance

Ralph Reeve
Westbury College, Westbury-on-Trym, Gloucestershire,
Sunday the 23rd of July 1643, two o'clock

They waited outside the high walls of Westbury College, all seven troops of the regiment together again, three ranks of mounted dragoons lining the street, Colonel Washington at their head. Ralph Reeve looked along the line. They looked very different, smart in their new red coats, all those that had marched from Oxford. All except the little troop that had been detached to join Prince Maurice and his Western Army. His own coat was faded, tattered, thin at the elbow. They'd accompanied Prince Maurice from Bath to Sodbury to meet his brother, Prince Rupert, on the march towards Bristol. Now, they were reunited with the rest of the regiment, back with the King's Oxford Army. There'd been slaps on the back, questions, stories to tell, jokes about their dress. Now they waited for the two princes, a shabby little troop at the far end of the parade.

Trumpets blared and the two princes emerged from the old college gatehouse followed by a half-dozen general officers, their retinues and Prince Rupert's Lifeguard Troop of Horse.

They turned to ride along the line as Colonel Washington swept off his hat and lowered his head in salute.

Ralph sat as high and upright as he could on his little dragoon pony, the ranks beside and behind him bracing up, horses heads twitching as trumpets sounded and officers' hats were lowered in salute. The princes passed in silence, with just the hint of a nod from Prince Maurice to his ragamuffin troop at the end of the line.

'The regiment will march in column of divisions!' Colonel Washington replaced his hat on his head. 'Prepare to March! Wheel your front to the left, by divisions! March on!'

One by one, the troops wheeled from the right to file past, following the princes down the street. Finally, Ralph and the rest of the motley dressed little troop wheeled on the road to join the back of the column. They clattered down the street and out onto Durdham Down.

The down stretched out, flat, still and empty, shimmering in the summer heat; just a lone shepherd minding his flock under the shade of an oak tree and the chatter of martins swooping on a Sunday afternoon. For two long, slow miles they followed the track across Durdham Down and Clifton Down, the horses' heads hanging, tails and manes flicking in a cloud of dust, grass seed, mugwort and flies. Somewhere beyond the edge of the down lay the River Avon and the City of Bristol in its hollow crook.

The horses' hooves thudded through a village, silent and still, except for a dog barking and a few geese hissing, flapping, running to the shade of an alley. Doors and shutters were closed to keep out the heat, dust and unwelcome soldiers. Finally, they halted to dismount and walk their horses the last few yards to the edge of the graveyard. The princes, officers and a troop of dismounted dragoons walked on to the church beyond, its nave and chancel quiet, empty after Sunday service.

Ralph waited under an old yew tree, thanking God for its shade. His little mare looked up at him, her eyes swimming, blinking. He gently wiped away the dust from around them, from her lashes and tears, trying to wipe away the image of Breda's last look at him in that bloody ditch before he pulled the trigger. The mare bobbed her head in gratitude, shook herself from ears to tail, in a shower of dust, pawing the ground lazily.

'Have a care, now.' Sergeant O'Brien was striding back through the graveyard. 'The enemy – the rebel line – is only a musket shot beyond that there church. Horses to horse holders! The rest o' yiz, make ready and follow me. Let's be a-movin now, skirmish order!'

The sergeant led them away to the left, skirting the edge of the graveyard and rectory to fan out across the slope of the hill. Cautiously, they crawled forward in the long dry grass to look out across the slope of the down. Beside him, Sam slithered forward low and silent, the poacher, in his element. Jack worked his way forward on knees and elbows, determined and ready. Luke frowned, earnest. Behind them, Clem smiled, Jewkes glowered and Tandy looked sharp. Only Kibler wheezed and grunted, sweating in the heat, his arse stuck high in the air.

'Easy does it now.' O'Brien stopped them on the brow of the hill. 'The rebels have a fort on yonder hill beyond the church. Keep your heads down. It won't be long before they know we're here. Not with all those bloody officers wandering about.

'Now, this here they'll be callin' Clifton St Andrew. And that rebel fort is on top of Brandon Hill. Yiz can see Bristol sat down aways, all in a hollow like, behind Brandon Hill, with our fine, brave Cornish friends on the far side of its walls. And beyond the city, you see that great hill on the far horizon? Well now, that is Lansdown bloody Hill, with Bath beyond it. So, you could be sayin' we've come around in a great big circle.'

The sergeant turned in the long grass to point across them. 'Now, that there next hill to the left is St Michael's Hill. Yiz can see the windmill and the fort on its top now. And beyond that, at the far end of the ridge, is Prior's Hill. There's another fort there, with a redoubt between the two, next the highway. Yiz'll want to be markin' them all well now.

'The rebel line on this side of the city runs up from the river to Brandon Hill Fort. Then, it runs down to a barn beside the lane down aways from Clifton village to Bristol. From there, it runs up the other side to the Windmill Fort. Yiz can see the ditch and rampart runnin' aways up the slope now?'

'Yes.' Ralph nodded towards the line. 'But what is that projection, that bit sticking out from the wall? Half way up the far slope to the Windmill Fort.'

'Ah. That'll be a ravelin, a tenaille as the French would call it. A triangle sort of work thrust out, forward of the line. The defenders'll fire from it across the front of the rampart and along the ditch, in a flankin' fire, across the ranks of them attackin', a scourin' fire if you like. There'll be one of those between every two forts, within half a musket shot of one another. The rebels'll probably not be havin' enough men to defend along the whole length of the rampart. But they won't need to y'see. They'll cover the line from the forts and ravelins, so they will.'

'Thank you, Sergeant O'Brien. It sounds rather effective.'

'Ah well, that it is.' The sergeant looked at them. 'Now, after

CHARLES CORDELL

the Windmill Fort, the line runs along the back of the ridge, past the redoubt to Prior's Hill Fort. Then, it'll be turnin' right, back down the hill aways, to another river and the city walls. Between the line and the city walls are the suburbs.'

'Sergeant O'Brien. . .' It was Luke, his forehead creased. 'So, the line of defences is up on the ridge to defend the suburbs and to stop our cannon from bombarding the city. But it's a-runnin' along the back edge of the ridge, set back from the crest. Is that to shield the line from our guns on the down?'

'Ah, you're a clever one, Luke, so ye are. They'll be making an engineer of you, they will. The line is set back behind the crest just enough to protect the rampart from cannon. But it's not so far back that them in the forts and ravelins cannot see to the crest. Think on't this way. . . yiz never want to be lookin' out further than you can shoot. If youse do, some bastard with a bigger gun than yours will surely sit back and shoot you as he pleases. And yiz don't want be sittin' there like a stuck goose with your arse in the air now.'

For a moment, each lay in silence, considering the sergeants words, studying the hills, forts and line. Fuck. This was no easy nut to crack. It was not like Marlborough with its couple of little sconces and a barn. This was a city, England's second city, with a line of forts filled with cannon, a continuous line of ditch, rampart and ravelins, well sited, well prepared, well supplied. Best Prince Rupert and his brother have some sort of cunning plan to take this city easily.

Ralph plucked a grass stalk and chewed its end; the sweet taste of summer. What would he give to be home, with the mowers in the fields, scythe swinging rhythmically, the scent of new-cut hay, the girls singing as they raked, laughter and ale in the shade at bevering-time and afterwards in the barns and late into the night around the supper table. The sun

183

burned hot on his back. Beetles, earwigs and a ladybird clambered through the grass. Grasshoppers chirped and martins chattered as they swooped over the down.

The air shook with shrieking iron, a cannon's thunder crashing out from Brandon Hill, thumping against Clifton and its little church, echoing back against St Michael's Hill and Bristol in its hollow beyond. Ralph spat the grass stalk from his mouth, grabbing his carbine to his shoulder. It had started.

'I said it wouldn't be long now didn't I.' Sergeant O'Brien shifted. 'Some bloody officer pokin' his silly plumed head out. Let's be hopin' Prince Rupert hasn't lost his now.'

There was a flurry of activity around the church as another cannon ball screamed overhead. Horses whinnied and stamped. The horse holders would be trying to calm them, Hodge soothing them, the boy holding the mare and three others. And then Prince Rupert's Lifeguard of Horse were mounting, preparing to leave, the princes with them.

'Sergeant O'Brien!' It was Captain Norwood, striding from the graveyard. 'Please remain in place. We are to cover the princes' withdrawal. Their reconnaissance is, shall we say, complete. The regiment is to remain here. To occupy and hold this hill until morning. We should expect a pair of demi-culverins and a battalion of foot to join us.'

VII

Bristol Venture

Jeremy Holway
Redoubt, Mile Hill gate, Bristol, Monday the 24ᵗʰ of
July 1643, a quarter to eleven o'clock in the morning

Jeremy Holway leant against the parapet of the redoubt staring out over Durdham Down. Nothing moved. Not even a shepherd, or a sheep. The down was deserted, an empty sea of grass shimmering in the sun. The highway was closed, barred below the redoubt. No traffic had passed along it for days, all trade between Bristol and Wales halted.

He should be in his shop, in the town, checking his stock. Instead, he was on guard, at Mile Hill, out beyond the suburbs, while his poor wife minded the business and tended to his affairs. He should be home, with Sarah now, helping her, caring for her. Not playing at soldiers on the down. She was heavy with child again, suffering in the summer heat, worried about the little ones with the sweating fever abroad in the city, killing the weak, the old and young alike.

He'd enjoyed being a musketeer with the Bristol Trained Bands. It'd brought respect and good contacts. But the new governor had turned them into a foot regiment – his own regiment. Now they were Colonel Nathaniel Fiennes' Regiment of Foot. Some had even been ordered to march away to fight at Bath and Devizes. Half of them hadn't returned after Sir William Waller's terrible defeat at Roundway Down. Those who did, crawled back with wounds.

Trade was poor. For the last years, it had been stifled, crippled, ruined, ever since the King's damned Spanish Alliance. The King had supressed all trade with the Moors, with Barbary, the Orient and Turkish Levant, in a fool's attempt to appease Popish Spain. It was hopeless to think that the King of Spain could be lured away from an alliance with his Roman Hapsburg cousin, the Emperor, and their war with the Dutch, the Elector Frederick and the Protestant princes. Anyone with the slightest mercantile sense could see that.

Bristol had traded with the Moors of Barbary for two hundred years. Its merchants had traded cloth, tin and muskets for saltpetre and sugar, for timber, for oranges, lemons and dried barberries. The trade brought profit and protection to the city, and to the commonwealth of all England. It was a trade that was good for the nation.

But more than that, the Moors were allies against Papist Spain. They'd helped protect England's ships and coasts against the Spaniard since the time of the Armada. Ambassadors, emissaries and merchants had been exchanged between the Sultan and the court of good Queen Bess, living and trading in safety. Now that ally had been slighted, insulted, starved of England's aid against its old enemy, Spain. In their hurt and anger, the Moors had turned away. Weak and enfeebled, they let pirates, brigands and corsairs sail from their shores, let them take English ships and cargoes on the high sea.

There were some that said a Mahometan could not be trusted, that they were all thieves and lechers, covetous, cruel and base. But they were merchants like any other. They understood the value of trade and trust as well as the value of their merchandise. And they were merchants that traded far and wide across the Turkish lands, across Africa, the Levant and beyond – infinite lands, peoples and markets. And they could open the way for trade in all the luxuries of the Orient: gold, ivory, ostrich feathers, silks and spices; perhaps even negroes to work the colonies, a trade in black slaves.

England needed such trade and its markets open. Trade and traffic were vital to the commonwealth, their ebb and flow curative, healthy, natural. It needed to be nurtured. Instead, they faced decay; trade stifled, ruined by favourites at court who knew nothing of things mercantile, fools who sought to control trade through monopoly and intrigue, as if markets were something that could be bent to their petty design. The King had even tried to patent the making of soap! As if they hadn't been making good, soft Bristol Soap long before it was made in London. They made it with olive oil from the Levant. Not like the hard *Popish Soap* of the Court that scarred the soul as much as it scoured fine linen and the poor washerwomen's hands.

He'd rather trust a Moorish merchant than a corrupt courtier or cavalier, or a Catholic. The King had demanded more Ship Money, promising to put an end to the corsairs. But it was just a ruse to tax the well affected, the funds to be squandered. The King's navy was a laughing stock, incapable of catching the so-called Barbary pirates. Their expeditions against Algiers and Salé had only made things worse – inflamed hostility, and all whilst Spain's Flemish pirates were left to infest the seas, sailing free out of Dunkirk and in league with the Catholic Irish rebels.

Neither were their own sailors to be trusted. Their humours unbalanced, made fluid and unstable by the tumbling of the sea, the heat and vices of foreign shores, they were just as likely to fall in with the pirates – turn renegade. And as for the Cornish, they were a damnable nation of liars, their feeble lamentations pathetic, primitive, Popish. If the Turks were such a threat, why did they not defend themselves? They were ready enough when it came to fighting their own Parliament – biting the very hand that fed them!

Neither the King nor his court could be trusted. But then again, neither could half the Members of Parliament. Most of them were only there to look out for themselves or their interests in London. Bristol needed to stand up for itself. It was England's second city, with a harbour near as good as London, a port that traded with Iberia, Barbary, Virginia, the West Indies, Newfoundland and Ireland. But were was Parliament now? Sir William 'the conqueror' Waller had fled to Gloucester with half the garrison and two-thousand pounds in Bristol coin. And that fool Sir Arthur Haselrigge had taken ship to London with what was left of his armoured knights, while Essex skulked about Reading. Now Bristol stood alone against the King's armies.

It was said that Prince Rupert had brought an army from Oxford to lay siege to the city. And that the Cornish would march to join him. There were cavaliers about Clifton St Andrew, with shots fired between them and Brandon Hill Fort the night before. But all was quiet now. Nothing stirred on Durdham Down, just the wind in the grass, the sun beating down and the larks' song.

And yet. . . there was something else. A far-off sound. A thumping, rattling, drumming sound. A sound that came to them, rising and falling, snatching on the breeze. A noise that grew louder, closer, wider, building from every side across the down. The noise of drums!

And then he saw it, far out across the down. A grey-brown

smudge on the horizon. A thin smear that grew taller, rising up from behind the crest, swaying, glinting in the sun.

'I don't like it, Jeremy.' Young Richard Hort stood pale beside him. 'What is it?'

'I don't rightly know.' Jeremy pointed. 'Look, there's another. And another.'

'They's pikes.' John Friend spat. 'I reckon that's Prince bloody Rupert and his army come to pay us a visit. I seed them like that at Lansdown Hill.'

'Shit! We need to tell Mister Taylor. Go now, Richard. Fetch him here. And Major Woods. 'Tis urgent!'

They stood and stared, the little redoubt's parapet filling with men, as the stands of pikes grew taller and sprouted colours billowing in the breeze, men's heads, bodies, flanked by wings of musketeers on either side. All the while the drumming grew louder, stronger, incessant, thrashing out their march, hundreds of them across the down, drawing steadily nearer.

'To your posts!' Major Wood stood in the centre of the redoubt. 'Pikes to the parapet!' The old soldier knew his business. 'Musketeers, make ready!'

Jeremy took one end of the match from between the fingers of his left hand and blew the ash from it. He'd almost forgotten about it, almost let it go out. He blew again on the coal until it crackled bright and hot in the sun and wind. He fumbled to press it into the cock with his thumb, pressed the trigger arm to try its length against the pan.

And then the drumming stopped. The cavalier army stood still, just its colours billowing in the wind. Battalion after battalion stood before them, a dozen or more pike blocks flanked by musketeers, lined across the down, regiment after regiment of horse on either flank. The King's army stretched as far as the eye could see, from Clifton to Cotham and beyond.

VIII

Tha'n Mor!

Kendall Tremain
Bath Road, outside Bristol, Monday
the 24th of July 1643, midday

An mor! The sea! The smell of salt, mud and tide – creek, estuary and open sea! It was in the air, on the breeze, *gwenz an mor*, blowing in up the river. Strong, sure, certain now. Kendall thought he smelled it first back on the road after Bath, at Saltford. He was surer he smelled it when they crossed Keynsham Bridge. Now there was no mistake.

He stepped out, his musket thrown over his shoulder. God, to stare out to sea again. To watch it heave and tumble, glinting in the sun; the whisper and call of the *mordroz*, the sound of the sea, its pull and draw, *leav an mor*, the voice of the ocean, sucking, tugging, dragging a man's soul back. It was enough to lift the heart. '*Tha'n mor!*' To the sea!

And then they crested the rise. Before them was a city, not the open sea, but a city and harbour. Bristol. Ships' masts jostling with church spires, roofs and chimneys, wheeling gulls and jackdaws, as the river twisted and turned about the town. The sea was hidden, calling, blowing through its gorge. He'd heard tell of Bristol from old sailors: of its quays, backs, wharfs and warehouses; its merchants, porters and whores; its silks, spices and loaves of sugar; its taverns, alehouses and houses of ill repute; a city and harbour where a man could get anything he wanted, and a few things he didn't – for a price.

Kendall had thought Bath was a fine great city. But it was nothing like Bristol. The city stretched near as far as the eye could see. It was huge, enormous, with high great walls, towers and gates about it. And the chimneys and smoke! He could smell the city now, its filth mingling, overawing the freshness of the sea. It smelled of piss, tar, soot and shit.

'Slanning's Regiment of Foot!' It was their colonel, at their head, preparing them for his order. 'Battaile will move to the left. . . by divisions! Wheel your battle. . . to the left! March on!'

The column wheeled to turn off the Bath road, the drums crashing out, *piphet* pipes blaring, *crowdy-crawn* thumping. Kendall stepped short behind his file leader as his division of musketeers made the half turn. Off the road, they stepped out again, marching along the crest of the ridge, the army in a single column across the front of the city. Only Prince Maurice and the guns remained beside the road, unhitching, preparing a battery.

'Slanning's Regiment of Foot will advance! Wheel your battle. . . to the right!'

Orders flowed now from captains, ensigns and sergeants as each division wheeled into line, one after another. Kendall listened for the orders from his own sergeant as they marched past the rear of those turning ahead of them.

Finally, their sergeant raised his halberd. 'Division will wheel to the right! About!'

Kendall stepped out, following his file leader in a tight arc back to face the city.

'March on!'

They stepped forward again until level with the ranks to their right.

'Stand!'

Slanning's tinners stood in battalia, six ranks deep, division by division, pike block and musket wings in line of battle. Already to their right stood Prince Maurice's Devons, the Marquis of Hertford's Somersets and Colonel Buck's Hampshires. To their left, Lord Mohun's Regiment swung into line, followed by Trevanion's, Grenville's and Godolphin's, Cornishmen all. On either flank stood a wing of cavaliers. As the pipes and drums fell silent, Hopton's Western Army stood together, as one, in line, colours unfurling on the breeze, facing the city of Bristol.

A single drum rattled out the order to advance. Its long roll and urgent bars repeated by every drum along the line, thundering out their call.

'March on!'

The line surged forward, colours streaming, snapping in the wind, drums thrashing. They marched forward, out over the crest of the ridge into full view of the city, twenty paces. Then the drums were suddenly silent, just the sound of tramping feet.

'Stand!'

The line halted, stood in silence; battalion after battalion lining the hill. The ground sloped away to meadows, a great church and the city beyond. Bells tolled out across the city, sounding their alarum. The Cornish had come!

And then came a single shout. *'Perh co Grenville!'* Remember Grenville. *'Kernow bys vycken!'*

Together, as one, they yelled their response. *'Kernow bys vycken!'* Cornwall forever!

IX

Encompassed

Abel Cowens
St Nicholas' Back, Bristol, Monday the 24ᵗʰ
of July 1643, one o'clock in the afternoon

Abel Cowens leant his weight against the capstan bar, his crippled arm tucked under it. Aye but, it was good to be back on a ship's foredeck, to feel the deck beneath his feet, to be with a crew again. He'd known nothing else since he was a lad shipped aboard a Newcastle collier. Until his hand was broken.

The boatswain stepped back from the gun carriage. 'A'right now. Together. Heave!'

Together, they stepped forward, Abel, Israel, the Swede and the laddie. The capstan turned, the line straightening, stretched taut, twisting, squealing in the blocks.

'Belay! Hold her there!'

They stopped, straining against the bars. Suspended on the tackle, a foot above the deck, the gun spun slowly.

The boatswain looked aloft at the yard arm braced back, the creaking block and stretched tackle. 'A'right now. Gently does it. Together. Heave!'

Together, they forced the bars to move again, the capstan turning slowly clockwise; feet, legs, bodies labouring.

'*Hail and Howe!*' It was Israel, the boatswain's mate, calling for a shanty.

Together, they followed, chanting out the words, stepping out the beat.

'*Haile and Howe,*
Rumbylowe!
Steer well the good ship;
And let the wind blow!'

The gun rose steadily higher, turning gently in the breeze off the river.

'Belay!' The boatswain took up the line's slack from the deck. 'Hold her there!' He took a turn around the samson post, hauled it tight, made it off with another turn and a half-hitch. 'A'right, ease away. Braces now.'

They eased back, carefully, letting the samson post take the strain before stepping away from the capstan and its bars. The gun hung above the deck, twisting slowly in the sun. It was only a four-pounder minion on its squat, wooden ship's carriage, but it weighed two-thirds of a ton, enough to tear a hole through the deck and hull.

They shifted to the base of the foremast and took up the port mainbrace. Abel joined the end of the line, wrapping the rope around his back, over his crippled arm, ready to haul.

The boatswain loosed the port brace from its belaying pin, held it ready to run out. 'A'right now. Gently does it. Together. Haul in!'

The yard arm slowly braced around the mainmast, creaking, haulyards straining, the gun swinging out over the quay, the deck canting as the ship listed under its weight.

'Steady! Belay!' The boatswain held the yard firm. 'That'll do. Make her fast there.'

The gun swayed above the stone quay as merchants,

foremen, porters, sailors and soldiers hurried past on St Nicholas' Backs. Slowly, carefully, they loosened the hitch on the samson post and eased the rope out, lowering the gun down onto the flagstones, ship and crew righting themselves as the tackle slackened.

Now they needed to shift the gun to Temple Gate. It was to add its weight to the defence of the city. Abel was there to show the crew the way, act as their guide, help them rig it in the round tower next to the gate, join them in manning it against the cavaliers and Cornish that had now encompassed the city.

Prince bloody Rupert and his bastard cavaliers filled Durdham Down to the North, from the Avon Gorge to the River Frome. And now the Cornish stood all along Pine Hill, to the south, from the Bath road to Bedminster. They were still up there now, with their guns, flags, shrill pipes and bloody drums; hordes of them, yelling, chanting worse than Scotchmen in their wild barbarian tongue.

An army of Cornishmen was worse than any army of cavaliers or Spaniards. Worse than North Country mosstroopers or Dunkirk pirates even. More like Irish rebels, or Turks, a heathen horde that would likely rape, pillage, burn the city and ships in the harbour. A host of half-wild fisher-folk that lured ships onto the rocks, drowned crews and cut the throats of any that got ashore to rob them of cargo, victuals and gear. Their womenfolk were worse – half-naked, half-starved, wild-haired harpies, each with a long knife to slit and gut fish or man. Rich or poor, they would take from all, leave the poor with nothing. Unleashed by a tyrant king, his bastard lords and so-called gentlemen, their chaos would destroy the commonwealth, turn back the rights and freedoms won, halt the rebellion, plunge the common man back into oppression and servitude.

Well, they'd have to face this gun first. While the crew coiled the breach ropes around the barrel, fixed traces to the eyebolts and gathered up their stuff, Abel carried a keg of powder ashore. With a nod from the boatswain, he hefted a barrel onto his shoulder and led the way along St Nicholas' Back, past the crane to Bristol Bridge.

They had to push their way through the crowd that poured across the bridge, that collided with those scurrying along the backs and down Baldwin Street, all jostling to get through St Nicholas' Gate under the church and up the High Street or Shambles. Folk had gone mad. They were all rushing backwards and forwards to the Castle, their coin and precious things in barrows or on their backs. The Governor had offered them safe keeping for their belongings behind the Castle walls. A merchant was shouting at his servant on his hands and knees in the gutter, a chest of coins, papers and silver plate scattered across the cobbles. Abel touched his pocket. He'd barely two copper farthings, let alone silver shillings or gold crowns to stick in the Castle.

He'd never had much. He'd gone to sea when he was just a laddie, when his father had died. The parish magistrate said he had to go, put him aboard a collier out of Newcastle, apprenticed to a bastard bully and drunkard mariner. He was just eleven years old. He had jumped ship in London, just as soon as he was fourteen and joined as a sailor aboard a merchantman bound for Muscovy. He got back to Newcastle with a bit of coin in his pocket. But it was too late: his mam and younger brothers and sisters were all dead and buried in a plague pit. Rated paupers they were. The city hostmen couldn't give a shite for the likes of them. Buried them on waste ground like they were only fit for a midden heap. And his father was a carpenter, building grand ships and all.

There was nothing for him in Newcastle after that. So, he put about and went straight back to sea. He'd sailed the North Sea and Baltic, the Mediterranean and Atlantic, he'd seen Moscovy, France, Spain, Portugal, Virginia, New England and Newfoundland, the Levant, Barbary, Africa and the West Indies – wonderous lands, strange peoples, things that could scarce be believed. It was no easy life aboard a merchant-man. But it was better than what many got ashore. The poor wretches they landed in America had nothing but hope. Half of them were dead before the year was out. He'd seen those that were left beg to be carried back to England. But there was no leaving without a licence. Providence Island they called it. And the ship was named *Charity*.

But then came the storm, his hand broken and maimed. Half the fingers were cut away, smashed by a parted sheet and flailing block, the wind shrieking through the shrouds. He had to leave seafaring for good. He couldn't climb, work aloft or tie a reefing pennant. Nobody wanted a cripple on the crew. Not even as ship's cook. Not with only one good hand. And all because the bastard captain and his bloody share-holders wouldn't pay up to refit worn-out rigging, instead of sitting on their tidy profits.

He'd washed up ashore in Bristol. All that was left was to queue in the rain and cold on the backs at dawn each morning for a job as a porter, a dockside labourer, a hireling. He had to fight with the others there just to beg to be hired. Those that were lucky enough to get picked, slaved all day shifting a cargo to some poxy merchant's warehouse. And all for a few pennies.

But the foremen all knew him and favoured others, said that he was a useless cripple, northern scum and a trouble-maker. He'd once taken a loan from one of them, just to get a job. Now he was trapped, forced to take what job he could to pay thruppence a week on a shilling loan. The worst were in stinking tannery hides, the foul slime slipping from them to coat his arms, neck and back. Each night he fell into his cot exhausted, only to crawl out again with the dawn. His life was little better than that of a Barbary slave. At least they were fed. A slave was worth something, was valued by his master. He was just another labourer in the crowd fighting for a day's pay. And to think he'd been an able seaman who might have made a boatswain himself.

They left the bridge behind, dragging the cannon down St Thomas Street, past the church and the tenement off St Thomas' Lane he shared with a whore when she had no punter. The street reeked in the summer heat, its gutter clogged with rotting scraps, a thousand turds and the carcass of a dead dog all alive with flies and their maggots. They were South of the river now, where few merchants lived or visited. These were the parishes of the city's poor, the haunts of boat-builders, smiths, tanners, butchers, footpads and whores.

Abel led the way, turning into Long Row, dark and narrow between the overhanging houses. The smell of burnt pitch rankled, strong, stark and harsh. A house fumigated, its lodgers' bodies carted away; folk hurried past in the street, handkerchiefs held to their noses. The ague, the burning fever, infested these streets. It had come with the summer heat and the soldiers that were lodged on the city. Now it was amongst them, the poor were unable to shake it off, while the rich city merchants kept to their fine houses and open suburbs.

They turned South again into Temple Street, the sun slicing between the buildings, past Petticoat Lane and Temple Church with its leaning tower. They dragged the gun on down the street past inns, taverns and whorehouses, on to Temple

Gate. And there they stopped, staring up at the great round tower beside the gateway that led out onto Temple Meads, Redcliffe Meadows and the Bath road.

'A'right now.' The boatswain spat on his hands. 'Let's get that tackle rigged and this little beauty hauled up where she can do some damage.'

X

Escape

Moussa Dansocko
Boucher House, Christmas Street, Bristol, Monday
the 24ᵗʰ of July 1643, a quarter to midnight

Moussa sat at his master's table. A single candle burned low, the door closed, the windows shuttered, the house silent. He dipped the quill in the ink and touched it to the paper; a black teardrop upon pure white. He traced a long diagonal line. Slowly, deliberately, he drew the Sufi star, its interlocking lines filling the page; the symbol of divine light, of man's union with God, of God Himself. *And that it is He alone who is the Lord of Sirius* – the Mighty Star, the brightest star, the leader, the lantern that guides the way.

Within the star he carefully spelled the name of God in flowing Arabic script, *Allah*, the *Blessed and Exalted*. Calming his shaking hand, he traced the name of the Prophet, *Mohammed, blessings of God be upon him as well as peace.* He took a deep breath, dipped the quill again and wrote the required *hadith*, the sacred words flowing from right to left across the page.

And whosoever fears Allah – He will open a way for him to escape.

And He will provide sustenance for him from where he does not expect.

And whoever relies upon Allah – then He is sufficient for him.

He dipped the quill and drew a crescent moon: the *hilal,* the new moon of the *hajj,* of pilgrimage, the heart responsive to the light of truth, reflection of the light and reckoning of time. He sketched the mystical Zulfiquar, the double-bladed sword of Hazrat Ali, *peace be upon him,* the brave, the chivalrous, the Lion of Allah, standard bearer and defender of the Prophet; the Door to the City of Knowledge: the Cleaver of Spines with its blades of *zikr* and *fikr,* remembrance and contemplation of God. He traced the Hand of Fatima, *peace be upon her*: five fingers outstretched, an eye within the hennaed palm; the magical *khamsa,* the five letters of Allah, the law of the Prophet, the Five Pillars of Islam; a daughter's protection and bloody battle flag; a ward against *al-ayn,* the Evil Eye.

Finally, carefully, separately, in flowing curves about the star, he wrote the five mystical letters of the Quran; the *Muquatta'at,* the mysterious opening chant of the Surah Maryam, the Chapter of Mary, mother of Jesus. Each letter a holy name of God. Secret names, names greater than the ninety-nine known names of God.

The names

and attributes of creation:

ك　　　　　　　　　ه

The letter *kaf,* the totality of being, the cave in which every being took shelter.

Ha, the waiting dominion, the kingdom prepared for us.

ي　　　　　　　　　　　　　　ع

Ya, the spring; *'ayn,* of springs

and mine of the hidden secret. *Sadd*, the attributes possessed.

ص

Together, as one, the five letters spelled out the message of God, the sufficient, the guide, the guardian, the scholar, the true promise.

He sat back, breathed deeply, his heart racing, hands shaking. It should have been written by a *marabout*, a holy man. But he had no marabout, no imam, no teacher. He was alone in this land. *Oh my Lord, forgive me, have mercy upon me, for you are the most merciful.* He stared at the *taweez* on the page in front of him, the page he'd created. He dared not pick it up, dared not touch it. It had force, resonance. The letters, words and symbols rose from the paper, combining, drawing, holding secret meaning, secret power. It was dangerous. He should not have drawn it. He should burn it, now, in the candle. But he needed its strength, its sustenance. He needed its protection.

Gangs of soldiers and citizens roamed the streets, ready to arrest any they suspected of sympathising with the enemy outside, looking for an enemy within – a scapegoat. They had come to the house in the evening, demanding to search it, to question all within. Mistress Elizabeth had hidden him and turned them away. But he could stay no longer. It was not safe. Enid watched his every move – suspicious, vengeful. She was possessed by that *shaytan* Mistress Hazzard and by her soldier. He would be hunted down, taken, sold again into slavery – or hanged.

A floorboard creaked – someone outside the chamber door. The mistress's dog snuffled under the door then padded away. The house was silent once more. Moussa exhaled. He had to escape. Tonight. Before the battle started. He would go

to the *Askia,* the King, and plead for his protection and a clear
end to his indenture. If he had to, he would fight for the King
until he could find a way home, find a ship that would carry
him back to Africa. He would have to get to London to find
a ship going to Africa. Those sailing from Bristol only traded
with France, Spain, Barbary and the Americas. All would enslave him again.

But first he had to finish the amulet. The *taweez* was written, drawn, cast. Now he must add the *barakah.* He needed
its blessings to feel God's force within him, to feel it within
his heart. He needed to feel the *hadith* sustain him, to let the
barakah guide him. He took the leather pouch from around
his neck, pulling it from under his shirt, opened it carefully
to remove each item within. He placed them on the table, in
a circle about the *taweez*: a brass coin, a hollow bead, a seashell; things he'd collected and carried with him as a slave,
his only belongings, his childhood treasures. He added a date
stone he'd found discarded on the floor one Christmas. With
a smile, he ran his thumb over its dry, rough texture, feeling
its contours. He'd chewed the last of the sweet flesh from it,
savouring the sweet taste of the desert, sucking it and sucking
it till the stone was dry and cloying in his mouth. He would
carry it home and plant it, watch it grow in the sun. It could
never grow tall, never thrive or bear fruit here on this wet
and cold island. He held the tiny ball of *hashab* to his nose,
an amber piece of hard gum arabic stolen from the kitchen,
the faint scent of acacia transporting him home; the sweet
warm incense of sun. Finally, he placed on the table a chicken
bone and a dried bean. The bone was picked clean, white and
smooth; the bean notched with the cut of an iron knife. It was
pale and flat, not like the big red beans of home. But it held
barakah. It had brought him blessings of luck, kept him safe.

203

He had to offer *du'a* to God. He had to pray before binding the *taweez* and *barakah* together. He had to pray before he could wrap them tight in the amulet, to be kept about his neck, against his skin, close to his heart. He turned towards the east, from where the sun would wake the house and find him gone. He knelt in the dark, the flash and thunder of cannon fire in the distance, raising his hands as he'd been taught, palms upwards in supplication, eyes closed and whispered the Surah al-Fatihah, the opening of the Holy Quran.

'Allah in the name of The Most Affectionate, the Merciful.
All praise unto Allah, Lord of all the Worlds.
The most Affectionate, The Merciful.
Master of the Day of Requital.
We worship You alone, and beg You alone for help.
Guide us in the straight path.
The path of those whom You have favoured.
Not of those who have earned Your anger,
Nor of those who have gone astray.'

———

A light flickered under the door. Somebody was in the master's old chamber. Enid Powell stepped carefully, quietly, feeling for the creaky floorboard with her bare feet. She had woken restless, sleepless, troubled by dreams, sweats and a full moon in the still heat of the night. She eased the door open and stepped in.

The candle on the master's writing table fluttered, the light wavering on white paper, inkpot and quill. Beside them lay a coin, a seashell, a shiny bead, a date stone, gum arabic, a bean and a chicken bone. The candlelight swirled over the paper, a page marked with lines, symbols, strange signs. She grasped the paper, held it to the light: a crescent moon, a double-bladed sword, an eye in the palm of a hand, strange swirling marks, coded signs, occult ciphers around and within a great five-pointed star.

She gasped, her hair prickling, sweat soaking her chest, chill down her back. It was a pentacle! Sorcery! Witchcraft!

Something moved. A shadow rising from the floor – the Devil himself!

Moses stood before her, his eyes wide, nose flaring. 'Give it to me.' His hand stretched out, shaking. 'It is *haram*. Forbidden. Sacred. You are not clean.'

'Yes, Moses.' She shook the paper in her hand. 'It is forbidden!'

'You do not understand. It has divine power.'

'It is witchery!'

'It is a *taweez*. A prayer to God. For His protection.'

'To Satan more like!'

'We worship the same God, the one true God.'

'Mahomet is a false god!'

'Do not insult the name of the Prophet, *blessings of God be upon him as well as peace*. Enid, you must give it to me. Quickly, before you wake the others.'

'It is something evil, Moses. They'll hang you for it!'

'Give it to me!'

'No, Moses. Mistress Elizabeth and Master Francis shall see it first. And then Mistress Hazzard and Reverend Cradock.'

Moussa lunged, snatching at the paper. Her back crashed against the table, the candle rolling, spluttering, the round bead, date stone and bone falling on the floor.

She felt for the door, pulled it open and ran. The floor-boards and stairs squeaked and thumped, gasping as her bare legs fled in the moonlight. She didn't care, didn't slow. She had to wake Master Francis and tell him – show him the pentacle. He'd know what to do.

———

Moussa grasped the candle, its wax dripping. Held it upright, flaring as he groped for the precious pieces of *barakah* scattered on the floor. He dropped each one on the table, the bone, date stone and tiny coloured bead beside the coin, seashell and bean.

Quickly, carefully, he spread out the *taweez*. The page was torn, ripped, a corner missing. With a shaking finger, he traced the shattered fifth point of the star, the missing crescent moon, the new moon of the *hajj*, the light of truth that guided the heart, reflection of the true light, the reckoner of time. The invocation was broken. Its resonance, its force, unbalanced, dangerous.

He should burn it now, in the candle. But he needed its strength. He needed its sustenance. He needed its protection, whatever was left of it. *Oh my Lord, forgive me, have mercy upon me, for thou art the most merciful.*

———

Francis Reeve lay awake, the night still, sticky and sultry, his loins hot, balls burning, his manhood stiff, slick, aching. His old enemy Asmodeus haunted him. The Prince of Lechery, the demon of lust, whispered to him in the moonlight, tempted him, urged him to touch it, to rub it, to ease his own pain. Images of flesh possessed him, burned his soul, clawed at his will, dragging him towards eternal damnation.

Mistress Elizabeth would be in her chamber, the covers thrown back, with only a shift to cover her beauty, her form stretched out in the moonlight, tall, slender, silent. The maidservant, Enid, would waken, hot and restless, naked, her hands wanting, searching, feeling. . .

A floorboard creaked. Somebody was at the door. It was opening! He dragged the sheet over himself, damp sweat sticking to it.

'Master Francis?' It was her, the maidservant, Enid.

'Yes.' He pulled himself up. 'What is it?'

'Oh, Master Francis.' She was at the door. 'You've got to come quickly! There is evil doing in this house!'

'Where? What is it?' He pulled his shirt over his head. 'What sort of evil?'

'In the master's chamber. It's Moses. He's a witch!'

'Are you sure? How do you know?'

'I saw him. Just now. He drew a witch's pentacle! With ink. On paper. Look. . .' She stepped into the moonlight, her tiny frame silhouetted against the window, her shift translucent, transparent in the silver light, the contours of her body, breasts, hips, legs, naked, visible. 'Look!'

He stepped out of the bed, gulping, his manhood stirred, jutting, swinging, wet. He dared not step from the shadows. Lust still pulsed in his veins. Her musk was strong and heady.

She held a scrap of paper, the torn corner of a page. 'Look. See, it's a moon. Do you see? It was one part of a star, with five points. And there was more. A sword with two blades. A hand holding an eye. And strange marks, like signs, symbols. And writing like I never seen before. He said it was a prayer. But it looked like it was writ back to front.'

Francis took the piece of paper, stepped into the light, closer. He could feel the heat from her body. His hand shook and the light was weak.

But the image was clear: a crescent moon between two sides of a triangle. *Thou shalt not suffer a witch to live!* He turned to her, this brave maidservant who had come boldly to him, this handmaiden sent by God. 'Quickly now. . . fetch a light. I must prepare myself to do battle with evil. *For all that do these things are an abomination unto the Lord.'*

———

With tears in his eyes, hands shaking, Moussa folded the paper, tighter and tighter, until it slipped into the leather pouch, the torn corner unseen. Quickly and carefully, he slipped each piece of *barakah* into the pouch beside the *taweez*, coin, bead, seashell, date stone and bone, binding the whole together, wrapping them tight, the amulet made, cast.

A floorboard creaked. Someone was coming. He slipped the pouch strap over his head.

Someone was outside the chamber; the door opening.

The amulet slid inside his shirt, against his skin, close to his thumping heart. He turned slowly to face his accusers.

Mistress Elizabeth stood before him, tall and beautiful in the fluttering candlelight. He'd never seen her in just a shift before. She was even more lovely than he'd imagined. 'Moses. I heard noises – voices. . . someone running. What are you doing in my father's chamber at night? Is something amiss?'

'Mistress Elizabeth, it was Enid. We argued. She has gone to fetch the soldier, Master Francis. He will take me from you. They will sell me as a slave. Perhaps they will kill me.'

'I should have dismissed her. But the executors would not allow it. I am sorry, Moses.'

'No, Mistress, it is I that am sorry. I must leave. I must go from this house.'

'But must you go now? I don't know what I will do without you?'

'Mistress, every day now they look for someone to blame for this city's misfortune, someone to hang like the poor master, like your poor father. I am sorry. I must leave you.'

'It is true, I cannot protect you any longer. God alone knows what will happen in the coming battle. I fear for us all.'

'I will fetch help. If I stay, I will be taken. I will be of no use, unable to serve you.'

'But what will you do? Where will you go?'

'I will go to the King, beg for an audience, tell him all that has happened here in his city, plead with him to come to your aid. I will fight for him, defeat these rebels against God, these evil doers that stir hatred between neighbours. I will guide him to you.'

'Very well. But you will need a letter of introduction, a letter explaining who you are, a letter explaining that you are released from your indenture, that you are a free man. I will write it. I see you have prepared paper, quill and ink.'

Moussa fell to his knees, touched the hem of her shift with shaking hands. 'Thank you. Mistress Elizabeth, thank you. May the blessings of God be upon you.'

'Moses, please. Prepare yourself.' She sat at the table, the quill scratching across the paper in her quick, delicate hand. 'I am writing to Colonel Henry Lunsford. He fought at Marshall's Elm and will be with the King's army outside the city. He will know of my father and will know what to do. You must take my letter to him and guide him here to this house.' She stopped, looked up, looked at him. 'And Moses, you must not leave the town by the bridge. Frome Gate will be closed to you. The guards will be suspicious. Take my father's boat to cross the river.'

———

Francis crashed down the stairs, his spurs ringing with every step, pistol in one hand, guttering candle in the other. The handmaiden, Enid, skipped behind on bare legs. He crossed the hall and threw open the door to the plotter's chamber.

Mistress Elizabeth sat at the writing table, dressed only in a shift, her delicate hands on the table before her. The room was silent, empty in the wavering light.

'Where is he?' He stepped forward. 'Where is the witch? Where is your slave, Moses?'

'He is not my slave. And he is not a witch.'

'He is so!' Enid waived the evidence at her, the torn piece of a pentacle. 'He was making witchery! The Devil's work! In this very room. I saw him with my own eyes. He was casting a spell!'

'Where is he?' Francis stepped closer. 'Harbouring a known witch is a heinous sin in the eyes of the Lord. And a felony in the eyes of the law.'

Mistress Elizabeth stared back at him. 'He is gone. He is a free man.'

———

Moussa lowered himself into the boat. The River Frome was dark and ominous below the house and garden wall. The boat lurched, wobbling, ripples spreading outward in the gloom as he untied it from the steps and pushed off. *Zin*, *genii*, spirits, the *dya* of the dead, all haunted the *Jeliba*, the River Niger, resided in its waters, waiting to suck the unwary into their watery lair. Spirits lurked here too, swirling and clutching in these dark waters.

He paddled gently, quietly with one oar, careful not to knock it against the gunwale, out from the wall, away from the house to let the current and tide float him under Frome Bridge, below Christmas Street. A splash echoed under the arch – a fish or spirit rising. A light shone from the courtyard behind, in the stable.

The boat emerged into the moonlight beyond the bridge,

a dark shadow disturbing the bright silvered calm. He paddled harder now, pulling the boat across the stream to bump against Prior's Slip. Quickly, he tied the boat to the slip wall and stepped out into the shadow of a house. The slipway was dark, wet and slippery with the ebbing tide. A rat scurried across a pile of slimy weed.

He rounded the end of the house and turned into Horse Street, careful to keep out of sight of the guard on Frome Gate. He dared not use Christmas Steps; they would be too obvious, too visible. Instead, he crossed the narrow street and slipped into Zed Alley.

———

Francis turned his horse onto Christmas Street, dug spurs into its flanks to clatter between the houses on the Frome Bridge. 'Open the gate!' he yelled. 'Open the gate!'

'On who's order?' The corporal of the guard appeared at the guardroom door in his shirtsleeves.

'On the Lord's!' Francis gathered his reins, the horse tossing. 'I am in pursuit of a witch!'

The corporal stared at him, an eyebrow raised. 'An' what does this 'ere witch look like then? Just in case we happenstance see 'er. In 'er flight as it were.'

'He is a blackamoor.' Francis pulled his pistol from its holster. 'From the Boucher House, at the other end of Christmas Street.'

'Aye, we knows the one.' Unsure now. 'Moses they call him. What's he done then?'

'He was caught casting a spell. Casting it over a pentacle!'

'Well, where is 'e now? He ain't passed this way. Not unless he flew. The gate's barred.'

'He crossed the river by boat. Beneath you. Did you not keep a lookout on the river?'

'Shit!' The corporal turned. 'Get the gate open!'

The gate creaked slowly open, enough for Francis to force his horse through the gap. He turned into Horse Street and looked up Christmas Steps. Nothing moved. It was empty, silent, save for a cat that stared and hissed at horse and rider. He spurred the horse into a canter, sparks flying on the cobbles as he rounded the corner into Steep Street. The horse put its head to the slope as the road curved uphill. He clattering past the Ship Inn, tiered jetties overhanging the narrow street in dark shadow.

He drove his horse on up the hill with another deep rake of spurs. On past the top of Christmas Steps and the bottom of Stony Hill, on up St Michael's Hill.

———

Moussa ducked back into the alley, as a horseman cantered past, his mount lurching, rasping, iron shoes scrabbling for purchase on the steep cobbles. He waited, pressing himself into the shadow, trying to calm his breath, listening. The horseman was alone.

He slipped across Steep Street and ducked past the end of the Ship Inn to climb the steps behind it to Trencher Lane. Long and narrow, the lane ran between houses and high walled gardens, half in moonlight, there was no escape if he was caught on it. But he dared not use Stony Hill. He had to avoid the guard at the Essex Work. With one last look behind him, he stepped out, walking quickly and quietly down its length.

With a deep exhale of breath, he turned off Trencher Lane to climb the hill again, up the winding path that led out to join the lane to Clifton beyond the Red Lodge and the Essex Work. At the top, he slipped across the road to head out beyond the last houses and gardens of the suburbs. The moon was bright and full, flooding the parks on either side as he stepped out towards Clifton and the line of defences – the ditch and earth wall he'd been forced to dig.

It was the best place to cross. The ditch was not deep, on stony ground. And it was out of site of the soldiers in the forts on Brandon Hill and St Michael's Hill. He lengthened his stride; almost running now.

———

Francis reined in his sweat-soaked horse. The road was empty. There had been nobody moving on St Michael's Hill. The highway up Mile Hill was deserted. He had ridden as far as Alderman Jones's house. The highway beyond was barred and guarded. The witch had not passed this way on foot.

He turned and retraced his steps, urging the animal on, only to drag at the reins as its iron shoes slipped and slid downhill. At the top of Christmas Steps and Horse Street, he turned right up Stony Hill. With a deep rake of bloody spurs, the beast careered up the cobbled street to the Essex Work.

A sergeant stood in the moonlit road, lantern and halberd in hand. 'And where now, sir, do you think you're going in such a hurry?'

'I am in pursuit of a witch.' Francis reined in again. 'A blackamoor man. I believe he is in league with the malignants and trying to escape to them. Have you seen him?'

'Nobody, nor nothing has passed this way since Sergeant-Major Langridge made his rounds before midnight.'

'Very well.' Francis kicked the horse forward. 'If you see him, kill him!'

He crossed the ditch across the road, between the Essex Work and Red Lodge, before driving the sweat lathered animal on again with his spurs. They cantered past the last of the houses and gardens, out beyond the suburbs, the moonlight clear and bright, the lane towards Clifton stretching out between parks to the Spur Work, a barn and line of defences that ran between Brandon Hill Fort and the Windmill Fort. Nothing moved on the road. He was too late.

———

Lightning flashed as thunder crashed out, rolling over the hill, echoing back from the city below. And then another, and another, as a ripple of flame lit the night sky above him. Moussa turned to stare.

The horizon above the suburbs was ablaze with flame and roaring thunder, from St Michael's Hill to Prior's Hill. It burned with God's wrath, with the fire and wind of *jinns*. All along the line of the defences, a battle raged: men fought one another with fire and steel; the *nyama*, the magic force, the secret power of *Ogun*, the strength of the god of iron, was unleashed to rain havoc and destruction.

Moussa opened his stride, stepping out faster – running now. A burning star arched its way across the night sky to land with a thunderous explosion in a ball of flame. The battle had started. *And indeed, We have adorned the nearest heaven with lamps, and We have made such lamps as missiles to drive away the shayaateen. And We have prepared for them the torment of the blazing fire.*

———

The line from Windmill Fort to Prior's Hill Fort was ablaze with gunfire. Another mortar bomb bright in its arced flight, exploded with violent light and thunderous roar behind the rampart. The battle had started. The apostates were storming the city. There would be a general alarum. He should go to his place of duty, stand with his troop behind the line.

Ahead, a figure moved on the lane – a man on foot. Francis bent low, raking the beast into a gallop. The witch must be stopped, the devil slain. He must be stopped before he summoned Satan's hordes to join the battle, before he joined with the accursed cavaliers, before he gave to the apostate hordes the keys of hell and death.

———

Moussa heard the horseman behind him on the lane, saw him between the flash of gunfire and the moon, bent low over his horse's neck. It was Master Francis, come to take him, to kill him. He ran. He ran as fast as he could in his ribboned shoes. He ran as if the Tuareg chased him once more.

Ahead lay the barn and earth wall across the lane. There would be a guard in the barn. But they would be looking the other way, out towards Clifton and the King's army.

The horseman was closer now, hooves pounding, breath rasping.

Moussa leapt at the wall, scrambled up over it rolling down the other side into the ditch, his fine valet's clothes covered in dust and grit.

———

Francis dragged at the reins of his horse, the beast turning to slam into the wall. He pitched sideways, grasping at the saddle to haul himself back up.

He levelled his pistol, aimed at the dark figure crawling from the ditch as gunfire flashed out again from St Michael's Hill. He squeezed the trigger. The pistol whipped back and up as the charge exploded, his horse leaping, tossing, rearing.

———

Hot wind swept Moussa's cheek as the pistol ball smacked into the grass ahead of him. Another shot crashed out from the barn to his left as he ran into the night and the wide open down.

He was free! He'd escaped the city. He was a free man. He was Moussa Dansocko of the Bambara. No longer Moses the slave. *In the Name of Allah, the All-Beneficent, the All-Merciful. May Allah bless Muhammad and his Family and damn their enemies.*

XI

Bombardment

George Merrett
Colonel Belasyse's Battery, Cotham Hill, Tuesday
25ᵗʰ July 1643, three o'clock in the afternoon

They were ready. Finally, they were ready to start the bombardment proper. They had tested the defences with alarums, fire and shot the night before. Now it was time to start the real work of preparing the way for the foot tertias, of silencing the forts, of blasting breaches in the rampart, of showing what artillery could do.

It was three o'clock; five hours until sunset, perhaps six before darkness would finally stop them. It was hardly enough time. This was not work that could be rushed. They could not afford to overheat the guns, to burst a barrel. It needed deliberate, careful, precise execution. They needed another day at least. But the hour for the assault had been appointed, the time set for the foot to fall on the defences: they were to storm the rampart wall at daybreak. George Merrett stepped forward, up behind his two great culverins. 'Load your pieces!'

Old Nick Busy returned just the briefest of nods as his Number Two thrust the long-handled ladle into the budge-barrel. The full scoop of course black gunpowder was slid down the bore, the ladle twisting to release its contents. The ladle was filled and pushed home again and again, until twelve pounds of precious gunpowder filled the breech to be tamped hard against its base with a double thud of the round-headed rammer.

A wad of oakum was stuffed into the gun's muzzle and thrust home to hold the compressed charge in place. The first round shot was hefted up and rolled into the muzzle, fifteen-pounds of solid iron, five-inches across. It was pushed home, followed by another wad, and seated up hard against the charge with three more thumps of the rammer.

The great culverin was loaded. Old Nick sighted along the top of the barrel, signalling with an outstretched hand as his Number Two and six matrosses forced hand spikes under the trail and shoulders against wheel spokes to turn the gun. Inch by inch they eased near two tons of iron and oak into line. Now the wedge-shaped quoin was tapped under the base of the breech, eased out and tapped again until, with a grunt, the gun captain was satisfied with the angle of elevation.

Now, Old Nick leant over the touch-hole, working a hole in the powder charge with a copper pricker. Finer grained priming powder was poured, the grains carefully crushed yet finer with the end of the powder horn. Finally, the gun captain turned and doffed his cap, one hand still clasped over the touch-hole to protect the fine priming powder. The gun was ready, loaded and laid. Within moments, the second culverin followed. They were ready.

Now they had to wait for the great demi-cannons and the order to start the bombardment. It had already taken them too long to prepare: to site the battery; to level the gun plat-forms, to put up and fill the gabions; to get the guns, powder, shot and stores into position. They had issued powder, match and small-shot to every foot regiment, enough to assault the line. And they had readied more to resupply them if needed. They had issued hand-grenades. And they had made and issued fire-pikes to every battalion. Finally, they were ready to start the bombardment. But still they waited.

And there was still so much to be done. They must prepare the way for the foot. Ensure the minimum of loss, safeguard the foot regiments for the assault on London. They could not afford to weaken them now, not while so much hung in the balance, not when this was the one real chance to crush the rebellion before it recovered. Already, there was news that the Earl of Essex was marching on Aylesbury, that the King had written to Prince Rupert urging him to send horse regiments, urging him not to delay.

They must be efficient and effective in their work. But they had to be given time. The foot should wait until the artillery had done their work; wait while they broke down the defences. Only when this was done should the foot be sent in to secure the victory. It was clear that there was not time for a full siege. But they could not afford to waste the King's precious foot in a costly storm against well prepared defences. They needed more time. And they could not afford to delay. But still they waited.

The Parliamentary line was well sited, back from the crest, with forts, ravelins and spur works along its length. The line itself was reckoned to be no more than a ditch six-foot across, six-foot deep at the base of the scarp, with a sloping earth rampart built of the spoil as high again from its top. It was not manned along its length, only at the ravelins, spur works and forts.

But the forts were something stronger, well sited, well-built and well-armed. Prior's Hill Fort was at least twenty paces square, its ditch nine-feet deep, the rampart and parapet as high again. It was armed with three six pounder sakers that commanded the ground on three sides and a swivel-mounted murderer that swept the ditch. Against this were emplaced the King's two demi-cannon and Lord Grandison's tertia of foot waiting to fall on against its walls.

In the centre, opposite Colonel Belasyse's battery and tertia, stood a redoubt at Mile Hill built out on a crook in the line to cover the highway to Aust Ferry and Wales. Smaller than Prior's Hill Fort, it still mounted a three-pounder minion and a falcon. But George's guns had also to deal with the Windmill Fort, within a musket shot of the redoubt. It mounted another two sakers and a minion. The ditch of each was as deep as that about Prior's Hill Fort, the sloping scarp, rampart and parapet as dauntingly high and well built.

Further right, beyond St Michael's Hill, lay Brandon Hill Fort: eighteen feet square and as many feet high, on the crest of a steep hill. It was reckoned to mount three minions and a little robinet. Colonel Wentworth's tertia waited about Clifton and the valley between to storm its slopes. They had not ceased in pressing the defenders, day and night, even shooting an insolent rebel who dared to stand on the parapet, capering in his shirt, his arse bared.

On the other side of the city, the King's Western Army waited to storm the town walls on either side of Temple Gate. Their battery was emplaced and ready, their tertias issued with faggots of wood to bridge the town ditch, ladders to scale the city walls. The walls were old, without the protection of a modern sloping earth glacis, bastions or fausse-braye parapets. But they were high and the towers mounted with cannon. Forward of the wall the rebels had constructed a gun platform, a hornwork and a demi-bastion. And they had turned the great church of St Mary Redcliffe into a fortified outwork.

The Council of War had specified the signal for the combined assault to be the firing of the two demi-cannon against Prior's Hill Fort at first light. At the signal, the six tertias of foot were to fall on, to assault their allotted section of the defences. Those that broke through were to throw down the wall and fill up the ditch to create a breach for the horse regiments to enter. Every man was to wear something green, a ribbon or sprig of leaves, as their sign to know one another. They were to wear no band or handkerchief about their neck. And the watchword for all was to be 'Oxford'.

But before all this, the artillery had to silence the Parliamentary forts. If not, the foot battalions would be cut to pieces as they assaulted the line. They would face slaughter from great shot, case-shot, iron slugs and small-shot fired from the cannon and muskets emplaced behind the fort parapets; cannon and muskets that would sweep the ditch, scarp and rampart wall along the line with enfilading fire; a fire that would cut down swathes of men as it struck the ranks in their flank. *God, grant them time to break those forts.*

George took the perspective glass from under his arm and trained it on the redoubt once more. The parapet in focus, he studied the single gun muzzle that stared back, a few heads beyond, shimmering in the heat. But that was as much as he could see. The rest of the fort, the rampart and ditch, was hidden below the crest of the down. There was nothing between him and the redoubt but a pair of cottages, bright white in the sun, nestled in a hollow beside the highway. He trained the glass on the Windmill Fort again; nothing but the parapet showed itself visible above the down.

He pulled the watch from his pocket again and flipped

it open. A quarter past three o'clock. A quarter of an hour waisted, lost, discarded. He snapped the lid shut and thrust the watch deep into his pocket. He could stand still no longer. He paced backwards and forwards behind his two culverins that stood idle, waiting. All was silent save the incessant chattering of bloody martins. *For Christ's sake, let the bombardment start!*

The down shook with the thunderous roar of a demicannon. The signal! *Thank Christ!* It had started. George turned back to face his own guns. 'Mister Busy! Give. . . fire!'

The gun captain blew upon the smouldering match in his linstock before whirling it in the air to bring the smoking coal down upon each touch-hole. George whipped the perspective glass to his eye, instinctively opening his mouth to save his eardrums from bursting.

The great culverin leaped back in a ball of smoke, flame and thunder; the fifteen-pound iron ball shrieking across the down. Two tons of iron and oak hung in the air before crashing back down upon the gun platform, clashing carriage bolts, iron locks and trunnion plates. Thick sulphurous smoke billowed back between the gabions to wreath through the grass.

The smoke finally clearing, George looked for the damage inflicted upon the fort. The fort stood defiantly staring back at him, only the faintest graze visible across the top of its parapet. The culverin had fired high. It was not yet hot. Old Nick would need to work his magic if they were to reduce the two forts, silence the rebel guns and save the King's foot from certain slaughter before dark.

George thrust the perspective glass under his arm. 'Mister Busy, put back your piece. Load!' He turned to his second gun. 'Mister Berkeley! Give. . . fire!'

George flipped open the lid of his watch and turned the face towards the setting sun. It was a quarter to eight o'clock. They had barely an hour of light left. Already, long, dark shadows cast their path across the down creeping towards the Windmill Fort and the redoubt. Gunsmoke hung in the hollows, twisting through the still grass, the two cottages almost hidden.

Old Nick Busy had silenced one rebel gun. The redoubt and fort were battered and torn. But it was not enough. Too many guns remained to cut down the King's precious foot battalions at dawn. They needed more time. They needed another day. He should go to the General of Ordnance, ask for more time, plead with him, beg Prince Rupert to delay the assault.

'Stand clear!' Captain Fawcett stood beside the mortar, its short stubby barrel pointing skyward, match coal glowing brightly in his linstock as he lowered it into the wide, open mouth. The bomb fuse spluttered and then flared, spitting sparks as he stepped back to blow on the match again before bringing it down against the mortar's touch-hole.

Priming powder flashed in the gloom, the mortar exploding in a ground shaking sheet of flame. The thirty-pound bomb soared high over the redoubt, its fuse bright against the darkening sky; tumbling in a trail of smoke to land behind the rampart in a flash of burning light, shattering blast and shrieking iron.

George slipped the watch back into his pocket and turned back to his own guns as a saker hurled its own six-pound ball at the fort. Old Nick was bent over his breach, his brow furrowed as he ground the priming powder more urgently now, the great iron barrel shimmering with heat in the still evening air.

George sensed rather than heard the hot shriek of the cannon ball as it tore the air apart. It struck the culverin barrel with a searing screech to ricochet away across the down in a whining blur.

The great gun shook on its axle trees, then settled, dust scattering. Thank God, only a bent lifting dolphin, the gun was barely damaged, still serviceable.

Something moved in the shadow behind the gun trails – young Flash, pale and shaking, covered in blood. George stepped closer. The boy was slumped against a budge barrel, as if he had been thrown there. Across his lap lay another figure, legs kicking, an arm flailing, grasping, clutching at a dark, bloody stump. 'No!' *Christ, no!* 'Nick!'

George fell to his knees, hands shaking, eyes swimming, clasping the old man's hand. Blood pumped, spurting, hot, bright, vital blood – *affluent* blood, blood that caried heat and spirit, blood that carried life – gushing in great steaming jets, slick, sticky, sickly.

This was Harvey's motion of the heart and blood, the *de Motu Cordis* – the heart a pump, circulating one's blood within the body. There was no separate *natural* blood in Galen's liver and veins. He had to keep the blood within the body. He had to stop it escaping.

He grabbed at the shattered stump, torn flesh and bone bulging between his fingers. The blood still squirted, seeping and running through his hands. He forced his fingers deeper, searching for the artery, feeling it slipping away from him, fumbling, gripping, squeezing.

The flow was slackening, the squirts less often, feebler now; the heart slowing, blood draining. The old man's face was pale, his breath ragged, eyes staring. Still. Unmoving.

George let go of the shattered stump and fell back against

an empty barrel. He pulled Flash to him, held the shaking boy in his bloody arms, clasped him to his soaking chest. Tears rolled down his face as the last of Old Nick Busy's lifeblood dripped, seeping away into the dirt of the gun battery floor as the sun slipped below the skyline, the last light of the day all but extinguished.

Part Four

Bristol

It was the hottest service that ever was in this kingdom since the war began.

AN EYE-WITNESS, *A TRUE RELATION OF THE*
TAKING OF BRISTOL, 1643

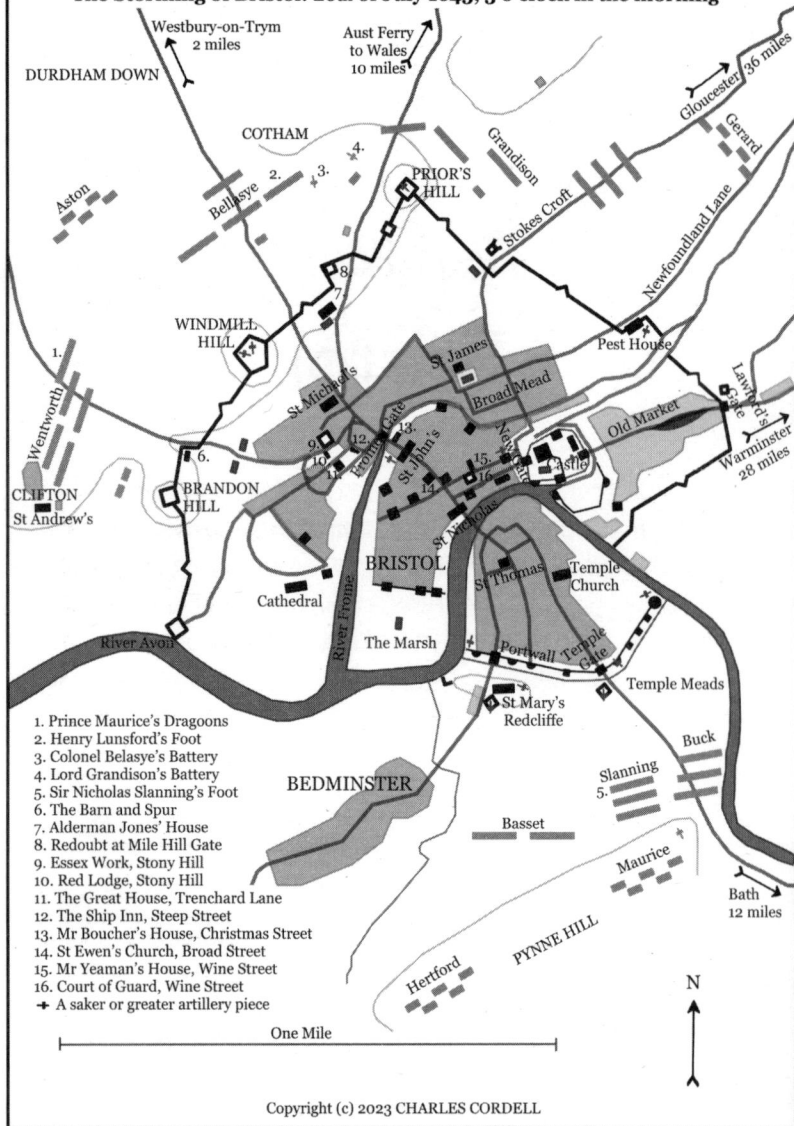

The Storming of Bristol: 26th of July 1643, 3 o'clock in the morning

Westbury-on-Trym
2 miles

Aust Ferry
to Wales
10 miles

Gloucester 36 miles

DURDHAM DOWN

COTHAM

Grandison

Gerard

Aston

Bellasye

2.

3.

4.

PRIOR'S
HILL

Stokes Croft

Newfoundland Lane

Wentworth

WINDMILL
HILL

8.

7.

St Michael's

St James

Broad Mead

Pest House

Lawford's
Gate

Old Market

Warminster
28 miles

CLIFTON
St Andrew's

6.

BRANDON
HILL

9.

10.

12.

11.

Froome Gate

13.

St John's

14.

15.

16.

Newgate

Castle

River Frome

St Nicholas

BRISTOL

Cathedral

The Marsh

St Thomas

Portwall

Temple
Church

River Avon

Temple
Gate

Temple Meads

St Mary's
Redcliffe

Buck

BEDMINSTER

Slanning
5.

Basset

Maurice

Bath
12 miles

Hertford

PYNNE HILL

N

1. Prince Maurice's Dragoons
2. Henry Lunsford's Foot
3. Colonel Belasye's Battery
4. Lord Grandison's Battery
5. Sir Nicholas Slanning's Foot
6. The Barn and Spur
7. Alderman Jones' House
8. Redoubt at Mile Hill Gate
9. Essex Work, Stony Hill
10. Red Lodge, Stony Hill
11. The Great House, Trenchard Lane
12. The Ship Inn, Steep Street
13. Mr Boucher's House, Christmas Street
14. St Ewen's Church, Broad Street
15. Mr Yeaman's House, Wine Street
16. Court of Guard, Wine Street
✦ A saker or greater artillery piece

One Mile

I

Kernow Kensa!

Kendall Tremain
Bath Road, before Bristol, Wednesday the 26th
of July 1643, three o'clock in the morning

The waggon creaked in the dark as they pushed it towards Bristol. Kendall Tremain stepped carefully, cautiously. The road was rutted, baked hard. Ahead, the spire of St Mary Redcliffe stretched towards bright Arcturus, a dark pike-head against the western stars. Fat, ripe, the swollen Hay Moon hung over all, flooding the open meadows between them and the city's walls with light. The stench of charred timber and cob rankled in the cool night air, an inn burnt to the ground.

The waggon rattled, lurched, jarred on a divot, the ladder on it clattering.

'Abarh Deew!' someone cursed.

A dog barked somewhere up ahead.

'Senj tha glapp!' The corporal beside them snarled – *Shut it!*

The dog barked again. A light in a tower. 'They spied us now, they have.' Kendall turned to the corporal. 'We ought-a go now. Afore they wake.'

'We can't go yet. We've got-a wait for the gun, for the signal.'

'Since when? When did we wait for no bugger?' Another light showed on the city wall. 'I say we go now. Afore they man their guns. *Brabm an garth* on Prince bloody Rupert and his signal!'

'*Kidgia!*' The corporal spat. Fuck it!

'Come on.' Kendall put his shoulder to the waggon. It rocked but fell back. Others joined him. 'Together!' They heaved. '*Onen hag oll!*'

The cart lurched forward crashing into the next rut. It was moving now – faster, gathering pace down the slope to the meadow, to the black ditch and town wall beyond. Together, they ran, the waggon yawing and bouncing on the road, the rest of Slanning's behind them. They would be the first to the walls. Theirs was the glory. The *Sowsen* English would know that Cornwall waited for no man. Cornwall first! '*Kernow kensa!*'

Behind them, the dark mass of Hopton's Cornish army surged forward. Unstoppable. Lansdown Hill or Bristol wall, they'd scale it for themselves. Again, together, one and all, they yelled their ancient cry. '*Kernow kensa!*'

———

Abel Cowans woke flushed with sweat. Something had started him from sleep, from the dream. The same dream. Aloft, the dark tropical storm shrieking through the shrouds as he fought to gather in the topsail, his fingers refusing to tie the knot, unable to reef the flailing canvas, to hold the yardarm, the ship pitching, yawing, the black sea hissing as it reached up.

'Abel.' It was the boy, shaking him awake. 'Abel!'

Abel dragged himself up. His broken hand ached. The boy was on watch, alone, the others sleeping on the cold stone underfoot. 'What's wrang, son?'

'Some int's movin' out yonder. I heard he. Some int's out there.'

Abel stood at the tower battlement, the cool night air cutting through the sweat, washing the dream away. He shivered. A dark shadow spread across the moonlit meadow, wavering, murmuring, like a great wave rising, hissing, the sound of feet, thousands of feet running. And then a call riding on the wave: the shriek of a siren; a strange, unearthly cry; a barbarous yell.

'*Kernow kensa!*'

'Shit!' Abel grabbed the smoking linstock. 'Wake the others, son.' He blew on the smouldering match. 'Howay, now. Look sharp.' No time to wait for the gun captain, or aim the gun. He had to warn the city, before the Cornish horde broke upon them. 'Stand clear!'

He swung the linstock through the air, the match flaring as he brought it down upon the great gun's touch hole. A jet of sparks, smoke bursting skyward. The charge erupted from the barrel in a great ball of searing flame that lit up the tower, walls, ditch and meadow beyond as the guncarriage flew back, breach ropes snatched taught and crashed back down on the stone tower roof, ring bolts, locks and tackle flailing.

II

The Signal Guns

George Merrett
Colonel Belasyse's Battery, Cotham Hill, five
minutes past three o'clock in the morning

George Merrett heard the gun. There was no mistaking it: a cannon firing on the other side of the city. He threw back his cloak and was up, standing, listening, holding his breath. Another cannon, then more, a continuous bombardment, flame lighting up the night beyond the city.

The attack had started. Why had he not been woken? 'Up! Up now!' He kicked the nearest gunner under his blanket. 'It has started. The attack has started!' God, how he missed old Nick Busy. He would not have let this happen. 'Stoke the brazier! Get the linstocks lit!'

It was still pitch dark; no dawn light above the far hills. The attack had been ordered for daybreak – it was too early. He fumbled for the watch in his pocket, flipped open the lid and held it to the glow from the brazier, the flames still feeble, almost out as young Flash added fresh wood. It was three o'clock, an hour before daybreak, an hour before the attack should have started.

Damn the Cornish for attacking early! Damn them for not

obeying the order, for their wildness, for their disobedience! Now the attack would be disjointed, the rebels ready, manning their defences, the element of surprise gone – wasted. The Oxford Army had to attack now, before it was too late. If not, the Western Army would be slaughtered, all hope of overwhelming the rebels lost in needless chaos.

But they still had to wait for the signal, wait for the firing of the siege guns, of the two great demi-cannon against Priors Hill, wait for Prince Rupert's order. George snapped the watch shut and thrust it back deep into his pocket, safe from muck and chaos, ordered time enclosed in its silver case. He could stand still no longer. He paced backwards and forwards as the gunners and their matrosses blundered about in the dark to sweep away the mess of their bedding and ready the guns.

Someone had to tell Prince Rupert. Someone had to wake His Highness. Somebody had to give the signal. . . fire the guns. . . start the attack. Could he, should he start the bombardment now? Here, with his own guns? What if he was wrong? What if the prince wanted to wait? He would be cashiered, dismissed, ruined. The Earl of Newport, his old patron, could protect him no longer. There were too many ready to step over him to seek preferment. He dared not risk it.

'Mister Berkeley, I am going to Sir John, the General of the Ordnance. I must speak with him.' He stepped into the dark. 'Be ready for the signal guns.' He walked out from glow of the embrasure, away from the battery, his place of duty, past his two culverins, away from the platform soaked in Old Nick Busy's blood, on past the mortar, stumbling in the long grass as his eyes adjusted to the dark, seeking out Lord Grandison's battery across the down on Cotham Hill.

The down lit up with flame, the siege guns stark, recoiling

in their own glare and thunderous roar. The signal! They were followed by the rest of Lord Grandison's battery pouring its fire against Priors Hill fort. The bombardment, the attack had begun. Thank Christ!

'Stay that!' George turned back to face his own battery. 'Give. . . fire!'

———

The redoubt shook, earth and stones raining down, dust filling the night air. Jeremy Holway crawled, fell, rolled to lie against the parapet, curling tight, his arms wrapped about his head as another iron cannonball thumped into the earth rampart; yet more shrieking overhead. How much more could the walls take? How much more could any of them take?

A dark comet spat flame and sparks as it arced its path across the stars to land behind the redoubt. The night exploded in white flame, shrieking iron shards and scorching heat, the earth quaking. Black night rushed in to cover the scene, but it could not hide the screams of those torn apart by the violent burst of a bomb fired from the cavalier mortar.

Pray to Christ, it won't last. Not like the bombardment the day before. Oh Jesus, please make it stop.

———

The drums beat all around him while great iron guns lit the night with flame and thunder and soldiers gathered in line upon line, their lighted matches glowing in the dark. Moussa Dansocko picked up the drum he had been given and slung its strap over his shoulder. It was like the *dunun sangban* of Africa, of home, hide skins stretched tight over either end. But these drummers played with two straight sticks, not with curved drumstick and open hand.

234

This was not the *djembe* drumming of his childhood. These drums did not call people to gather in peace, *anke djé, anke bé* to hear the tales sung by a travelling *jali*. These drums shouted of battle. Could he play their song? It is what his new master wanted, what the *horo* Colonel Lunsford expected, what the *jatigi* warrior-prince needed. But could he make the drum talk?

Moussa grasped the drumsticks, one in each hand, listened to the beat, let its *nyama* flow through him, reach inside, resonate within, touching him, feeling its power. It pulled at his *dya*, tugged at his spirit, compelling, demanding obedience. He struck the drum, gently at first, let the rhythm guide his hands, building slowly in strength, his drumsticks rising and falling in time with the others, louder and stronger, the drum vibrating, pounding, calling, pulling the soldiers into line, drawing them to its call, dragging them to battle.

At a nod from the drum-major there was silence, the drumming stopped. *Ogun's* great guns had ceased their thunder, their smoke lying in stinking wreaths that slipped through the damp grass and coiled themselves around men's legs. Their thunder would bring no rain, no lucky stork or hornbill, no joy, no children running into the street to sing of '*banikono kili da, kili da, samiya sera*', the gift of life that ended the long months of dry heat. Their iron thunder spoke only of war, of destruction and of death.

Colonel Lunsford stepped forward, filled his lungs. 'Musketeers, shoulder your. . . muskets!' Together, the long ranks of glowing match rose and fell in the dark. 'Pikes, advance your. . . pikes!' As one, the pike block hefted their pikes into the night sky with a rattle and slap. A thousand men were ready, awaiting their colonel's command. 'Battaile. . . will advance! Prepare to march!' The colonel turned to face the city, the earth walls and army that defended it. 'March on!'

'Up!' Major Wood stood in the centre of the redoubt. 'Get up!'

Jeremy Holway raised his head. It was still dark. The guns had stopped, their deafening thunder replaced by the beating of drums.

'Get up! To your posts!' The major kicked at a prostrate figure. 'The damn cavaliers are coming!'

Jeremy stood, earth falling from him, the taste of dust and gunpowder clogging his mouth and nose. The drums were beating the march, hundreds of them across the down, thrashing out the order to advance, drawing steadily nearer in the dark. He reached for his musket, shook the grit from it.

'Gunners, put back your pieces!' Major Wood strode about them. 'Pikes to the walls! You are to keep these royal-arse-licking whore's sons from climbing the scarp. If they have scaling-ladders, push the bastards back into the ditch!' The old soldier knew what they must do. 'Musketeers, make ready!'

Jeremy stepped forward to the parapet, brought his musket up across his chest. He took the match from the cock and blew on it. It was almost out, smothered under the bombardment. He blew again, the coal flaring, crackling, alive. Others passed a lighted match between them, faces glowing in the dark as they stepped forward, taking their places along the line. He pressed the glowing match back into the jaws of the musket cock, checked it would strike the centre of the priming pan and blew on it once more as the drums came on, nearer, louder, incessant.

He looked along the line. Order was returning, nerves calming with sure instruction, fear ebbing in familiar drill. But would they be ready? Could they hold the line, hold this redoubt against the cavalier hordes, against the King's army? Behind them, beyond the city, came the noise of another battle as their brethren fought to hold back the heathen Cornish. How long could they hold on?

Major Wood was beside them, the dark night thundering with the sound of drumming across their front. 'On my command!'

III

Temple Meads

Kendall Tremain
Temple Meads, before Bristol, a quarter
past three o'clock in the morning

The waggon plunged into the ditch with a splintering crash, a welter of flying planks, mud and water. It was supposed to fill the gap, form a bridge, let them charge across. Its shattered remains barely half filled the trench.

Another waggon disappeared into the ditch beside them. The ditch was vast, deeper, wider than they'd expected. It just swallowed the waggons whole.

'*Kidgia!*' Kendall slithered down the bank to the broken waggon. 'Come on! We can still cross.' He stepped warily in the dark, his feet seeking out the loose, twisted boards that formed a bridge across the void, steadying himself with his musket balanced across his chest. A leap and he was clambering up the far bank, out onto the far side. 'Come on! Are you *cog*?'

All along the ditch, men poured over the lip, disappeared into its dark depths, emerging again into the moonlight on the far bank, an army of tinners rising from the ground. Together, they surged forward, charging the last yards to the town wall. '*Onen hag oll!*' Again, together, one and all, they yelled their war cry. '*Kernow kensa!*'

———

Abel looked up from loading the gun. They were close now, the charging Cornish horde, the first wave swarming across the ditch to crash against the walls. Behind them, more battalions loomed out of the dark, an army of wild, heathen, barbarians that would plunder, rape and kill – soldier or citizen, rich or poor – without distinction. They would destroy all, leaving the common people, the oppressed, with nothing.

Flames lit up the night as the great guns crashed out from every tower along the wall, from Tower Harris to the hornwork at Bedminster Gate and from St Mary's Redcliffe. Beyond the town wall, the great church stood like a ship. Its great demi-culverin and sakers raked the heathen waves with case-shot, but still they came on. Muskets along the wall added their fire to pour shot down upon those that crossed the ditch. But still they came.

Israel ladled powder into the barrel, quickly, hurriedly, tamping it home, wadding and ramming as the Swede clamped the lid on the powder barrel. Abel cradled the next case-shot, a three-pound canister of saltpetre-soaked canvas that would burst on firing to spray its 234 pistol balls in a lethal hail. With a nod from the boatswain, he slid the case-shot into the muzzle, Israel driving it home before whipping the rammer out.

The boatswain looked up from priming the breach with pricker and horn. 'Run her out boys!' Together they grabbed the tackle. 'Heave!' The gun slid squealing across the stone floor on its ship's carriage, the muzzle jutting through one of the embrasures.

There was no need to aim the gun with staves. The bloody horde filled the meadow. With a grunt, the boatswain lifted the breach, knocked the quoin hard under it to force the muzzle down, pointing its lethal hail of shot at the ditch below.

'Stand clear!' The linstock came down against the breach. Again, the bright bursting jet of smoke, sparks and burning powder corns before the muzzle exploded in a ball of flame and thunderous roar, the gun leaping back and up against taut ropes to crash back down on the stone in a welter of tackle and iron fixtures.

———

Where were the ladders? Where were the bloody ladders? Shot rained down around them as they clung to the wall, pressed into its shadow, desperate to hide from the moon's glare. Kendall dragged his musket closer. Beside him, a pike-man cradled a boy with a shattered arm. They had crossed the ditch. They were ready to scale the walls. But where were the bloody the ladders? There were supposed to be teams following with ladders. Well, where the bloody hell were they?

Another group were moving forward towards them, across the meadow in the moonlight. Again, great tongues of flame lit up the night with their whistling hail of case-shot, the shadows of men caught in their blast swept away. Each time a group came forward, the great cannon on their mount beside the church swept the meadow in a murderess crossfire. The church rose like a fortress, stark in the moonlight, surrounded by open ground in the middle of the meadow. It was enormous, a wonderous great church – a cathedral. But this was a church filled with Puritans and their bloody cannon. St Mary's Redcliffe they called it.

'Alright boys! There's nothing more to be done!' It was

Colonel Slanning, still with them. 'If the ladders won't come to us, we must go back to fetch them. It's no good just sitting here. We can't scale the walls without them. On my order, we go back. At the double. We reform on the far side of the meadow and we come back with the bloody ladders.'

Back? Back, across the ditch and meadow? In the moonlight, with the bloody Puritan gunners on the walls and around St Mary's awake and watchful? *Re Satnaz!* This was bloody madness. Was there no other way? Where were the bloody *Sowsen* English? Were they just waiting for Cornwall?

'Alright! Everyone ready?' Slanning yelled. 'Carry the wounded. Together boys! Now!'

As one, they ran – out from the wall's shadow and into the moonlight – sliding, slithering down the bank into the dark ditch as the first shots from the wall behind smacked down around them. No time to find the waggons to cross over. Water black and deep up to his chest, Kendall waded, floundered, the taste of rank mud in his mouth, nose and throat. He clawed at the far bank, wet feet slipping in the mud, dragged his sodden body to the top, back into the moonlight.

Behind him, the pikeman struggled to drag the boy up the slope beside him, unable to get a purchase in the mud and clay. Together, the older man and boy slid back into the water.

Kendall looked across the meadow. Men were already running, following Colonel Slanning back to the safety of the hill. Kendall turned, let go of his musket and let himself slide back into the water. Together, he and the pikeman pushed and hauled the boy up the bank. The boy's body was limp, barely able to grip a hand, a lifeless wet lump of whimpering pain that sobbed with each heave. They lay at the top gasping for breath.

Together, they picked the boy up between them and

stumbled forward across the meadow. St Mary's Redcliffe loomed black against moon and stars as they tried to pass it. And then the open field filled with burning light, flame, crashing cannon fire and shrieking case-shot.

IV

'Oxford!'

Jeremy Holway
The Redoubt at Mile Hill, half past
three o'clock in the morning

Jeremy Holway stood at the wall of the redoubt. The cavalier drums were louder now, still hidden in darkness. They thrashed out the Preparative, the order to close ranks for the attack. Pinpricks of light ran in lines across the down, thousands of them, rank upon rank of musketeers, their burning match cords bobbing and swaying as they came on.

He looked about the redoubt: just one gun, a tiny falcon that fired a shot weighing barely more than a pound, the three-pounder minion upended and useless, a file of six pikemen and twenty musketeers. One gun and twenty-seven men to hold back an army, an army of delinquent cavaliers that would show no mercy, that would lynch and hang those they did not slaughter in their assault.

There was little chance of relief or reinforcement. Already, to the right, Priors Hill Fort was ablaze with the flash and thump of grenades and the rattle of musket fire, its bigger guns lighting the down with tongues of fire. To the left, flame lashed out from the Windmill Fort. Beyond it, Brandon Hill

Fort was engaged in an artillery duel with the cavalier battery on Clifton Hill. Across the harbour, beyond the city, another battle raged where their brethren fought to keep out the Cornish. And to the rear, behind Priors Hill, the sounds of attack rolled up from the hornwork at Stokes Croft and the highway to Gloucester. They were encompassed, surrounded, pressed on all sides.

To the front, the cavaliers were closer now, their drums loud, the rattle of kit and tramp of feet – thousands of feet – moving closer, faster. They were running, charging, led on by a block of fire-pikes. They would come out of the darkness, span the ditch and scale the walls. There was no stopping them. It would be too late.

Why here? Why now? Why him? This was not what he'd expected, not what they'd said would happen, not what he'd signed the muster roll for. He shouldn't be here. It'd been a misunderstanding – a terrible mistake. He should be protecting his wife, children, home and stock.

He needed to piss. He must beg leave from his corporal. He needed to go, to go now, to slip into the dark. He would feel better if he could just leave for a moment, leave to take a piss.

'Have a care!' It was Major Wood, his partizan raised. 'Gunners! Give. . . fire!'

———

They were running now, charging, the ground gently rising, dark against the stars. Moussa Dansocko slung the drum across his back and ran to keep up with Colonel Lunsford. They followed the road across the down, the road that came from a great river and the place where a boat crossed to Wales. They ran past a pair of cottages.

Great balls of flame flared ahead. The air vibrated, shrieking as it was ripped apart. A whirling *jinn* hurled earth, stones and grit from the road, smashed into the cottages. Thunder rolled over Moussa as his *dya*, his shadow, his spirit, was lost again in darkness. But no *jinn* could harm him. He was protected by the name of God in the *taweez* around his neck. *And whosoever fears Allah. . . He will open a way for him to escape.*

———

The guns had not stopped them, even with case-shot. Still the cavaliers came on, their shouting, yelling, clattering charge almost upon him. The down was afire with their flaming fire-pikes and dancing match-cords.

'Musketeers. . . have a care!' Major Wood was beside him, staring out across the ditch. Could the old soldier halt these cavaliers? 'On my order! You are to stay back from the parapet until I give the order to present.' But what if he left it too late? What if the cavaliers scaled the walls before they could present and fire?

The night burst with fire as the cavaliers poured a volley at the redoubt, ragged but vicious, shots drumming into the wall and wailing overhead in a welter of lead, grit and dust. A fizzing, spluttering hand-grenade thumped down on the floor of the redoubt. Jeremy stared at it as an old gunner stepped forward, snuffing out its fuse.

'Present!'

Jeremy stepped forward with his musketeers, stared down at the mass of cavaliers swarming into the ditch below, shadows leaping at the wall, driven on by their fire-pikes.

'Give. . . fire!'

The ditch exploded in flame, smoke and kicking, screaming bodies.

'Make ready! Fire at will!'

V

Washington's Breach

Ralph Reeve
Clifton Lane, daybreak

They were moving now, quickly, suddenly, downhill towards the rebel lines, stumbling in the twilight, the long, damp grass and furze snatching at boots, spurs, scabbards. Ralph gripped the fire-pike as another man fell cursing in the gloom. Ahead, the first sliver of dawn etched bloody Lansdown Hill on the far horizon. To the right and left, Brandon Hill and St Michael's Hill each loomed black, hunched, sullen. Between them, a dark hollow, ink black in their shadow, the moon unable to penetrate its depths, the rebel lines hidden, waiting.

They had woken with the sound of cannon on the far-side of the city, the Cornish army attacking early. Last-minute preparations, hurried orders, frantic packing of cloaks in the dark, loading of weapons and feverish pissing had followed before the horses were led away to the rear and the regiment stood in line, just in time for the signal, the two great demi-cannons firing on Priors Hill Fort. Colonel Belasyse's battery and the guns at Clifton Church had followed in a volley that echoed and shook the dark night, reverberating between the down and hills.

Now they were moving forward, on foot, the left-hand regiment of Colonel Wentworth's Tertia. To their right, Sir Jacob Astley's boys from Hereford, Fitton's Cheshire's, Bolle's Staffords and Herbert's Welsh descended the slope from Clifton to storm Brandon Hill. To their left, Colonel Belasyse's Tertia advanced on the line between St Michael's Hill and the Cotham road and, beyond them, Lord Grandison led his tertia in the assault on Priors Hill.

Still the rebel line lay in silence. Had they abandoned it? Were they running now, back down the hill to the old town walls and castle, to their homes and wives? Or were they waiting, holding their fire, keeping back until they were sure of their target, waiting for the moment when they would have greatest effect?

Ralph looked up at the fire-pike. Its tar-soaked rags blazed against the dark sky. A useful rally and marker for his division to follow in the gloom, it equally marked them out as targets. Other fire-pikes burned bright in the front rank of Washington's Dragoons, they swayed and dipped as the line swept on downhill.

And then the first great tongue of flame flared from the Windmill Fort on St Michael's Hill, followed by the shriek and crash of iron ripping through the cool night air. The fort on Brandon Hill followed in a lethal cross-fire, sheets of flame lighting up the hollow as the five and six-pound balls cleft paths of steaming flesh, grass, earth and stone.

The line was more ragged now, broken and disjointed as men either fell behind or stepped out, keen to close with the rebel line, to get beyond the cannon fire, beyond the killing ground, to get it over and done with. His own men were straggling in the dark. He had to keep them together. 'Keep close!' He lifted the fire-pike. 'Keep together!'

Almost at the bottom of the slope, the first volley of musket-shot crashed out from Brandon Fort. Thank God, it was aimed at those climbing the slope towards it. And then came a volley from up ahead, balls of flame in the dark, lead hissing past – musket fire from the rebel line. Etched in stark relief with each explosion, a ditch and wall blocked the lane at the base of the hollow. A half-dozen muskets fired, a single file of musketeers. Above them was a barn overhanging the track. Then darkness again.

'Close up!' Colonel Washington urged them forward. 'Keep moving!'

'You heard the colonel!' yelled Sergeant O'Brien. 'Shift yer feckin arses!'

More musket shots flared out from the line running up Brandon Hill. But they were below the forts, running now. Hidden from their cannon fire, they surged forward. They had to reach the ditch and wall before the next volley. Ralph levelled the fire-pike, boots flapping about his legs as he charged the last yards. 'Come on! With me!'

The barn loomed dark and solid above them, its bulk form- ing an angle, a spur in the rebel lines. Beyond it, the ditch and wall turned again to cut across the lane, a black void and dark solid mass. Ralph slid to the bottom of the ditch, the fire-pike dipping and spluttering to illuminate its rocky depths. It was six feet across, almost as deep, the far bank rising in a contin- uous slope to the top of the wall ten feet above.

Luke slid into the ditch beside him, then Sam, Jack, Jewkes, others he did not recognise. They had become disordered in the dark. From above them came the clatter of musketeers loading behind the wall. Fuck! Where was Clem? 'Clem? Where's Clem?'

Luke peered back into the dark. 'He was just behind me.'

'He stopped to help Sergeant O'Brien.' Jack caught his breath. 'Back on the road there.'

Above them, scouring sticks rattled in musket barrels. 'Present!' The order to take aim rang out from the wall above.

'Fuck!' Ralph leaped at the wall, his boots scrabbling for purchase, hauling at its surface, only to slide back down in a welter of earth and stones.

'Give. . . fire!' The air above their heads exploded in sheets of flame.

'No!' Ralph clawed at the bank, slipping, sliding back again. 'Clem!'

'Master Ralph?'

It was Clem. Thank God! 'Clem, are you alright?' He was alive. 'Where are you?'

'I be here.' Clem came around the corner of the ditch, from under the barn, wreathed in gunsmoke. 'Lost you in the dark I did. Well, are we going to just sit in this here ditch waiting to be shot or are we going t' git over that there wall?'

'Make ready!' Already, the musketeers were loading above them.

'Ralph, Clem is right.' Luke looked concerned. 'We must clear the wall before the next volley. Can we use the grenade? Or must we wait for orders?'

'Where is Sergeant O'Brien?'

'He be the other side of that barn. He were following the colonel and Captain Norwood.'

'Fuck it. We use it. Clem, take the fire-pike. Luke, do you have it?'

'Yes, it's here.' Luke handed him the grenade.

Ralph weighed the unfamiliar iron sphere in his hand, checked its fuse was firmly in place. 'Luke, please cover me, shoot any rebel that sticks his fucking head out. Clem, be ready with that fire-pike. The rest of you, keep low, keep your heads down.' He stood in the corner of the ditch. What if the grenade exploded early? Or if it rolled back into the ditch? Or the fuse was too long and the rebels threw it back? His division would be decimated if it exploded in the ditch amongst them. He braced a leg against the bank. 'Now Clem. . . hold the fire-pike steady.' He touched the end of the fuse to the flaming pike. It spluttered alight, crackling, spitting, showering sparks over his hand.

Ralph weighed the grenade again, watched the fuse burn, guessed that it was the moment just before it would ignite the charge. He leaned back, arm extended and lobbed the great iron ball over the wall. He saw it clear the lip, a fiery blur in the night sky, before he too put his head down. A sheet of flame, crashing explosion, shrieks of pain and terror and a trickle of earth rolled back from the top of the wall.

'Come you on Master Ralph!' Clem was handing him the fire-pike, holding out cupped hands, bracing himself against the wall. 'Let me give you a leg-up. Git yourself up there afore they know what hit 'em.' Ralph thrust a boot into Clem's open hands. 'Just like going a-scrumping for apples.' Another boot on Clem's shoulder and he was up on top of the wall. Beside him, others were helping each other up the wall, scrambling up its slope. 'Come on!' Fire-pike in hand, Ralph stood on its flat top, fanned the flames in a sweeping arc. 'Get over while you can!'

Luke was up beside him, others rising around them. Together, they slid down the far side to stand with their backs to the wall. A body at their feet, the stench of black powder hanging in the dark. To their right, the barn ran back into the hill, light spilling out at its far end. A door. . . Musketeers filing through it into the barn. Then darkness – the door slammed shut. 'Luke, the barn! We must storm the barn!' A musket exploded from a window above them. Others fired on the far side of the barn. 'Now! Before they can defend it properly!'

'Who put fire to that grenade?' Fuck! It was Sergeant O'Brien. His bulk dropped down the wall beside them in the dark.

'I used the grenade, Sergeant O'Brien.'

'Did I tell ye to use it? Did I give ye permission? They're not for throwing around as you like. And why have yiz not pulled down this wall like yiz were ordered?'

'I thought we should clear the barn of rebels first. They are still firing from it.'

'You were thinking were ye? Well, come on then! Let's be getting on with it. Before they shoot us all down. Or are you wantin' for a grenade to do the job? It's as well I still have the other one, so it is. Now this is how we are goin' to do it. We get up close under the barn wall. I drop the grenade through a window slot. We keep our heads down until it has fired. Then, Ralph – an' only then – you stick the fire-pike in and the rest of you give fire. I don't care if you cannot see your mark. You shoot inside the barn. Then, we storm the door and club the bastards to death. Do I make meself clear? Good. Now, let's be getting on with it.'

The grenade exploded inside the barn in a burst of light, noise and shower of slates from the roof. Ralph rammed the fire-pike into the darkness, dust and smoke that followed as the others fired through the slatted door and window slots, each shot crashing out in the enclosed space until silenced by yells for quarter from inside. Finally, the great barndoor swung open.

As each of what was left of the defenders staggered out of the barn, Sergeant O'Brien knocked them to the ground.

'Now, get these feckers bound, hands an' feet. And get that wall pulled down to let the others through, like the colonel ordered.'

Ralph left Sergeant O'Brien kicking the prostrate prisoners in the dark. He, Luke, Clem, Hodge, Jack and the others set about the wall. They stuck swords into its face to prize out rocks and clods of turf. They dug into the loose earth behind to drag it down, dust and damp filling their nostrils, gritting cuffs and collars. On the top of the wall and on the far side, more dragoons kicked and dug at the slope to fill the ditch. Soon, they had made a gap wide enough for four men abreast to march up and over. It was enough.

'Well done.' Captain Norwood strode through the breach. 'Well done all. Well done indeed. Ah, Sergeant O'Brien.'

'Thankin' you, sir.' Sergeant O'Brien appeared beside them, doffing his hat. 'I took the liberty of storming the barn, sir. Four rebels taken. One of them is an officer, wounded he is. And a couple killed.'

'Very well. Please find Colonel Washington and inform him that we have breached the rebel lines. Reeve, take your division along the wall towards the Windmill Fort. Hold back any rebels that charge from that direction while I get the rest of the troop across. Mister Bellamy!'

VI

Wildfire!

Francis Reeve
St Michael's Hill, a quarter past
four o'clock in the morning

They were inside the lines. The army of Satan had breached the wall. They had entered at the spur-work, beside the barn. They must be thrown back, the breach made good. This was the work of the horse, of God's troopers. Francis urged his horse forward in the grey half-light, pricking it into a stumbling trot with his spurs.

Praise God! At last, they were moving! They trotted downhill, out from behind the Windmill Fort, down St Michael's Hill towards the breach. They rode across open ground. To their left lay the suburbs, harbour and old town, still dark in the valley, lights at the windows of Godly citizens waking to Hell's host at their gates. Beyond the city, cannon fire flashed from Temple Gate and great St Mary Redcliffe fighting to hold back the heathen Cornish horde.

To their right, the line's earthen bank swept downhill to the barn and spur. Beyond, Brandon Fort still blazed out with cannon and musket fire. But at the base of the slope, around the barn, dark figures poured through a gap in the lines, a hundred pin-pricks of burning match led on by devils with fire-pikes; the wall breached, their scourge spilling out onto the lane that led downhill to the city.

———

Ralph led the way as they steadily climbed St Michael's Hill, following the rebel line. They stuck to the inside of the wall, fire-pike held high, the open ground sloping away to the city below. He did not want to be mistaken in the half-light for a rebel and shot by those still outside the breach.

Above them, ahead of them, the Windmill Fort still belched flame, iron and lead. Thank God, its fire was aimed at Belasyse's Tertia and those still fighting to get inside the rebel line. There had been a couple of musket shots from further up the wall, from the ravelin, but now it seemed clear, empty, abandoned. And yet. Something was moving. To the rear of the Windmill Fort, something, somebody, some troop was on the move.

Ralph stopped, put his hand up for silence, stared into the gloom. Fuck! 'Horse! Rebel horse! There – behind the fort. They are coming this way.'

It was too late to warn Captain Norwood. The breach was a hundred yards behind them now. He must try to halt the rebels before they charged, before they smashed into those still in disorder around the breach. Stop them before they plugged the gap, before they sealed the breach. But, could he do it, could they do it? They were just eleven men – half of them boys. He was alone. No sergeant. No officer.

He thrust the fire-pike into the ground. 'Come on, up onto the wall. We form a line! *On* the wall. We must fire on the rebel horse before they charge. We must break them. Before they cut our boys down.'

———

Francis gripped his pistol as they rode in line across the open ground towards the breach and the apostates pouring through it. Where was Major Langrish and his troop? This was their part of the line. They were supposed to throw back any cavaliers that breached the wall between the Windmill Fort and Brandon Fort. That was how it was ordered by the Governor. But where were they? The cavaliers were filing through the breach unmolested. There were a hundred, perhaps two hundred of them inside the walls already. Thank the Lord, they were only foot soldiers. And they were not yet formed in a body. There was no cavalier horse and no pike block.

Now was the time to break them, to cut them down, to secure the breach, trap those inside and throw back those that followed. He and his troop must strike now. Strike them before they formed in a body, strike hard with pistol and sword – with or without Langrish and his troop – before it was too late. The line jerked into a trot, the horses shaking out their stiffness as the troop gathered pace. Theirs would be the glory, the glory of saving this city and its precious harbour. The Lord was bountiful in his offering. *As birds flying, so will the Lord of hosts defend Jerusalem; defending also he will deliver it; and passing over he will preserve it.*

Ahead, a single fire-pike burned beside the wall. He had not noticed it before. They would pass close to it. Was it some sort of mark, some devilish trick?

———

Ralph checked the flint was firmly held in its jaws before pulling back the snaphaunce cock of his carbine. The lock clicked into place. He slid the weapon up into his shoulder. "Those of you with matchlocks, guard your coals, keep them hidden till we fire. On my command, we give them one salvee, then fire at will. We keep firing until we break their charge."

He looked along the line, looked at his division, a line of anxious faces peering into the gloom ahead of them. Jack, grim, determined; Jewkes glaring; Sam's furrowed brow; a nod from Clem and Tandy; Kibler missing; and Luke. . . Luke calm as ever, at the far end. They lay across the top of the wall, their legs hanging down the bank. At least it would give them some protection. Thank God, the down and sky behind were still in darkness. They would cloak their silhouette.

The fire-pike spluttered, wavering in the pre-dawn still. It cast a pool of acrid light where he had stuck it into the ground a little down the hill, perhaps ten paces to their right. With any luck, it would draw the attention and fire of the rebel horsemen, while his boys lay in the shadows. God, let the rebels ride within range before they saw them on the wall.

Memories of the ambush before Aylesbury came flooding back. The tension of waiting, hiding until the right moment. Then the chaos of the ambush sprung, the terror of the escape and shear bloody joy of getting away with it. But this time there was no Corporal Nisbet to give the order, no Sergeant O'Brien and no Captain Norwood. It was up to him now. He had to judge the moment, make sure they stopped the rebels. And he had to keep his boys safe.

———

They were close to the line now, almost past the lone fire-pike. Nothing moved about it. Just the shifting of its own light against the dark earth of the wall. Francis gathered in the reins, held his pistol high and focused on the Babylonian horde disgorging from the breach. Now was the time to strike, to strike with the sword of Christ.

He clamped spurs to his horse's flanks as the line jerked into a canter. Boot to boot, they surged forward. This would be the Lord's victory.

———

Ralph pulled the carbine into his shoulder. The rebel troop were closer now, dark shapes against the lightening Eastern sky, a long line of armoured horsemen, three deep, thudding hooves and jangling harness preceding them. There were too many of them. He could not hope to stop them. He had been foolish – foolhardy. O'Brien would delight in his failure. He should have run to warn Norwood. It was too late. And yet. . .

'Aim low.' Ralph curled his finger around the trigger. 'Aim for their mounts. Make your shots count. On my command. . .'

They were almost level now. A horse snorted, shaking its head, dancing sideways. It had seen them, sensed them. It was now or never.

'Give fire!'

———

The wall burst in a blaze of light, the air fizzing with shot as the crash of muskets hit them. A horse collapsed in a ball of screaming, thrashing, whinnying legs, iron shoes and leather harness. Another bolted, throwing its rider as it kicked and bucked across the front of the troop. There were curses and shouts as a second trooper slid from his saddle under the hooves of the ranks that followed.

Francis hauled on his reins as his horse leaped sideways cannoning into the next file, crushing his leg between them as the whole line staggered sideways. Riders fought with their mounts as each beast tried to flee, eyes white, ears back, teeth bared in terror. Together, as one, the herd turned away from the wall and its crashing muskets to gallop in a wide arc across the open ground and back uphill towards the Windmill Fort.

Gradually, yard by yard, Francis slowed his horse, holstering his pistol to haul back on the reins with both gauntleted hands. All around him, troopers hauled in their mounts, turning their tossing heads back to face downhill again. The animals stood shaking, bathed in sweat, before walking stiffly back into line, heads and tails twitching in the cool grey light.

Sweat soaked the inside of Francis's buff coat, clammy about his tightly tied collar and under his helmet. He pushed back his visor and let the heat and frustration rise from him. Damn the devils that hid along the wall. Damn them for their raking fire. Damn his horse for its fear and brute strength. Damn his fellow troopers for their failure. Did they not see the import of their task? Did they not feel God's purpose?

Thank God they had run no further. Thank God they had not fled after Langrish and his troop of faithless sinners. There could be no more than a dozen musketeers on the wall. Now they knew what faced them. Now they must finish the Lord's work with pistol and sword.

———

'Well done, Reeve!' Captain Norwood rasped. 'Well done all of you. . .' He was out of breath, from climbing the hill, the rest of his troop straggling behind him, Sergeant O'Brien bringing up the rear, pushing Kibler before him. 'You did well. But they may be back, and soon. They cannot leave the breach unchallenged. And while we have barely formed a rank to defend ourselves. The pikes are not yet formed.'

'Thank you, sir.' Ralph slid down from the top of the wall. 'I am sorry we did not scatter the rebel horse completely. They are reforming now. We can see them from the top of the wall, on the crest of the hill, just behind the Windmill Fort.'

'Very well. Mister Bellamy, please get the troop formed up, three ranks, rear rank on the wall, the first two ranks in front of it. Sergeant O'Brien, please re-join your division.'

'Right ye are, sir.' O'Brien gasped. 'Yiz heard the captain! Luke, Hodge, Jack, get your arses down here. Where the feck d' ye think yer goin', Kibler? You stay down here, where I can see you. Clem, and the rest o' yiz – as you bloody well were on that wall. Form three ranks. Now! If your piece is not loaded, make ready!'

———

They were moving forward again, slowly, hesitantly at first. Again, Francis pulled his faceguard down to meet his breast-plate. Again, he drew a pistol from its holster. He pulled back the cock, releasing the doglock. He dug spurs into the flanks of his horse as they lurched stiffly into a trot. Another touch to the beast's bloodied belly and they sprung into a canter. Tight-packed, they surged forward, three ranks of horsemen.

Ahead, the mass of cavaliers about the breach, clearer now in the blue pre-dawn light. Perhaps three hundred were inside the line, a half-formed pike block and a ragged line of musketeers before them. God had been generous. There was still time to break them, to seize the breach, seal their fate as lambs to the slaughter, to cut them down and offer them up, a worthy sacrifice. *For into his hand hath God delivered Midian, and all the host.*

The fire-pike was still there, beside the wall. Now there were two more, a dozen musketeers or dragoons on the wall, more lurking in front of its dark mass. Their path was further from the wall this time, but they would still be within range of these cavaliers. There was no choice if they were to charge downhill, no time to take a wider route. The Lord had ordained it, they must trust in Him. *Be strong in the Lord, and in the power of his might.*

———

'Make ready to give fire by salvee!' Captain Norwood stood with sword raised. 'Present!'

Knelt in the front rank, Ralph pulled the carbine butt into his shoulder. The rebel horse were further away this time, but still the drumming of hooves and rattle of harness swept across the slope to wash against the wall behind. He steadied his breathing, squinted along the barrel. They were almost level with them now. It was now or never. Thank Christ, it was not up to him this time. Fuck, it even felt good to have Sergeant O'Brien beside him.

Captain Norwood stepped forward. 'Give. . .' His sword sliced down. 'Fire!'

———

The wall exploded in a sheet of flame, shot shrieking through their ranks as the thunder of a musket volley crashed into them. The line staggered, faltered, men and horses falling, flailing, screaming as the ranks behind rode over them.

Francis forced his horse on, digging spurs into its heaving flanks. And then the trumpet call, the call to charge. His horse's head came up, the line recovered, surged forward. *Now will I arise saith the Lord, now will I be exalted, now will I lift up myself!*

They careered downhill, drummed the last yards, reigning

back hard, hooves sliding to a halt just yards from the cavalier horde, horse heads tossing, snorting, stamping. A hedge of pikes swayed before them. But, praise the Lord, the pike block was barely formed, a knot of apostate scum in a jumble of coats pushed together, their pikes disordered, wavering in the dawn light. The musketeers were no better, sergeants still pushing men into line with their halberds. Now was the time, now was the moment to break them.

Francis stood high in his stirrups, levelled the pistol, took aim at a blue-coated pikeman – some poor farm-labourer dragged from his village to fight for a Babylonian king. It did not matter. Just another depraved sinner to be cut down. His soul was stained, damned from creation, irredeemable. No matter what good deeds he had accomplished, they would not save him. He lacked perfect faith. He stood with the apostate horde. Those who moved against the children of the promise shall be rooted out with the *sharp arrows of the mighty, with coals of juniper*.

Tongues of flame flared along the line of horsemen, pistols crashing in a ripple of fire. His gauntleted finger closed around the trigger. The pistol whipped back and up as the charge exploded in his grip – horse leaping, tossing, stamping, ears flat with fear, teeth bared. Francis holstered the smoking weapon, grabbed at both reins, hauled the beast back into line.

The pikeman was on his knees, clutching at his belly, blood, gore, sin spreading in a dark stain about him. His prayers for redemption were too late. His death was ordained, the blessing of absolute faith ungiven. He was not chosen. His name was not written.

The pikes staggered back, musketeers recoiling with them, pressing back against the mass about the breach. All along the cavalier front, men grasped at wounds or writhed on the ground kicking, clawing, choking in their own blood. Better they die now than fill the ranks of Satan's horde in the final battle at the End of Times.

Now was the time to break them, to seal the breach, to reap the sacrifice, to cut them down. *And the slain of the Lord shall be at that day from one end of the earth even unto the other end of the earth. They shall not be lamented, neither gathered in, nor buried. They shall be dung upon the ground!* Francis drew his sword, its heavy blade rasping in the scabbard's steel mouth. *And their carcasses shall be meat for the fowls of heaven, and for the beasts of the earth.*

———

The rebel horse were forcing back those around the breach, threatening to charge home, seize back the barn and wall – cut them off. Ralph thumped the scouring stick down in the barrel, ramming the wad, ball and charge home. He whipped the stick out, reversed it and slid it back into its groove before bringing the carbine back up across his chest. But there was no chance of a second shot. The bloody rebels were too close to those at the breach. A shot that missed its mark would strike their own men.

'With me!' Norwood stepped forward. 'Stay close! We hit them from the flank!'

'Right. You heard the Captain!' Sergeant O'Brien barked. 'Down from that feckin' wall! Look lively now! You too, Kibler. I'm watching ye.'

Ralph slung his carbine, plucked up the fire-pike hissing and spluttering as he swung it forward to step off beside O'Brien. Norwood strode ahead, Gabriel the trumpeter trailing behind him. They moved quickly, striding across the rough open ground: a nod from Luke; Sam hunched, ready;

Jack, his scar vivid, musket butt before him; Tandy behind him, grinning; Jewkes wild and glaring; only Kibler lagging, stumbling at the rear.

'Alright, Master Ralph.' Clem, dear Clem strode a pace behind him, covering his back as always. 'I'm a-with you.'

———

Francis pushed his horse forward, his gauntleted fist tight around the sword hilt. The Babylonian horde shrunk back, a fearful rabble. Here and there an officer wielded a devilish fire-pike urging, pushing, prodding them into line like frightened cattle. The stench of their fear hung in the cool morning air the reek of beasts, of saltpetre, of sin.

———

'Give. . .' Norwood's sword swung down. 'Fire!'

The carbine kicked in his shoulder. The dark bulk of a horse staggering, falling sideways. Ralph threw the smoking weapon across his back, snatching up the fire-pike again.

'Now!' The captain levelled his sword as he leapt through the smoke. 'Charge!'

It was madness. Insane. To charge mounted horsemen, on foot.

'Jesus save us!' O'Brien turned to follow. 'Well, come on then! Kill the bastards!'

Fuck it! Ralph leapt forward, the fire-pike held high. 'Oxford!'

———

The air was suddenly filled with flying shot. A horse collapsing, kicking, iron hooves thrashing in the ranks. Another rearing, screaming. Two, three troopers slumped in their saddles. Francis yanked his horse back, twisting the iron bit in its mouth to keep it from bolting.

'Right!' Captain Nevill was yelling, turning his horse. 'To the right!'

———

Norwood was almost amongst them. A horse turning, an armoured horseman, his pistol levelled. Jesus, no! The pistol sparked, flared, exploded in a ball of flame throwing Norwood back, his sword falling, face clutched in his hands.

'No!' Ralph thrust the fire-pike at the horseman, swung it at the horse's head. The animal reared, eyes white, teeth bared in terror. He thrust again, ramming the flaming torch into its neck, mane flaring, sizzling.

The animal shrieked, reared higher, forelegs flailing. The armoured rider fell crashing to the ground as the horse bolted. Norwood was on his feet again, his sword driving into the horseman's neck.

Captain Norwood stepped back. He spat and swore. 'God damn!' He turned, his eyes bloodshot, face livid with powder burns. 'Thank you, Reeve! I am grateful. That fire-pike did the feat better than carbine or sword.'

Beyond the captain, the rest of the rebel troop were turning away, fleeing, their horses terrified by the fire-pikes and sudden charge, lost in a kicking, bucking race to stay with the herd. Luke and Sam held a wounded prisoner while Clem knelt beside a dying horse. O'Brien stood over a writhing horseman, his sword raised. The sword thrust down through the bars of the man's helmet. Again and again, O'Brien drove his sword into the man's flailing arms and face until the bloody corpse finally lay still. Over all hung the smell of gunsmoke and burnt horsehair.

Francis hung onto the saddle as his horse careered after its fleeing companions. There was nothing he could do to slow or halt its headlong gallop. He was not a skilled or strong enough rider. As a herd, they raced across the open ground in a great arc across St Michael's Hill. Below them, the suburbs, oldtown and harbour lay open, unprotected in the valley. The defensive lines were breached. Hell's host were inside the walls.

Why did God try them so? He must not question. It was the Lord's will, part of His unknowable, divine plan. He must trust in the Lord. He alone could carry the light out of darkness, create order from confusion. He alone controlled nature. The setting and rising of the sun were above the comprehension of man. God alone would bring deliverance.

'Well done, Norwood.' Colonel Washington clapped the captain on the shoulder. 'Well done indeed. Ah, O'Brien. I thought you might be involved. Well done. Well done all.'

All about them, officers and dragoons, musketeers and pikemen congratulated them. Ralph could not help but return Clem's grin and Luke's nod as the first rays of sun broke over Lansdown Hill and the horizon. The breach was secure, with yet more of Colonel Wentworth's Tertia pouring through it in the dawn sunlight. The lane that led downhill towards Bristol was theirs. It was open, unguarded, the last of the rebel horse gone.

Cannon and musket fire still hammered out from the fort on Brandon Hill, from the Windmill Fort and beyond, on the line to Priors Hill Fort. And then the crash of cannon far below, across the river at Temple Gate. The Cornish must be attacking again. They must still be trying to scale the town walls. After an hour and a half, with two armies assaulting on three sides of the city, this was the only breach.

'Now. We need to press on, seize the moment.' Colonel Washington pointed to the lane. 'I want to thrust into the suburbs. I don't care about widening the breach. That can come later. Leave it to the bloody foot. I don't want to wait for Colonel Wentworth, or Prince Rupert for that matter. I want to press on into the suburbs now. I want to seize the Frome Gate, the town if we can, before the damned rebels recover.

'Captain Norwood, your troop has done well. They are in better order than most. You are hurt, but I must ask you to lead the way, as vanguard. Can you lead them?'

'It will be an honour, sir. Just a few powder burns, nothing more. Thank God.'

'Very well. The rest of the regiment will follow. Are there any question? Good. Then lead on. Let us take this city.'

VII

'They Run! They Run!'

George Merrett
Colonel Belasyse's Battery, Cotham Hill,
half past four o'clock in the morning

George Merrett snapped the watch shut. It was a half past four of the clock. Almost sunrise. For an hour and a half, the foot had assaulted the rebel defences and still there was no breach. For an hour and a half, they had thrown themselves at the ditch, scarp and forts only to be beaten back. Now it was daylight, all surprise and advantage lost in a foolish attempt to seize the city quickly. He thrust the watch into his pocket, turning to pace backwards and forwards behind his battery. There was nothing more he or his guns could do.

Damn the Cornish for attacking early. Damn them for not waiting for daybreak, for not waiting for the signal guns. Damn them for their wild, stupid disobedience. And damn the rest of the foot for attacking without preparation. Damn them all for insisting on an assault. Why could they not wait for the guns to affect a breach, approach trenches to be dug? At the very least, they should have taken time to prepare wood faggots to fill the ditches and scaling ladders for the walls. As it was, all sense and advantage were squandered, lost in the charge to be the first amongst the King's enemies, the first to show their valour, discarded in the scramble for honour and preferment, all hope of overwhelming the rebels lost in needless chaos.

The cost was counted in the ever-growing numbers of dead and wounded that lay on the down around the battery. The King could ill afford to lose yet more of his precious foot. Not here, not when they should be building their forces for the push on London, the real prize. Seizing Bristol would clear the West Country and give the King a port for his army in Ireland to return, if peace in that accursed realm could ever be achieved. But not at any cost. Not if it weakened the King's forces, not if it put seizing London in jeopardy.

Captain Fawcett had returned from the attempt on the gate at Stokes Croft. He was exhausted, cut, dust-covered. He had succeeded in fixing his petard to the gate, despite the high hornwork, gun and musketeers that protected it. The petard had blown as it should, shattering some of the timbers. The Lord General's Regiment of Foot charged with hand-grenades, forced pistols and pikes through the bars. But the gate held. Twenty men lay dead about the gate, lost to no advantage.

At Priors Hill, Colonel Dutton's boys and Earl Rivers' Cheshires had reached the ditch a second time, only to be cut down by case-shot and musket, thrown back, unable to scale the walls. Lord Grandison had been shot through the leg and Colonel Owen shot in the face. And all for nothing. They had thrown themselves at a fort, well built with ditch, scarp and palisade of stakes and mounted with four guns. And they had made this assault with only one ladder between them, one ladder prepared for an entire tertia of foot. Not a single man had got upon the top of the wall.

George had seen for himself Colonel Belasyse's Yorkshire-men, Stradling's Welsh and Lunsford's local Somerset boys charge the rebel redoubt and line in front of his battery. Again, they had attempted an assault, running at the defences with no faggots or scaling ladders. Colonel Belasyse and so many had been wounded. Now they licked their wounds, huddled together in clumps on the down. Others lay dead before the line. The attack had been a disaster. Only God knew if there was enough powder and shot for another attempt.

George stopped pacing, stood, stared. Before him was old Nick Busy's culverin, the grass still matted with the old gun captain's blood. Why? Why could they not have done it properly, carefully, with preparation and order? Why did it have to end in chaos? He sat on the empty budge barrel, his hand shaking, exhaustion washing over him.

———

Moussa Dansocko beat the drum. They were beating the call again. They were almost back where they started, beating the call that began the attack. It was a mess. They had woken in the dark, charged against the great guns of *Ogun*, run into the ditch. But they had no ladders, no way of climbing the wall. It was chaos. The King's soldiers were cut down, slaughtered. They had been forced back, forced to retreat, run from the enemy walls. Now they beat the drums to call the soldiers back to their flags, call them back into line, while shots still whirred overhead.

Nobody had told him what was to happen. Nobody had explained what to do. Colonel Lunsford was wounded, shot through the arm, huddled in council with the great *jatigi*, Prince Rupert, his chiefs and captains – messengers running in all directions. Corporal Stokes stood in line with his blue-coated musketeers. The drum-major just shouted. Moussa had done his best to follow the other drummers, to learn their beats, to master the drum with its two sticks. He wanted to play well for his *jatigi*. He beat the drum. But he could not make it talk, the skins were dead, the sound dull. There was no *nyama* – no power in it.

He had thought these men were great warriors, thought that they knew what they were doing. God in his infinite wisdom had given the English the power to sail the oceans, master iron and gunpowder. But these *'ajanib* lived like pigs – unclean, unshaven, drunk and stinking of sour cheese. They knew nothing of true faith, charity, abstinence. They knew nothing of duty, of respect for women or their elders. And they were incapable of *jihad*, of striving to live and die in the true cause of God. They were savages that preyed on those that were weaker, poorer, older. They delighted in their conquests, bragged of their humiliation and abuse of others. They were no better than a pack of dogs that had turned upon themselves, fighting over this cold, damp dunghill of an island.

How was he to fulfil his duty to his mistress if the *jatigi* and his soldiers could not break the enemy walls? He had promised to guide Colonel Lunsford into the city to rescue her, her mother and the young ones. Did God expect him to do it alone?

A rider reigned in hard, swept his hat from his head, bowed low to the prince. The drum-major gave a nod, the drumming stopped. A great shout rose from among the captains, the clapping of backs, shaking of hands. Prince Rupert mounted, smiling and gathered the reins of his great warhorse. Colonel Lunsford bowed stiffly. Lieutenant-Colonel Moyle faced them, faced Colonel Lunsford's Regiment, raised his hat and yelled. 'They run! They run!' A great roar rose from the ranks. Again, the chief yelled. 'To the breach, boys! The rebels run!'

The prince gave a wave of his hat, his horse rearing before thundering away at a canter towards Priors Hill and the tertia still fighting there, his dog racing after him.

Jeremy Holway stood at the parapet, on watch while others rested, slumped down where they'd fought. A lone cavalier rode across the down. A damned officer, a poxy plumed courtier on a great charger, only a dog for escort. His path would cross in front of the redoubt set forward of the line, bring the delinquent close enough for a shot. He should wait for an order, save his powder and shot. There was little chance of hitting a man, let alone a moving rider at this range.

Pox on it! Jeremy blew on his match and levelled the musket. Resting it across the parapet, he took aim. He pulled the butt tight, held his breath, braced, gently squeezing the trigger arm. The match thrust down, a jet of sparks from the pan, the musket thumping into his shoulder.

Gunsmoke rolled back over the wall, clearing. The cavalier was gone. No! There. The horse thrashing and whinnying on the ground, the dog barking. The poxy delinquent cut down!

Major Woods was at his side, others waking, standing, staring out. The cavalier stood, dusted himself down. The horse fell back, unmoving, dead. Damn the cavalier whoreson for living. But he'd think again before riding so close. The major clapped Jeremy on the shoulder. 'Fine shot, Holway! Fine shot!'

Christ was with them. They'd halted the cavalier charge, thrown the recusants back, held the line against cannonade, grenade, pike and shot. Now the delinquent fools were marching away, gone to lick their wounds. Bristol was saved. *For the Lord fought for Israel.*

———

Moussa saw the prince fall. The ranks swayed, shook in horror. Praise be to God, the great *jatigi* prince stood, waved his hat again before setting off again on foot, alone except for his dog, across the down, as if nothing had happened.

VIII

The Essex Work

Ralph Reeve
Stony Hill, Bristol suburbs, sunrise

The lane sloped gently downhill towards the suburbs. They moved quickly in loose order, Captain Norwood striding ahead in the sun's first warmth, Gabriel beside him. Ralph could not help but smile. They were inside the defences, the suburbs and oldtown open before them. They had made the breach and beaten back the rebel horse. And now they were the vanguard, leading the way for Colonel Wentworth, Prince Rupert and the whole of the King's army to follow. From across the lane, Luke returned a nod, Sam loped, alert as ever, Jack stepping out. Behind them, a grin from Tandy, Jewkes shambling, Clem smiling back. Behind them, Kibler still wheezed, puffing and chuntering under his breath.

The lane curved and steepened – darker, in shadow between high garden walls. The fire-pike sputtered, spent, black and charred. Ralph chucked it aside, unslung his carbine and checked the flint in its cock. A house loomed tall and solid, its windows staring out over the lane and city. It was quiet, thank God. More houses lined the road and suburbs beyond. The pace slowed. They moved more cautiously now, the smiles gone. And then Captain Norwood stopped, his hand raised.

Ahead a dark scar ran across the road. Beyond, a structure jutted out from the hillside, high banked, massive – a fortification. It dominated the road and the suburbs around, looking out over the hillside and houses to the harbour and old town beyond. They had not expected this. There had been no intelligence, no warning of an inner ring of defences, just the old town walls and castle to deal with.

'Sergeant O'Brien. . .' The captain looked grave. 'Please take your division to the left. Encircle this defensive work from the hillside above. Find a way through the gardens. Find a place where we can fire down into it. If needed, where we can gain entry. The rest of the troop will follow. Mister Bellamy. Please remain here on the road. Inform Colonel Washington and those following that we have encountered a defensive work and that the road is ditched.'

'You heard the captain.' Sergeant O'Brien spat on the road and gave a flick of his chin. 'Reeve, take Sam, Tandy, Clem and lead the way, now. I want to find a house that looks down on this here little fort. I'll follow along with Luke and the rest of them. Kibler, you stick close to me, now, where I can see ye. Well now, let's be getting on with it.'

They forced open a gate in the wall, slipped into the garden beyond and fanned out across its neat parterre, gravel crunching underfoot. Clem and Tandy cut a way through a hedge to an orchard beyond. Ralph led the way quietly, stealthily between the fruit trees. Memories of the garden in Brentford flooded back, memories of an innocent touch and of furtive lovemaking under a pear tree, rolling on the warm damp grass. But that was a year since, a lifetime ago. Now he was a soldier, a corporal leading a division of dragoons to attack a fort deep inside a rebel city.

The back door of the house gave in with a splintering crash. They were in. An old man, a hunched old merchant, blocked the passage, shaking, his stick raised. Ralph pushed him aside.

'Tandy, guard this doorway and show Sergeant O'Brien the way in. Sam, check for others and secure the ground floor. Don't let anyone escape. They must not warn the fort.' Ralph took the stairs two at a time. 'Clem, upstairs with me. Check each room.'

Ralph pushed the chamber door wide. There was a shriek – a frightened old woman and two gasping maids. 'Stay still and stay quiet, and nothing will befall you.' The window looked down on the fort. He raised his carbine. But the fort was empty, deserted, abandoned, its far gate open.

IX

Slanning's Charge

Kendall Tremain
Pine Hill, before Temple Meads,
five o'clock in the morning

Kendall crouched behind the hedge. His musket gone, the ladder lay at his feet, ready for the charge. Beside him, others waited with great faggots of wood and more ladders, mixed with musketeers in open order. Behind them waited more plotoons of musketeers and Slanning's pikes in reserve. To left and right stood Lord Mohun's Regiment and Trevanion's Foot, beyond them, Grenville's and Godolphin's – Cornishmen all – then Prince Maurice's Devons, The Marquis of Hertford's Somersets and Colonel Buck's Hampshires. Hopton's Western Army waited for the order to advance, waited for the signal gun.

On the far side of the hedge, the meadow stretched out: open, flat, swallows skimming low over the grass warming in the dawn sun. Overhead, larks rose singing while gulls circled high in the still, blue sky. But beyond the meadow was the ditch – deep, waterlogged and mud filled – and then the town walls with their towers, guns and muskets. And looming over all was St Mary's Redcliffe, serene spires, pinnacles and buttresses stretching heavenward, glinting in the sun, a majestic cathedral to God, bigger even than Bath Abbey. He'd never seen a building like it. It had to be wonderous up close, its great nave glorious to sing in. But at its base, Puritan cannon crouched, waiting to sweep away the old ways, the true Church and all that was beautiful. In the far distance, along the ridge beyond the town, beyond the harbour, a battle raged as the roundheads threw back Prince Rupert's Oxford army, the sound of their cannon rolling over all. Before him, an angry robin shouted from the top of the hedge while a wren bobbed in and out.

'Alright! Not long now!' Colonel Slanning faced them, a watch held in his hand. 'On my order! We wait for the signal guns to fire! Not before!'

Kendall picked up the ladder, lifted his eyes to Heaven and prayed. He prayed as he had been taught, in the way of his church, the way his father had prayed, the way his grandfather had prayed and his grandfather before him, the way they'd always prayed in Cornwall, for God's protection, for His Grace, for a safe homecoming, for Morwenna and for the little ones. Tears ran down his face as all about him men prayed openly, piously, aloud. They offered up the Lord's Prayer, together, chanting as one, the ancient words filling his soul, the sky and meadow.

'*Gun Taz nei dr'ez en neav, benegas veth gus hanow;*
Gus gwlasketh a toaz,
Gus bonogath veth gwreaz
En noar, pokar hag yn neav.'

Cannon fire crashed out from behind them, Lord bloody Herbert's battery firing as one, a single salvo. The signal.

'*Ro tha nei an jorna'ma gun bara deth,*
Ha gav tha nei gun pehazo.'

Colonel Slanning stepped forward, turning to face the town walls and bloody rebels.

Pokar ha dr'era nei gava an pehadurrian war gun pedn.'

The colonel filled his lungs. 'Slanning's Regiment of Foot. . .'

'Ha na raze gun lewia tha demptacion.'

'Will advance!'

'Bus gun gweetha nei thurt droag.'

'By your right!'

'Amen. . .'

'March!'

'Andelha re bo!'

The drums rolled, thrashed out the call to march, beating the time as they stepped off together as one. All along the line, in every regiment, the drums beat the order to advance. Kendall forced his way up and over the hedge, dragging the ladder and his mates with him. The meadow stretched before them, flat, easy going. Ahead, musketeers led the way in open order.

They were supposed to advance at a steady pace, the drums keeping time. They were not supposed to leave the musket plotoons and pike block behind. But Kendall could not help stretching his stride, those around him pushing on past the first of the bodies that littered the meadow. Gradually, imperceptibly, as one, they stepped out, the pace quickening.

Ahead, the town walls lay silent, basking in the morning sun, Temple Gate beckoning. St Mary's Redcliffe silent, unmoving. Overhead, the larks still sang, the battle distant on the other side of the city.

And then the cry they knew would rise, the cry that no Cornishman could ignore. It only took one. But there was always one. And all would answer the call. One and all, together, *onen hag oll*. An ancient cry, a single voice calling. '*Kernow kensa!*' Cornwall first!

Together, as one, with a single mighty yell, an army answered. '*Kernow kensa!*'

And then they were running, charging as one across the warm meadow grass.

———

'A'right, now here they come agin.' The boatswain stood up from checking the breach. 'But we wait. We wait for the buggers to get close. On the captain's order, one volley of case-shot, a broadside.

The Cornish were coming again. No longer were they dark shadows in the moonlight. This time they were plain to see. They came on with the dawn sun at their back. Thousands of them. Eight regiments, colours flying, a swarm of musketeers before them, an army advancing on the city, an army that would rape, pillage, burn houses, tenements and ships. A Cornish army; a horde of half-wild heathen fisher-folk and the harpies that followed them ready to swarm over the city with their long knives and wild heathen shrieks.

They were yelling now, chanting in their wild barbarian tongue as they gathered pace. They were running, charging across the meadow towards the ditch and wall, a wave of musketeers and others leading them. There were men pushing great faggots of wood over the ground, rolling them across the meadow, and men carrying ladders to fill the ditch and climb the walls. The noise of their coming rolled across the meadow ahead of them, washed against the walls, the noise of drums, shrill pipes, yelled chants and running feet – twenty thousand feet charging. The noise washed over the tower, mingled with the noise of battle behind them on the other side of the town, beyond the harbour and suburbs where another army threatened to storm the city.

Fire and thunder lashed out from St Mary's Redcliffe as the great demi-culverin and two sakers at its base raked the Cornish line with ball and case-shot, tearing gaps through the nearest battalions. But still they came on, the first musketeers almost at the ditch.

'Have a care!' The captain of the wall yelled out his caution. 'Gun captains, check your lay! Musketeers, present!'

The boatswain squinted over the gun barrel with a grunt, tapped the quoin a quarter inch under the breach and stood up, smoking linstock in hand.

'On my order!'

They were at the ditch, the first of them swarming across it. More followed close behind with ladders and faggots. The rest pressing forward in a great yelling, surging wave – wild savages all.

'Give. . . fire!

Kendall stumbled, almost fell. The back of the ladder was on the ground, dragging. His mate was on the ground, rolling, trying to sit, one foot a bloody flapping mess. Kendall pulled at the ladder with both hands. He lurched forward, step-by-step, hauling it behind him, others passing. And then another picked up the back of the ladder and again, together, they surged forward.

At the ditch. His feet went from under him, the ladder crashing down, sliding forward to hit the far bank with a jarring thud. Gasping and spluttering, he reached the far bank, dragging himself half out. Brown mud-roiled water sucked him back as a great faggot of wood rolled down the bank, thrusting aside waves that washed over all. Clawing, crawling, he pulled himself up the muddy bank. Together, they dragged the ladder free to haul it across the churning water, the faggot bobbing to the surface.

Musketeers were already firing up at the towers as lead shot smacked into the mud around them, threw up bursts of water and flung men back into the ditch bleeding, shrieking, crying out. Hands slippery with mud and clay, Kendall gripped the ladder, rose up, as together they flung themselves over the last yards. Behind them, men surged over the precarious bridges of waggons, faggots and shattered wood to cross the ditch's boiling slick of mud, flotsam and floating bodies.

On they surged – on to the foot of the town walls.

———

They were at the walls, scaling ladders crashing against the stone.

'Load!' The boatswain was at the breach, sealing the touchhole with his bare hand, Israel raking the embers from the bore. The mop plunged in to swab and dowse, steaming, black and stinking as it came out. Israel ladled in the charge, tamped, wadded and rammed, working like a machine. Abel thrust in the case-shot, Israel driving it home, the screaming Cornish climbing at their back.

'Re-lay! The side-port! We rake the wall. Israel. . . Abel. . . the breach ropes and tackle!'

Abel fought to loosen the heavy breach rope and tackle from its merlon driven into the parapet, his broken hand burning as he forced it between rope and stone, the skin raw, chaffed and bleeding over shattered bone stumps.

The rope ran free. They turned the gun on squealing wheels, thrust it through the last crenel, levered it into position, forced the quoin under the breach, made the ropes fast again. But the gun's muzzle was still too high. Their shot would pass over the ladders and Cornish that swarmed at the base of the wall.

'Staves! Under the back wheels. Jack 'em up!'

Together, they rammed hand spikes under the back of the gun, forcing it up, pointing the barrel down, down towards the yelling, climbing Cornish hordes.

The ladder swayed, wobbled, as they thrust it upright. With a scraping rattle, it landed against the town wall. Kendall grabbed it, held it steady as the first man, a young lieutenant, stepped up and began to climb. The ladder sagged, swaying as the man climbed. The next man stepped up, ready to climb. A shot ricocheted from the wall in a shower of mortar.

'It's too short!' The officer looked down. 'The ladder's too short! I can't reach the top of the wall.' The ladder shook, lurched, as the lieutenant fell, his body thumping limp, groaning in a bleeding heap beside them.

No! It could not be. Kendall pulled the ladder upright, thrust it into the air, forcing it higher, stuck his shoulders under the first rung, staggering, as it crashed back against the wall. 'Come on! *Onen hag oll!*' Others leaped to hold him steady, the ladder sagging and swaying.

A sergeant lifted a boy up onto the first rungs. 'Go on lad! *Kernow kensa!*'

The ladder pressed heavy into Kendall's shoulders, shaking with every step. He staggered, heaved, bracing his legs, sweat and tears running down his face.

Together, one and all, they yelled as the boy climbed. *'Kernow kensa!'*

———

'Stand clear!' The boatswain swung the burning linstock through the air.

Abel leaped aside, the match on the touchhole, a ball of flame, the gun and carriage flying, smoke and thunder filling the tower, smashing back from the wall, ground and ditch.

X

Holding the Line

Enid Powell
The highway, Mile Hill, six o'clock in the morning

Enid Powell climbed the hill towards the line. She'd risen at daybreak, as she always did. But, instead of lighting fires, cleaning candlesticks and tending to the mistress, she'd piled a basket with bread, cheese and a jar of small-beer and left the house to climb the hill. She'd slipped out through Frome Gate, climbed Christmas Steps to St Michael's and the highway up Mile Hill.

The basket was heavy, pulling, knocking at her leg. She shouldn't have taken the food or beer from the kitchen. They'd beat her if they found her out, throw her back out on the street. But she wanted to find him, find Master Francis Reeve, give him the breakfast she carried for him, feed him, tend him, wait on him. He deserved it more than they. He was a trooper of God, engaged in the fight against the persecutors of the Godly, against the empires of Rome and the Antichrist; against the Pope, the King of Spain, the Grand Turk and Satan himself. He deserved it. He deserved her. Not they.

Master Francis had saved her, saved her from heinous sin, saved her from heresy, saved her soul from immortal damnation. He'd saved her from the clutches of *Barabbas*, saved her from possession by a blackamoor, from certain sodomy, saved her from Moussa. He was a Mahometan. She knew it now. The shifter had hidden it, like the chameleon of Africanus that he was – called himself Moses, let her think he was one of them, like her. But beneath his fine clothes his heart was stained black with sin, his skin shaven, his manhood cut with the Mark of the Beast. She'd seen his witchcraft, the symbols written, his spell to conjure all the devils of the air, earth and water against her, against Master Francis, against Jesus. Master Francis had saved her, taken her to Mistress Hazzard, shown her the way. She would do anything for her saviour.

At the brow of the hill stood Alderman Jones's great house. This was where Master Francis was stationed, where he waited with Colonel Fiennes, where he and his troop stood guard over the city. But there was no troop. The highway was empty, its surface scarred, burnt, the smell of saltpetre and horseshit steaming in the morning sun. They were not here. He was not here. Her arms ached at the weight of the basket.

The highway was barred beyond the house and garden wall, a massive timbered gate closing it, barring the way to Aust and the ferry that crossed the River Severn – the way to Wales, to Monmouth, Llanvaches, the way home. A cannon thundered. The noise of battle was suddenly close. To right and left were the sounds of cannon and musket shot, from Priors Hill to St Michael's Hill and beyond to Brandon Hill. Behind her, from beyond the old town, harbour, Portwall and St Mary's Redcliffe, the noise of cannon fire rolled over the city. And at Stokes Croft, muskets fired.

She should go back. She'd been foolish to come here, to think that she would find him. If she hurried, she would not be missed. She could return the bread, cheese and beer before they were missed.

But beyond the gate, the line turned to run beside the highway, by a great earth wall, fresh built, before turning to run across the top of the down again towards Priors Hill. In the corner, where the wall turned, was a small earthen fort with great guns and soldiers. It was no further than four-score yards. Perhaps, the soldiers would know where the troop had gone, where she could find Master Francis.

———

Jeremy Holway sat, slumped at the back of the redoubt, the morning sun warm on his face. He was tired and thirsty, his belly empty. A young woman walked towards him – a skinny maidservant weighed down by a basket. 'Alright maid. Where't thou going with that there basket, now?'

The maid looked at him, barely more than a girl. 'If you please, sir.' A scrawny Welsh maid – he might have known. 'I'm looking for Master Francis Reeve. He's with Colonel Fiennes Regiment of Horse. Posted by Alderman Jones's house he said. But he isn't there just now.'

'They've gone, maid. Along the line. To capture the cavaliers that got over the rampart. Some of them got across you see, down between St Michael's Hill and Brandon Hill. Our horse have gone to stop up the breach and round up the delinquents.'

'I hopes they kill the lot of them, the reprobate sinners.'

'Well, that's strong fighting talk. We could do with more of thy sort on the line.'

'Send the devils back to Hell I say.'

'Maybe thou seed something of them on thy way here. Which way did thou come now?'

'I came up Frome Gate way. Up the steps to Sant Michael's. I didn't see nothing. The way was empty. Not till I got here leastways.'

'Well let's hope they've killed all the cavaliers and thy master gets back here soon.'

'Oh, he isn't my master. Leastways, not a proper master.'

Jeremy eyed the girl. 'What's in the basket, maid? We've had nowt to eat or drink and the fighting do make a man dry. And some of our boys are hurt and all. That wouldn't be a jar of ale would it now?'

'I suppose it wouldn't do any harm – you all fighting for Jesus Christ, our Saviour. I've got small-beer and bread and cheese. It doesn't make sense to carry it back down the hill now.'

Jeremy took a long draw from the jar, tore off a piece of bread and cut himself a snap of cheese. 'Thank. . . ee.' He swallowed the first mouthful. 'Wouldst thou share it with the others? the wounded first?' The girl nodded. 'Bless ee maid. And pass on my thanks to thy master.' She blushed and turned away. He watched her as she moved among the others, doling out bread, cheese and welcome beer – a brave, strong girl.

———

Enid looked up from the boy she tended, a boy with an arm that would not stop bleeding. She'd ripped the hem from her own shift to bind his wound but the blood still seeped through. He was weak, his skin hot and clammy. She'd helped him drink from the jar and mopped his brow. But what else could she do? Mistress Hazzard would know what to do. If only she were there. Enid wiped away a tendril of hair that had fallen, hanging lank from her coif.

A man rode towards them. He was coming from Priors

Hill, riding, cantering along the inside of the wall. A soldier. A gentleman in a fur hat. He was something special, riding out in a fur hat on such a sunny warm morning in July. An officer.

The rider reined in beside the redoubt, flushed red in the face. 'Major Wood, you are to remove your command into the town.'

'But why, sir?' The old soldier in charge looked down from the fort. 'Who will replace us here on the line?'

'All are to draw off from the line and repair to the town. With all haste.'

'But why, sir? What is the reason for this alteration? I know that the cavaliers have breached the line in your sector, Colonel Clifton, but surely, we should all hold the line while our horse and the reserve of foot stop the breach? We have the advantage of the hill here. The damned cavaliers will be trapped between us and the Essex Work.'

'The Essex Work has been. . . evacuated. The enemy has entered the suburbs, possessed themselves of the College Green. They are at Frome Gate – may have taken it by now. You must march into the town via Newgate. The reserve is marching that way now. If you do not shift immediately, the enemy will get betwixt you and the town. You and your men will be cut off.'

'And these are the Governor's orders?'

'The Governor doth command every man, upon pain of death, to come off the works, to march under their colours and commanders into the town at Newgate.'

'And what of our horse? Will they cover this retreat?'

'Major Langrish and the horse are already come in.'

The redoubt exploded in uproar, soldiers cussing, shouting, raising their muskets in the air. Enid leaped to her feet, stepped forward, waved her fist at the rider in the fur hat. 'This is Satan's work! You would let those devils in? Abandon this city to them while you hide in the castle? This is Satan's work, I tell you! I say, here is Judas! Judas!'

'Silence!' Major Wood yelled while the rider fought to control his startled horse. 'I will have silence in the ranks!'

'Major Wood, you are to keep your men in order. I say again, the Governor doth command every man – upon pain of death – to march under their colours into the town!' The rider turned. He scowled down at her, more red-faced than ever under his fur hat. 'And take this vixen with you!' And then he was gone, spurring his horse towards St Michael's Hill and the Windmill Fort.

'I'm not one of your soldiers!' Enid stepped out onto the road after him. 'I'll go where I please.' She yelled at the back of his silly fur hat. 'And I'm not afraid of no bloody cavalier neither!'

———

Jeremy watched the girl go, striding down the highway, past Alderman Jones's house and on towards Frome Gate. She was just a young girl, an ignorant Welsh maid. But she was right.

'Gunners, spike your guns!' Major Wood glared out across the down. 'Burn any powder you cannot carry. And dump the shot in the ditch!' He turned, took one last look around his redoubt and cursed. 'Sergeant Gale! Get these men formed up and ready to march.'

Jeremy looked about him. 'Damn! But that Colonel Fiennes is an honest man. Otherwise, I should think we were betrayed.'

'Silence in the ranks!'

He wanted to do his duty, but he had responsibilities too,

as a husband, a father, a mercer. This was his city. These were his suburbs. 'I ain't going with you. I got a wife and children over by St Austin's. I ain't marching away and leaving them. I'm for staying and fighting.'

XI

The Red Lodge

Ralph Reeve
Red Lodge, Stony Hill, seven o'clock

Ralph Reeve crouched beside the lodge as yet another shot ricocheted up off the lane to smack against its fine red stone wall; the thump of a musket echoing between the houses, gardens and walls. Somewhere out there was a marksman. Already, he'd killed a captain from Sir Edward Fitton's Cheshires and wounded others. And he was not alone. There were other shooters that fired from the houses that overlooked the lane.

The ditch across the lane, between the Red Lodge and the Essex Work, was almost filled in. But every time there was a shot, the men filling it froze or scattered, while the dragoons and musketeers searched for a target. But the rebel marksman had learnt to keep back from the windows from which he fired, leaving no smoke or sign of his hiding place. Again, there was nothing to be seen of this bastard. Again, men dashed back out into the lane to fill the ditch, digging as fast as they could before the next shot claimed its mark.

Drums echoed down the lane from the breach, louder now as a battalion of foot rounded the corner between the garden walls. It was a blue-coated battalion, Henry Lunsford's, one of Colonel Belasyse's Tertia. They must have broken off their attack against the Windmill Fort and Redoubt to follow Wentworth's Tertia through the breach by the barn. Fuck. It must still be the only breach on this side of the city. This must be the only way yet open to take the town. Thank God they had found the Essex Work empty. And thank God they'd managed to hold on whilst they were almost surrounded and cut off from support.

Ralph watched as the redhaired Colonel Lunsford halted his battalion and came forward to talk with Colonel Wentworth and Colonel Washington. He was accompanied by a drummer, a blackamoor drummer, in the fine clothes of a page.

———

Jeremy Holway rammed home the fresh ball and charge in his musket barrel, the smoke from his firing still thick within the chamber. It was time to move. He'd seen at least one of the damned cavaliers drop. But they'd work out where he was soon enough.

He'd not marched back into the town with his company. They'd left the redoubt and line to march back in via Newgate. But he, John Friend and Richard Hort had slipped away down the highway to St Michael's and Church Lane. There they'd found the Essex Work abandoned, the garrison sent away by that fool colonel in his fur hat. Under pain of death! Worse, they'd found it occupied by damned cavaliers. So, they'd found a place from which to fire down on them.

But now it was time to move. More of the King's bloody foot were coming down the lane from Clifton. He'd heard their drums. There was no way back to St Austin's this way. No way back to Sarah, to his wife, family and shop. He'd try his luck down Steep Street and Trenchard Lane, or along St Austin's Back.

———

'Reeve!' Sergeant O'Brien called from the door of the Red Lodge. 'Yiz are moving now. You're to be going along with Mister Bellamy and Sergeant Willetts and his division, down the hill to occupy the Great House beside the river.'

Ralph slipped inside the doorway. 'Are you not coming with us?'

'No, not this time. I'm to stay here with the Colonel, Captain Norwood and the cornet's division. Young Mister Watson has no sergeant and Captain Norwood wants me here beside him. We are to prepare this here lodge for Prince Rupert.'

'Very well.' Ralph swallowed. He wished O'Brien was going with them. 'I see.'

'You'll be doing fine enough without me. Now, some of our horse are inside the line. Our boys have occupied the cathedral and a pair of churches besides. But there's another rebel work down by the river that plays on them, so mind who yiz are shooting at. Do you have any questions?'

'No sergeant. I don't think so. And. . . thank you.'

'Off with you, now. Get your division in through this here doorway and away with Mister Bellamy. He's waiting now in the garden beyond.'

———

Abel Cowans dropped the keg of powder beside the gun on the Quay Head. It was another three-pounder minion, just like the one at Temple Gate. He and the gun crew had stopped the bloody heathen Cornish out on Temple Mead. Now they'd been shifted, sent by Mister Hazzard, the Master of Ordnance, to the other side of the town to man this gun facing out over the River Frome. The boatswain, Israel, the Swede and the boy all followed with shot and gun tackle.

The river was packed tightly with ships, boats and lighters. Beyond them lay St Austin's Back, the Great House and the suburbs rising to the Essex Work and line beyond. Smoke and the sound of gunfire rose, crackling and thumping out from the College Green, St Austin's and the Water Fort below Brandon Hill. The little fort must still be holding out against the bastard cavaliers that poured into the suburbs from the line above.

'A'right now.' The boatswain spat on his hands. 'Let's get this little beauty loaded.'

———

Ralph led the way through arched doors and oak panelled rooms, cool and dark inside the Red Lodge, past fine great stone fireplaces and under strapped plasterwork ceilings, their thumping boots and dust worrying the ordered hush. On the far side of the building, they emerged into the bright morning sunlight. Ornate gardens and orchards ran down the hillside before them to the Great House, the river, quays and town beyond.

They descended brick steps to a knot garden, where Lieutenant Bellamy waited with his division. With a nod to the officer, his sergeant and corporal, they brought up the rear, following on down the slope between clipped beds, trimmed shrubs and fruit trees. Ralph looked back at his own division: Sam alert, scanning ahead; Jack grim, determined; Jewkes scowling, out of place and uneasy in such a fine formal garden. Tandy grinned, spitting out a cherry stone, more of the dark fruit in his hand. Clem smiled and Luke nodded. Only Kibler worried him, pale and sweaty, blowing on his match and fiddling with his bandolier as he lumbered along at the rear.

Ahead, a high garden wall ran across the slope at the end of the orchard. They slipped through a wicket, stepping quickly across a lane and under the arch of an ornate pillared gateway. The courtyard of the Great House lay open, empty, square. Chequered flagstones lay surrounded on three sides by walls with high windows, pinnacled gables and lofty chimneys.

Lieutenant Bellamy thumped on the great porticoed oak door. 'Open up! In the name of the King! Open up! Or we break down the door!' They pushed past a frightened old footman, into the vast chequered hall. 'Reeve, you and your division upstairs. Find a place where you can shoot across the river. Break the windows if you need to. I will join you shortly.

Sergeant Willetts... please secure the ground floor. Barricade the doors with what furniture you can find. Make sure the courtyard and any approaches are covered. Any men you can spare, please send upstairs to me.'

———

Abel stood back from the muzzle, the iron ball rolled into the bore. Israel stepped forward to push it home with a thump.

The boatswain looked up from priming the breach. 'Bring her round boys! Lay her on the big house now.' Together, they levered the carriage round with staves. 'That'll do!' With a grunt, the boatswain knocked the quoin under the breach, squinting over the barrel.

Abel could not help but grin. The gun was trained on the Great House, the grandest house in all Bristol, staring out over the backs, quays and shipping in the river. This was the pleasure house of Sir Ferdinando Gorges, owner of the whole Province of Maine, feudal lord over a thousand poor New England colonists, a royalist merchant venturer who'd never sailed the Atlantic nor set foot in America. It was a palace big enough to house a hundred families. And the bastard did not even live in it! Now it was filled with bloody cavaliers and he and this gun were going to knock holes in it.

'Stand clear!' The boatswain swung his linstock through the air, the coal crackling and smoking as it plunged into the priming powder. Smoke, sparks and burning powder corns burst skyward from the touchhole, the gun leaping backward from the cone of flame at its muzzle to land on the quay flagstones with a thunderous roar, crash and rattle of tackle.

The Great House shook, plaster falling from the ceiling, dust swirling in the sunlight.

'Out!' It was Lieutenant Bellamy, yelling from the stairs. 'Everyone out! We cannot hold on any longer. Sergeant Willetts, get your division outside!' Feet running, Willetts's men descending the staircase. 'Reeve, you too! Come on! Out!'

Ralph took one last look across the river packed with ships and boats, across the quay on the far bank to the old town. Smoke billowed back from a cannon on the quay, a gun at the head of the quay, where it met the end of the bridge across the river. 'Come on! We can't stay without the others. Luke, get everyone downstairs. Into the courtyard!'

The others clattering out of the chamber and down the stairs, he turned to leave. Something, someone was behind the door. A body sat hunched in a ball, shaking, covered in dust and plaster, arms wrapped about its head. 'Kibler?' Ralph pulled the door back. 'For God's sake. Come on!' He shook the man's shoulder. 'We are leaving!' Desperate eyes looked up, stared back blankly, the face pale and twitching. The man was terrified.

'Clem!' Ralph yelled through the door. 'Clem! Back up here, please! I need help!'

'I'm a-coming Master Ralph!' Clem burst back into the room. 'What is it? What's wrong?'

'It's Kibler. He needs help. I think it's been too much for him.'

Together they lifted Kibler to his feet, Clem supporting and guiding him, swaying as they lurched out of the room. 'Come on, I got you. Wow, steady now! That's the way.'

Ralph gathered up Kibler's carbine and followed, down the stairs and across the hall as again, the great building shook, the sound of falling bricks and rooftiles above. The old footman cowered by the door, unsure whether to stay or leave, torn between duty and fear.

Ralph touched the older man on the shoulder. 'Come away, now. It isn't safe here. Take this man up the hill to the Red Lodge. He needs help. Can you do it?'

'Bless you, master. I weren't sure as to go or to stay, like. The Red Lodge belongs to this here house. Tis the garden house of my master, Sir Ferdinando Gorges.'

'Find Sergeant O'Brien there. Take this man to him. Sergeant O'Brien will know what to do. But he may need your help. He is expecting. . . an eminent visitor.'

'Right you are, master. You can count on me. I ain't no bloody roundhead, if you gets my meaning.' The footman took Kibler from Clem, holding him up. 'Come on then. Let's be getting you up to the lodge and that Master – that Sergeant O'Brien.' The rest of them watched Kibler and the old man stagger through the gate, the footman still talking. 'Eminent visitor your master says. Well now, I remember when good

Queen Bess came to stay in this very house. Them were the days. . .' Jewkes glared after Kibler, hawed up a gob of flem and spat.

There was no sign of Lieutenant Bellamy, Sergeant Willetts or his division in the courtyard. They'd gone. Ralph looked at his division. He was damned if he was running back to the Red Lodge. But would they all follow him? They were tired, exhausted, caked in dust and plaster, running low on powder, shot and match. The strain showed in their eyes. It had been too much for Kibler.

All but Jewkes flinched as a chimney above collapsed in a welter of falling bricks. 'Come on!' Ralph led them out through the gate. 'We can't stay here.' He led them out onto the lane behind the Great House. The wicket gate to the gardens and Red Lodge was ajar. Fuck it! He turned to follow the lane, to lead his division deeper into the suburbs, to lead them towards the bridge over the river and the town beyond.

They moved cautiously, between houses and high garden walls. The lane was narrow, straight and flat; an inn at its end, alms houses across the street beyond. Ralph quickened the pace; Tandy opposite him, his carbine cocked.

———

Jeremy Holway blew gently, the match spluttering and hot in the dark chamber. He, John Friend and Richard Hort had found a place in the old Ship Inn, a place where they could give fire on any damned cavalier that came up Steep Street or along Trenchard Lane. The delinquent whoresons were all over the College Green and St Austin's now. There was no way open to get back to his wife, family and shop. Christ alone knew what the bastards might do to his poor Sarah. He should never have left her, the little ones and the shop in danger.

He flicked open the pan. 'The first one is mine.' The cavalier came on, stepping quickly now in the sun, others behind him. 'Come on you bastard.' He aimed low, low for the kick and low for the angle. He aimed at the pox ridden shit's belly. 'This is for Sarah.' He took up the slack in the trigger arm. 'Now!' The musket slammed into his shoulder, the little chamber exploding in a ball of smoke, dust and thumping crash.

———

The shot crashed out in the narrow lane; Tandy thrown against the wall, writhing in the dirt. 'Fuck!' Ralph leaped across the track, another shot smacking into the wall, he and Sam dragging Tandy back into the shadow – blood and kicking feet.

'Sam. . . Luke. . . stay with him!' Ralph turned back and raised his carbine. 'There in the inn! We should charge now. While they reload.' But he could not ask them to charge. They would not follow him. It was madness. He'd been foolish. They should go back. Tandy needed a surgeon.

Behind him, a growl and snarling oath. Jewkes crashed past, running, charging, roaring his anger. A spurt of dust – another shot ricocheting off the lane.

'Now!' Ralph charged. Jack and Clem behind him.

———

Jeremy heard the window shatter, the scrape and thump of bodies climbing through it. 'Shit! They're inside!' He banged the butt of his musket on the floor to seat the ball. 'Downstairs! We gotta get out! Now!'

———

A shot exploded, bright blinding light in the darkness, an ear-splitting roar, heat and flying splinters. Ralph blundered forward, a chair crashing over. Feet pounding on floorboards, down stairs, a door crashing open. A woman screamed. Jewkes was yelling, roaring in his bloodlust. A musket butt smacked into flesh. A groan. The sound of the butt coming down again. And again. And again.

———

Jeremy turned and fired once more down Trenchard Lane as the others ran staggering back up Steep Street. 'Come on! Christmas Steps! We find a place to stop them at the top. The top of Christmas Steps!'

———

Ralph thrust the tankard under the barrel tap, let the liquid fill it, slopping over the top, his hand shaking. It wasn't ale, but cider. The cool draft sank sharp and clean in his throat, harsh and clean, clearing his head, washing away the dust, smoke and blood, soothing his breathing, calming his shaking fist.

Tandy sat in a broken chair while Luke cut away his bloody shirt and bound his arm with a fresh, clean torn sheet. He was alive. Thank God! He would live.

In the corner, Jewkes sat slumped on the taproom floor, covered in blood and half a tankard of cider, exhausted. Jack had dragged away the innkeeper's body, the old fool's pistol now in his belt, while Clem calmed the wife and Sam kept watch.

XII

The Sally

Francis Reeve
Christmas Street, inside Frome Gate, eleven o'clock

Praise God, at last they were to move! Finally, they were to sally out from behind the town walls, throw back the Babylonian dogs that infested the suburbs, return the devils to the pit from which they had crawled.

The great iron portcullis clanked, clanged, rising foot by foot as it was hauled up into the tower of Frome Gate. Francis pulled down the barred visor of his helmet, drew a pistol, pulling back the cock to release the dog lock. Only a plotoon of musketeers stood before them, a forlorn hope, ready to clear the way beyond the gate. Behind them, three more musketeer plotoons waited. Just one troop of horse and two hundred musketeers to clear the suburbs. There should have been more. The whole garrison should be ready to charge. Instead, half of them sat drinking their fill of ale in the oldtown taverns. They should never have been recalled from the line. They should be descending on the enemies of the Lord from every side, encircling those within, enclosing them for the slaughter, sacrificing them to Christ.

The gates swung open; the trumpets blared, drums

beating, echoing between the overhanging shops on the narrow bridge, the forlorn hope charging out through the gap. Francis twisted spurs into his horse's bloody flanks. The animal leaped forward, iron-shod hooves crashing on the flagstones, echoing under the gate's vaulted roof as they burst out onto the narrow street.

———

Ralph Reeve heard the trumpet call, a call echoing up the hill, rising from the river. It was not one of their own, not one of the king's troops of horse; they were all still behind the inn, beyond the Great House, out of range of the shots from across the street. Fuck! This was rebel horse, rebel horse advancing, sallying out from the town.

Ralph slammed down the mug of cider. 'Up!' He grabbed his carbine. 'Stand to your posts! Luke!' He ran across the tap-room to the stairs his boots crashing on the stairs, two at a time. 'Luke, they are sallying! The rebels are sallying out from the town!'

'I know, Ralph.' Thank Christ, Luke was upstairs. 'They are at the bottom of the street!'

———

Jeremy Holway heard the trumpet call, heard the drums thrashing down Broad Street, Christmas Street and across the Frome Bridge. They were coming. Finally, the garrison were coming, sallying out from behind the town walls, coming to retake the suburbs, to save the city. Thanks be to Christ, they were coming.

He slid across the floor to the smashed window. Already, the drums echoed up Christmas Steps, hammering out their march as they climbed the narrow street. He checked the match in his musket's cock, blew on its smouldering end. 'Alright, we just gotta keep them blue-coated devils back up Stony Hill till our boys get here.' He, John Friend, Richard Hort and the others would hold the cavaliers back until the garrison joined them at the top of Christmas Steps.

Perhaps Major Wood would be with them. Perhaps he'd re-join his company, take his place in the ranks again. They would see that he'd been right, welcome him back as a hero.

———

Moussa Dansocko heard the trumpets' shrill call echoing over the city, shouting out their challenge. He heard the drums beating, thumping in the streets below, shouting their *nyama*. The enemy were marching, coming out from the old town. They would be marching down Broad Street, through St John's Gate under the church, past the Boucher House on Christmas Street and over the Frome Bridge.

Mistress Boucher would be frightened by the drums outside, hiding in her chamber. Mistress Elizabeth would be comforting her now, holding her hand, stroking her hair, her arm around the young ones. She would be waiting for him, waiting for him to guide Colonel Lunsford to the house, waiting for them to rescue her from the factors, creditors and dogs that circled ready to seize what they could. He had to save her before she was taken, forced into marriage, sold like a slave in the market to some drooling old merchant.

Colonel Lunsford stood before them, staring down Stony Hill, his wounded arm bound in a cloth about his neck. He turned to face the murmuring blue ranks stretched across the road below the Essex Work. 'Stand straight in your files!' The whispering ceased. The ranks stiffened. 'Lunsford's will prepare to receive horse! Battaile, advance your arms! Port your arms!'

With a nod from the drum-major, Moussa and the other drummers beat the Battaile driving the files to close up, to close-order. His drumsticks rose and fell with the rhythm, the drum resonating, pounding, pulsing, its *nyama* flowing out, pulling at his *dya*, lifting his spirit, echoing down the street to crash against the enemy drumming, to beat it back, to smash it down.

———

Francis turned the corner into Steep Street and drove his horse at the hill with bloody spurs. The animal put its head to the slope, lurching, rasping, iron shoes scraping at the cobbles.

The Ship Inn loomed over the street, overhanging in tiered storeys. The narrow road below curved uphill, dark in the inn's shadow, all sunlight blocked. A window burst open. Flame, smoke and the crash of muskets filled the street, shot smacking off the cobbles, whistling past.

The horse stumbled, scrabbling on the cobbles. He yanked on the reins, hauled its head up, forced the beast on with another deep rake of spurs.

———

Ralph pulled the carbine back from the window, smoke streaming from the warm barrel. 'Fire at will!' He pulled back the cock, dug his thumb into the priming pan to wipe it clean of gritty residue. 'They'll be trying to retake the work on the street above us.' He poured powder into the pan, snapped the frizzen shut. 'Luke, there may be more troops following.'

'I know, Ralph. Clem is watching that way.' God, what would he do without Luke?

'I can't see nought. Not yet leastways.' It was Clem. 'But I hears drums. Down by the river. I doubt that'll be foot a-coming on.'

'Fuck!' Ralph poured powder down the barrel. 'That's all we need.' He dropped in a ball, shoved in a wad of paper and rammed the charge home. 'Rebel bloody foot!'

———

They were here! The garrison were with them, a troop of horse streaming up Steep Street. 'They're here, boys!' Jeremy could not help but yell. 'The garrison are here! They're with us!'

The armoured horsemen were turning up Stony Hill. They were pouring past the shop to turn up the hill towards the Essex Work. From behind, the noise of drums was louder, the garrison foot climbing Christmas Steps to join them at the top. More drums and foot followed their horse up Steep Street. Together, they would throw the bloody cavaliers back from the suburbs, retake the Essex Work and line.

———

Francis reigned in, his horse heaving, sweat lathered, steaming in the sun. Ahead, stretching across Stony Hill stood a battalion of blue-coated foot. Apostates, sinners all, they would be the first to be thrown back. Cut down and sacrificed.

Beside him, the rest of the troop came into line, horses jostling, pushing, stamping on the sloping cobbles, the line heaving. Slowly at first, the line advanced, pistols drawn, gathering pace. They would ride down this Babylonian horde – send them back to Hell.

———

Moussa stood behind Colonel Lunsford. The wounded *horo* stared down the hill at the enemy horsemen. 'Stand straight in your files!'

The line of armoured horsemen stretched across the road.

They were coming up the hill, horses snorting, champing, harness jangling, iron shoes stepping high.

'Pikes. . . charge your pikes!' The great spears swung forward and down to form an iron tipped wall. 'Musketeers. . . will fire by salvee! Present!' On either side of the road, the muskets came up to the aim in three ranks.

Still the horsemen came on. Faster now, they gathered pace.

'Gunners!' Lunsford's own gun sat at the edge of the street. 'Give fire!' It crashed out in tongue of flame and smoke. It was not a great gun, but its noise thundered over the city.

———

The horse collapsed in welter of shrieking, flailing hooves. Francis pulled his leg clear as the heap of horseflesh and steaming guts convulsed, jerked then stiffened. He dragged himself up from cobbles running with blood, hot, shimmering in the sun. His leg buckled, searing pain running up the long boot, but he stood. The visor of his helmet was buckled, the bars of the faceguard bent, twisted, untrue. With shaking hands, he forced them up and back, away from his face.

The rest of the troop had halted. They were pulling back, turning in the street, sliding back down the hill. They were leaving him. The street was emptying, the last of the troop turning the corner, melting back down Steep Street.

Francis bent, picked up his fallen pistol, dragged the second from its holster. He had been ready to charge the apostates. But he could hardly walk. He turned away, back towards the town, towards the drums that climbed Christmas Steps. He tried a step. His boot slipped in the blood, spur rowel catching on a cobble as he crashed back down on the stone, armoured breast and back jarring, his leg burning with pain.

Again, he pulled himself up. Jeers and laughter echoed about him, rolling down the street from the ranks of bluecoats. *There shall come in the last days, scoffers, walking after their own lusts.* He took a step, stumbled, the leg weak, shaking. His blood heating with the pain and humiliation. *Judgements are prepared for scorners, and stripes for the backs of fools!*

As the last of the horsemen disappeared back down Steep Street. Jeremy stared after them. They were riding away, re-treating, back the way they'd come. They hadn't given fire to, let alone charged the blue-coated cavalier battalion. They'd turned and ran at the first shot – a shot that killed a single horse!

The horseman was dragging himself away, stumbling back down Stony Hill alone, abandoned, hurt. Again, he fell, sprawling on the cobbles. The garrison foot were almost at the top of Christmas Steps. He would be caught between the two forces, shot by one side or the other.

'Damn!' Jeremy leaped down the stairs, opened the door onto the street, the noise of drums louder. 'Cover me!' He dashed across the cobbles, grabbed the horseman under an arm and half carried, half dragged him back inside, the door slamming shut behind them.

Ralph watched the rebel foot marching up the road. The first musketeer division was rounding the bend at the bottom of the hill, drums thrashing in the narrow street. 'Make ready!' He and his dragoons would try to slow them, give those at the Essex Work time. 'We will give them one salvee! Then, fire at will.' If nothing else, they would gall them from the inn windows, perhaps thin out an officer or two. 'But make every shot count!'

He fumbled in his bullet bag. Only six balls remained. He needed to conserve what powder and shot they had left. Those still with matchlocks would be getting low on match, its stench filled the chamber despite the smashed window panes. They had not yet reached the walls of the old town, let alone fought their way into it. This fighting from house-to-house cost time, shot and lives. They must make each shot count.

'Present!' He pulled the butt into his shoulder, squinted along the barrel, aimed at an officer striding in front of the division, waving them on, partizan in hand.

A horseman cantered past, almost knocking the officer down. Then another, careering down the hill, hooves skittering on the cobbles as horse and rider squeezed between the marching musketeers and the front of a shop. Then more horses, the whole troop of rebel horse streaming back down the hill, filling the street, cannoning into the ranks of musketeers, knocking them aside in panic and disorder.

'Hold!' Ralph turned to the others. 'Hold your fire! Save your shot.'

———

The drumming was louder now, nearer, thundering within the walls of Christmas Steps, rolling on up Stony Hill to where they stood below the Essex Work. It was as if some beast was rising from the earth, a giant *wuluwulu*, the *bama-fa Niare*, the terrible *Sâba*, climbing the steps towards them, up from the river, its great clawed feet thumping, pounding the earth as it came, dragging its scaled belly and tail over the steps, long jaws and ragged teeth grinding, growling, come to tear men apart, to drag them half dead back to its watery lair.

Its head was rising, swaying, up over the last step to the street. The drumming stopped. Silence. A line of enemy musketeers formed across the top of Christmas Steps. They must have marched out from Frome Gate to climb the steps. Now they stood in three ranks facing their own warriors. Moussa took a long breath.

'Battaile... will advance! Prepare to march!' Colonel Lunsford stared ahead, down the street. 'March on!'

Moussa beat the call to advance, a long drumroll and eight bars, followed by the slow, steady beat as Lunsford's bluecoats stepped off. He marched behind Colonel Lunsford, his colonel, his *horo*. They were marching towards the town, to throw back this last enemy. They would march down Christmas Steps, through Frome Gate and across Frome Bridge to the house on Christmas Street. He, Moussa Dansocko, would bring the colonel to his mistress.

'Pikes! Port your... pikes!' The pikes swung forward, over the heads of the ranks in front. 'Pikes! Files close to your centre. To your closest... order!' The pikemen wedged themselves together, as a block, on the march, without breaking step, each pace in time with the drum, drawn on by its rhythm, by its power, its *nyama*.

Ahead, the enemy musketeers waited in three ranks. They held their fire. But shots rang out from the houses around. Men fell on the cobbles crying out in pain and blood. Others were left behind to limp away clutching at shattered limbs. The rest cursed and swore, put their heads down, hunched their shoulders and pressed on. They passed the dead horse, ripped and bloody. But still the enemy musketeers waited at the bottom of the hill.

—

The delinquent blue-coats came on down Stony Hill, drums beating, but still the garrison musketeers did not fire. Jeremy was damned if he would wait with them, even if Major Wood was with them. He, John Friend, Richard Hort and the others fired freely from the shop while the injured horseman loaded for them. This was their battle. This was how they'd kept the malignant papists back from storming the old town. They weren't going to stop now.

Jeremy slid the warm barrel over the window sill, looked for a mark. These bluecoats were Lunsford's Regiment, Somerset boys, local lads, dumb farm labourers. But the man who led them was Harry Lunsford, one of an evil brood. His mother was a known witch, a spinner of evil, of ungodly fictions of the 'Rosy Cross'. His brother was a murderous outlaw, a godless, brawling fugitive pardoned and knighted by a king who would use any means, any sort of man to bend all power to himself. It was said that the Lunsfords feasted in secret on the flesh of poor Puritan children.

A cavalier urged on Lunsford's bluecoats, a big man with flowing red hair, an arm bound in cloth, followed by a black devil drummer. The cavalier was Harry Lunsford. There was no doubt. Jeremy pulled the butt into his shoulder, sited through the shimmering heat of the barrel. He aimed for the man's chest, steadied his breath, curled his fingers around the trigger.

———

Colonel Lunsford raised his hand. 'Battaile. . . halt!'

Moussa stood still, let his drum calm. All must hear the great *horo* colonel speak.

'Pikes! Charge your. . . pikes!' The long spears swung down to the level. Their iron tips only a few paces from the enemy's faces. 'Musketeers! Make ready to give fire by salvee. Front rank... kneel! Rear rank close forward to your closest... order!' Bandoliers rattled on either side, then silence. The enemy musketeers simply stood, silent, their muskets at the present.

'Present!'

A shot crashed out, echoing back and forth between the houses, not knowing how to escape, trapped, held in the crossroads. A twist of smoke curling from the window of the shop above the steps.

Colonel Lunsford staggered, half turned, opened his mouth, closed it and crashed to the ground.

Moussa held him, cradling his head. The *horo* lay on the cobbles, soaked in his own blood, his heart pierced, his *ni*, his soul, leaving the body, all life slipping away, a fading shadow.

The air about them exploded, filled with fierce *yeelen* light, desert wind, angry bees – men falling, screaming and bleeding, the enemy musketeers wreathed in gunsmoke.

'Fire!' Lieutenant-Colonel Moyle had taken charge. 'Give fire!' Their own muskets crashed out. But the salvee was ragged, half-fired. The ranks were collapsing, men running, crawling, dragging each other to shelter, away from the open street.

'Moses!' Corporal Stokes stood over him. 'Moses! Come on!'

Moussa shook his head. He could not leave the *horo* colonel.

'Jesus!' The corporal grabbed the colonel's arm. 'Moses, come on!'

Together they dragged the limp body across the cobbles, slumping down beside the Chapel of the Three Kings, amongst its alms houses, a bright trail of blood marking their path.

311

———

'Fuck!' Ralph looked back from the inn window. 'Lunsford's are falling back.' He looked at Luke. 'How much powder and shot do you have left?'

Luke checked his bullet bag. 'One loaded and four shots left.'

'Me too. Sam, how much powder and shot do you have?'

'Three shot, three charges.'

'Tandy?'

'Four shot and four charges.'

'Good. Just keep loading for the others. Jack, what have you got left?'

'I've got five all told an' our Jewkes's got four.'

'Clem, what about you?'

'I've got enough for four more shots.'

'All right. Jack, give Sam one shot and one charge.' Ralph looked across the chamber. 'Clem. . . what're the rebel foot doing down the hill?'

'They ain't stirred further since their hoss retreated.' Bless Clem. 'I recon they've seed our hoss away down the street. I don't suppose they'll move much now.'

'Right. We're going to cross the street. I want to get into that alley and see if we can find a way through to the next street. I want to get behind the bloody rebel foot at the top of it. I will lead with Clem, Jack and Jewkes. Luke, you follow with Sam and Tandy. Any questions?'

Ralph eased the inn door open. The steep curving road was empty. The sound of shots and drumming echoed from the next street across: a second battalion marching down the hill above to throw back the rebel sally.

He ran, boots thumping on the cobbles, dived into the alley, down the first steps. Thank God! It was empty.

He waved for the others to follow. One by one they crossed until they were all bunched together in the narrow space. A gate in the wall to the left led into a garden. They crossed it quickly to the back of a house. The drumming was louder now, from the next street the other side of the house. With a splintering crack, Jewkes had the backdoor open with his tuck. They were in.

'Jack. . . you and Jewkes hold below stairs. Bar the doors and windows.' A woman, a maidservant, two children and a babe cowered in a corner. 'Clem, put these ones somewhere safe. In the cellar, if there is one, watch them. The rest of you, upstairs.'

The street below was narrow and stepped. It resounded with the noise of drums. The windows were thin, too tight to get a clear shot up the street. Ralph led the way on up to the chamber under the roof, the maid's garret. He kicked free the tilestones, laths and rafters, kicked them into the street below, forced a way out onto the roof. Across the top of the steps stood a line of rebel musketeers. Beyond, a battalion with blue colours advanced down the hill towards them: Stradling's Welshmen.

'We must try to break the bloody rebels. Luke, Sam, fire at will. Their officers first. But, for God's sake make your shots count. Tandy and I will load.'

———

The volleys from the top of Christmas Steps were ragged, the ranks thinner, men shrinking back, hiding themselves in houses, alcoves and doorways while another damn battalion came on down Stony Hill, a battalion with blue colours, Stradling's malignant Welsh scum.

Jeremy emptied a powder charge into the barrel of his

musket. Where were the rest of the garrison? Why did their grandee bloody Governor not lead them out to throw back the damned cavaliers? Was he hiding in the castle already?

The ounce lead ball slid down the soot-caked bore with a bang of the butt on the shop floorboards. He and the others in the shop had fought to hold them back. The injured horseman, Francis, had stuck by them. Those who had sallied out were hard pressed. But where were the rest of the horse and garrison?

Jeremy pushed a paper wad into the muzzle, rammed home the ball and charge. Were they to be abandoned after all?

———

The drumming was louder now, filling the suburbs with its noise, drawing on the next battalion of soldiers down Stony Hill. Moussa touched the drum beside him. He was ready to join in, to make the drum talk, to add its power, to call the soldiers on. But his *horo* was dead. Instead, he must wait, huddled beside an alms house with Corporal Stokes, the remains of Lunsford's bluecoats and their dead colonel.

The battalion came on, cheering, shouting, strange words Moussa did not know, in a language he did not understand. With a single salvee and terrifying yell, they charged. Savage, wild, warriors, they poured down Christmas Steps; knocking down the last of the enemy that stood.

Moussa laid the colonel's head gently on the ground. He unslung the drum and placed it beside the body, pulling the colonel's pistol from his belt. The great *horo* was dead. He must be avenged. The enemy musketeers were broken. But the man who shot Colonel Lunsford was still in the shop above the steps.

Corporal Stokes had turned away, busy with his soldiers. Moussa leaped up, ran out into the street and sprinting across the top of Christmas Steps. Weaving between the soldiers, he threw himself at the shop window.

———

Jeremy heard the glass panes shatter. It was the shop window. Somebody was inside, downstairs. 'Francis! The stairs! Watch the stairs! Somebody's inside!' He brought the musket up to his shoulder. 'John! Find a way through to the next house. Cut a hole in the wall. Quickly!'

———

'I have it!' Francis dragged himself to the top of the stairs, his pistols ready. A black face below. The witch, Moses! The Barabbas had returned – returned to haunt him! To drag him from salvation, drag him to a Turkish Doom. 'Devil!' The first pistol crashed out on the stairs, filling it with smoke, then the second, dust flying.

———

Splinters flying, smoke, flame, and falling plaster filled the stairs. Moussa felt the pistol balls strike the wooden banister and newel post beside him. He heard the horseman's shriek. The pistol in his own hand leaped backwards in its fire and fury as he charged, throwing himself at the stairs, clawing his way up in the swirling dust and smoke.

———

John was through the cob wall into the next house. 'Francis!' The wounded trooper was still at the top of the stairs. 'Come on!' Jeremy grabbed him, dragging him across the floor,

315

pushing him through the hole. 'Richard, hold them off, then follow me!'

———

The horseman was gone, no longer at the top of the stairs. Moussa burst into the next room, the door crashing back on its hinges. A man, a soldier, was climbing through a hole in the wall, disappearing backwards, escaping. *Was this Colonel Lunsford's killer?*

Moussa leaped across the room, his hand on the assassin's collar. The *shaitan's* pale frightened face was upturned, arms struggling to pull away, to escape.

The pistol butt struck down, thumping against the side of his head. The head and arms jerked, thrashing out, then slumped, as Moussa brought the pistol butt down again and again, again and again.

'Easy Moses.' Corporal Stokes was holding him. 'Easy now.' The corporal pulled him back from the body slumped in the hole. 'What the devil's got into you?'

Blood and gore spattered the wall, soaked Moussa's hands, face, coat and breaches. It dripped from the misshapen head in great lumps to run bright and dark across the floorboards. The room was suddenly quiet. There was just the sound of dripping blood and the drums beating again in the street outside.

Moussa followed Corporal Stokes back outside. He knelt again beside Colonel Lunsford's body. '*Inna lillahi wa inna ilayhi raji'un.*' Slowly, gently, he closed the great man's jaw and eyes as he whispered the sacred rite. *Surely, we belong to God and truly to him shall we return*. Lieutenant-Colonel Moyle was his *horo* now. He must follow him, be his *jali*. Perhaps, *inshallah*, he would guide the lieutenant-colonel to

Mistress Elizabeth. Was this the will of God? Even now, the lieutenant-colonel was gathering what was left of Lunsford's Regiment to lead them forward again.

Moussa pushed the pistol into his coat, the butt still sticky with blood. He slung the drum over his shoulder. Corporal Stokes gave a nod as the lieutenant-colonel led them down the steps. Slowly, cautiously at first, they moved from doorway to doorway, looking up at the windows, watching for and anticipating the next shot.

The street echoed to the sound of doors splintering and windows shattering as others broke their way into the shops and houses. A pair of wild heathens uttering unintelligible oaths burst from a doorway, unkempt, ragged, fearsome, laughing, wrapped in bolts of satin and velvet cloth.

Gradually, the pace quickened, relaxed, the strides longer, muzzles lowering. Together they strode down Christmas Steps towards Frome Gate. Ahead, the last of the enemy threw down their weapons or ran.

———

Ralph eased the door open. 'Oxford!' God, let these bloody Welshmen understand he was a friend. 'Oxford!' He yelled their watchword again stepping out into the street. A mass of foot descended the steps, Lunsford's bluecoats, Stradling's Welsh and the Lord General's in red, all mixed together. At their head strode Lunsford's lieutenant-colonel and the black-amoor with a drum.

The others stepped out behind him, Clem like a shadow, Sam wary, Tandy pale and bound, scarred Jack, shambling Jewkes and dear Luke. Together, they joined the throng, striding out, close behind the lieutenant-colonel.

The blackamoor was pointing, almost dragging the

lieutenant-colonel down the steps. 'Master, the gate. Frome Gate is just beyond these steps. Just across Horse Street.'

The pace quickened, the bottom of the steps in sight. Beyond it lay a narrow street and the old town rising on its hill. The smell of mud and tide told of the river between. They plunged down the last steps, boots thumping on the flagstones as they raced to seize the gate and take the city.

———

Francis staggered, limping across the courtyard, his leg burning with every step, sweat drenching him beneath buff coat and armour. In front, Jeremy and John Friend beckoning him on. Together, they had crossed a garden, climbing its wall to fall into an orchard. Now they were running, stumbling across the Grammar School yard, boys peering agape from windows.

Ahead was an arched cloister. Beyond it was Horse Street and Frome Gate. Francis threw himself forward, boots crashing in the narrow passage. Together, they burst out onto the street.

———

Moussa pulled the pistol from his coat. They had to get to the gate before it was closed. He grasped the drum, ran the last yards, tore around the corner into Horse Street, Frome Gate yards in front, looming over the narrow road.

The great iron-studded gates were closed, shut tight. Too late. They were too late!

Three men ran across the street, out from the Grammar School, two musketeers and limping horseman.

———

Jeremy stopped. Frome Gate loomed over the narrow street, blocking out the sun. It was only yards away, across Horse Street. But the gates were shut, barred. Were they too late?

The last of the garrison foot soldiers were at the side of the gatehouse, disappearing through the narrow side-door. 'Come on!' The postern gate was still open. 'Francis! The postern!'

———

Moussa heard the name, the name of the evil one, the soldier devil in league with the witch, Mistress Hazzard, the one who had poisoned poor Enid, whispered evil in her ear, the man who would steal Mistress Elizabeth. Master Francis! He charged. *'Shaitan!'*

———

Francis heard the shriek of the Mahometan, the black demon that pursued him, that would infest his soul, drag him to a Turkish Doom, the Barabbas that would pull him back from the gates of salvation. He turned to face his tormentor. 'Devil!' The pistol exploded in his hand, the barrel whipping back in smoke and flame as the street shook at its percussion.

———

The lieutenant-colonel staggered, pale and swaying. He dropped to the ground, blood and urine flooding his breeches, pain, fear and exhaustion etched across his face. 'Oh Christ. No!'

Ralph, Luke and others dragged the older man back into the shelter of Christmas Steps, sat him propped against the wall of a house in a growing pool of his own blood. There was little more they could do for him. A slow and painful death awaited.

The sally-port door slammed shut. Behind it, the muffled noise of a wooden bar thumped down between stone and iron. Frome Gate was sealed.

Moussa sank to his knees. The *shaitan* Francis and the musketeers had escaped. They were inside the gate, inside the town. While he, Moussa, was locked outside. Colonel Lunsford was dead, Lieutenant-Colonel Moyle dying.

He looked down at the drum, touched it with shaking hands. It was broken, holed, shot through, its shell splintered. How was he to save Mistress Elizabeth, save her from her tormentors, from Francis, Enid and the witch, Mistress Hazzard?

XIII

Frome Gate

Enid Powell
The Governor's Lodging, Broad Street, midday

Enid Powell stood with the women of Bristol, two hundred of them before the Governor's lodging. Mistress Joan Batten was there, Mistress Dorothy Hazzard from St Ewen's and Mary Smith from the Castle. She'd never seen anything like it before, not in her whole life. They stood there, a great congregation of women, filling Broad Street, shouting for the Governor to come out. And Mistress Hazzard had recognised her in the crowd, smiled at her, with a nod. Now Enid stood near her, almost beside her, shouting with the others.

A window opened, a head thrust out, a gentleman's head. It wasn't the Governor. He held his hand up for silence. 'Ladies, goodwives, maids! Please! What ails you?'

'We wish to see the Governor!' Mistress Batten spoke for them.

'The Governor is detained. He is attending to urgent matters of duty.'

'We would speak with him!' Mistress Hazzard held up her bible.

'Aye!' Enid joined the clamour. 'The Governor!'

'Ladies! Please!' The gentleman held up his hand again. 'Some of you will know me as the Governor's brother and second, Lieutenant Colonel John Fiennes. You may speak to me. What is it that you wish to say?'

'We wish to offer ourselves!' Mistress Batten hushed them, stepping forward. 'We are ready to offer ourselves for the fortification, the defence of the city!'

'Aye.' Enid nodded in assent.

'We are ready to march out, ourselves with our children, to stand before the cannon, to keep off the accursed cavaliers' shot from our soldiers!'

'Aye!' The crowd swayed.

'We are determined to go into the mouth of the cannon, to dead their shot. Rather than consent to see this city yielded up to the forces of darkness!'

'Aye!' They were jostling now. 'Amen!'

'Oh, brave ladies!' The young colonel held up his hand again. 'Who speaks of surrender? Rather than consent to the surrender of this city or its castle, I would consent to be hanged!'

'Mark thy word!' Mistress Hazzard's fist was raised. 'As Christ is thy witness!' Her finger pointing to Heaven above.

The colonel looked pale. 'Ladies, let me speak a while with the Governor on your behalf.' His head disappeared inside the window.

The crowd fell to an excited hubbub. Enid felt the Lord's presence, the warmth of the Redeemer himself upon her. She had been good, clean and pure. And now Mistress Hazzard and these Godly women were showing her the way to redemption. Master Francis would smile on her, come to her.

The young gentleman was at the window again, his hand raised. 'Good ladies, goodwives, brave maids! I bring a message from the Governor!'

They fell silent, expectant, waiting to know the Lord's bidding.

'He thanks you for your brave words and determination. But he begs you not to endanger yourselves or you children. Rather, he commands you to go to the Frome Gate. And there to make a bulwark of earth, to block up the gate, so that none may enter. Or exit. So that this city cannot be yielded up to the enemy!'

'Come!' Mistress Batten turned to lead them. 'Let us march to Frome Gate!'

'Aye!' It was clear, decided, ordained. 'Amen!' The Lord had given them their mission. They surged down Broad Street, through St John's Gate and out under the church tower to march down Christmas Street as one.

Enid glared up at the Boucher House as she passed. The Mistress and Mistress Elizabeth would be hiding in their fine chambers instead of marching with these Godly women of the city, instead of marching to do the Lord's work.

On they swept, across the bridge to Frome Gate.

———

Ralph Reeve sat slumped under the cloister arches of the Grammar School gate, his carbine across his lap. They could go no further. Frome Gate was defended, barred and barricaded. The sound of earth and sacks being piled against the inside of the doors carried across Horse Street. Not even a cannon or petard could open it now. And there was no way around the gate. The houses across the street, on either side of the gate, backed onto the river. On the far side of the river were the town walls and cannon commanding the quays. Even if there was a way into the town, they had barely enough powder and shot left between them for one volley.

He looked back at what was left of his division. More than anything, they did not have the strength to go on. Exhaustion overwhelmed them. And he did not have the will to ask them. Jack sat in a ball, his head on his knees. Jewkes slept, twitching and fitful. Tandy's head lolled, his eyes drooping, the binding on his arm bloody and dirty. Sam stared back out across the schoolyard. With them sat the blackamoor, Moses, slumped beside his broken drum, not wanting to leave, refusing to retire with the rest of Lunsford's bluecoats. Only Luke looked up, eyes red, brow furrowed with worry. And Clem, dear Clem, still trying to crack a smile through the dust and sweat that streaked his face. They could go no further. They were done.

Thank God, for the last hour, the only sounds of battle were far off, intermittent, indistinct, echoing up the river from the quays. Silence, cool and still, had steadily overcome them. The old stones of the cloister slowly wore down their resistance, sapping away their strength, exhaustion seeping up into their bones until they could no longer fight. Until they could no longer stay awake.

———

Enid pushed the straw mattress up on top of the bulwark, stuffing it into the gap between the woolsacks and the gatehouse ceiling. It was Moses's mattress. She'd dragged it from the Boucher House to add to the fortification. The accursed Mahometan witch wouldn't need it any more, not in Hell. Now it would serve the Lord. Not Satan.

She wriggled backwards, lowering herself back down the mound of woolsacks, grain sacks, earth and wood to stand on the bridge. It was a fine great barricade, as deep and high as it was wide, filling the gateway behind the wooden doors and portcullis. No one would get past it, neither in nor out of the town. Master Francis would be pleased with her.

They'd done it all themselves, ladies, goodwives and maids, all women together, with Mistress Batten leading them on and Mistress Hazzard encouraging them with her Bible. There'd been a man, an engineer, to show them what to do, and a few soldiers helping, but it had been their own work that had done it.

'Well, ladies!' Mistress Batten looked at them. 'It is a fine piece of work!'

'Christ be praised!' Mistress Hazzard stepped forward, her Bible open. She read aloud. '*And Abimeleck came unto the Tower of Thebez, and fought against it, and went hard unto the door of the Tower to burn it with fire.*

'*And a certain woman cast a piece of a millstone upon Abimelech's head, and all to break his skull. Then he called hastily unto his armour-bearer, and said unto him, draw thy sword and slay me, that men say not of me, a woman slew him. And this young man thrust him through and he died. And when the men of Israel saw that Abimeleck was dead, they went every man to his place.* And Thebez was saved!

'*Thus, God rendered the evil of Abimelech. And all the evil of the men of Sechem did God render upon their heads. And upon them came the curse of Jotham the son of Jerubbaal!*'

'Amen!' The crowd nodded devoutly.

'I say we go to the gunners on the quay!' Mistress Hazzard closed her bible and raised it high. 'That we stand by them in their need!'

'Aye!' Enid shouted her assent out loud with the others. 'Amen!' She would follow Mistress Hazzard anywhere.

Together, they swept back across the bridge, up Christmas Street and past the Boucher House to turn into Jewrie Lane and out onto the Quay Head. Before them, staring out across the River Frome, stood a great gun and its gunners.

Abel Cowans sat beside the gun on the Quay Head, staring out across the river to St Austin's Back and the suburbs beyond. The boatswain, Israel, the Swede and the boy all lounged in the shade beside St Giles' Gate, across Jewrie Lane.

The river was packed tight. The ships, boats and lighters all sitting on the mud at low tide. The bloody cavaliers could nigh on walk across. That's if they didn't set fire to the ships first. The flames would carry on the wind, burn the city. There would be no stopping it. The warehouses, tenements and fine merchant houses were as dry as tinder in the summer heat.

They had to be ready to stop the bloody cavaliers; to sweep the quay and river with iron shot or cannister. It was quiet now, but maybe they were just readying themselves and waiting, waiting for the bottom of the tide to rush across. The minion was well placed. It would do some damage. But they had no protection out on the open quay. They needed a wall or some sort of barricade to stand behind when it started. They could do with some of those woolsacks the women had used to block up Frome Gate.

He turned towards the growing noise behind him, a stirring hubbub. A crowd of women marched down Jewrie Lane and out onto the Quay Head.

'Ladies!' Abel stood, stepping towards them. 'It is not safe! Please! Stay back!'

'We are not afeared!' A fearsome woman led them with her Bible. 'Christ is with us!'

The boatswain was on his feet. 'Ladies! Please be keeping

yourselves to the shelter of the street. The cavaliers may shoot at any moment!'

The woman with the Bible stared at him. 'We will not hide ourselves away!' She looked at Israel, the Swede and the boy behind him. 'It is time to stand out and fight! Be not afeared. We will stand by you! We will shield you from the shot of the accursed!'

'We was just resting awhile.' The boatswain shuffled, uncomfortable. 'We were in the fight at Temple Gate.'

'Come now, Christ will sustain you! You shall not want for provisions.' The woman turned to a young maid beside her, a scrawny wee thing. 'Enid dear, you are from the Boucher House. It is nearby and still needing to pay for its sinful ways. Run and fetch bread, cheese and ale for these brave sailors. And, Enid dear, if anyone tries to stop you, tell them that Christ, the Governor and Reverend Hazzard have sent you.'

———

Ralph's head snapped back, his eyes open. There was the sound of drumming beyond the cloister gate. It was getting closer, louder, rattling down Christmas Steps. Fuck! Surely, they could not be attacking again. Not without powder and shot. But this was different, a single drum, beating a call, a summons, not a march.

A single drummer stepped out cautiously from the bottom of Christmas Steps. Beside him walked an officer, Colonel Charles Gerard, commander of a wing of Prince Rupert's horse. A younger officer held a torn white sheet stuck on a partizan, a flag of truce. They halted in front of Frome Gate. The drumming stopped, echoing away down Horse Street.

Colonel Gerard looked up at the gatehouse. 'Your governor has sent for a parley. We come on behalf of his Highness

Prince Rupert, Prince Maurice and the Marquis of Hertford to agree articles. Please fetch your officer to escort us in.'

A head disappeared from the parapet. Another peered over, then disappeared. Shouting and clattering sounded inside the gatehouse, then silence. Colonel Gerard started to pace up and down the street in front of Frome Gate. Finally, a window creaked opened above the gate. An officer's head stuck itself out cautiously.

'Ah, thank God! At last. An officer. I am Colonel Charles Gerard. And this is Captain William Tyringham. We come on behalf of his Highness Prince Rupert, Prince Maurice and the Marquis of Hertford to agree articles and terms of surrender. Your governor has sent Major Langrish and Captain Hepsley to us, as hostages for a parley. Now, please open this damn gate and escort us to Colonel Fiennes.'

'I am sorry, sir, but I cannot let you in by this gate.'

'God damn me! We will come in by this gate! If not, we will return to the princes and your governor will have no damn parley. And no terms at all!'

'Colonel Fiennes, the Governor, is ready to receive you. However, he says that you should not come in at this gate, but at Newgate.'

'This is most irregular. It is against all expectations of war. Why in God's name should we not enter at this gate?'

'I am sorry, sir. In truth, we cannot open the gate. It is barricaded on the inside. I have had to climb to this window to converse with you. Newgate is but a short walk.'

'God damn me! Very well. But it is ill done. What is your name?'

'Thank you, sir. I am Captain Taylor. As I say, sir, Newgate is but a short walk. If you would go along to your left, sir, along Lewin's Mead, then turn right into Silver Street and St James's

Back. Take the second street on your left hand, into Broad Mead, then right into Merchant Street, at the end of which you will be on The Wear and Newgate will be to your right. I will meet you there, sir.' And then the head disappeared and the window was shut.

'Damned impudent!' The colonel turned away and stopped. He peered into the cloister, sensing the presence of those watching him. He glared at Ralph and his ragged division. 'And who the hell are you?'

'Corporal Reeve, sir.' Ralph stood, his hat by his side. 'Prince Maurice's Dragoons.'

'One of Colonel Washington's damned dragoons. I might have known. I suppose you were at the breach. Well, well done. Keep your men together and no more shooting now, do you hear? His Highness, the Prince has ordered a complete ceasefire.' The colonel turned away again. 'Well, come on, William. We have articles of surrender to negotiate on behalf of his Highness. I hope you can remember the damned way to this Newgate. It is but a short stroll!'

'We are betrayed!' Enid dragged Mistress Elizabeth by the wrist, pulling her, stumbling to the Quay Head and the gun. 'Mistress Hazzard! We are betrayed!'

'What?' Mistress Hazzard looked at her. 'No! How be this?'

'I heard them!' Enid stood firm, heat rising in her bodice. 'At the gate. When I went for the provisions, for the gunners. That Captain Taylor. He was talking to the cavaliers – through the gatehouse window. Colonel Fiennes, the Governor, has sent for a parley! The cavaliers are to come in at Newgate. To agree terms. Terms of surrender!'

Mistress Hazzard raised her Bible to the sky. '*The Lord thy*

God hath pronounced this evil upon this place. Now the Lord hath brought it and done according as he hath said. Because ye have sinned against the Lord! We are undone. *The Lord hath done this unto this land. How fierce is his great wrath!'*

'Amen!' The crowd of women wailed, starting to turn away.

'No!' Enid stepped forward, pulling Mistress Elizabeth. 'I say we are not yet undone. Remember Thebez! Remember how a woman cast a millstone. And it did break that King Abimelech's skull. And when the men of Israel did see it, they went again to their places on the wall. And Thebez was saved!'

They all looked at her.

'I say we fire the cannon! We shoot it at the bloody cavaliers. We shoot it and shoot it. We cast it like a great millstone and break their parley. And all the while we stand with the gunners. Until all the soldiers do see and go again to their places to save the city.'

'Oh, my child!' Mistress Hazzard smiled at her. 'Ye are as *a firebrand plucked out of the burning!'* She pointed at Mistress Elizabeth. 'But who is this woman?'

'It is the Boucher bitch!' Enid dragged her forward. 'Mistress Elizabeth bloody Boucher! She was with that Mahometan witch, Moses! I saw her! When he was casting his spell. She helped the accursed devil escape, let him join with the cavaliers. To cast his evil against us! Against this city!' She forced the bitch's arm up, up between her shoulder blades, made her gasp, pushing her forward to stand beside the cannon. The knife was thrust up against her perfect neck, pale and damp with sweat, the fine hair falling astray. 'Now the bitch can stand with us! She can stand against their accursed shot! Let's see how she bleeds when they shoot holes in her pure bloody hide!'

'Come ladies!' Mistress Hazzard stepped forward, stood

beside Enid. 'Let us stand with these brave gunners! And let us cast a millstone for Christ!'

Enid turned to the sailors over her shoulder. 'Now shoot this bloody cannon!'

———

Abel Cowans looked at the boatswain. This was not right. It would end in chaos, the city destroyed, too many would suffer, the poor more than the rich.

The boatswain shook his head. 'Nae lass. I canna do that. For me, it's over.' He turned to leave. 'Israel, Job, laddie, it's time we were getting back to the ship.' He looked at Abel. 'Are ye coming along wirr us, Abel? Or stopping with these here women?'

Abel looked back at the women about the gun. It was not right to leave the young mistress held against her will. He was happy to see her father hang for the self-seeking, privileged bastard that he was. But this lass had done nothing. She did not deserve to be yoked to these she-fanatics. 'Let the young mistress go now.'

The maid turned on him, her knife flashing in the sun. 'Damn you! You crippled prick! Be gone!' She shook it at the boatswain, the blade twisting. 'You and this pathetic crew! You cowards!' She tore the match from the linstock, held it in her hand, blowing upon it; smoking, crackling, burning bright. 'For Jesus!' She thrust the match down upon the breach.

The burning coal stabbed down upon the back of Abel's hand, his crippled hand held over the touch hole. Searing pain tore through the old wounds, his shattered hand and stumps flinching, twitching. He held it there, over the priming powder, flesh burning as the blade sliced the air between them and a woman screamed.

He caught her wrist with his good hand, turned it, brought it down upon the breach, the knife clattering onto the flagstones. Her eyes burning, wild, seething anger as he grasped the match, tore it from her fist, hurled it over the edge of the quay.

With a weather eye on the bitch maid, Abel plunged his burning hand into the mop bucket beside the gun, let the water cool and sooth the pain as the match gave a final splutter and gasp, sinking amongst the wet mud of the Frome.

The young mistress ran from them, back up Jewrie Lane, wiping tears from her face as the rest of the women began to melt away. Soldiers poured from St Giles Gate, Fish Lane and St Stephen's churchyard, throwing down muskets and pikes as they ran across the quay to clamber over the ships, boats and mud to the far side of the river, to join the cavaliers.

Finally, Abel stood. He picked up the bucket and poured it over the gun's touch hole, the last of the priming powder running over the breach to drip, black, wet and useless on the quay. He turned to the maid, the fearsome woman with the Bible and the staring women. 'It's finished! Now, get yersels home!'

XIV

Return

Moussa Dansocko
River Frome, Thursday the 27ᵗʰ of July 1643, first light

Moussa lowered himself into the cold dark water, his feet sinking deep into the thick mud, the last of the tide eddying about him. The old master's boat had gone from where he left it. But he had to cross the river, he had to cross now, before the dawn light and the waters rose again. Already, the first hint of grey streaked the far sky beyond the city.

Carefully, he took a step out from the slip wall, his feet feeling for the bottom, the *taweez*, pistol and drum held above his head, his shoes around his neck. The water flowed faster, deeper, darker under the arch of the bridge, swirling thick and black, its echo lapping over his head.

Something touched his leg: the water tugging, pulling, clawing at him. His foot slipped, the drum scraping against the wall, his breath sharp and fast.

The *Faro*, the supreme power, lived in the *Jeliba*, the River Niger. The dead must cross the river, their *dya* trapped in its waters until reborn. Trapped amongst the *jinn*, the *ghulah* that lurked there, that lurked in these waters, ready to drag a man down to devour him in their dark haunt. He should have offered prayers, made a sacrifice before trying to cross.

He dragged himself out from under the arch, stood with his back against the first pier, the gatehouse of Frome Gate and the houses on the bridge above him. He let his breathing calm feeling the strength of the *taweez* in his hand. Slowly, gingerly, he waded deeper, out across the river, moving from one pier to the next until he stood in the shadow of the far wall, under the Boucher House, listening and waiting. The house was silent, just the gurgle of water under the bridge.

Cautiously, he climbed the wet and slimy steps, his coat and breeches dripping. The garden lay still and quiet in the grey dawn. He stepped carefully across its neat parterre – once his place of solace, almost like the little Arabic gardens of Gao he'd known as a boy. Beyond it lay the courtyard.

The stable was empty. Mistress Elizabeth's own horse gone. Had she fled or was it taken, an asset seized. He slid the drum and shoes inside. The drum was broken, holed, but he could not leave it behind. Colonel Lunsford had given it to him. He could no longer bring the brave *horo* to Mistress Elizabeth, but he carried his *nyama* with him. He slipped the *taweez* over his head and under his wet shirt, against his heart.

The window was unlocked. Enid never remembered to twist the turnbuckle catch at the end of the day. Time and again, he'd had to check that it was locked at night. Slowly, he eased the casement open, creaking on its hinge. The kitchen lay silent within. Enid not yet at work. He squeezed himself through the gap.

The pistol gripped in his hand, he carefully opened the kitchen door and stepped into the passage. The house silent, sleeping – or waiting to kill him? Slowly, quietly, he slipped into the hall, his muddy feet padding damply on the flagstones.

Something moved. Someone, something, sniffed. Then a

growl, padding claws and snuffling, skittering feet and a wet nose. Mistress Elizabeth's dog licked the damp salt from his legs its tail wagging, thrashing on the panelled wall. He tried to calm the dog before it woke Master Francis and the soldiers, before they found him, before they killed him.

A noise above: a chamber door opening, the stair creaking.

'Who's. . . Who is there?' Mistress Elizabeth's voice.

She would wake the others. The soldiers would hear her.

'Good dog, Pepper.' She was almost at the bottom. 'What is it, boy?'

Moussa stepped out from the shadow, heard her gasp. 'It is I, Mistress. Moses.'

'Moses. . .' She choked. 'You came back.'

'Please, Mistress,' he whispered. 'Do not wake the soldiers.'

'They are gone, thank God. They left the house at cock-crow.'

'God be praised!' He breathed, the pistol dropping to his side.

'I don't believe they mean to return. They have taken all their stuff. And what provisions they could carry. And my own riding horse. My father's last gift to me.'

'Where is Enid?' He felt the *taweez* hung about his neck, torn, incomplete. 'She took something that is precious to me.'

'She left with them. With that bigot, Master Frances. God knows what she may have taken with her.' She shook, her cheeks glistening wet with tears in the dawn light. The dog nuzzled closer, brushed against her bare ankles, sensing her distress. 'But I could not. . . I could not face her. Not again.'

'Mistress, I am sorry. I was not here to protect you. And I am sorry, I have failed to bring Colonel Henry Lunsford to your aid. He is dead. I was with him, on Christmas Steps, when they. . . when they killed him.'

'But, Moses, you came back. I did not think. . . I thought you had gone.'

'Mistress, I must leave you again. I will bring help. There may be more fighting. The soldiers may return. I will bring the King's soldiers. You must let me out, but bar the door behind me. And lock the kitchen casement. The turnbuckle was undone.'

Cautiously, Moussa looked out from the courtyard of the Boucher House. Christmas Street and Frome Bridge were empty. Only a wary cat slipped past in the grey dawn. Nothing moved on or about Frome Gate. No soldiers. No one.

He stepped out into the street, the drum at his side, pistol tucked into his breaches. He walked between the houses that lined the bridge, faster now, the way clear. A door opened. A maid stepped out, scurried past him, a look of recognition and shock on her face.

The gatehouse was empty of soldiers. Silent, unoccupied, abandoned. Just a great mound of woolsacks, timber, mattresses and earth blocking the gateway. He climbed up, pulling at the sacks, dragging them away at the side to tumble into the street behind. He worked alone, feverishly, his arms aching. He did not stop until the little postern door would open enough for a man to squeeze through.

Finally, he climbed the winding stair to the top of Frome Gate. He stood in the first of the morning sun, bright and clear on his back, his *dya*, his spirit, his double, his shadow stretching out over Christmas Steps.

He slung the drum, touched the splintered hole in its side. With stick and hand, he struck the skins. He struck it as a *djembe*, the drum of his childhood. The drum was dulled, wounded, sullen, refusing to respond to his touch. Gently at first, his beats soothing, he warmed it, caressed its skins, let the rhythm guide his hands, building slowly in strength. He played the call, the summons. Louder now, stronger, the drum vibrating, pounding, its *nyama* flowing through him, reaching out, resonating within, reverberating without, echoing over the roofs, its power booming over the city. It called the great *jatigi's* soldiers, pulled at their *dya*, tugging at their spirits, compelling, demanding obedience.

The street below was filling, the King's soldiers emerging from doors and alleys, rising up. They saw the open postern door. They were cautious still. The drum reaching out, louder still. The soldiers from the Grammar School entering the gatehouse. More following behind. They came down Christmas Steps. Still, he played, the drum filling him, his hands flying, the power flowing through him, melding, mixing, fusing with the drum, the city, earth and morning sun. He was Moussa the *jali*, Moussa the *nyama* worker, Moussa the *nyamakala*.

———

Ralph squeezed through the half open postern door. The inside of the gatehouse was stacked with woolsacks, grain sacks, piled earth and balks of wood. A narrow gap had been cleared, pulled away, behind the postern. He climbed up over the crude barricade, his carbine at the ready, emerging on the far side of Frome Gate.

He was inside the town. Except for the lone drummer on its roof, the gatehouse was unoccupied, unguarded. The narrow street that crossed Frome Bridge was empty. 'It's clear!' He looked back at Luke's head poking past the door. 'Come on! They've gone. The gate is unguarded. We're inside the town!'

Luke clambered out of the gatehouse to stand beside him, followed by Clem, Jack, Jewkes, wounded Tandy, and Sam.

Ralph led them forward, slowly, out between the tall, fine houses and shops that lined Frome Bridge. The lone drummer that had called them from the top of Frome Gate finally stopped, the last beats of his call echoing away down the street.

A clattering on the gatehouse stairs stopped them. The drummer burst from the gatehouse behind them. It was the blackamoor, Moses.

'Master Ralph, you came. You all came.'

'Moses, was it you that opened the postern gate?' Ralph had not expected that of him.

'Yes.' Moses grinned back. 'I cleared the sacks to open the door. I am sorry I could not open it better.'

'How did you get inside the gate?'

'I crossed the river, in the dark, when the water was low. My mistress's house is just on the far side there, at the end of the bridge. I will take you there.'

Ralph let Moses lead them forward across the bridge. Already, others were emerging from the postern behind, a few more of Washington's dragoons, the Lord General's redcoats and Stradling's wild Welshmen.

Moses continued to talk, as he led them on, pointing the way to the quay, into the town, explaining that they were on Christmas Street. 'My mistress needs your help, your protection. They hanged her father, three months back, when he tried to open the gates to Prince Rupert. You will see, it is a fine house.'

It was indeed a fine merchant's house, big enough to quarter what was left of his division of dragoons, with stables for the horses. There was even a garden that backed onto the river. Better to occupy it now, than wait for the quartermaster to allot them billets in some rundown tenement when the best quarters had been taken. They might be moved later, but they may as well enjoy it while they could. They would need to guard it, keep it safe from looting.

Ralph looked at them, the morning sun on their tired, dust caked faces. They deserved – *needed* – good quarters. 'Sam, guard this place. Some of the foot may get out of hand. We will quarter here tonight. Keep Tandy with you and get his arm dressed by the ladies inside. If anybody questions you, you tell them that this is the house of a loyal citizen and that you have orders to guard it.'

But there was more that needed to be done before they rested. He turned to Jack, grim as ever. 'Try to find us snaphaunces or dog-lock carbines, enough to arm every man. It is time we replaced the matchlocks. Take Jewkes with you. And pistols. We need a horse pistol for each man. The rebels will be forced to leave their firearms behind, under the terms of surrender. Start by searching their rendezvous place. They will likely have stacked their arms there.'

He looked at his old school friend. 'Luke, you and Clem find us horses, *good* horses, chargers if you can. The rebels will not be allowed to take more than one horse each. They must leave their spare riding horses behind. Search the inns first and take the best horses you can find. Enough for all of us, Hodge and the boys as well. I don't care if we are dragoons, I want us all to be mounted on *horses*. No more ponies.'

Finally, he turned to the blackamoor. 'Moses, please show me the way to the centre of the town and the castle. I want to see the route the rebels are leaving by.' Already, the sound of drums echoed over the city; the rebel garrison starting to march out.

XV

Surrender

Jeremy Holway
St Peter's Street, outside Bristol Castle,
seven o'clock in the morning

Jeremy Holway stood in the crowd about St Peter's Church, outside the castle gate. The gate was closed. It should have been open. The Governor had promised to keep their goods safe inside. Now they had to retrieve them. They had to rescue their belongings before the city and castle were surrendered to the damned cavaliers, before it was taken as booty, or stolen to fund a tyrant king and his Papist army.

The crowd pushed and jostled, men, women, rich merchants and poor shopkeepers, all desperate to reclaim their stuff. It was already seven o'clock. The garrison was to march out at nine. Just two hours were left before the castle and all that was in it was handed to the delinquents.

And then came a yell from the front of the crowd, from those nearest the gate. Jeremy strained to see what was happening, the crowd pushing from behind. Like a rippling wave spreading outwards, a great wailing moan, frothing with anger, rolled back through the gate.

The castle was already in the hands of the cavaliers! The

Governor's men had already abandoned their posts, had marched away to The Marsh, had let free the prisoners inside. The delinquent bastards had closed the gate, barred the citizens entry, were ransacking their belongings, laughing at them from behind the high castle walls.

He was ruined! His precious stock lost, given away by that fool Fiennes.

———

Enid Powell held tight to the back of her saviour as the horse moved, wrapping her arms around his battered armour, drawing in his scent of leather, iron and Godly manhood. They'd left the Boucher House together in the pre-dawn dark, on Mistress Elizabeth's horse. Served the perfect bitch right, it did. She'd have thrown her out on the street with nothing.

But Master Francis had swept her up onto the back of the horse with him, saved her from a life of sin, from selling her body to sailors and dockside porters on the streets, backs and quays. Together, they'd joined what was left of the garrison on The Marsh at dawn. Now they were moving, part of a great column of soldiers and citizens leaving the city. They marched under Marsh Gate and along St Nicholas' Back in the morning sun.

He'd come back from the battle wounded, hurt, limping, exhausted, his faith tattered and torn. She knew his torment, his inner struggle and self-loathing. She'd helped him upstairs, fed him, tended him, nursed him again. And he'd taken her into his bed. He'd chosen her, wanted her, loved her. Not Mistress perfect Elizabeth. He was shy, vulnerable, unsure, no more than a boy. But she'd soothed him, stroking, guiding him in the dark, driving their demons away to lie wrapped together in perfect sleep. Now she was his. She held him tight in her grasp.

———

The Lord has forsaken his altar. He hath abhorred his Sanctuary. He hath given it into the hand of the enemy. They were leaving, surrendering the city, abandoning it to the forces of Satan. Francis Reeve touched the Bible under his breastplate. Now the King and his Popish cavaliers were free to unleash upon England the forces of darkness that ran amok in Ireland. The last bulwark was gone. The keys of Hell and Death relinquished. Cornish barbarity, Welsh malignancy, demonic Irish Papacy, Spain, Rome and the Antichrist had their harbour, had their hold from which to spread their darkness.

For *Babylon the great is fallen; is fallen and is become the habitation of devils, and the hold of every foul spirit. And the kings of the earth, who have committed fornication and lived deliciously with her, shall bewail her and lament her, when they shall see the smoke of her burning.*

And the merchants of the world shall weep and mourn over her. But they had brought the wrath of God upon themselves. *For thy merchants were the great men of the earth; for by thy sorceries were all nations deceived. And in her was found the blood of prophets, and of saints, and of all that were slain upon the earth.*

They had been forsaken. For this was a Godless city. Its merchant venturers cared only about their profit. Half of them would have sold their city and souls to the Devil if they could. It was a harbour, a port an inlet for all the sins, pestilence and plagues of the world. It was a city that fornicated with Satan. *And they shall answer because they have forsaken the Covenant of the Lord God of their fathers.*

The city's militia were no better. They had shown themselves to be faithless, cowardly, treacherous. The women citizens had done more to hold back the heathen horde. The maid Enid had fought with the witch Moses, taken food to the soldiers on the line, tended wounded, built the bulwark inside Frome Gate, stood with the gunners on the quay. She was braver than most of the garrison of this city.

And yet, she had debased herself to lie with him, slid herself into his bed when he was weak. She was a seductress, a night hag that rode him. She clung to his back now, her arms coiled about him. He shifted in the saddle, his loins hot, balls aching, his manhood stiffening, slick, images of flesh burning his soul, tormenting him, turning his thoughts from God.

They rode in silence with Colonel Fiennes' Regiment of Horse, following the Governor, what was left of the garrison and righteous citizens following in a great column. Up ahead, a crowd, spilled out of Baldwin Street and onto the backs. 'Where is now your Puritan God?' The crowd were shouting, yelling gesticulating. 'Where is your Calvinist King Jesus?'

More blocked the way under St Nicholas' Gate, the way to the Castle, Lawford's Gate and the Great Road to London. 'Where are your fastings, your prayers and profession?' There were soldiers amongst them, apostates, cavaliers, Cornishmen. 'King Charles shall be King, for all!' They were inside the town already. 'Remember Reading!' They poured across the bridge, grasping at the horses ahead. 'God is a cavalier now!'

But there was one in the crowd that was different. One that stood out. A dark devil. A blackamoor. The witch, Moses!

———

Moussa Dansocko pushed through the crowd, men and soldiers stepping aside as they saw him. The garrison soldiers were leaving, the head of their great column turning to cross Bristol Bridge. The Governor looked pale and frightened, officers and rich merchants crowding around him as the King's soldiers yelled and spat, waiving their fists and weapons in the air.

Behind him rode a troop of armoured horsemen. The crowd pulled men, women and baggage from the backs of horses. Further back marched the foot soldiers and poorer citizens. They were without pikes or muskets to defend themselves. The crowd dragged some away to be stripped and plundered of what they carried on their backs and in their purses.

And then he saw her. She rode behind an armoured trooper. On Mistress Elizabeth's horse. Her arms wrapped about the *shaitan*, Francis. The *qarinah* bitch, Enid!

———

Ralph Reeve followed Moses through the crowd. The blackamoor suddenly stiffened, lunging forward at an armoured trooper and the young woman that rode pillion on his horse.

The woman was yelling, a scrawny maid waving a scrap of paper, pointing at Moses. 'Witch! He is a witch!' She was falling, pulled, kicking, clawing and screaming from the horse. Moses wrestled with her, fighting to prise the paper from her fist as her teeth and talons bit and scratched, drawing his blood.

Ralph grabbed at the reins of the skittering, whinnying horse. Its eyes bulged wide with fear, its ears flat. The trooper tried to back away; shock and anger bursting from under a bent visor. Francis!

The bastard had taken Breda from him at Winchester, broken the horse's leg at Roundway Down, left Breda for crowbait. He did not deserve another horse. Not this fine mare, or any other. The bastard could walk! Ralph stepped closer. But he'd promised their mother, promised her on her deathbed, promised her that he would look after Francis. Always.

Moses was drawing back, licking his wounds, the scrap of paper in his hand. The crowd were swarming forward, yelling wildly, pulling at Francis, reaching up to drag him down. Then came the sound of breaking glass. . . a window smashed. . . a pistol shot. . . all order collapsing in frenzy.

Ralph grabbed the maid by the back of her bodice, picked her up, still kicking, and threw her across his brother's saddle bow. He pushed a wild Cornishman aside and smacked the mare's rump to send it leaping forward, back into the column. 'Go! Go now!'

———

George Merrett stood outside Lawford's Gate, beside the King's Great Road to London. He waited with others, behind the princes and general officers, waiting to take charge of the ordnance, arms, colours, powder, match and shot that were to be surrendered with the city at nine of the clock. All was arranged, the terms and articles of surrender agreed and exchanged the evening before.

The Governor and officers were permitted to march out with their arms, horses and baggage, the troopers with horses and swords only, the common foot soldiers without any arms but their musket rests. Carriages and carts were permitted to carry their baggage, sick and hurt soldiers and those citizens who wished to leave were permitted to do so with *their goods, wives, families, bag and baggage*. All were to be escorted in safe convoy as far as Warminster. The King's forces were not to enter the town until the Parliamentary soldiers had marched out at nine of the clock, when all prisoners held in the city were to be released and delivered up. The city, its inhabitants and their estates were to be secured from *plundering and all other violence and wrong whatsoever.*

But something was terribly wrong. The garrison was already marching, the sound of their drumming echoing over the town. George looked at his watch again. It was only half past seven o'clock. They were marching early – far too early.

But worse, there were other noises echoing through the streets and Old Market, the sound of shouting, yelling, of tumult and riot. And now they had heard the sound of a shot. The drums were not getting closer. They were not approaching Lawford's Gate. They had turned. They were moving obliquely south, not east – south towards Temple Gate. They were marching away from the princes and the escort waiting for them. Instead, they were heading towards the Cornish.

An officer trotted back from Lawford's Gate and swept off his hat to Prince Rupert. A whisper ran back through those waiting beside the road. The gate was unguarded, open to all.

George shifted in his saddle, snapped the lid of his watch shut. What if the other gates were unguarded? The King's soldiers were bound to find out. It was the way of soldiers. They would find the gates unoccupied, unguarded. They would enter the town. They would not wait for their officers to restrain them.

Christ! They were inside now. They would be roaming the streets unchecked. There would be plundering, pillage, perhaps even rape. Those who had been badly treated by Essex's army at the surrender of Reading would seek revenge. And the Cornish... Oh, Christ! the Cornish would run amok! They were wild and unruly as it was. And they had suffered

346

terribly in the storming. There would be no controlling them once loose inside the city.

Why? Why did it have to end in chaos? Why could it not have been done properly? Damn the Governor and his officers for marching early, for failing to keep the gates guarded, for failing to keep to the articles. Damn the Cornish for their wild, senseless disobedience, for their not waiting for the guns. Damn the rest of them for insisting on an assault, for storming Bristol without proper preparation, for throwing away the King's greatest hope of seizing London, for squandering his advantage in the charge, in the scramble for honour and preferment. And damn them all for killing Old Nick Busy!

What good would the port and riches of Bristol bring if it was now lost to plunder and chaos? There could be fire, the city burned, the ships in the harbour destroyed – all hope of taking and equipping a fleet for the King lost in stupidity, in unruliness and anarchy. What good would it bring if all that was left was a graveyard for the King's precious foot? How would they ever have the strength or standing again to take London?

George thrust his watch deep into his pocket, his hand shaking, anger and exhaustion washing over him.

———

Abel Cowans lay curled under a dirty blanket in his rotting tenement, the drums echoing down St Thomas Lane. The Governor, rich merchants, so called gentlemen and soldiers were leaving. Only the poor remained, those who had no money and nowhere else to go. Another governor, more merchants and soldiers would come to take the place of those that left. But the poor always stayed. They always stayed put. And they always stayed poor.

There was no place on a ship for him, not with only one good hand. He couldn't climb or work aloft. He couldn't tie a knot even. All that was left was to wait in line on the backs at dawn, to fight to get hired, to slave all day in the rain and cold, shifting stinking tannery hides on the dockside, in hock to a bastard foreman for a few pennies. Only to crawl out again with the dawn to do it all again. He might have made boatswain once. Now, he was no better than a Barbary slave – valueless, worthless, just another hireling labourer in the crowd in a foreign city fighting for one more day's pay.

One day, one day, the common man would rise up and be heard. One day, there would be true rebellion, an end to oppression and servitude. There would be common wealth, rights and freedoms for all, not just the privileged few. *One day, poor men will speak!*

———

Kendall Tremain lay beneath the town wall beside Temple Gate. He'd lain there all through the night, since they'd charged the walls for a second time. His leg was smashed, bloody, swollen, black and stinking. The tears had long since burned dry on his cheeks and neck, hot with fever.

He was not alone. Too many others lay with him. Sir Nicholas Slanning was mortally wounded, his thigh broken by a case-shot. Young Colonel Trevanion had died at midnight. Colonel Buck, Major Kendall, Captain Rich were all gone. Colonel Basset was wounded and Sir Bernard Astley gravely hurt. Three-score and ten more lay dead in the ditch or under the wall and as many and more again were wounded, almost all true Cornishmen.

They'd won the day. Taken Bristol. The Puritan bastards were leaving now, marching out of Temple Gate to jeers and shouts. But there'd be sorrow and pain in so many villages and coves at the cost, pain and want for lost fathers, sons, brothers, husbands, shipmates and lovers.

He dared not think of Morwenna and the little ones. She'd be minding Hedrek and little Merryn, feeding the pig or tending her little garden, barefoot in the sun, her hair falling down like it did. The moon hung fat and full, high in the blue morning sky. Perhaps she'd look up and see it, think of him and what might have been.

It was the Feast of St Anne, Breton queen and mother of the Virgin Mary, patron saint of sailors, of fishermen, of mothers and of infants, guardian and protectress against the storm. Please God, let St Anne watch over Morwenna now. Watch over her and the little ones.

A seagull wheeled overhead, calling to him. The smell of saltwater over mud, the tide rising in the ditch, flooding in, *an mor*, the sea coming for him, coming to claim him, to take him back, to wash him clean, to bathe his wounds, to take him home.

The water was rising about him, cool, calm, soaking the pain away. His legs and arms were cold. . . numb. . . floating. The *morvorenyon*, the merfolk, were all around him, singing gently on the breeze, *an morwyns*, the sound of the sea, the *mordroz*, calling to him.

He could see Morwenna and the little ones on the beach. They'd come to see him, to see the sea, to play on the sand. He tried to wave, to shout, to tell them that he loved them. But his arms were heavy, his voice lost, the waves washing over his head.

A beautiful *morvoren* held him, sinking, down into the depths, deeper into the cool, dark sea to join all the old fishermen lost under the waves. They were taking him back, taking him home, taking him back to the sea, *tha'n mor*.

—

The seagull wheeled overhead, rising higher with every turn, high on the warm air blowing in from the sea. With one final circle and cry over the city, it turned west, following the river, out past Hot Wells and Clifton, over the Avon Gorge, Shirehampton and Morgan's Pill, out over the ships that lay at anchor in the King's Road, out to the Bristol Channel and the sea.

High over Porshut Point and Black Nore, it turned to follow the coast, out past Flat Holm and the Mendip Hills, sweeping over Minehead and Exmoor, on past Appledore and Lundy Island to the rolling Atlantic Ocean. Lower now, it skimmed the swell, surf and spume under Hartland Point to rise again, arcing over the cliffs of Morwenstow.

Racing inland on a Westerly wind, the great gull swooped over Kilkhampton to follow the River Tamar south, past Holsworthy and Launceston then dropping lower, down between Bodmin Moor and Dartmoor, the river twisting and turning, over Horsebridge, Gunnislake and Drakewalls, the quays at Morwellham, over Calstock and Danescombe. It swept low over the great house at Cotehele and up the little valley to Metherell to land on a pigsty in the corner of a tinner's cottage garden.

Morwenna Tremain looked up from hoeing the beans. A great ugly black-backed *gullan* stood on the pig *crow*, staring – staring at her with its evil yellow eye. It ruffled its feathers, dipped its chest, raised its beak and called, a long choking, piercing, hawing *galow*.

'*Re Varia!*' The hoeing stick dropped between the beans. *Cool ew!* An omen, a message! *Ankow*, death! Morwenna grabbed Merryn, pulling Hedrek inside, holding them tight to her, her back against the rough door, tears flooding down her cheeks and straggling hair. He wasn't coming back. He wasn't coming home. He was gone. Kendall was gone.

Gloucester

George Merrett
The mine, beneath Eastgate, Gloucester,
Friday the 1ˢᵗ of September 1643,
nine o'clock in the evening

George Merrett groped for the watch in his pocket, pulling it free. He flipped open the lid, held it up to the candle guttering at the base of the mineshaft. It was almost nine of the clock. Quickly, he snapped the lid shut, pushed the watch back deep inside his pocket, where it was safe, away from the wet and earth that dripped and fell from the shaft's sides.

Nine of the clock at night. Just nine hours before first light. They had to finish the mine before then. It was their last chance to seize Gloucester. Already the Earl of Essex was at Brackley Heath with a fresh army of London trained bands, intent on relieving the city.

They should be marching on London. But the King had been persuaded to first take Gloucester by siege. The Welsh refused to march further until the city was taken and old slights repaid. And the Cornish had gone, back to the South, angry and sullen after their losses at Lansdown and Bristol. Even the King's Oxford foot insisted on siege, not storm.

The city was expected to fall quickly, easily. Governor Massey was supposedly ready to surrender. They had surrounded it, bombarded it day and night with mortar grenades, heated shot, iron ball, great stones and beams of timber. The King's engineers had devised siege engines to bridge the moat. But now they were short of powder and iron shot.

Still Gloucester defied them. For twenty-three days it had withstood their siege. Still the city's walls stood, backed up by the citizens with an earth rampart. Still, the garrison defied them with false parleys, marksmen on the walls, their psalm singing and sallies into the King's earthworks. And they had killed two more of his skilled gunners. Mister Berkeley and Mister Scott were dead, killed beside their guns in the trenches.

The mine was their last hope. Day and night, they had been digging it, the Welsh miners labouring to cut their way through the gravel, mudstone and clay, underground springs flooding the bottom of the level.

He had measured it, and measured it again. They were under the moat, almost under the Eastgate walls. By morning, they should be there. Then they would pack the mine with gunpowder and blow a breach for the King's army to storm.

John Barnwood climbed down into the shaft, the light from the lanterns in the Eastgate dungeon disappearing above him. The countermine was narrow, wet – hurriedly built. At the base of the shaft, he stooped, crawling into the adit that led down and out under the city walls. His hands and knees sank into the cold mud; water dripping from above, trickling beneath him. They'd had to abandon the other shafts for underground springs. Pray to God that this one held tonight.

The moon would be rising outside, full and bright. It had to be now, between last light and high moon, while the shadows were still long. They had to stop the bastard cavaliers and their Welsh miners before they got under the Eastgate, before they blew a breach in the wall and stormed the city. They had to hang on until the Earl of Essex or Sir William Waller came to their relief. There were only four barrels of gunpowder left in the city to face the storm. It had to be tonight. They had to stop them tonight. He felt for the satchel across his chest, the pistol and grenade inside, checked it hung free of the mud and wet.

Slowly, softly, carefully, he pushed aside the wooden boards and turf that covered the end of the adit. Fresh, cool night air rushed in. The moat was still in shadow, dark, dry, silent, the stars filling the sky above. He crawled out of the adit, waited beside it, counting out the sergeant and four musketeers that followed him.

They crept across the dry moat, watching, listening for the accursed malignant sentinels, pistol in hand. They climbed the counterscarp, crawling forward over the earth spoil thrown up from the damned cavaliers' trenches, galleries and mine. The moon rose slowly, full and ripe.

A pair of sentinels stood whispering in the glow of their match, moaning about their officers and their victuals, their smoke dark and bitter in the night air. Closer, below the parapet, a miner dragged a bucket of wet mud from the shaft to empty it and descend again into its wavering candlelight. Then silence.

The musketeers were in place, ready to rake the trench with their firelocks. Quietly, gently, John pulled the grenade from the satchel, checked its fuse was uncoiled, still in place. He'd cast it himself, like the bells that he'd cast for the churches and the shot he'd made for the garrison. Pray to God it would work. The sergeant held his tin open, the lighted match shielded, ready within.

The grenade fuse spluttered, sparked, crackled into life, brilliant and ruinous. The mouth of the cavalier mine lay open, gaping wide, waiting to swallow it down.

Historical Notes

The General Crisis of the 17th Century

The 17th century was a golden age of European art, science and progress. But it was also a black age of religious persecution, slaughter, famine, disease and destruction. In parts of Germany, more than half the population perished. Bohemia saw worse. The civil wars that tore apart England, Scotland, Ireland and Wales remain the bloodiest conflict in British history.

This was a period of extraordinary upheaval and change. It marks the birth of the modern world, a secular, materialistic world based on rational, scientific thinking and the independence of man. However, change was not sudden or universal. Faith in ancient, medieval and superstitious practices, local lore and the centrality of God remained fundamental parts of life for many, as they do in much of the world today.

Overpopulation led to huge disparities of wealth and living conditions, exacerbated by climate change. Life expectancy of the poor in England had dropped to thirty years, significantly lower than a century before. The 'Little Ice Age' is now acknowledged as an underlying contributor to the violence that swept the globe in the 1640s.

The medieval world no longer provided adequate spiritual, moral or societal answers to maintain stability. This was a period of fundamental intellectual change. The ideas of William Gilbert (1544 –1603), Kepler (1571–1630), Galileo (1564 –1646), Thomas Hobbes (1588 –1679), Descartes (1596 –1650), Newton (1642 –1726) and John Locke (1632 –1704) irrevocably challenged the perceptions of the ancient and medieval worlds. Ultimately, they placed mathematical calculation as the basis for scientific advancement, a concept taken for granted by most today.

Whilst the need for change may have been clear, there was no agreement on its course. Some saw a strong centralised state as essential. Others believed in the natural rights of man, some in a 'levelling' of society. Many sought answers in religion, in glorifying or appeasing God, some in religious extremism, in defeating Satan and in building a heaven on earth.

Ultimately, the 17th century is marked by violence. The 1640s was the most violent decade in world history, ever. The conflicts that swept the globe in this decade are now recognised as symptoms of the General Crisis of the 17th century. Continental Europe was ravaged by the Thirty Years War and the endless Wars of Religion that accompanied it. These brutal religious and political wars saw the destruction of large areas of Germany, Bohemia, Lorraine and the Low Countries. Callot's *Miseries of War* provides a glimpse of the horrors of this conflict which remains a deep scar in the European psyche.

Huge numbers of English, Scottish, Irish and Welsh soldiers fought in these wars, joining the Imperials and the Catholic League, as well as the protestant cause. In many cases, complete regiments served on the continent. Others served Russia or fought against the Ottomans. The British Civil Wars should not be seen in isolation, but as part of the wider European conflict.

The British Civil Wars: The War of Three Kingdoms

Charles I was king of England, Scotland and of Ireland. His reign started with seven 'fat years' (1629 to 1635). These were followed by poor harvests, severe hardship and discontent. The years 1642 (Edgehill), 1649 (the year of his execution) and 1659 (the end of the Interregnum) were particularly bad. These were caused by the Little Ice Age. However, many in 1642 saw God's wrath and biblical parallels with Pharaoh.

The old medieval system of communal farming was inefficient. However, the process of enclosure led to social tension and civil disorder in the years running up to the First Civil War. It was a contributory factor in the Great Rebellion. The disenfranchised rural poor had little legal recourse but to swell the numbers of vagrants on the streets of London, Bristol, York, Norwich and other towns across England. They also filled the ranks of armies.

Economic depression contributed to a crisis in government. King Charles I's attempt to rule without Parliament and his use of royal prerogative to raise taxes such as ship money is well known. However, it is worth noting that Parliament voted Charles only one year of Customs and Excise revenue on his accession; a tax granted to all previous English monarchs for life and essential for maintaining the national administration, including the navy.

Religious tensions between Charles and his Scottish subjects came to a head in 1639. Abortive attempts to impose religious uniformity, the 'devil's whore', resulted in the

Bishops' Wars. These were rapidly followed by the rebellion of disenfranchised Catholics in Ireland from the summer of 1641. Reports of atrocities stoked political and religious division to the point of crisis, with both King and Parliament claiming the sole right to raise an army to protect England.

The final breakdown came when, encouraged by his queen, Charles made an abortive attempt to seize five MPs from the House of Commons on the 4th of January 1642. However, the 'birds had flown' and London apprentices mobilised to force the King to leave London for York. The Queen left for Holland to purchase arms and munitions.

King and Parliament both raised armies. At the centre of the divide were supporters of what were to become the Tory and liberal Whig parties, the basis of British politics today. However, each was forced to ally with political and religious extremists. The King appealed to those who sought strong central patriarchal government, Catholics and reactionaries. Political Levellers, recognised today as early socialists by the British Labour Party, and radical sectarians seeking Godly Rule sided with Parliament.

The armies raised by both the King and Parliament each drew on recent military practice from the Thirty Years War and Wars of Religion in Europe. The 17th century saw a military revolution that was to dominate warfare for the next two and half centuries. Linear formations of pike and musket progressively replaced the great Spanish *tercio* squares of pike, shot, sword and buckler, finally defeating them at Rocroi in 1643.

Inspired by classical Roman tactics, the Dutch reforms of Prince Maurice of Nassau brought greater firepower to bear and strength in defence. These were adapted by King Gustavus II Adolphus of Sweden to deliver both firepower and offensive mobility. Both sides in the British Civil Wars adopted these 'pike and shot' tactics. Each was relatively well matched in terms of manpower, equipment and training.

Civil war was unleashed upon the mainland of Great Britain when the armies raised by the King and by Parliament collided at Edgehill, on the 23rd of October 1642. Most had anticipated a single show of force or token battle – a letting of blood to 'purge the nation'. But this first major battle descended into a shockingly lethal and drawn-out slog, with no conclusive victor.

A close-run campaign to seize London followed. Had the King taken London, the English Civil War would probably have ended after only three months. As it was, after a late start, Essex forced marched his army from Warwick to London to arrive before the King. The armies clashed again at Aylesbury and at the barricades in Brentford. Finally, the King's advance was halted on the very edge of London, on Turnham Green.

What followed was the protracted slaughter of the British Civil Wars – through four civil wars, reconquest and suppression, across three kingdoms, lasting over ten years. We should never forget that these wars saw a greater loss of life across Britain and Ireland than even the Great War of 1914–18.

The Western Campaign:
The Battle of Lansdown Hill to the
Storming of Bristol in 1643

In the spring of 1643, the small but fiercely Royalist Cornish Army fought its way out of Cornwall and across Devon. It was joined by Prince Maurice, the Marquis of Hertford and a force of mostly cavalier horse at Chard in Somerset. Together, the combined Western Army continued its march towards

Oxford. However, Parliament's Western Association Army threatened any attempt to cross the open Wiltshire down country that lay between.

On the 5th of July 1643, the King's Western Army stormed the heights of Lansdown Hill, outside Bath, in an attempt to free itself from pursuit. We know a good deal about the Battle of Lansdown Hill from the eye-witness accounts of Sir Ralph Hopton, Colonel Walter Slingsby, Richard Atkyns and an official Parliamentary report. It was a brutal affair. The actions depicted within *The Keys of Hell and Death* are as accurate and authentic as possible. Much of the battlefield remains, including the gun platform taken and held by Sir Bevil Grenville and the pits. The account of a soldier being sent out to discover that Sir William Waller and his Western Association army had slipped away is taken from Hopton's account.

Demoralised at the appalling cost of their victory, the death of Grenville and near fatal burning of Hopton, the Western Army staggered on towards Oxford. They were threatened again at Chippenham, forced to turn back and face Waller once more. The Battle of Chippenham amounted to no more than a standoff broken by skirmishes. But there were losses.

On the afternoon of the 9th of July, the Western Army withdrew over Chippenham Bridge and resumed its march. However, lacking ammunition and dependable cavalry to face Waller's horsemen on the open Wiltshire downs, it turned off the Great Road towards London and headed south for Devizes. The Parliamentary horse caught the straggling Western Army again at Rowde. A rear-guard defended the ford long enough for Hopton's foot regiments to drag themselves into Devizes. But they could go no further.

The Siege of Devizes followed. The King ordered that a

relief force be dispatched from Oxford with ammunition. The Earl of Crawford's convoy was ambushed and taken during the night of Monday 10th of July. The exact site of the skirmish is unknown. However, the point where the Great Road (now the A4) crosses the River Kennet and rises to skirt Silbury Hill seems most likely.

Prince Maurice did break out with the horse, on the same night as the ambush. His route to Marlborough is not recorded, but across the downs via Etchilhampton and All Cannings makes sense. Atkyns gives an account of the ride and the exhaustion of those who rode with the Prince to Oxford to seek reinforcements, returning on Thursday 13th July.

Meanwhile, Waller's Western Association army bombarded Devizes and assaulted its defences. The tower of St James' Church, almost certainly an outwork, remains holed by cannon fire to this day. St John's Church is also scarred and its rectory destroyed in the assault. Hopton and his foot regiments were reduced to boiling bed cords to make match for their muskets. But they hung on long enough for Prince Maurice to return with a relief force under Lord Wilmot.

Waller faced Maurice and Wilmot on Roundway Down. Sir John Byron gives us a good report of the battle, while Atkyns writes of his action against Sir Arthur Hesselrigge and his 'lobsters'. The battle really did end with many of the Parliamentary horse careering over the precipice into Bloody Ditch. Those who escaped dragged themselves to Bristol.

Byron's report includes a footnote that states, 'redelivered of ours that were prisoners with them 113, and Mistress Parsons'. It is not clear who was this Mistress Parsons or why she had been taken prisoner by Waller's army. However, *Mercurius Civicus* describes 'lewd strumpets which go under the name of Parsons' and 'lie with the great [Royalist] commanders' at Oxford, one of whom 'goes most comely in man's apparel'.

The description of the King's Bath, or Roman Baths, in Bath, is taken from John Wroughton's work on *Stuart Bath*. The scenes in Bristol draw on *A Letter Written by a Reverend Minister now residing in Bristol*, as well as the confessions of the plotters, Robert Yeamans and George Boucher. Dorothy Hazzard has long been seen as a heroine and early Baptist. However, she did call for the brains of the plotters' children to be 'dashed out against the stones'.

We know of a number of black Africans in Bristol in 1630s and 1640s. Their status was that of indentured servants, bound to serve for a limited term. In theory, there was no legal basis for slavery in England or its colonies. But their status was increasingly in doubt with the arbitrary extension of indentures and the sentence of John Punch, by the Virginia Governor's Council, to life servitude in 1640.

We know a good deal about the defences of Bristol in 1643, from the reports made by Bernard de Gomme and Samuel Fawcett after its capture and from archaeological evidence. It is possible to trace the line of defences from Brandon Hill Fort at the base of the Cabot Tower to Prior's Hill Fort. We also know a good deal about the Storming of Bristol on the 26th of July 1643 from the trial of Nathaniel Fiennes, its governor, for surrendering the city too easily. It is the eye-witness accounts of that trial that provide the stories told in *The Keys of Hell and Death*.

Finally, John Barnwood was a Gloucester pewterer and bell founder. On the night of Friday the 1st of September 1643, with a sergeant and four musketeers, he 'crept forth of a hole made in the dungeon at the East-Gate, and came very softly to the mouth of the besiegers' mine there'. Looking down upon the Royalist miners, he 'cast in a grenade amongst them'.

Further Reading

More detailed historical notes to accompany this book can be found on the website at www.charlescordell.com. These include background articles on the impact of the Little Ice Age and the General Crisis of the 17th century, the English Revolution and 17th century military theory. Historical pages to accompany the text of *The Keys of Hell and Death* include notes from research of the Battle of Lansdown Hill, the Siege of Devizes, the Battle of Roundway Down and the Storming of Bristol in 1643.

If these do not provide what is needed, please do post questions via the website contact page, or via social media. Alternatively, you may wish to consider following the monthly Early Modern history blog, or joining the Divided Kingdom Readers' Club for more.

The focus of my research and writing has now shifted to the next book in the Divided Kingdom series. It will feature some of the survivors of the books so far but will also include new characters. It will find them at the Massacre of Bolton, the Siege of York and the Battle of Marston Moor in 1644.

Acknowledgements

The journey from Army to author has been an extraordinary, sometimes bumpy ride. There are very many to whom I owe my thanks, for their support, their help, confidence and good company along the way. I offer them all my sincere thanks. Any mistakes are mine alone.

But firstly, to you the reader: thank you for your time and trust. Without you, there would be no books. Thank you for selecting this book from the very many that fight for space on your shelves. I hope *The Keys of Hell and Death* repays you in full. I would love to know what you think of it. If you enjoy reading it, please do spread the word and post a review. Positive ratings and reviews make a very big difference to a new and relatively unknown author.

I feel hugely grateful for all the support I have received from so many of you so far. To all the 'Clubmen' of the Divided Kingdom Readers' Club, thank you for joining and sticking by me on the march. It has meant a lot. Your kind messages of support have kept me going. I am also very grateful to all those who are friends and followers on social media or who follow my 17th Century Almanac blog posts. Your likes and comments make a real difference.

I hope to meet as many of you in person as I can. Please do look out for an opportunity to say hello and tell me what you think of the books. It is always a pleasure to meet, chat to and sign a reader's book. If you can, please do join me for an author talk, book signing, history lecture or battlefield walk. Whenever possible, these are posted on the website at Charles Cordell Events. I am also a fan of Living History and historical re-enactment. I think they play an important role in making history both accessible and tangible, in letting crowds touch and be touched by history. They are also great fun events to be part of.

Sometimes, writing can feel a lonely pursuit. However, the author is only a part of the story of publishing a book. It requires an extraordinary range of professionals to bind art and craft into a physical book, let alone market, sell, print and distribute copies in the thousands. I feel extraordinarily lucky to be published. However, I feel blessed to be part of a chain of people who pride themselves in producing quality books. I hope you can appreciate and love your copy of this book for many years to come.

The publishing industry is a sector fraught with risk. I am indebted to Myrmidon for taking that risk with my manuscript. I feel very fortunate to have an editor that really gets the period and how to wring the best out of my writing. Ed Handyside's patience, advice and editing have been both light and illuminating. My thanks also go out to Myrmidon's partners: to Joe at Blacksheep for the stunning cover; to the printers at CPI; to Sophie O'Neill, Jane Pike, Ceris Jones and all at Inpress for their marketing and selling and to the troops at Gardners, Ingrams and BookSource who store, pack and distribute.

I also want to thank the staff of all the wonderful bookshops that have found space on their shelves and tables. This includes the many Waterstones, Foyles, Blackwells and Toppings outlets, and the host of smaller independent bookshops that stock the Divided Kingdom books. My thanks also go to those that work at Amazon and Booktopia for making these books so widely available to an international audience from the USA to Australia.

I am hugely grateful and indebted to David Gilman, Professor Ronald Hutton, General Richard Nugee and Jeremy Fowler for their generous words of endorsement. To have such public support on the book cover is humbling. I can only hope that others feel the same way about the writing. I am also extremely grateful to Simon Scarrow and Charles Spencer for their time and words of encouragement. It has meant a lot to have their support.

On a more personal note, I owe my sincere thanks to many others who have helped to make this story as historically authentic and accurate as possible. I am grateful to Dr Bernard Deacon and Andrew Climo of the Institute of Cornish Studies at the University of Exeter for their help with 17th Century *Kernewek*, or Cornish language. My thanks go out to Ian Chard for his archaeological reports on Civil War Bristol defences and Lansdown Hill, and for his historical notes on John Friend. I am grateful to Keith Genever for his mapping of finds on Roundway Down; to John Litchfield for his advice on Civil War foot drill and military etiquette; to Bob Burgess for his rare insights into horse formations on the march and Wiltshire bridle paths; to Stewart Peachey for detail on fire pikes; to Dr Keith Lawrence and Tony Rowland for their help with *Jehovah-Jireh: God on the Mount* by John Vicars; to Graham Evans and the Northamptonshire Battlefields Society for their advice on local history and dialect; to David and Lalla Soumaya Ashworth for help with Berber and Darija names; and to Dr and Mrs Dermot Shier for their knowledge of Cornish chapels, holy wells and standing stones.

The writing of a second book is often said to be as difficult as a musician's second LP. This one was certainly not easy. I had nothing to lose with the first. This was much more of a test. Again, I owe a very deep debt to Chris Warner for all his time, thoughts and encouragement during the long months of writing. But I also want to thank General Stuart Skeats, Peter Thompson, Sam Hearne and Dr Beth Roberts for their kind words, encouragement and support. I am grateful to Julian Humphrys and to Andrea Zuvich – the 17th Century Lady – for their support, and to Torin Douglas and Jo James for a brilliant Chiswick Book Festival. Finally, friends and family I thank for their patience and good will. I am sorry it took so long.

I am a veteran who was lucky enough to come home. I have a few scars. But they are nothing compared with others. So many veterans are still battling the impact of conflict and struggling to find home. It is an enduring Misery of War. I remain indebted to the Armed Forces charities that watched my back for so many years, ready to pick up the pieces. I pledge to give 2% of any royalties I receive from this book to support those veterans in need.

To Clio, Fortuna and Mars, I offer up eternal thanks. But more than any other, I thank Tommy Atkins. He remains a sheer bloody inspiration in an ever more fractured world. It was my honour to have stood beside him.